RONA

(Incomers: Book 3)

Jim Forbes

A Kinord Book

Published by Kinord Books
Edinburgh
www.kinordbooks.com

ISBN: 978-0-9928080-8-2

To Elinor with love and gratitude

'La vengeance se mange très bien froide'
– Eugène Sue, *Mathilde* (1874)

'Revenge is a dish best served cold'
– Klingon proverb, *Star Trek II: The Wrath of Khan* (1982)

PROLOGUE

COLD VENGEANCE

TEN WHITE JEQUIRITY SEEDS. *Check.* How innocuous they looked, lying on the kitchen worktop. Though not to the Avenger, who knew each one packed enough abrin to kill an adult man or woman.

Ten 600-gram packs of Fairfield's Premium Organic Muesli. *Check.* Scottish rolled oats enhanced with an eclectic mix of seeds, nuts and dried fruits, sold in health food stores and 'better' supermarkets at an eye-watering price. Each of the ten artist-designed, consultant-approved light cardboard boxes, emblazoned with quasi-scientific nutritional claims, enclosed a generic inner heat-sealed bag containing the product. The Avenger had bought these in ten different towns throughout Scotland and the north of England.

A pack of heat-sealable bags. *Check.* Indistinguishable from those used by Fairfield's.

A heat-sealing machine, purchased on EBay for £55. *Check.*

Pound-store glue-stick. *Check.*

Nail file. *Check.*

The process the Avenger had worked out was simple.

The outer cardboard packaging was carefully slit open so that it could be re-glued as invisibly as possible. Not on the top, where minor signs of tampering might be noticed, but on the bottom of the box.

Then the contents of the inner bag were transferred to a new bag. One whole white jequirity seed was dropped in about half-way through, so that it ended up in the middle of the pack. The new bag was sealed and slipped into the box; finally the task was completed with a dab of glue on the bottom flap.

Next step: a second visit to each of the ten supermarkets around the country. Meticulously and inconspicuously the Avenger had put a coded mark on each box to ensure it would be returned to its proper origin.

Ten times, the identical procedure would be followed. It would not be a case of taking the product to the customer service desk. Nor would it do simply to replace it on the shelf – too risky, with all those CCTV cameras. The packet to be returned had instead to be in the bottom of a trolley from the car-park, hidden under a pile of multi-use grocery bags. Security had no concern for what was coming *into* the store, only what was being taken *out*. Inside, a second pack of Fairfield's Premium Organic Muesli would be selected from the shelf, joining a number of additional purchases in the trolley.

At check-out, the entire contents of the trolley, including the poisoned muesli, would be placed on the belt. Then an apology to the cashier: 'I seem to have taken two of these by mistake. I only need one. Sorry about that.'

Invariably, the cashier would say, 'No problem.' The marked box of muesli would be back in stock within the hour, waiting for another discerning customer.

The plan had gestated in the Avenger's brain for a year or more. Its key elements, white jequirity and Premium Organic Muesli, had been selected after much research.

Abrin was well known. One of the most toxic substances in nature, it had been deployed before by criminals and terrorists and was the agent of death in a few fictional crime dramas, but the Avenger's plan took a novel tack.

First, the common jequirity with its bright scarlet seeds was too conspicuous to use as a contaminant. Hence the selection of the rarer white-seeded variety. It was the same species (*Abrus precatorius*), with at least the same content of deadly abrin. Only the colour of the seed-coat was different. The Avenger had

learned all about these seeds on the Internet, had known exactly what to look for and had flown to Indonesia just to collect some. No more than ten for the muesli 'enrichment' plan plus a few spares to plant at home. Not out of mere botanical curiosity but to generate larger numbers of seeds for possible future use.

Second, there was no need to extract the pure toxic principle. Nature had helpfully wrapped a lethal dose of it in a neat package: why mess with it? All that was necessary was to abrade a small area of the surface with a nail file. That ensured the seed could not pass undigested through the gut.

Third, muesli was a product designed to be poured from the packet directly into the bowl, with addition of chilled fresh milk or yoghurt. Abrin is destroyed by cooking; even moderate heat will lessen its potency. So forget porridge oats as a vehicle. *Revenge is a dish best served cold*: never was the adage more literally true.

Fourth, just one whole seed was to be added to each pack of the chosen food product. One person would swallow it and die; others eating from the same pack would be totally unaffected. And no trace of the poison would be detected if the remaining contents were ever analysed.

Premium Organic Muesli was an ideal carrier for white jequirity as it contained whole grains and nuts covering a broad spectrum of sizes. A single smooth little 100-milligram seed fitted right in with the flax, hemp, pine nuts, sunflower, cashew and macadamia. What a delicious, healthy last breakfast!

The significantly cheaper non-organic version of Fairfield's Premium Muesli would have done just as well. But the white jequirity had grown in Indonesia without artificial pesticides or fertilisers; it was certifiably 'organic' and deserved to be delivered to a connoisseur of foods free of residual amounts of those nasty chemicals.

Up to ten people were going to die. It was collateral damage, an unfortunate side-effect of war, however just or unjust the cause. The real enemy was Fairfield's Cereals, more particularly the individual who owned and ran that company. Donald Swainson was his name. A 'toff' he was – doubly so, for he had been born into the Earldom of Fairfield and had acquired the Barony of Bracklinn through foul play by his mother.

For six centuries, Swainsons had been Earls or Countesses of Fairfield. Fifty years ago, in financial difficulties, they had coveted the wealth of the Argills of Bracklinn. By 1970 the sinister 23rd Countess, Rona Swainson, had married and murdered her way to the Argills' barony and wealth, making her three-year-old son Donald 6th Lord Bracklinn. Though Rona had not been charged with any wrongdoing, the Avenger was in no doubt she was guilty and had got away with it.

Problem was, Rona had vanished from the scene in 1990, shortly after abdicating the Fairfield title in favour of her son. Her live-in lover – some said he was her third husband – took off around the same time. Icelandic he was, by the name of Haraldsson. The Avenger's inquiries through a detective agency in Reykjavik had failed to turn up a Haraldsson sharing an address with a British woman called Rona anywhere in Iceland.

Yet, if she was still alive, that was most likely where she had been hiding all these years. One day, the Avenger would track down the former Countess and make her suffer for her crimes. In the meantime, Donald Swainson, his Fairfield's Cereals company and his family were still very much in Scotland and a suitable target for cold vengeance.

1

A PIECE OF THE ACTION

FROM THE PATIO OF HER PRETTY whitewashed house on the edge of Akureyri, Ragna Enjudóttir admired her colourful garden in the evening sunshine. The last house on Ketilsgata, a road that led nowhere except to the entrance of the municipal park just beyond, was little disturbed by passing traffic and Ragna felt blissfully alone. Solitude had been her friend since that day in 1990 she had embarked on her new life, leaving her old identity and so much trouble behind ...

Not that she ever wished to be parted from her beloved Ari. He was still out in the fjord on his boat and would be there for at least two more hours. She had eaten dinner alone; when he got home Ari would fix himself something he had caught. Unless, that is, he stopped off at Adda's Café as he often did.

In peaceful moments like these, Ragna liked to reflect on the life she had come to love, here on the north coast of Iceland not seventy kilometres from the Arctic Circle. Who could have foreseen it?

And yet, was it not strangely fitting that Rona Fay Swainson, as she once was, would find peace and happiness in this Nordic land? Here she would enjoy her good health for as long as it would last, together with the man she had loved for fifty years; here she would be content to die when the time came. If the narrative arc of her life were ever written down, its logic would be plain: the seeds of her present existence were sown across the sea in Scotland from the day she was born.

Except: in the early years she had found herself in some nasty situations. Had she not taken control, the arc could have deposited her somewhere very different. Not the happy ending towards which she was now cruising.

At Gordonhall, Kincardineshire, 30th September 1944, to Captain Philip Swainson, RN, 22nd Earl of Fairfield and Aenea, Lady Fairfield, a daughter, Rona Fay. Mother and baby well.

Thus was her arrival announced in the *Daily Telegraph*. That Lady Rona Swainson would ultimately inherit the Fairfield earldom was not, of course, presumed at that time. A later-born son, if there were any, would scoop that prize.

One of the most ancient Scottish peerages still extant, it had been created for its first holder by Robert I (the Bruce) around 1308. A reward, it was believed, for crucial support to the king in defeating John Comyn, Earl of Buchan at Inverurie and in the subsequent 'harrying' of the north-east to extinguish all opposition from the Comyn family and their supporters.

The Earls of Fairfield down the centuries had a semi-mythical tale of their family origins: they believed their ancestors were Norse, among relatively few who settled inland south of the Moray Firth. The Swainson name, they maintained, was, like Swanson or Swinson, an Anglicisation of *Sweynsson*. Had their forebears made their home in the Western Isles, as many Norse incomers did, their name would have become MacSween.

Philip Swainson, the 22nd Earl, served with distinction in the Royal Navy throughout the Second World War, but in later years would have little to say of his active service. The only exploit he did recount from time to time occurred one night in December 1943 when, under his command, HMS *Metis* was patrolling the north Atlantic. On sighting distress flares, he directed his ship towards them through dark and mountainous waters.

By daybreak, *Metis* was in the vicinity of a remote island. An eerie calm had descended; the ocean offered some respite from its normal winter fury, allowing a search party to go ashore. They were drawn to the ruins of an ancient chapel, the only remaining indication that this dot of land had ever seen human habitation. Huddled within its walls was the entire 49-man crew of a German U-boat. Surrendering without a fight, they told their captors that their craft had struck offshore rocks and, as she was irreparably damaged, they had been ordered to scuttle her and await rescue. They had waited eight days in vain for a vessel of their own navy to pick them up; now they were relieved to be in enemy hands rather than spend one more winter's night on this godforsaken rock.

The submariners would give no hint as to their mission, but Captain Swainson suspected covert activity of some kind, using the island as a base or radio relay station. Once the German prisoners were securely on board his ship, he set out alone on a reconnaissance of the bleak half-square-mile surface. He found nothing to confirm his suspicions.

However, his brief foray on that wind-blasted, sea-spray-soaked speck of land affected him deeply. In later life, he would sometimes talk of the ghosts of islanders lingering in the caves and geos of the shoreline. They spoke to him, he said, in words he recognised as Old Norse, the language of his own ancestors, on which his father the 21st Earl had been something of an authority.

On Christmas Eve, *Metis* put in to Wick to disembark the prisoners and Swainson took a few hours' shore leave. His young wife Aenea had arrived the previous evening by train and was staying in the Temperance Hotel. It was in those lodgings that their only child was conceived.

The island where Philip Swainson had just encountered his 'ghosts' was Rona. On the birth of his daughter on the last day of September 1944, he was adamant that Rona would be her name. Aenea was given little say in the matter, but was allowed to select a middle name for the infant.

Some while after VE-day and the repatriation of German prisoners of war, Philip received a letter from Klaus Strohmann of Dortmund, manager of a print works and formerly the captain of the U-boat crew uplifted from the island of Rona in December 1943. In grammatically faultless if slightly stilted English, he wished formally to express his gratitude and that of his men for their rescue and for the humane way they had been treated aboard the *Metis*. He hoped that the enmity of a war not of the making of either one of them could be replaced by a bond of mutual respect, as one sailor to another. That letter began a lifelong friendship, renewed each year by exchange of Christmas gifts.

Rona Fay Swainson enjoyed as comfortable an early childhood as the daughter of a landed earl could expect – which is to say, not very. Cared for by a succession of nannies then packed off to boarding school at the age of seven, she developed an independent streak which often got her into trouble with her teachers and housemistresses.

Queen Alexandra's School for Girls in rural Stirlingshire did not in those days put great emphasis on academic achievement. Focused as it was on turning out marriage-fodder for the aristocracy, it aimed to develop the arts of social interaction as well as proficiency in country pursuits, particularly those involving horses. By the time she reached her early teens, Rona found the whole programme stultifying and despised her airhead schoolmates.

Salvation was to come from an unexpected quarter: her father. Though not out of any concern he may have had for the quality of the girl's education.

In April 1958, Philip Swainson received an unexpected visitor at Gordonhall: an ex-navy colleague who, like himself, had returned to civilian life after the war. He knew him as Commander Harry Fitzwarren, but was interested to learn that in 1956 he had inherited the title of Lord Wythorpe from a distant cousin.

'My dear fellow,' Swainson said, sitting down with him in the library, 'what brings you to this neck of the woods?'

'I've been travelling up and down the country renewing old acquaintances ... you know, friendships forged during the war. What has surprised me is the number of men I thought of as comrades in arms who have no desire to stay in touch. I've a feeling – perhaps you can relate to this, Philip – it's my recent elevation to the peerage that has alienated them.'

'I wouldn't have thought so, Harry.'

'Nor would I, old chap. But there it is. All that post-war socialism under Attlee changed people's attitudes to the aristocracy. Even seven blessed years of Tory government haven't undone the damage, although if Eden hadn't got himself unstuck by that damn Suez mess, I think we'd be in a better place. Macmillan's not a bad prime minister but he's not one of *us*, if you catch my drift. Doesn't have the *blood*. Comes from the *business* world – publishing, if I'm not mistaken.'

Swainson was about to disagree politely with the visitor's political analysis but was distracted by the arrival of Mrs Gibbon, the housekeeper, with tea and crumpets.

'Anyway,' Fitzwarren continued, sensing his host did not share the view he had just expressed, 'it doesn't matter *why* some people are giving me the cold shoulder. It's good news for those who don't – and I earnestly hope, Philip, that I can number you among them. You see, I've come into possession of some information that stands to make me a lot of money, and I want as many as possible of my friends to get "a piece of the action" as they say in the City.'

'What kind of information?'

'Let me answer with a question. What's the biggest money's-no-object commercial opportunity at this moment? Don't just think Britain, think the planet.'

'When you say "money's-no-object" I have to think you're talking about the Space Race.'

'Exactly.'

In 1958, the whole world was galvanised by the US-Soviet competition for dominance in space. Following the shock of *Sputnik 1* the previous October, the US response had initially been beset by failure, most humiliatingly the televised launch-pad explosion of *Vanguard TV3* that was to have carried the first American satellite into space. On 17th March 1958, *Vanguard TV4* had gone successfully into orbit; the 6-inch sphere derisively called 'the grapefruit' by Nikita Khrushchev marked a new beginning for the US programme. (Nearly sixty years later it continues to circle the Earth once every two hours and thirteen minutes, having logged its 100,000th orbit on 14th April 2015.)

'But I don't understand, Harry. It's an American government project, top secret, no opportunity for the likes of us to get involved, isn't that so?'

'Not so, as it happens.'

Looking his visitor in the eye, Swainson saw the sincerity of a fellow naval officer who, like himself, had faced the enemy with distinction. 'This tea's a little weak, don't you think? Why don't I pour us something a little stronger while you share this "information" of yours?'

Fitzwarren laid out his stall. Contacts he maintained in the upper echelons of the British Navy had dropped some friendly hints, which he had gone on to confirm through other networks. ARPA, an agency recently set up by US President Eisenhower in response to the 'Sputnik crisis' to promote space technology for military purposes, was working with UK defence procurement to access certain products of scientific research. The problem was, the companies engaged in such research lacked the capital to meet ARPA's needs.

Harold Macmillan's government could not countenance an American takeover of these companies, nor would it fund them directly, either of which solution would invite parliamentary and press scrutiny. A public share offering was likewise out of the question. Instead, a highly selective call was going out to private investors who had been vetted for their wealth and discretion. Fitzwarren's visit was, he explained, part of that process.

'What rate of return do you expect?' Swainson asked, suddenly all ears.

'Are you ready for this? Fifteen percent, guaranteed; could go even higher. Paid as a dividend once a quarter.'

'Macmillan says we "never had it so good", but bank rate is four percent and the best I can get on my stocks and shares is about six. I'd certainly be interested in a small punt. Can you put me down for £5,000?'

'No can do, old chap. The minimum investment is £50,000. To keep out the spivs and riff-raff, you know. How quickly could you raise that?'

Swainson was nonplussed for a few moments by the amount needed, but quickly recovered. 'Er ... a few days, that's all.'

'Okay, I'll send you details of where to remit the money. If you're happy with your investment, you'll have a chance to increase your stake at any time. Now, enough of business. Have you heard anything of Toothy Turnbull since he left the Navy? Somebody told me he was on to his third wife, just since the war.'

The two men enjoyed a couple of hours of gossip and reminiscences over fine whisky and cigars. Coming into the library, Aenea Swainson, delighted to witness her husband talk uncharacteristically – and animatedly – about his wartime experiences, invited Fitzwarren to stay for dinner.

A few days later, an official prospectus headed 'M31 HOLDINGS' arrived in the mail. Careful perusal confirmed everything Fitzwarren had said. Having liquidated almost his entire brokerage account, Philip Swainson wrote a cheque for £50,000 and sat back waiting for the dividends to roll in.

In June he received the first £1,875, and in September the second dividend, in the same amount but with an additional £500 'bonus'. A signal, he thought, that he should increase his investment. Without telling Aenea – she would worry unnecessarily – he took out a bank loan, three-fourths of the assessed value of the entire Gordonhall estate, and put it all into his M31 account. After paying interest to the bank, his net return would be 8 percent, more if bonuses kept coming.

Or so he thought.

When no dividend cheque was delivered by the middle of December, he tried to contact M31 Holdings. The phone number printed on the prospectus was unobtainable; letters were returned as undeliverable.

It took a few days to sink in fully: his erstwhile friend Harry Fitzwarren, the self-styled Lord Wythorpe, had pulled a huge scam on him. Not only had he lost all his savings, he was now colossally in debt. Confessing to Aenea how he had been duped was almost as painful as the financial ruin now staring them in the face.

The police could offer little hope of tracking the fraudster down. Fitzwarren had almost certainly disappeared abroad with his ill-gotten wealth.

What kept the Swainsons' heads above water in the months that followed was a small nest-egg Aenea had brought to the marriage back in 1938 but had kept in her own name for tax reasons. That money, together with the meagre rental income from the Gordonhall estate and the occasional sale of heirloom silver and paintings, covered the interest they owed the bank and supported a frugal lifestyle in their draughty mansion.

Among the luxuries that could no longer be afforded was Lady Rona's private schooling. In January 1959, at the age of fourteen, she was taken out of Queen Alex's to complete her secondary education at the local state school, Banchory Academy, less than three miles from home. What for her parents was an embarrassing come-down was for Rona a blessed release.

2

BOOKPLATE

DELIA COBB'S INTERNSHIP in Edinburgh* was up and she had so far been unable to secure a new position. Her work experience and academic qualifications, including a Master's degree in environmental science, were not the issue. She was a citizen of the United States, not of the United Kingdom, and arbitrary limits on employment of immigrants had been imposed by the Home Secretary in response to a perceived 'threat to the British way of life'. Delia had to convince a prospective employer not just to hire her but to make the case to the Home Office that her skills were special enough to warrant employing a foreigner.

'Aren't there jobs back here in the States that you could be applying for?' her parents repeatedly asked her. 'You're in your mid-twenties. Soon you'll be too old to get a foothold in the American market.'

The truth was, she wanted more than anything to make her career in Britain. Quin, the long-distance boyfriend who had remained steadfast during almost all of her time here, had fallen for a colleague in the University of Chicago and was no longer a factor in her life. Plus, there was a personal matter binding her to her adoptive country.

From DNA evidence, Delia knew she had Scottish ancestry, at least on her mother's side, but an online genealogical search had drawn a blank. Her quest for ancestors was not driven by

---

* The dramatic events that unfolded during Delia's stay in Edinburgh are the subject of *Scotch and Water* (*Incomers*: Book 2).

mere curiosity; a commitment she had made to identify the Keeper of Taran's Wheel depended on it, for the most likely candidate was herself. (Taran's Wheel was a pre-Christian religious talisman whose custody was entrusted to a bloodline of female 'Keepers' stretching back into antiquity.*)

Her challenge was to establish a link from Jane Wilson, her five-times-great-grandmother, to one Agnes Cromar, through the female line. That would confirm Delia's rightful status as Keeper, with all the ancient privileges and obligations that entailed. Jane had emigrated from the UK to America in 1800; Agnes died in 1874 at the age of 69, so was born after Jane emigrated. To complicate matters, no reliable trace of Jane could be found in old British records accessible online.

Delia planned to search though all the old graveyards, about thirty in all, within an arbitrary 15-mile radius of Agnes's final resting place in Tarland, Aberdeenshire. What she hoped to find was a headstone bearing both the Cromar and Wilson names. A week should be sufficient, she reckoned.

She had no reason to expect a week in May to turn into a whole summer, nor a brief stay in Aberdeenshire to result in travel to more remote parts of Scotland – and beyond – in a totally different pursuit. Nor had she the slightest inkling that she might once again be putting herself in harm's way.

In the study of the comfortable north London home he shared with his wife Emily, Frank Jamieson cast an eye over the volumes on the bookshelves. He was not looking for anything in particular. Many of them were titles he had kept to read, or re-read, in his retirement; five years into that happy phase he had not yet found the time to dip into any of them.

Today might just be the day, he thought. From a shelf of antiquarian books inherited from an aunt in Scotland over thirty

---

* See *Taran's Wheel* (*Incomers*: Book 1).

years ago he took out first one then another, leafing through them in a search for something he might want to sink his teeth into.

The third one he opened caught his interest. There was something puzzling about it.

It was a weighty tome – 847 oversize pages of closely-packed text with 2,236 engravings and 25 colour plates – bound in red cloth bearing the legend *Illustrated Natural History*. Frank was impressed by the sheer scale of the work, and surprised that it bore no author's or illustrator's name, and no date of publication. It appeared to be a 'new' edition of an earlier book with the expansive title

THE ROYAL NATURAL HISTORY,
BEING A SYSTEMATIC ARRANGEMENT OF DESCRIPTIVE ZOOLOGY
FROM MAN TO THE LOWEST FORMS

and credited only its editor: James Wylde.

Wylde was a mid-to-late nineteenth-century science writer whose interests ran more to experimental and industrial chemistry than to zoology. Almost certainly, he was not the primary author of this colossal opus.

A listing of the book on the Internet gave 1881 as its publication date; this seemed a reasonable estimate given the mention Frank found at page 115 of David Livingstone's remains having been 'lately' returned to Great Britain – an event which occurred in 1873. Yet the author rejected out of hand all the teachings of Charles Darwin, whose transformative *On the Origin of Species* had appeared in 1859 and *The Descent of Man* in 1871.

Torn between his disgust at the colonial-era racism of the chapter on man and a grudging admiration for the far more objective, and amazingly comprehensive, scientific treatment of non-human animals, Frank made to close the book and return it to its shelf, where it would probably rest unopened for another five years or more. As he did so, he caught a glimpse of the inside front cover, noticing for the first time that it bore an intricate bookplate.

EX LIBRIS GORDONHALL, it read.

Gordonhall was a name Frank recalled from the late 1960s, almost fifty years ago. It was a seventeenth-century mansion on the south slope of the Hill of Fare near Banchory in what was once Kincardineshire. He had gone there one day with his Aunt Barbara and Uncle Al – it must have been in 1969, by which time the great house was uninhabited. Some kind of scandal had befallen the family who had owned it – several suspicious deaths were involved, best he could remember. Peering through the windows of what had been a library or study, the sight of hundreds of books scattered on the floor had left an impression on the young Frank.

Now he found to his astonishment he had a book from that very library, as testified by its bookplate. How had Aunt Barbara acquired it? Uncle Al, a motor mechanic, had probably accepted a selection of volumes from the abandoned Gordonhall library in part-payment from a customer – someone charged with looking after the house and grounds, perhaps – for repairs to a vehicle. Barbara had come by several of her rarer books in just such a way.

Frank well remembered his aunt's sorrow at what befell the handsome building shortly afterwards: a devastating fire that spared no combustible material. What remained standing was deemed unsafe and pulled down for the site to be levelled. Only a walled garden, still being tended, remained as evidence that a house once stood there.

Looking again at the bookplate, Frank read the motto inscribed on a belt or ribbon near the top: *FAER FJALL*. Words that meant nothing to him; he had no idea even what language they were in.

An Internet search quickly provided the answer: the lairds of Gordonhall had been Earls of Fairfield, a title derived from Old Norse *Faer Fjall* meaning 'sheep hill'. The Hill of Fare that rose behind Gordonhall might, he thought, have been that hill.

More of a mystery was the object near the centre of the bookplate: what appeared to be a pyramid bearing a strange symbol. An inverted copy of the pyramid lay immediately below, like a reflection. The symbol, Frank found, was similar to a Scandinavian rune from around the tenth century: a letter corresponding to the modern *F*. Together with its reflection it could be read 'FF' – perhaps another reference to the *FAER FJALL* motto. But the symbolism of the reflecting pyramid remained a puzzle.

So, a few surprises. An unsuspected connection to a long-lost stately home had been in his possession since his aunt's death 35 years ago. A book, at once mysterious in its authorship and embarrassingly awful in at least part of its content. But a much bigger surprise awaited Frank as he hoisted the heavy tome on to a high shelf. The back cover, which threatened to break free of the binding, fell open to reveal a large envelope taped to the endpaper.

3
TEMPORARY

RONA ENROLLED AT BANCHORY in January 1959, midway through third year of secondary school. That forced her to choose between modern languages and sciences, mid-session. Having had pathetically little exposure to science at Queen Alex's, she felt languages would be her better option. Though she struggled to catch up in maths and Latin, she soon shone in English, French and especially German. Her curriculum was completed by choosing geography over history, more because of the recently-graduated young man who would be her teacher than for any particular love of the subject.

She was surprised and, at first, hurt by the unwelcoming reception from her female classmates, who over the years had formed themselves into cliques that resisted penetration by incomers. Her only ally was an outsider like herself, a Polish girl called Lidia Jaracz.

Physically, Lidia was everything Rona was not. The bodily changes accompanying puberty were more evident in Lidia. Her bobbed dark hair contrasted with the blonde waves that cascaded down to Rona's shoulders. Though not conventionally pretty, she had the kind of face that drew the eye. And, at the early age of 14, she possessed a sense of style that made Rona feel frumpy, even when both were dressed in the uniform of blue blazer, grey pleated skirt, white blouse and school tie.

Where Rona showed no great interest or prowess in sports, Lidia was the fastest in her year on the athletics track. She regularly left the other girls so far behind that, on the annual school sports day in the King George V Park, she raced with the boys instead – and gave them a good run for their money. None of this made Lidia any more popular with her female classmates.

'I pay no attention to those bitches,' she told Rona in her first week at Banchory. 'The boys are much nicer, and more fun. I'll introduce you to my friends: Keith, Alan, Dougie and Stewart. You'll like them.'

'I've never been pally with a boy. Aren't they just interested in football, trains and stamp-collecting?'

'Some of them, yes. But the ones I hang around with are also into films and music, especially rock'n'roll.'

'Are they in our year?'

'No, third-year boys are still babies. I like the fourth-years better.'

Less than a month after Rona's arrival at Banchory, news broke of the death of Buddy Holly. Popular music having been more or less banned at Queen Alex's and never played at home in Gordonhall, the fatal crash of a small plane in an Iowa snowstorm on 3rd February 1959 meant little to her – though it moved Lidia almost to tears. Clearly Rona had been missing something. She resolved to become more knowledgeable.

'Where do you hear this music?' she asked her new Polish friend.

'Radio Luxembourg. You can only pick it up after dark, since we're so far away. Beats me why the darkness helps. Right now, any time after six is good, but in the summer you can hardly get it at all.'

'So what then? Can you get rock'n'roll on the BBC?'

'The BBC's rubbish. No decent music at all. The only thing worth listening to is *Pick of the Pops* with David Jacobs on the Light Programme, Saturday evenings.'

As her parents' wireless, a walnut-trimmed item of furniture about the size of a cabin trunk, had to remain permanently tuned to the Home Service, Rona was not allowed to select the Light Programme, let alone turn the dial to the 208 metres wavelength beamed from Luxembourg, with its heady diet of pop music and ads. She got into a habit of walking over to the gardener's cottage after dinner, school homework permitting, where Bert and Ada were happy to tune in 208 for her enjoyment.

A violent storm that October caused serious damage to the roof of Gordonhall. Having cancelled their building insurance to save money, the Earl and Countess faced a repair bill that was far beyond their straitened means. Nor, as winter approached, could they afford to heat even the few rooms they occupied to a tolerable level.

It was Aenea who took charge of the situation – after all, it was her money that now supported the family. At dinner one evening, she laid out a plan. 'Let's face it, we can't continue to live in this old barn. We have to lock it up, leave it to the mercy of the weather, and move into a much smaller house. And Mrs Gibbon will have to go – she'll easily get a chambermaid job at the Raemoir Hotel, probably for more money than we're paying her.'

'And where will we find this smaller house?' her husband asked.

'Right under our noses, dear. The gatehouse at the bottom of the drive has two bedrooms and a decent-sized living room.'

'The *lodge*?' Philip questioned. 'I don't fancy that, not one bit. It's noisy down there, with all that traffic going past the windows. And where would our furniture go? Our oriental rugs? Our library of two thousand books?'

'The furniture that won't fit in the gatehouse we'll sell. The rugs too. We've already sold off most of our art collection. And as for your books – well, they can stay where they are meantime. The library's about the only room in the house that's dry.'

Philip had no answer, at least none that he could voice without his wife bringing up the subject of who had got them into this mess in the first place. He turned to his 15-year-old daughter. 'Rona, what do you think of this idea of your mother's?'

'It's okay. In fact, it would be better for me as the school bus could pick me up right at the door. I wouldn't have that long trek down the drive in all weathers. But don't the Latimers live in the gatehouse?'

'They're our tenants,' Aenea explained, 'but they gave notice a few weeks ago that they intend to give up the lease at Martinmas. They're moving into a council house in Banchory.'

Philip Swainson, 22nd Earl of Fairfield found the whole idea of living in the tiny lodge profoundly distasteful, but he realised his wife was right. For outside consumption, he thought, the story would be that this was a temporary move while Gordonhall was repaired and upgraded. In his heart he knew there would be nothing temporary about it.

4
BEYOND REPROACH

OLIVIA LAPOTAIRE SAT HUNCHED over her laptop compiling her grocery order for Saturday morning delivery. Waitrose was out of her usual brand of cereal, but was instead offering Fairfield's Premium Organic Muesli, which she had not previously bought.

Always a checker of online reviews, some would say obsessively so, Olivia did her homework. The Fairfield's product scored high marks for its composition, taste and organic credentials, and she decided to give it a try.

Had she searched a little further, she would have come across a tweet from a disgruntled former Fairfield's employee. The 'big secret' was that the company's non-organic products, which sold at about half the price, were in fact identical in all respects to those it labelled 'organic'. Not that there was anything dishonest about the label: all ingredients were indeed certifiably organic. It was just that the very same ingredients went into the lower-priced product line. Fairfield's scored a healthy profit at that lower price, and made out like a bandit at the premium price.

It would probably have made no difference to Olivia's purchasing decision. Seeing the word 'organic' on the box was a comfort. It made her a good wife and mother.

A week later, the Lapotaire family were having breakfast together at the kitchen table in their detached villa in an upmarket Manchester suburb.

'Jules, darling,' Olivia said, attempting to draw her husband's attention away from an item on TV about funding for the arts. 'Did you notice anything different about the muesli this morning?'

He harrumphed at the interruption, then noticed his wife's annoyance. 'Er, yes I did, as a matter of fact. Nuttier than usual, I thought. New packet, isn't it? Nuts tend to rise to the top, I suppose.'

'Like in theatre management,' she commented, in a sideswipe at his profession.

'If you say so.'

Ambrose, twelve going on twenty-four, piped up, 'Actually, Daddy, it's not the nuts that rise, it's the smaller stuff that sinks to the bottom. It falls through the gaps between the bigger pieces.'

'Yeah, yeah,' his ten-year-old sister Electra said with exaggerated world-weariness. 'That packaging project you did last year. Hope I don't have to do anything as stupid.'

Always keen to head off an impending argument between the kids, Olivia said, 'It's not just a new packet. A different brand. Fairfield's, it's called. I like it.'

'Me too,' Ambrose said, pouring some more of the muesli into his bowl.

His father was immersed again in BBC Breakfast and paid no attention.

Later, in his office at the theatre, Jules Lapotaire was putting the finishing touches to a PowerPoint presentation he planned to use at a 3 pm meeting with a group of councillors at the Town Hall Extension, when he became aware of an abdominal pain. He had eaten a sandwich at his desk half an hour earlier and was on his third, maybe fourth cup of coffee of the day. Putting the uncomfortable sensation down to indigestion, he chewed a couple of antacid tablets.

They had no effect. Gradually the pain became more acute. If he lay down for a few minutes, he thought, it would pass. He walked along the hall from his office towards the deserted theatre. In one of the boxes was a sofa on which he could recline, with the additional advantage of being close to a toilet should an urgent need arise. It was a ladies' room, but that didn't matter as there was no one but Jules in the whole building.

Half an hour later the pain had become almost unbearable and his whole body was shaking uncontrollably. He fished out his phone to call Olivia. No signal.

Have to get out of here, he thought, struggling to get to his feet. That was when the delirium started. Totally disorientated, he made a lunge towards the rail at the front of the box and fell twenty feet to the floor of the auditorium. He vomited copiously on the shabby maroon carpet before losing consciousness.

The councillors who assembled for the three o'clock meeting with theatre director Jules Lapotaire hung around for fifteen minutes before returning to their more important business. Nobody considered calling him – not that he was in a position to answer in any case.

As a freelance writer on 'lifestyle' topics for newspapers and women's magazines, Olivia worked at home, irregular hours. When, as today, she had a tight deadline, the kids would go from school to their Grandma's for tea.

It was after seven in the evening when she realised Jules had not come home yet, nor had he called to say he would be late. She rang his mobile and his office landline several times, getting no reply.

Before heading to Grandma's to collect her offspring, she drove to the theatre, which she knew was dark, between productions. Letting herself in through the stage door, for which Jules had given her a key, she made first for his office. He was nowhere to be seen, but his desk looked busy, his computer was turned on, and his jacket hung on the back of his chair. He had to be in the building somewhere.

In the theatre auditorium, the only light shone from one of the boxes. She called Jules's name. A little nervously, she made for the illuminated box, but found no one there. Looking over the rail into the darkness of the stalls below, she could see nothing. A strange unpleasant odour, like vomit, wafted up from the depths. An empty-theatre smell, Olivia assumed.

Ah well, she thought, *he'll show up at home when he gets hungry.* It was time to pick up the kids.

'Missing, you say, Ms Lapotaire?' the voice on the phone said at one in the morning.

Olivia told the police dispatcher what she knew of her husband's movements the previous day, and reported her own unsuccessful visit to the theatre premises. It was arranged that a constable would come to her house for the stage-door key, so that the building could be thoroughly searched.

Only at 4 am did the call come.

'Ms Lapotaire, I'm sorry to tell you your husband has been found, injured and unconscious but alive, in the stalls area of the theatre. He's in an ambulance, on his way to Manchester Royal. As soon as we've more information, we'll let you know.'

Jules's physical injuries from his fall were the primary focus of attention for the busy accident and emergency unit. It was not until after nine in the morning that one of the junior doctors on duty began to pay more attention to the fact that Jules had thrown up.

A sample of the vomitus revealed that his most recent meal had consisted of a roast-beef sandwich with mustard on whole-wheat bread. Most probably from the convenience store next-door to the theatre.

At the hospital, Olivia reported what her husband had eaten for breakfast. She was careful to mention that the muesli he had consumed was organic – therefore beyond reproach as she saw it.

'Nonetheless,' the doctor told her, 'if there's any left in the packet we should have it analysed. It looks as if Mr Lapotaire is suffering from acute poisoning of some kind.'

'I ate the same muesli, yesterday *and* today,' Olivia said, 'and I'm okay. My son even had two helpings, and is perfectly fine.'

'Sounds like it's not the muesli, then, but we'll check it out just to be sure. What else did your husband eat?'

By 6 pm, an endoscopic study had led the team of doctors, who now included a consultant clinical toxicologist, to suspect poisoning by ricin, unlikely though that seemed, or – an off-the-wall possibility – abrin. Blood tests, however, were negative for both.

The toxicologist pointed out that L-abrine, the blood marker for abrin poisoning, was quickly metabolised and could give a positive result only within about 24 hours of ingestion. Abrin could not be ruled out, but was so improbable that the patient's condition would have to be put down to 'poisoning by an unknown agent', pending analysis of the foods he was known to have consumed.

Jules Lapotaire was kept comfortable and hydrated. He regained consciousness fleetingly at midnight and again at 3:30 am. At 5:47 am, forty-six hours after his breakfast of Fairfield's Premium Organic Muesli, he was pronounced dead.

5
SENSATIONAL

JANUARY 1960 BROUGHT ONE OF the worst winter storms anyone could remember. School closed for three days, then reopened only for pupils who lived in the town of Banchory. Kids from further afield enjoyed a whole week of fun in the snow before buses began operating again.

Bert the gardener adapted his Allen Scythe – a two-wheeled walk-behind contraption driven by a two-stroke engine – to make a small snowplough. With it he cleared two-foot-wide pathways around the Gordonhall grounds as well as a small area where fodder could be put out to attract deer. Residents of the estate, including the Earl and Countess and Lady Rona, dined well on venison in the storm's aftermath.

It was during this surreal period that Rona began exploring her father's library. As the big house's electricity supply had been disconnected to save money, she had only the limited winter daylight hours in which to scan the shelves and dip into any books that caught her interest. An Aladdin paraffin heater took the worst chill off the air but the draughty room never warmed enough to tempt her out of her wool coat, scarf and tammy. She cut the fingers off an old pair of gloves to make what Bert called *hummel doddies*; these kept her hands reasonably warm while allowing the turning of pages.

The books were not arranged according to any logical classification that Rona could discern. Fiction and non-fiction were freely interspersed; Volume 2 of a work might turn up across the room from Volume 1. The giants of English, Scottish, Irish and American literature were all well represented, along with more than a smattering of Scandinavian writers, mostly in English translation but sometimes in the original Norwegian, Swedish, Danish or Icelandic. There was a collection of the works of Ibsen in an edition with Norwegian and English texts on facing pages. Rona knew that her grandfather the 21st Earl, who died before she was born, had been expert in the Nordic languages; she assumed he was responsible for this aspect of the library.

Among her finds were some of the Norse sagas, including the thirteenth-century *Orkneyinga Saga*, which featured in the Gordonhall library in a number of different English translations from the original Icelandic. Why she was so fascinated by these was not something she could fathom at the age of fifteen; much later it occurred to her that the fuzzy boundary between mythology and history was, like all boundaries, an inherently interesting place. She brought one of the *Orkneyinga* books home to the warmth and light of the gatehouse.

'Learning all about your ancestors, Peaches?' Philip Swainson remarked when he saw what his daughter was reading one evening.

'You've always told me we're descended from Vikings, Daddy,' Rona replied. 'Is it true?'

'Not Vikings. Norse, yes. The Vikings were pirates, the scourge of the seas and coasts. Most of the incomers who arrived from Scandinavia in the tenth and eleventh centuries were peaceable. Men, women and children, just looking for a better life.'

'But the sagas are full of violence,' Rona protested. 'Are you saying they're untrue?'

'No, of course not. Those *were* violent times, for all the peoples of Scotland, not only the Norsemen and their families. And the sagas are collections of folk-tales passed down by word of mouth. Inevitably sensational. Brave heroes and dastardly villains, that sort of thing. Not the everyday life of farmers and fishwives. What you're reading is a small window into that period, not the whole story.'

'Mm.' Rona returned to her book. A few minutes later, her father interrupted her again.

'Say, Peaches, have you come across a character by the name of Gudrun?'

'In this book? I don't think so. Not yet, anyway.'

'If I remember correctly, you will. Near the end.'

'Who was Gudrun, anyway?'

'She was a Norsewoman, from Sutherland I believe, who somehow came into possession of land – *our* land here on the Hill of Fare. Gudrun was said to be very tall – 'statuesque' might be the modern word. She built a grand house that became known as *Gudrun Ha* – a "ha" is what they still call a large country residence in Orkney and Shetland. Over the centuries, the name got corrupted into Gordonhall.'

'So our estate has nothing to do with the Gordons? I thought it was named after Whatsisname Gordon that fought the battle of Corrichie against Mary, Queen of Scots.'

'George Gordon, Earl of Huntly. Yes, that's the conventional explanation, especially since the battlefield is only a mile from here.* But the Gordonhall name is much older, going all the way back to Gudrun who came here around 1150.'

'Tall and elegant, was she?'

'So it was said. You know the Skairs, up on the hill?'

'Yes, those rocks above Cluny Crichton. When I was little, you told me not to go near them. And I never did.'

'Good. They're not on our land these days, but once upon a time, Gordonhall laid claim to the Skairs. Legend has it that Gudrun died there and her ghost haunts the place.'

Rona was sceptical. 'You don't believe that, do you, Daddy?'

'We shouldn't ignore these old stories. There's something eldritch about those rocks.'

---

* The battle of Corrichie features in *Taran's Wheel* (*Incomers*: Book 1).

'*Eldritch?*'

'Uncanny, evil.'

'Seriously?' She wanted to laugh it off, but something in her father's expression held her back. There was an uncomfortable pause.

'Anyway,' Philip said at length, 'Gudrun's land passed down through her descendants to the man created 1st Earl of Fairfield by Robert the Bruce ...'

'And from him all the way down to you, the 22nd Earl.'

'Eventually to you, Peaches. When I die, you'll be the 23rd Countess of Fairfield. Gudrun's legacy will live on.'

Soon afterwards Rona found a slim leather-bound volume in the Gordonhall library she had not previously noticed. It bore no words on the cover; inside, its pages were densely packed with ancient Gothic script that to her eyes was virtually unreadable. With a struggle she was able to decipher the title page, consisting of a single word in a language she was later to learn was Icelandic:

GUÐRÚNSSAGA.

Hoping to learn more about her twelfth-century ancestor, she hunted among the shelves for an English translation of this *Guðrún's Saga*, without success. At the time, she gave it little further thought.

Winter eventually turned to spring and spring to summer. Rona, who had been a gawky adolescent on her fifteenth birthday was now blossoming towards womanhood; by her sixteenth birthday on 30th September 1960 the strikingly beautiful lady she was to become was already evident. She no longer envied Lidia's precocious maturity. The friendship that had started through both girls' rejection by their contemporaries at school – one because she was Polish, the other because she was a 'toff' – became firmer.

Most Sundays they would get together, usually just the two of them but sometimes with one or more of the boys who had befriended them – Keith, Alan, Dougie and Stewart. For Rona it generally meant a five-mile round-trip by bicycle to a meeting-place in Banchory, as often as not Bongiovanni's café in the High Street. Her meagre pocket-money stretched to little more than a hot orange squash and perhaps three plays on the jukebox. The boys, especially Keith, seemed always to have plenty of cash and would occasionally buy the girls a special treat, such as a knickerbocker glory. They also paid for more than their fair share of spins of the latest hits.

Occasionally Lidia would come to Gordonhall, where the two girls would take a walk on the heather-clad Hill of Fare or, if the weather was inclement, spend a few hours in the library of the big house. Lidia, unsurprisingly, shared none of Rona's enthusiasm for the Norse sagas, but found other treasures, mainly illustrated books on sport and fashion from a bygone era.

One Sunday in early 1961, Lidia arrived with a book she had borrowed from Alan: *Lady Chatterley's Lover* by D.H. Lawrence, newly published as a Penguin Classic but written more than thirty years earlier. Alan had helpfully dog-eared a dozen or so pages of particular interest.

A few months earlier, Rona had heard talk about this book on the BBC Home Service. As usual, the news her mother and father tuned into was mostly background noise to her. But she gathered that a jury had been asked to decide whether or not *Lady C.* was 'obscene' and therefore unpublishable under the law at that time. She knew better than ask her parents to explain what precisely was supposed to be 'obscene' about it.

Now, with Lidia's assistance in the chilly privacy of the Gordonhall library, she was to find out what all the fuss was about.

Alan's dog-ears drew the girls' attention to passages that were shocking, yet somehow liberating, to see in print. That a serious novelist could write about sex in such explicit terms, and use the f-word and even the c-word so matter-of-factly, was startling. But Rona was drawn not so much to Lawrence's detailed description of a physical relationship between a man and a woman as to *who* the principal players were: Constance, a lady of culture whose marriage had propelled her into upper-class society, and Mellors, a working-class gamekeeper on her husband's estate.

Was that what the future held for Rona herself? Required to marry some aristocrat – another 'toff' in the vernacular – might she become a Constance Chatterley? Would she too turn to a Mellors for comfort?

She could not possibly have foreseen at that moment how closely, in a few short years, her life would mirror art. Nor that the art it would mirror would be something much older than a D.H. Lawrence novel.

6
CRIMES OF A PAST GENERATION

THE IDENTITY OF THE LEFT-WING blogger Toff Hammer was a mystery to all but Tim Heston himself. Without divulging his authorship of the blog, Heston drew it to the attention of his undergraduate students in sociology at Glasgow Caledonian University, but warned that the blogger's utterances, while they represented *a* truth, were not to be read as *the* truth. They were, he said, merely a counterpoint to establishment propaganda peddled by the right-wing media.

To his detractors, Toff Hammer seemed to have a huge chip on his shoulder, a desire somehow to see the targets of his venom, deserving or otherwise, get their comeuppance. Who were those targets? In short, Scotland's 'toffs': the landed gentry to whom, the blogger said, the rest of the population were still expected to tug their forelocks, metaphorically if not literally any more. He accused them of sins ranging from minor present-day infringements of civil liberties – denials of right-of-way across their land, for example – to massive historical injustices. Among the latter, he returned again and again to the still raw wounds of the Highland Clearances.

A recent posting gives the flavour.

DUNROBIN –DEMOLISH OR NATIONALISE?

by Toff Hammer

No visitor to Dunrobin Castle who knows anything of the odious family whose seat it is, can fail to see it as an obscenity, a vulgar blot on the landscape of

Sutherland. Some have argued for it to be razed to the ground. But as the most potent symbol of the ill-divided world of land ownership in Scotland, a better future for Dunrobin would be as a museum with free access to all. The castle and its grounds should be nationalised in the name of the Scottish people, without compensation to the present owners.

The museum I have in mind would not be one that glorifies the Earldom and Duchy of Sutherland, but quite the opposite. It would tell of the appalling crimes committed by past Earls and Countesses, Dukes and Duchesses in pursuit of wealth – the wealth that built Dunrobin and financed a breathtaking land-grab. In 1820, almost 1,500 square miles of the Highlands were in the hands of one woman, the unspeakable Elizabeth, 19th Countess of Sutherland.

Whereas Versailles and the Tsarist palaces of St Petersburg forcibly remind visitors why revolution was necessary in France and Russia, the museum of Dunrobin would be a monument to the conniving Scottish establishment – the lawyers, politicians, churchmen, educators and journalists under whose watch and with whose express approval the Sutherlands' crimes were committed. And what of the ordinary people of Scotland who kowtowed to them? They did not revolt. To this day they have continued to elect the same brand of weak-willed functionary that cannot face up to those who still benefit from their ancestors' crimes.

The rot started in the twelfth century when a Flemish nobleman received a generous grant of land in Scotland from King David I, and his grandson Hugh de Moravia (Murray) subsequently took possession of a vast tract of Sutherland. Whether that acquisition was legal (nominally, at least, Sutherland was still part of Norway) and why this family of incomers should have been the beneficiaries are open questions. In any case, by 1230 Hugh's son William had amassed sufficient feudal power to prompt King Alexander II to create a new Earldom of Sutherland for him.

In 1508, on the death of the 8th Earl, his eldest son John succeeded. However, John's sister Elizabeth had married the ambitious Adam Gordon of Aboyne and the couple coveted the earldom. The powerful Gordon family, through their connections to the judiciary, had John and his younger brother declared 'idiots'. This made them ineligible to hold the title, and in 1512, Elizabeth became 10th Countess and Adam Gordon the new Earl, residing at Dunrobin.

A legitimate heir, Alexander Sutherland, stormed the castle in 1518, but was soon defeated. In a nice touch, the Earl and his lady had their kinsman's head mounted on a spear atop the castle tower. The message was clear: the Gordons were here to stay.

But it was another Elizabeth, their direct descendant, who set the gold standard for nastiness among the Scottish landowning classes. Around 1790 she developed a plan to quadruple her rental income from Great Britain's largest landed estate, two-thirds of the county of Sutherland, to something over £20,000 per year (about £1.5 million in today's money). The plan involved repopulating her 900,000 acres with sheep in place of people – as many landowners were doing at the time – but needed more capital than she had at her disposal at that time.

When her husband came into a fortune in 1803 by becoming Marquess of Stafford, she might have thought, 'Why bother?' Instead the 19th Countess of

Sutherland, aided and abetted by the fabulously wealthy Stafford, set about torching the homes and crops of her tenants to force them out. Thousands of men, women and children perished for want of food and shelter, a consequence that left her unmoved. As she wrote to an English friend on witnessing the starving populace, 'Scotch people ... do not fatten like the larger breed of animals.'

Those who could, emigrated, mainly to Canada and the US, where the population of the diaspora is now vastly greater than that remaining in the Highlands. Some apologists for the Clearances argue that the Countess did Highlanders a favour: the emigrants were able to carve out a much more prosperous life for themselves and their descendants than would ever have been possible at home. Even if true, that would not excuse the Stalinesque brutality with which she organised the mass displacement of a people.

Such protest as the Highlanders were able to mount was quickly quelled. Elizabeth wrote: 'As the people resist by force, no one can complain if they are brought to reason by the same means.' The mere threat of military intervention was sufficient to intimidate a peasantry armed with no more than hoes and pitchforks.

Breathtaking though Elizabeth's barbarity was, the Scottish establishment loved it. The sadistic Patrick Sellar, who implemented most of the Clearances for the Countess, was acquitted of culpable homicide by a jury drawn from the landowning classes. The Kirk saw merit in the programme as a way to cleanse the Highlands of Catholics, though it transpired the majority of those driven out were Protestants. The press was almost unanimous in its praise for the Clearances; witness the view of The Scotsman *in 1851, to its eternal shame:*

> *Collective emigration is the removal of a diseased and damaged part of our population. It is a relief to the rest of the population to be rid of this part.*

The proto-nazi view from Edinburgh was that the 'Celtic' peoples of the Highlands were genetically inferior to the Anglo-Saxon and Nordic races and their extirpation was therefore a good thing. That the population of Sutherland had a rich amalgam of Scandinavian and Celtic ancestry was not allowed to spoil the story. The Strath of Kildonan, scene of some of the worst atrocities, was actually more Norse than Gael.

'Men of substance' were selected as the new tenants, each holding a vast tract of Sutherland that previously supported up to a thousand people or more. One such beneficiary in Kildonan was William Clunes, who was awarded the tenancy of half the strath as a sheep-farm. Scotland's pre-eminent portraitist Henry Raeburn painted him; for reasons we can now only guess at, the portrait – in the Scottish National Gallery – is dominated by a horse's arse.

The 19th Countess was enormously enriched by the Clearances. The Dunrobin we can visit today was built very largely on the wealth she amassed at that time and bequeathed to her successors. It is only right that those successors now be dispossessed, just as they dispossessed 'their' county's population two hundred years ago. It is never too late to recover the proceeds of crime against humanity.

Toff Hammer tended not to commit a story – or even a rant – to his blog without prior exhaustive research. His regular readers knew, when he went quiet, that a new attack on some unsuspecting aristocratic family was brewing.

Two such families, linked by marriage half a century ago in the 1960s, were about to become the unwitting subjects of his attention. They were the House of Bracklinn, with its seat at Ardwhinzean near Callander, and the much more venerable House of Fairfield, for centuries – but no longer – ensconced at Gordonhall to the north of Banchory. It was the ambition of Toff Hammer *alias* Tim Heston to force atonement for crimes of a past generation. Only one loose end remained: the fate of the key player, born Rona Fay Swainson, who had gone to ground in 1990.

7

END OF YOUTHFUL INNOCENCE

BY THE TIME RONA WAS approaching seventeen, in the summer of 1961, her parents' financial situation had become so straitened that she was obliged to find a holiday job. But how? As usual, Lidia came to the rescue.

'The boys have been taken on by Tillybarnie to cut broom,' she told Rona. 'It's a five-and-a-half-day week, total 44 hours. They're to get two and sixpence an hour. I'm going to sign on. You should too.'

Five pounds ten shillings a week, Rona calculated. *Four pounds to Mummy and Daddy for my keep, leaving one pound ten pocket money. I can be a big spender at Bongiovanni's like the boys!* 'Tillybarnie?' she queried. 'Don't they have estate workers to do that?'

''Course they do,' Lidia replied. 'But they planted more trees than they can handle, so Dougie says. If they don't cut back the broom, the trees are going to die.'

The Earl of Fairfield was distinctly unenthusiastic about his daughter doing menial labour at a neighbouring estate. The laird of Tillybarnie was head of a firm of solicitors in Aberdeen who took no part in the day-to-day running of his property, and was little more than a casual acquaintance, but the Earl gave him a call.

'It's about my daughter Rona. Seems she wants to come and work on your forestry plantations for the summer. Just to see first-hand how young trees are managed, you understand. Says she'd like us to do some planting here at Gordonhall. Would you be able to fit her in?'

'No problem, Philip. Lady Rona should put her name down at the factor's office and show up for work on Monday morning at 7:30. The foreman's name is Johnny Nicol. He'll keep her right.'

Broom-cutting was back-breaking, hand-blistering labour. The tool for the job was a *heuk*, a sickle-like implement with a curved blade honed to a lethally sharp edge. Expertly deployed, it could sever a woody broom stem up to an inch and a half thick. The trick was to bend the stem over with a slight twist, then sharply pull the *heuk* through the tensioned wood.

Rona had been forewarned that the work would be hard and painful. Bert the gardener lent her a pair of stout leather and canvas gloves to protect her hands; even so her palms and fingers blistered and bled until, after a few days, they began to callus against the onslaught.

Johnny Nicol proved to be a hard taskmaster. A wiry, dyspeptic-looking man in his fifties with bottoms-of-bottles glasses and a cigarette permanently dangling from his lip, he kept his young workforce from slacking with a constant stream of foul-mouthed invective. As a term of abuse for male and female minions alike he particularly favoured the c-word – not, Rona noted, in its Lawrencian sense.

'I don't think he knows what that word really means,' she said to Lidia one day during their short lunch break.

'Obviously it's been ages since he got any,' Lidia said, before repeating the conversation to the boys. Nicol caught them sniggering and immediately ordered everyone back to work ten minutes early.

Pay was doled out by the factor's cashier on Saturday at noon. The first Saturday there was no money for the girls, as he operated a strict requirement of one week's 'lying-time'. The boys had begun work a week earlier and were delighted with their sudden wealth: £5 10s each, at least ten shillings of which would be spent before they got home that afternoon.

A nasty surprise lay in store for Rona and Lidia. The following Saturday they received recompense for their first week's hard labour. Each was given in her callused hand three pound notes, a ten-shilling note and three sixpenny pieces.

'What's this?' Lidia asked the cashier. 'We worked the full 44 hours last week.'

'That's right,' he replied with a sniff. 'Forty-four hours at one and sevenpence ha'penny an hour.'

'But the deal was two and sixpence!'

'For men, yes. A woman gets 65 percent of a man's wage. Work it out when you get home. You'll find your pay packet is right to the penny.'

It was Rona's turn to remonstrate. 'But we cut just the same amount of broom as the boys did, not 35 percent less. Ask Mr Nicol.' She gestured towards the foreman, who was standing by the door, lighting a fresh cigarette from the butt of the last one. He avoided eye contact.

'It's the rule,' the cashier said. 'If every woman demanded a man's salary, imagine how ridiculous *that* would be!' He and Nicol laughed together, enjoying the girls' discomfiture.

To Rona's astonishment and delight, Lidia let loose a stream of oaths, making a point of emphasising Johnny Nicol's favourite c-word. 'We won't be back next week, except to collect the pay you owe us for *this* week,' she announced.

'What're we going to do for money now?' Rona wondered aloud as they walked along Banchory's High Street that afternoon.

'Dunno,' Lidia said. Then, on a whim, 'Come on, let's ask Mr Bongiovanni if he'll give us a job. This is his busiest time of the year. Look at all these day-trippers out for a run from Aberdeen. Every one of them dying for ice-cream.'

'Sorry, my dears,' the café proprietor told them. He pointed to two devastatingly pretty girls with glossy black hair moving among the tables. 'My nieces, from Perugia. They're all the help

I need just now. But why don't you try George Grant across the street? I heard he just fired two of his serving girls for stealing from the till. I'll put in a word for you, if you like.'

'That would be wonderful,' Rona said appreciatively.

He shook both girls by the hand. 'Ow!' he exclaimed, surprised by the blisters. 'What happened to you?'

'Just got our fingers burned, in a manner of speaking,' Rona replied, before explaining.

Grant's family restaurant was their salvation. Five pounds a week, plus tips.

Deeply uncool though it was to the two teenagers, with no jukebox and a menu that seemed stuck in the days of post-war rationing, it had the advantage that their cliquish classmates would never darken its door.

In August, just before school resumed for Rona to start sixth year, her Highers results arrived in the mail. A's in German, French and English; B's in Latin and mathematics. More than good enough for a place at university, and she still had geography to take in the coming year.

The four boys who had been their steady friends had finished school and were going their separate ways. Keith and Dougie would start university in October, at St Andrews and Aberdeen respectively. Alan had secured an engineering apprenticeship with the BBC at Beechgrove, Aberdeen, with day-release to 'Techie College' on Gallowgate. Stewart, always the quietest of the four, found a position on the very lowest rung of the management ladder at the Raemoir Hotel, meaning he did not have to leave home.

Lidia and Rona had been so popular with the restaurant's regular clientele that George Grant was only too happy to have them back in the summer of '62.

School was over; for Rona, university beckoned. She had been accepted into the Arts programme at Aberdeen, where it was her ambition to pursue a degree in German and Scandinavian Studies. Lidia, meanwhile, was set to train as a physical education teacher, at the 'Dunf' in Woolmanhill, Aberdeen.

With their academic year not starting until late September or early October, the girls had an extended period of summer employment at Grant's. Their art of innocent flirting with older men was rewarded with generous tips. The occasional half-crown, a satisfyingly heavy lump of silvery metal, was an excuse for a celebratory '99' after work, across the street at Bongiovanni's.

One day Lidia confessed that, while 'fooling around' with one of the Grant boys in the back seat of his father's Ford Consul, she had experienced 'proper sex' for the first time. Rona was shocked but curious, and strangely jealous, though she would not have admitted it.

To avoid the cost of lodgings in Aberdeen, Rona's parents insisted she stay at home for at least her first year of university. She could commute the sixteen miles each way by bus every day, an arrangement she hated. She had to miss out on the many extracurricular activities that being a student was all about, but began visiting Stewart late in the evenings when he was on reception desk duty at Raemoir.

Though obviously attracted to the beautiful blonde Rona, Stewart was too shy to make the first move. *She's too good-looking to really be interested in someone like me,* he was thinking. *Plus, she's a chum, and she's brainy, which I'm not. On top of all that she's a toff. An earl's daughter, for goodness' sake.*

It was up to Rona to make something happen.

'What are the bedrooms like?' she asked him one Friday night in February 1963.

'Pretty nice, most of them,' Stewart replied. 'A couple of them even have their own bathroom. *En suite*, it's called. That's French.'

'I know it's French, silly. But I've never seen an *en suite* room.' Rona ran her fingers over a row of keys hanging behind the reception desk – unoccupied rooms, she assumed. 'Which of these are *en suite*?'

'Only that one with the big green fob. I can take you up there if you like, but only for a few minutes, in case anyone rings. I'm on duty all on my own tonight.'

Looking back on that first dangerous encounter over half a century ago, Ragna Enjudóttir winced with embarrassment as she sat in her fragrant Icelandic garden waiting for Ari to come home with the day's catch. She recalled the awkward fumbling on the soft hotel bed, the unexpected urgency with which Stewart had to find his way in, the sudden stabbing pain and, above all, the mess of blood and seminal fluid. Thank goodness she'd had the foresight to grab a towel from the bathroom and lay it on the bed before they began.

The words of Philip Larkin's *Annus Mirabilis* came to her mind.

> *Sexual intercourse began*
> *In nineteen sixty-three*
> *(At least it did for me)*
> *Between the end of the* Chatterley *ban*
> *And The Beatles' first LP.*

For some reason, she had a vivid memory of meeting Lidia in Bongiovanni's the morning after. Though her experience with Stewart had been a bit of a disappointment, she reported it triumphantly to her friend.

While they talked, Mr Bongiovanni was adding some just-acquired 45s to the jukebox. 'Heard this one, girls?' he asked, putting sixpence in the slot and pressing one of the newly relabelled buttons. 'It's by a group called The Beatles.'

'Yes, it was on Luxembourg last night,' Lidia said as the music started. 'It's fab!'

Rona looked quizzically at her friend. *Fab? Where does she get words like that?*

The song was *Please Please Me*, the first of eighteen Beatles singles to reach the top of the British charts. It marked the beginning of a revolution in popular music. In Rona's mind it would be forever linked with the coming end of youthful innocence.

8
GUDRUN

THE TYPESCRIPT WAS OLD-FASHIONED, without doubt the product of a mechanical typewriter, perhaps a pre-war Imperial like the one Frank Jamieson remembered in his childhood home. From the sharpness of the letters he could see this was an original, not a carbon copy. Erasures had been made not with correction fluid or tape but by smudgy rubbings-out.

He settled down to read. The work was titled:

GUDRUN'S SAGA

*Translated from Icelandic by Rona Fay Swainson
assisted by Ari Haraldsson*

With explanatory notes by the translator

The work could already have been quite old when it came into his possession about 35 years previously. Had it been published? Not as far as he was able to determine on the Web. Though various references to 'Gudrun's Saga' could be found, none had links to Rona Fay Swainson or Ari Haraldsson. No book on Amazon; no library catalogue entry.

A more famous Gudrun featured in some versions of the myth of Siegfried and Brünnhilde, including the Wagnerian Ring operas; J.R.R. Tolkien had brought her to prominence in his *Legend of Sigurd and Gudrún*. No doubt it was *that* Gudrun after whom D.H. Lawrence named one of the principal characters in *Women in Love*, so memorably played by Glenda Jackson in the classic 1969 film. But it was clear from the opening paragraphs of the new-found manuscript that its eponymous Gudrun was of less ancient vintage than Wagner's and Tolkien's heroine – by at least 700 years. And she was not German but – originally at least – a citizen of the Norwegian Earldom of Orkney.

No, this was not the fifth-century Gudrun who, on the rebound from death of her husband Siegfried, married Attila the Hun and gave him two sons, both of whom she murdered and served to their father in a feast, in revenge for his slaughter of her entire family. She waited until he was very drunk before telling him what/whom he had eaten for dinner.

Rona Fay's Gudrun appeared housetrained by comparison, though her saga documented some bloody deeds and nasty people.

Frank found most of the major players of *Gudrun's Saga* to correspond to characters in the known Nordic sagas; many of them had entries in Wikipedia. By the time he reached the end, he had resolved to find out who Rona Fay Swainson was and if she was still alive. He felt he had to return the manuscript to its author or her heirs. Whether or not Frank was the rightful owner of the tome in which it was lodged, he considered that *Gudrun's Saga* was not his to do with as he pleased.

Swainson, he learned from Google, was the family name of the Earls of Fairfield, from whose library at Gordonhall his copy of *Illustrated Natural History* with its concealed envelope had come. Beyond that, he could glean nothing more. Links to the food company Fairfield's Cereals seemed irrelevant. He found no trace on the Web of the Fairfield family scandal he dimly recalled from his youth.

Several weeks later, Frank made the trip north from London to revisit the slopes of the Hill of Fare where the house of Gordonhall had once stood.

The site, as best he could remember, of the imposing mansion was now occupied by an avant-garde glass and timber dwelling like those often featuring on TV programmes of the *Grand Designs* genre. The walled garden he remembered was still there, now with a large modern greenhouse in one corner. Abutting the exterior wall on one side was a semi-derelict cottage that had presumably once been the home of the Swainsons' gardener.

'May I ask what you are doing here?' a peremptory voice behind him shouted as he peered through the gate.

Frank turned to see a tall lady in wellies and a Barbour jacket approaching him from the direction of the *Grand Designs* house. Her greying hair was cropped in a rather masculine way, though the effect was softened by large earrings. He stepped forward to meet her but was suddenly intimidated by her lady-of-the-manor demeanour, sharp features and cold eyes, set a little too closely together behind austere steel-framed glasses. 'I'm just revisiting some places I knew as a boy,' he said. 'I remember the original house of Gordonhall, and was pleased to see that at least the walled garden is still here. My name's Frank Jamieson.'

'You don't sound like you're from around here.'

'No, I've lived in London all my life, but my parents were from this part of Scotland.'

The woman's apparent hostility softened, though the glint in her eyes did not become any more friendly. 'I'm Faith Elliott,' she said by way of introduction. 'This property has been in my family since about 1970.'

'You're not one of the Swainsons, are you?'

'God, no. The Swainsons forfeited Gordonhall through non-compliance with some legal conditions, and the estate came into our hands. And it's been all the better for it.'

Stab in the dark, Frank decided. 'Wasn't there a Rona Fay Swainson who belonged to that family?'

Suddenly suspicious, Faith Elliott countered with a question of her own. 'What do you know of her?'

'Almost nothing. Only that I have a manuscript of hers, a translation of a Norse saga, and I'd like to trace her, if she's still alive, and offer it back to her.'

'I wouldn't bother if I were you, Mr Jamieson. She hasn't been heard of since 1990.'

'Mm. She's dead, then?'

'Probably.'

'Any surviving children?'

'As it happens, yes. Donald Swainson – have you heard of him? He's the chairman of Fairfield's Cereals, based in Dundee, but spends most of his time in Orkney. Telecommutes to board meetings. I'm on the board too.'

Ka-ching! went a bell in Frank's brain. The Fairfield's Cereals company was indeed connected to the family of that name, the former owners of Gordonhall. 'Maybe I can get in touch with him, see if he'd be interested in having his mother's manuscript.'

'Doubt it – family feud, you know – but I can tell him about it when I see him.'

'Thank you, that would be great.' He gave her a card with his contact information before returning to his car.

While he was in the area, he took a drive by the former home of his aunt and uncle (it had been extended and modernised, and Uncle Al's garage-workshop demolished), then paid his respects at their grave in Torphins cemetery.

9
NOBLESSE OBLIGE

'DO YOU REALLY WANT TO spend three more years of your life at university?' her father asked one day as they sat down to dinner. 'You've had a full year there, plus all that time immersing yourself in Scandinavian literature in our own library – too much for your own good. You're almost nineteen, old enough to be thinking about your future.'

'This *is* my future, Daddy,' Rona protested. 'I want to become an expert in Old Norse like Grandpapa.'

'That'll get you nowhere, Peaches. A wealthy and titled husband, on the other hand ...'

'*What?*' Rona screamed. 'You want to marry me off already?'

'Of course not. Certainly not this year or even next. But you need to start moving in the right circles. Aberdeen University may be a fine institution, but it's not the place where a future countess is going to find the right match.'

'For God's sake, I don't *care* about finding a "match". You should be pleased that I'm more interested in our heritage.'

'You're a young *woman*. You have different priorities to think about.'

'I'm a woman, yes, and as good as any man. I can have a career of my own, a *life* of my own.'

'Darling,' her mother said soothingly, 'we just want what's best for you. It's a man's world, and the best thing a young woman can do is ...'

'Hitch herself to some titled geezer, I know. Like you did. But we're not in Jane Austen land any more. We're over half-way through the twentieth century, in case you hadn't noticed. Women are doctors, lawyers, professors, members of parliament, even cosmonauts.'

'One *Russian* cosmonaut. We don't take our cue from the Soviets.'

'You'd better tell her,' Aenea said to her husband.

'Tell me *what*?'

The Earl of Fairfield drew a deep breath before speaking. 'There's something you need to know, Rona. We have promised Lord Bracklinn that you will become betrothed to his eldest son. A meeting has been arranged on the seventh of August, at Ardwhinzean House in Stirlingshire.'

Rona was struck dumb for a moment. Then her face reddened and she found the words to say, 'Who the *fuck* is Lord Bracklinn?' It was the first time she had ever uttered the f-word in front of her parents.

'That language may be what passes for conversation among your student friends, young lady, but we don't use it here. Let me tell you who he is. Ludovic Argill, 2nd Lord Bracklinn, owns a string of large grocery shops – "supermarkets", I believe they're called nowadays – up and down the country. He's on the boards of four or five financial companies including a bank and a brokerage. His lands in Stirlingshire extend to 3000 acres or more. He ...'

'What is it with Stirlingshire? You sent me to that pathetic school ... thank *God* I got out. Now you want me to marry some rich *jerk*, a chinless wonder, no doubt. Well, I've got news for you. He can have all the supermarkets in Great Britain, but he's not having me.'

Rona began to cry with rage. Her father looked as if he might burst into tears of his own. Aenea had to take the helm.

'We haven't told you about our present predicament, darling, because we didn't want to worry you. But here's the situation. The money – *my* money – we were using to keep paying interest on our loan at the bank has run out. We're on the verge of bankruptcy. The bank will take Gordonhall and sell it to the highest bidder. Gordonhall, that's been in the Swainson family for eight hundred years.'

'That's sad, but what has it to do with me leaving university to get married to this … this *grocer's* boy?'

'Lord Bracklinn approached your father at his club in Edinburgh. As a governor of the bank, he is probably aware of the parlous state of our finances and has made an offer that, frankly, is impossible for us to refuse. Here's the deal: if you agree to marry the Honourable Antony Argill, his son and heir, he will make good our entire debt. Gordonhall will be safe.'

'Why would he do that? It's a lot of money, just to buy a daughter-in-law.'

'Don't think of it like that, darling,' Aenea said. 'You can give a husband something money can't buy: a child who will one day be Earl or Countess of Fairfield. A much older and more prestigious title than Baron Bracklinn.'

The destiny Rona had dreaded was becoming reality. Deep down, she *knew* an arranged marriage was her lot. It was no good envying those 'lower-born' girls who could make their own choices. *Noblesse oblige* and all that. With the privileges of aristocracy come obligations, one of which is to enter marriages of convenience when circumstances dictate.

'I'll think about it,' she said at length. 'On one condition. I get to finish university, with Honours if I'm selected for the four-year programme. I have my graduation before my wedding. Deal?'

A huge weight was lifted off the shoulders of the Earl and Countess. 'Yes,' they replied in unison.

Rona left the dinner table without touching her food. Her father made to call her back, but Aenea restrained him. 'This is a difficult moment for her. She needs some time alone to come to terms with it.'

It was a beautiful summer's evening. Rona marched out of the gatehouse and set off up the drive towards the empty mansion. But on reaching its great front door she decided against going in. Instead she continued up through the trees behind the house until she emerged on the heather-clad slopes of the Hill of Fare – the 'Sheep Hill' or *Faer Fjall* that gave the Fairfield earldom its name.

On an impulse she strayed deliberately westward off the Gordonhall land, making straight for the Skairs, where she had been warned not to venture. Some ridiculous story about a ghost. Gudrun haunted that spot, her father had told her. *Rubbish!*

It was peaceful. Bees hummed contentedly among the rocks, seeking out the scattered bell heather that was already in bloom while awaiting the coming feast of nectar from the slightly later common heather or ling that would soon turn the entire hill purple. Rona sat down, resting her back against one of the great boulders of the Skairs, still warm from a day's toasting in the sun. She scanned the hills of the Mounth forming the southern horizon: Mongour, Kerloch, Clochnaben, Mount Battock, Mount Keen. Away to the west was Morven.

Alone with her thoughts, she allowed herself a tear, then a sob, then a full-blown cry. As if she were still a child, she cried herself to sleep right there on the hillside.

The sun sank lower in the north-west and the evening turned chilly. She awoke with a start, taking a moment to realise where she was. A light breeze had got up, playing among the boulders, and suddenly it seemed to speak. It said, with a startling clarity, 'Rona, tell my stories.'

She jumped to her feet and looked all around her. 'Who's there?' she asked.

But no one answered. Though she listened, all she heard was the light sough of the wind in the heather.

Lady Rona Swainson was formally introduced to the Honourable Antony Argill at a society ball in Callander. She was pleasantly surprised to find that her future husband was not only a good-looking man – albeit nine years older than herself – but courteous and charming.

In the weeks that followed, she learned from him that, although he had been linked with a number of young ladies in the society pages, he had formed no serious relationship with any of them. His brother Dominic, also easy to talk to, confirmed that Antony had been 'waiting for the right girl to come along'. The brothers, she discovered, had an unusual bond. Though Dominic was born within hours after Antony on 2nd December 1935, they were not twins. The elder was the only son of the first Lady Bracklinn, Nancy Telford. The younger was born to Edith Gauld. Their father divorced Nancy and married Edith in 1941, thereby legitimising Dominic and confirming him as second in line to the Bracklinn title.

Though Dominic was not blessed with Antony's handsome face and physique, Rona noted with amusement that he was, for some reason, a magnet for young women. He was sometimes described in the *Callander Advertiser* as a 'fun-loving' gentleman – good thing, the unwritten subtext went, that he wasn't the immediate heir to the barony.

Antony and Rona were duly dubbed an 'item' by society gossips within months of their first encounter. It was agreed between the families, however, that the official engagement would not be announced meantime, as the wedding would not take place until the summer of 1966, after Rona's graduation.

Suddenly spared from imminent financial ruin, Philip Swainson, Earl of Fairfield had a new spring in his step. No longer was all the income from his land swallowed up in interest payments to the bank. He and Aenea could now afford to repair the roof of Gordonhall and contemplate moving back into its stately accommodation.

Rona, meanwhile, could look forward to three more years of student life before giving up her freedom. The prospect of marriage to Antony Argill was not as awful as it might have been, and she consigned it to the back of her mind while she focused on her studies. Even better, she moved into lodgings – a single room in Fountainhall Road in Aberdeen's west end – and could now enjoy a full social life with her fellow students, something she had been denied in her first year.

Shock waves from a series of gunshots in Dallas, Texas were about to reverberate around the world. Hours before the news broke on Friday 22nd November 1963, Rona walked into Bruce Miller's on George Street, Aberdeen and bought a brand new Dansette record player, on hire purchase. Ten shillings and sixpence a week for 26 weeks – not bad for a machine with an autochanger you could load with up to eight records at a time. She also splashed out on six singles, all of them on that week's top twenty as featured on Radio Luxembourg, and her first LP, *With The Beatles*. But that sombre night the Dansette remained in its box.

She got around to unpacking it the following evening. Giving some of her singles a spin (*She Loves You* – The Beatles, *Be My Baby* – The Ronettes, *Memphis Tennessee* – Chuck Berry), she marvelled at the way the records dropped one at a time and the arm always positioned the stylus at the start of a new record. Then she headed out to a Scandi-Soc cheese-and-wine.

Most of her classmates, and a fair number of more sophisticated third- and fourth-year students, were at the get-together in the Students' Union. Rona had just entered the room when a young man wearing jeans and a colourful sweater, from which protruded a casually untucked shirt, approached her carrying two full glasses of wine. His hair was even blonder than her own.

'Red or white?' he asked in strongly accented English.

'White, please.'

'I'm glad you said that. I prefer the red. My name is Ari.'

'I'm Rona. Let me guess … are you from Norway?'

'Iceland.'

'I haven't seen you around at lectures.' *I'm sure I would have noticed him.*

'I'm a Forestry student. There are six of us from *Skógrækt Ríkisins* – the Iceland Forest Service. After we graduate we'll go back as researchers. We want to reforest our country.'

'It's a long way to come to get a degree.'

'I suppose so, but if we want to study forest science, Aberdeen is our local university.'

'So when will you graduate?'

'Sixty-six.'

'Same here.'

The conversation continued all evening, punctuated by trips to the bar to refill their wine glasses and fetch a variety of Danish and Swedish cheeses on sticks.

'How are you going home?' Ari asked at the end. 'By bus?'

'This time of night, they're few and far between,' Rona said. 'I'll just walk. Less than half an hour gets me back to my digs.'

'May I walk with you?'

'That sounded very formal,' she said, laughing. 'Sorry, didn't mean to make fun of you. I must be a bit tipsy.'

'I suppose that's a "yes",' Ari said, taking charge. As they set off into the frosty late November evening, he took her hand firmly in his. She did not resist.

In companionable silence, they walked briskly in the cold air. Nearing Fountainhall Road, he asked, 'When can I see you again? I've a hockey game next Saturday afternoon – did I tell you I was on the University team? We're playing St Andrews. But if you have no plans for that evening, would you go out with me? Is that too formal?'

Under a yellow street lamp she squeezed his hand and looked into his eyes. 'Not too formal at all.' Then she shocked herself by kissing him on the cheek.

'How is this for informal?' he said, putting both arms around her and kissing her full on the lips.

She drew back, dropping her eyes. 'Actually, I have to tell you ... I'm sort of engaged. We're supposed to get married at the end of my course.'

'You don't sound very enthusiastic.'

'Well ... it's something I have to do. I'm sorry if I've given you the wrong impression.'

The sadness in her voice led the young Icelander to probe a little. '*Have* to?'

'I'd rather not talk about it just now. It's been a great evening, Ari. Let's leave it at that.'

He walked her to the door of her lodgings. As they parted, he said, 'When you *do* want to talk about it, let me know. I would really love to see you again.'

10

A CHANGE OF SCENE

THE AVENGER'S SECOND VICTIM lived and worked in Durham.

Royston Perry, a 47-year-old married branch manager in one of Britain's biggest banks, had been having an affair with Leona White, an unmarried thirty-something teller, for almost a year. Their after-work trysts were usually in a seedy hotel near the railway station, unless Perry was able to secure the occasionally-available £29 room rate at one of the city's three Premier Inns.

'Miss White, close your desk after the next customer and come and see me, please.'

'Yes, sir,' Leona replied to the portly manager. Then, almost in the same breath to her customer, 'How can I help you today?'

Five minutes later, she walked into Perry's office and closed the door behind her.

'Leona, my dear,' the manager began, 'how about a change of scene tonight?'

'A change of scene?'

'Yes. You see, Mrs Perry – Norma – has gone off to spend a few days with her sister in Wales. Why don't I take you to my place instead of our usual ... rendezvous?'

'Oh, I don't know, Mr Perry ...'

'Royston.'

'... Royston, it doesn't seem ... right, somehow.'

'We won't be seen, if that's what's worrying you. We'll take my car, and I'll drive straight into the garage. A door leads from there directly into the house.'

Leona still looked doubtful.

'We'll have all home comforts, if you get my meaning. Better even than the Premier Inn. And you can stay the whole night, won't that be nice?'

'I suppose ... Oh, by the way, Mr Perry, when will that promotion come through, do you think? It's four months since you put my name in for the assistant manager position.'

'Any day now, my dear. I'll give head office a call this afternoon and check on progress.'

She insisted they use the guest bedroom. The marriage bed did not appeal – her backside would lie in the same hollow that Norma's normally rested in while he laid his sweaty paunch on top of her. Better to be on neutral territory.

He plied her with wine, got her a little drunk. The subsequent sex was the same as always, but in her mind she escaped his grunting, grinding routine with a vivid fantasy involving a young black actor from her favourite soap opera.

Leona woke at 1 am, alone in Royston Perry's guest bed. From the master bedroom through the wall she could hear his contented snoring. She turned over and fell into a deep sleep.

At seven, wearing a white dressing-gown she'd found in the guest-room wardrobe, she was hunting in the kitchen cabinets, ravenous. The Chinese he'd ordered in for dinner last night had left her long ago. Perry appeared in the doorway.

'What's this like?' she asked. 'Fairfield's Premium Organic Muesli,' she read aloud from an unopened box.

'Norma thinks it's great. Don't care for it myself. I'm going to have bacon and eggs. Join me?'

'No, I'll go with the healthy option. Where are your cereal bowls?'

As Perry stood grilling his bacon, she tucked into a large plateful of muesli, topped with plain yoghurt from the fridge. 'This is really good,' she said. 'Bet it's expensive.'

He turned to watch her eat. 'Tell you what was good. Last night.'

'Mm.'

Not a very enthusiastic response. What's the matter with her? 'We could do it again tonight, if you like.'

'Did you call head office?'

'Ah yes, the promotion.' He searched for a suitable lie. 'Only thing holding it up is they want you to start at the bottom of the assistant manager pay scale. I'm pressing for you to get a couple of rungs up the ladder, based on your performance record.'

'Thank you, Royston. And yes, why not tonight again? Long as Mrs Perry won't arrive home unexpectedly.'

'No danger. I had a text from her saying she and her sister had tickets for some kind of music event in Llandudno.'

Though Leona began to feel off-colour at work that afternoon, it was not until she and Perry were back at his home that evening that she fell violently ill. Sickness and diarrhoea, both laced with blood. 'Royston,' she moaned, 'you have to call an ambulance. I'm in terrible pain. I can't bear it.'

Can't have an ambulance coming here, he thought. *Too many questions.* 'Tell you what. Ambulance response times have been shocking lately. I'll drive you to A&E.'

'Whatever. Let's go now.' With that, she rushed back into the bathroom.

So much for tonight's entertainment. God, I'm going to have some cleaning to do before Norma gets home.

On the way to hospital, as she lay in the back seat, Perry began coaching her. 'We were working late at the bank when you got sick. Right? Right, Leona? I brought you straight from there to A&E. Got that?'

She just groaned.

A diversion for road works caused him to take a wrong turn into a vast council estate. He was hopelessly lost.

The moaning from the back seat gave way to incoherent babbling. By the time he drew up in front of the accident and emergency unit of the University Hospital of North Durham, Leona was unconscious.

'What has she eaten in the last twenty-four hours?' was one of many questions he was asked.

'Don't know. I only see her at the bank.' *I sure as hell won't be telling them she had breakfast in my kitchen.*

'Who would be able to answer? Who lives with her?'

'No one, far as I'm aware.'

Eventually, they had all they could get out of him. 'Okay, Mr Perry, you can go. Thank you for bringing her in.'

'Is she going to be all right?'

'Can't answer that, I'm afraid, until we know the cause.'

During the three days it took Leona White to die, investigators went through her one-bedroom flat with a fine-tooth comb, looking for any possible poisoning agent. Samples of every open food package were analysed; they all came up negative.

The post-mortem showed endothelial cell damage consistent with ricin or abrin poisoning, but in the absence of any trace of those toxins in her home no firm diagnosis could be made. The pathologist included in her report that the deceased had recently had sex with a person or persons unknown; DNA samples were preserved per standard procedure, and the police were informed.

11

INESCAPABLE TRUTH

IT WAS AFTER ELEVEN O'CLOCK when Rona let herself in, leaving a puzzled Ari on the doorstep.

As she got ready for bed, she knew no sleep would come. Shivering in her nightdress in the unheated room, she set *With The Beatles* on the Dansette turntable. Keeping the volume low so as not to disturb her landlady or fellow lodgers, she played the first few tracks. Though the Lennon-McCartney songs that dominated the album were her reason for buying it, the band's reinterpretation of an older Broadway number made her sit up and listen. It resonated with her feelings at that moment.

> *There were bells on a hill*
> *But I never heard them ringing*
> *No I never heard them at all*
> *Till there was you*

What *was* this sensation? Not love, surely. She'd only just met him, Ari Haraldsson the blond, untucked Icelander. She didn't *know* him or much about him. Yet he had awakened something in her heart, something the man she had agreed to marry would never do.

> *There was love all around*
> *But I never heard it singing*
> *No I never heard it at all*
> *Till there was you*

At half past one, still wide awake, Rona was struck with an awful reality, one she had buried deep in her consciousness: a

28th birthday party for Antony and Dominic Argill at Ardwhinzean House that coming Saturday, 30th November – St Andrew's Day. How she wished she had been in a position to say to Ari, 'No, I've nothing planned next weekend. Yes, I'd love to go out with you.'

Antony met her at Callander station on Saturday afternoon, and drove her to Ardwhinzean in his flashy new Jaguar E-type. 'She's the '64 model,' he proudly announced, though 1963 still had a month to run. In the passenger seat Rona sat tensely gripping her handbag as he sped along the narrow winding road, almost colliding with a roe deer on one corner. Gratefully she stepped out of the car at the house, to be welcomed by Antony's stepmother.

'Come on in, m'dear,' she said. 'You survived the journey here, then? Antony's a wild man when he gets behind the wheel. Just like his father.'

'So you've lived life in the fast lane.'

'Me? No, I'm still the woman I was before Ludo married me in '41. After his divorce from Antony's mother. I'd been their housekeeper for years. So no fancy cars for me.'

As Rona nodded understandingly, the second Lady Bracklinn held out her hand. 'You can call me Edith.'

The two women took an immediate liking to each other.

For the birthday celebration that evening, dinner was served in the Ardwhinzean ballroom for the family and their sixty invited guests. Later the floor was cleared for dancing to a Glasgow guitar group, who played current and recent hits.

This was Rona's first exposure to the entire extended Argill family. Presiding was 68-year-old Ludovic Argill, 2nd Baron Bracklinn. He had succeeded to his father's title in 1950, bought in 1918 to the personal enrichment of David Lloyd George,

Britain's last Liberal Prime Minister. His Lordship conspicuously aligned himself with the Liberal Party, though his political views were decidedly illiberal on many issues.

The 1st Baron had adopted the Bracklinn name for his peerage after a popular beauty spot on the Keltie Water near Callander. He had taken his ennoblement seriously: his coat of arms was prominently displayed over the faux-Regency fireplace at one end of the ballroom. But perhaps not seriously enough. The shield featured a sheaf of grain and a cow's head that would have been more at home on a Laughing Cow processed cheese wrapper, though to Rona's relief *sans* earrings. *Ah well, once a grocer ...*

Nancy, Ludovic's first wife who had reverted to her Telford surname following the 1941 divorce, was there, unexpectedly but in Rona's view entirely appropriately, given that she was the mother of birthday boy Antony. It was unfortunate, then, that she pointedly snubbed his intended when the two were introduced. *Bugger you for a mother-in-law,* Rona thought.

Besides Antony, Ludovic and Nancy had spawned two older daughters. Marjorie and her husband Angus were accompanied by their 17-year-old son Fergus, who had acquired the double-barrelled surname Argill-Hawke. Not to be outdone, Marjorie's younger sister Lucinda and her husband Roger had given their son Telford, now 16, the Argill-Elliott handle.

The present Lady Bracklinn, Edith, had given Ludovic only one child, the *other* birthday boy, Dominic. The inescapable truth that Lord Bracklinn had impregnated his wife and his housekeeper around the same date was something that was never mentioned.

Rona duty-danced with her future father-in-law and with the two teenagers, Fergus and Telford, who were closer to her age-group than anyone else. Strangely, dancing with Antony also felt like social duty, whereas with Dominic it was more fun – they even won a twist competition together.

The festivities ended just before midnight. As the non-resident guests were ushered out into the frost to make their way home, Rona stood in the front hall to bid them good-night, with the family she was destined to join. Only her future husband was nowhere to be seen. Twenty minutes later, alone in her room, she heard the unmistakable *Vroom!* of Antony's E-type, and looked out of her window in time to see its tail-lights receding rapidly down the drive.

At breakfast on Sunday Antony was a no-show. 'Don't worry,' Dominic whispered to her as they helped themselves to devilled lambs' kidneys from the buffet. 'His poker group meets every Saturday night, and they play until three, sometimes four in the morning. Don't say anything – Father doesn't know, and wouldn't hold with card games of any kind on a Sunday.'

'My Dad's the same,' she whispered back. Somehow Rona enjoyed the little conspiratorial chat with the man who was to be her brother-in-law.

By eleven-thirty, Antony had appeared, ready to drive Rona to the station for her train.

'Did you win last night?' she asked him in the car.

'Win? Oh … er … broke even, just about,' he said.

Something in his tone put her off asking him any more questions. The short journey continued in silence.

Had she known what her intended was really up to in the small hours, she would have been deeply shocked, and seriously confused.

End-of-term exams put a damper on social life of any kind for the next two weeks. But on the evening of Friday 13th December all the pressure was off, and Rona went with some female friends to a hop at the Union.

The Swinging Blue Jeans, a Liverpool group who were riding high in the charts with their cover of *Hippy Hippy Shake*, had been hired for the gig before they became hot property.

Their professionalism was a welcome change from the usual local bands at Friday night dances.

Though she would not admit it to herself, she had secretly been hoping that Ari would make an appearance. Yet if he did, what was she going to say to him? The problem, it turned out, did not arise. There was no sign of him.

In the spring of 1964, Rona took to strolling occasionally in the Cruickshank Botanic Garden, home to the university departments of botany and forestry.

Inevitably one day, her subconscious wish was fulfilled. Just as she was passing the main entrance to the Forestry Department, Ari Haraldsson emerged. He broke into a huge smile when he saw her. If she had tried to suppress her own grin, it would have proved impossible.

'Had lunch?' he asked.

'No,' she replied. 'I've a banana and a pot of yoghurt. I was going to eat it in the garden.'

'Very healthy. I was going to head down to the baker's shop on King Street for a Scotch pie.'

'I'll walk with you.'

The conversation was stilted:

– 'Are you still on the hockey team?'

– 'Yes, we're not doing too well this year. Still liking your Scandinavian Studies?'

– 'Mm hmm, it's a really good course.'

Soon, however, Ari could hold back no longer. 'The subject you didn't want to talk about last November. You ready now?'

Rona turned away, hoping he hadn't noticed her eyes welling up. But it was too late.

'Come here,' he said gently, taking her in his arms and hugging her close to him as she let the tears fall.

'I've ... I've a tutorial at two,' she said through sobs. 'Can we meet later?'

'My flat, Bedford Road, five-thirty. I'll make dinner.'

Rona protested lamely. 'My landlady will have dinner prepared. And what about your flatmate?'

'Call your landlady, tell her you've a late class or something. And Simon won't be there until much later. This is his band practice night.'

12
DOG

Y A CURIOUS ACCIDENT OF FATE, Delia Cobb and Frank Jamieson arrived at Torphins cemetery at exactly the same moment. The elderly Londoner politely held the gate open for the pretty red-headed girl and closed it behind her.

'Why, thank you,' she said in her Chicago accent.

'What brings you all the way from America to this little place?' Frank asked. 'Same errand that I'm on, I suppose – visiting a relative's grave?'

'If I'm lucky, yes,' Delia replied, and explained her search for a stone of the right vintage bearing the names Wilson and Cromar. 'It might be here, or in a different cemetery, or very possibly nowhere at all.'

Having time to kill after spending a few minutes at the grave of his aunt and uncle, Frank took a walk among the other stones. When he saw Delia making for the gate, he called out, 'Any luck?'

'No,' she replied. 'On to the next one.'

'It's chilly for May,' he said as he caught up with her. 'I was going to get myself a hot drink at Platform 22. Care to join me?'

'Sure, why not?'

At the coffee shop on the site of the old Torphins railway station, they made their introductions. She expanded on her Wilson/Cromar fascination, while he gave a potted history of his pre-retirement career before outlining his quest for Rona Fay Swainson.

Delia's ears pricked up to hear of a typescript lurking undiscovered in a book for 35 years or more. 'I'd love to see it,' she said, as she sipped an almost too-hot chocolate. 'I've been having an interesting time with old documents over the past two or three years.* Wouldn't mind having a crack at another one.'

'Here's your chance then,' Frank said. 'Give me your email address and I'll send it to you as a pdf.'

Less than twenty-four hours later, Delia had a copy of *Gudrun's Saga* as translated and annotated by Rona Fay Swainson with the assistance of Ari Haraldsson.

> *The great sagas tell of our heroic ancestors, whose lives, loves, battles won and lost, joys and sufferings have been preserved by the Skalds. Their epic tales, passed from father to son, are told in the words of men.*
>
> *But women, too, have tongues. The stories they tell their daughters recount the same events as those of the Skalds' sagas, only seen in a different light, as under the moon instead of the sun.*
>
> *Gudrun Ljotsdottir, who stood taller than any man, knew these moonlight-stories and was the first to put them all together. The scribe who now sets them in writing is her great grand-daughter.*

> *OF YRSA*
>
> *Long ago Denmark was ruled by a king who was only half Danish and for that reason was named Halfdan. He had two sons named Hrodhgar and Helgi. Both were strong and warlike, Helgi the more so, being of tall stature.*
>
> *(NOTE: The reign of Halfdan was probably during the late fifth or early sixth century.)*
>
> *The two brothers were fierce rivals and each in his turn tried to kill the other to be sure of succeeding to*

---

* See *Taran's Wheel* and *Scotch and Water* (*Incomers*: Books 1 and 2)

the throne. Their mother the queen, who was called Sigrid, was saddened by their constant quarrels. She devised a plan to make peace between them: on Halfdan's death, one of her sons would rule the land and the other the sea.

They accepted this proposal, but immediately began bickering as to which of them would secure the land. The queen, taking Helgi aside, reminded him that although Denmark was a great prize, the sea was even greater. Furthermore, across the sea lay lands that, if he conquered them, would become part of his realm. Helgi was initially convinced, and when his father died he willingly allowed Hrodhgar to become king of Denmark.

Before long Helgi regretted his choice, and began to hate Sigrid for having tricked him. It being unthinkable to harm his own mother, he resolved to find another queen on whom he could take his revenge for female duplicity. Somebody had to be punished.

One summer he set sail for Saxony with a band of warriors, where he raided a small town, put its citizens to flight and established a camp. Soon the Saxon king arrived with a small army.

The Danish invader was not intimidated. 'I am Helgi Halfdansson,' he announced to the king, 'ruler of all the seas. You must pay me tribute, otherwise I will destroy your petty kingdom.'

The king was scornful of Helgi's threat, and ordered his men to set upon the unwelcome visitors. A battle ensued, in which the Danes were victorious. In the resulting confusion, Helgi seized the Saxon queen, a beautiful young woman by the name of Olava, and took her to his camp. There, he cruelly beat and raped her in front of his men.

'Go back to your little husband, witch,' he told her, 'before I kill you for the crimes of womankind.'

Despite her pain and anger, Olava said not a word. Turning her back on Helgi, she left his camp with such dignity as she was able to muster. It is said that some of Helgi's men, hardened though they were, took pity on the queen and escorted her to a farmstead. The farmer and his wife gave her food and shelter while she recovered from the injuries inflicted by the vicious Dane.

The Saxon king, meanwhile, learned of his wife's ordeal. A vain man, he refused to have her back at his side, for she had been defiled. He wasted no time in finding another consort.

Thus Olava went from queen to simple milkmaid on the farm where she had taken refuge. Soon she was with child.

(NOTE: In some sagas, the woman raped by Helgi was called Thora and was never a queen.)

The following spring, she gave birth to a daughter, whom she named Yrsa after a puppy she had befriended. 'Though I wish you no harm, little mite,' she said as she cradled the infant, 'I cannot forget that it was a Danish dog who fathered you.'

Yrsa grew into a young woman as beautiful as her mother. Happily she tended her goats in the forests around the farmstead.

Before she was yet twenty, Saxony was invaded once again, on this occasion by a Swedish force under the command of their king, Eadgils. Among the Saxons seized as slaves was the comely goatherd Yrsa. The king, smitten by her beauty, fell in love with her and took her as his queen. Soon they had a daughter, Skuld.

Yrsa's fame as the beautiful queen of Sweden spread far and wide. Helgi, still seeking retribution for what he saw as his mother's deceit, launched a bold attack on the Swedish royal residence at Uppsala. He captured the queen and, not knowing she was his daughter, raped her just as he had Olava. Back in Denmark he kept her captive and treated her with great cruelty. The son she bore as a result of the rape was Rolf, later nicknamed 'Crow'.

(NOTE: Though the sagas differ greatly in the details of Yrsa's story, all have incestuous rape as an essential ingredient.)

Meanwhile, Olava burned with hatred for Helgi. She paid him a visit, having dyed her hair so that he would not know her.

'Gracious lord,' this peasant woman said, 'I have herbs and potions in my basket that can preserve the great beauty of your lady Yrsa, as befits the mother of the future king of Denmark.'

Helgi was contemptuous. 'My lady Yrsa is a withered rose. You come too late. In any case, I have pretty concubines aplenty to warm and perfume my bed. I have no need of your merchandise.'

Listening behind a door, Yrsa heard the conversation and recognised her mother's voice. Rushing in, she fell to her knees before her captor. 'Master,' she implored, 'do not send this poor woman away empty-handed. With her herbs and potions I can once again be more beautiful than all your concubines. Then, I promise you, we can together make a second child, conceived this time in love.'

He raised a hand to hit her, but withdrew it, suddenly aware of the peasant woman's menacing glare. He knew those malevolent eyes. They belonged to an elf-woman who haunted his dreams. A being who could change herself from ugly troll to beautiful siren, seduce him on a cliff-top then, at the height of his passion, push him off the edge into a raging sea.

'Very well,' he said at length. 'Take this creature to your quarters and let her show you her wares.'

In the privacy of Yrsa's chamber, mother and daughter wept with joy at their reunion. Olava turned out the contents of her basket.

'Most of what I have here is useless. Weeds of the wayside. But these mushrooms from a forest in our native Saxony will gain you your freedom. Let me explain how.'

The following night, Yrsa did exactly what her mother suggested. She had the cook prepare a mushroom sauce for Helgi's meat, while she made herself as appealing as she could with the aid of powders and perfumes borrowed from his concubines. After he had eaten, she invited him to her bed.

As she caressed him, he began to have difficulty in moving. Soon his whole body became rigid. Only his eyes could move in their sockets. She took his dagger from the pile of clothes he had flung on the floor and brandished it before his terrified eyes. 'Now, dog,' she said, 'you have had your last bone.'

With the dagger she cleanly castrated him, well practised as she was from gelding young billy goats back in Saxony. She watched with satisfaction for a few moments as his blood poured forth on the bedsheet, then jammed in his mouth a sealed letter Olava had given her.

Only when she met Olava again, having made her escape, did Yrsa learn that Helgi, the father of her son

Rolf, was also her own father. 'And he will learn,' Olava said, 'when, waking with searing pain in his groin, he opens that letter, that it is his daughter whom he has defiled and mistreated so cruelly, and who has now taken her revenge.'

Helgi's injuries healed, but shortly afterwards he threw himself off the cliff that had featured in so many of his nightmares. Some say he was heartbroken and stricken by remorse for the harm he had done to his daughter, others that without his manhood his life had become meaningless.

His son Rolf 'Crow' was adopted by Hrodhgar who, having no son of his own, declared him heir to the Danish throne. Yrsa returned to Uppsala to be reunited with her husband King Eadgils and their daughter Skuld. In due course she bore Eadgils a son, Eystein, whose descendants ruled Sweden for many generations.

Numerous tales survive of the later life of Yrsa and her kin. One tells of a Swedish conquest of Denmark after the death of Hrodhgar. As a calculated insult to the Danish people, the Swedes, at Yrsa's suggestion, proclaimed a dog as their new ruler. Only after the dog died was Rolf 'Crow' permitted to become king of Denmark.

13
TIRED OF WAITING

A RI OPENED TWO CANS OF LAGER, gave her one and sat her on a stool in the tiny kitchenette while he grilled sausages, boiled and mashed potatoes and opened a tin of beans. She offered to help but, as he pointed out, they would have got in each other's way in the cramped space.

'I hope you weren't expecting a gourmet meal,' he said apologetically. 'If you come with me to Iceland one day, you'll get to taste all the things I've been missing – *harðfiskur*, which is fish that has been hung in cold air to dry, *hangikjöt*, smoked lamb, and of course *skyr*. That's a kind of milk curd, delicious with blueberries or cloudberries.'

How can I ever do that? Rona thought ruefully. 'Sausage and mash will be just fine, thanks.'

They carried their plates into the living room, where they talked as they ate. Ari made no attempt to steer the conversation to the subject Rona 'didn't want to talk about'; she would get around to it in her own time. Eventually, over coffee and biscuits, it all came out.

The more she told him, the more outrageous it seemed to Ari.

'Your parents have sold you, Rona! Into the clutches of these Bracklinn people. My God, they can't do that to you, can they? This is 1964!'

'If my father was Joe Smith, a schoolteacher, or a plumber, or … I don't know, a post-office clerk, it couldn't happen. But he's the Earl of Sodding Fairfield. Even then, if he was rich, I'd have more choices. But he's the *poor* Earl of Sodding Fairfield.

I *have* to go through with this marriage, otherwise he'll forfeit his home, his land and such income as it brings. My mother will leave him if that happens, I'm sure of it. It'll be a disaster for both of them.'

'And what about you, Rona? Don't they care that it's a disaster for you?'

'The way they see it, I get a handsome rich husband, my children inherit the Bracklinn as well as the Fairfield title ...'

'And *is* he handsome?' Ari broke in.

'Oh, yes. A handsome *shit*. I don't like him, and I absolutely hate his mother.'

'Maybe it won't be as bad as you think.'

'You haven't met him. Jesus, even if it was his brother, it wouldn't be so bad.'

'You'd still have the mother-in-law problem.'

'Actually, no. They're *half*-brothers. I quite like Dominic's mother.'

Ari made an attempt at levity. 'In that case the solution is obvious. Bump Antony off and marry Dominic.'

'I do have a plan. And I'd like you to be involved, if you'd be willing.'

He looked startled for a moment.

She laughed. It was the first time she had shown a flicker of light-heartedness all evening. 'It's all right. I'm not asking you to be an accomplice to murder!'

'What then?'

'I found an ancient book in my father's library. It's a saga, in Icelandic. I reckon it was first written down in the thirteenth century or thereabout. My father's copy is not as early as that, obviously. Judging from the binding, and comparing it with other books in his library, it was probably printed around 1600 to 1700.'

'Have you shown it to anyone?' Ari asked. 'In the University library they know a lot about early printed books.'

'I will do that at some stage. But not right now.'

'So what is it you want me to do?'

'Before I get to that, I need you to suspend disbelief for a minute, while I tell you a ghost story.'

'Whatever it is, it won't be as unbelievable as you being sold into marriage with the Wicked Baron.'

Ari listened while she related her eerie experience at the Skairs, where a disembodied voice had said, 'Rona, tell my stories.' A voice in the wind that had to be Gudrun's, or at least her ghost's.

'Gudrun? Who was she?'

'A noblewoman of some kind who, my father says, left Orkney when the going got tough and eventually settled on *Faer Fjall* – the Hill of Fare, about sixteen miles from here.'

'Hey, I've been there on a field trip. Had to do a stand density analysis in a larch plantation.'

'Well, her place was known as *Gudrun Ha*, now called Gordonhall. My home. She's my ancestor.'

'And what are the stories she wants you to tell?'

'They're in that book. *Gudrun's Saga*, it's called. But her stories are in Icelandic which, as you'll know, is very close to the Old Norse once spoken in the northern isles of Scotland. I'm planning to work on a translation, whenever time allows. During holidays, for example. And you could be a tremendous help to me.'

'Wait a minute, Rona. The sagas have all been translated. Into every language you can think of.'

'I've checked the catalogues of the British Library, the US Library of Congress, you name it. *This* one seems to be unknown, might even be one of the "lost sagas" that are hinted at in the literature.'

'I'd love to help you, if I can,' Ari said.

Rona's face lit up. 'Then it's settled.'

Her boat sailed on through the calm waters of weekdays in Aberdeen and the stormier seas that were weekends at Ardwhinzean; all the while her friendship with Ari kept her on an even keel. But just over the horizon lay the rocky shoreline of marriage to Antony. Would it provide a safe landing-place? Or, more likely, would her boat perish on its skerries or be swallowed by a tidal maelstrom?

Inevitably, as she allowed herself to grow ever closer to Ari, the friendship turned to something deeper. When he went home to Iceland for the summer of '64 she missed him dreadfully, but kept her mind occupied by researching the sagas in the Gordonhall library. Once classes resumed they were virtually inseparable.

The Palace Ballroom on Bath Street became their favourite venue. One Friday evening in February 1965 they danced to a London band whose rendering of hit songs was almost indistinguishable from the original recordings by big-name performers. *Could they be miming?* they wondered – but when they got close to the stage it was clear the music was all live. The group had a contract with Woolworths to make 'covers' (knock-off copies, actually) of hit singles that would sell at two-and-sixpence each, a little over a third of the price of the originals. Their repertoire from the top ten of that very week included The Kinks' *Tired Of Waiting For You*, The Moody Blues' *Go Now* and, to close the set, The Righteous Brothers' *You've Lost That Lovin' Feelin'*.

It was, Rona believed, her slow-dance with Ari to that last number that pushed them over the edge. No longer could they pretend their relationship was a platonic stop-gap. It was love, and there was no going back.

Afterwards, in the second-floor flat on Bedford Road, they huddled together for warmth over the GEC single-bar electric fire. 'I've wanted to ask you something for a long time,' he said, 'and this is the night. Will you come to bed with me?'

She had known what was coming, from the moment he opened his mouth. And she had her answer ready. 'Yes, but not tonight.'

'Not *tonight*? That doesn't mean "not ever", does it?'

'No, but I want to go on the pill first. I can't afford to get pregnant at this stage.'

'I have protection.'

'Good, but not good enough. I've heard Student Health is giving out prescriptions now, no questions asked.'

Ari gazed into her eyes. 'I can wait, *elskan.*'

'It won't be long, sweetheart.'

'Are you sure? Won't Antony expect to marry a virgin?'

'If he does, he's going to be disappointed anyway.' She told him about her brief adolescent fling with Stewart in the vacant room at Raemoir. 'Are *you* disappointed in me, from what you know now?'

'Rona *min*, why would I be? Your future bothers me, your past not at all. My hope is that you will forget this ridiculous family debt and live life for *you*. I want your future to be with me, not with Sir Antony Argill.' He spat the name out.

'He's not a Sir. One day he'll be Lord Bracklinn, for now he's just Honourable. (Ha! *That's* a laugh.) But even if he was going to be king, I'd still prefer to spend my life with you. You know that.'

'So tell them the deal's off.'

'I wish it were that simple.'

The meter gave a click as the two shillings Ari had put in ran out. The bright red glow from the bar of the electric fire quickly faded to black. Almost as quickly, the chill February night air began to pervade the room.

In June 1965 Rona moved into the Bedford Road flat. At that time of year its north-west facing windows might catch an hour or two of evening sun. Opening them, however, admitted clouds of black dust from the Kittybrewster coal depot across the street. A fine residence for a future countess!

Her parents were furious, but powerless – they dared not risk pushing her into breaking the agreement to marry Antony Argill. All they could do was hope Rona's living with a young man would not reach the Argills' ears.

Ari made only a short visit home that summer, as he had to work on his thesis – a study of mixed birch-conifer woodlands. Rona found a summer job in the packing department of a tobacco wholesaler in Spring Garden, her weekly salary augmented with 60 Embassy Tipped. Neither she nor Ari was a smoker, but she found the cigarettes a useful currency in extracting small favours from various people, most especially their landlord.

For a year they lived, physically and socially, as man and wife, Rona determined to enjoy her last days of freedom and Ari hoping desperately to make her see sense and abandon her arranged marriage. Miraculously, the Argill household remained oblivious to her domestic arrangement. Edith, Lady Bracklinn occasionally let slip a remark to Rona, or gave her a sidelong glance, that suggested she might have had her suspicions, but that was as far as it went. Antony showed no interest whatsoever in how Rona occupied herself in Aberdeen.

At the end of the second term of her senior year in March 1966, Rona presented Ari with a carbon copy of a manuscript in her own neat handwriting, keeping the top copy for her own use. 'It's my first draft translation of *Gudrun's Saga*, she said. 'You'll see a lot of blank spaces and question marks. Those are where I'm stumped, or at least not sure I've understood the Icelandic correctly. And I still have one chapter to work on.'

'Do you have the original book here?' he asked.

'No, it's very fragile and I thought it would be safer to keep it at Gordonhall on the library shelf. I'd like to take you out there so you can check my translation against the book, help me fill in the gaps, correct my errors. When are you going home for the holidays?'

'I'm not,' Ari said. 'I've two mandatory field trips at the beginning of April.'

'Perfect. Let's go next Tuesday. My parents are off to Madeira for a fortnight. We'll have the place to ourselves, for as long as we need.'

'Pity. I'd like to have met them.'

'Not a great idea, lover boy.'

Ari was impressed with the Swainson family seat – its exterior masonry and interior timbers, its grand staircase, its ornate plasterwork. Roof repairs had once again made the house watertight but not yet fully habitable. The oak-panelled library with its thousands of dusty volumes was still the only furnished room in Gordonhall.

On inspecting the seventeenth-century printed copy of *Gudrun's Saga*, he remarked that Rona's handwritten translation was very accurate. Over the next three days they worked on it together, leaving just one chapter unfinished.

On Saturday afternoon they took a break. 'Let's go for a walk,' she suggested. 'The weather's too nice to stay in this musty old library all day.'

They followed a track up the hill from the back of the house, eventually leading to open moorland. 'Can we go that way?' Ari asked, pointing to higher ground to the west.

'I suppose so,' Rona replied.

They arrived at a place where the pink granite underlying the whole Hill of Fare broke through the heather. Rocks eroded by millennia of ice, water, wind and frost made a sudden contrast to the otherwise featureless landscape.

'The Skairs,' Rona said. 'This is the spot I told you about, where Gudrun supposedly died and where her ghost still hangs around. If you believe that kind of thing.'

'Gudrun was a big lady, wasn't she?'

'*Taller than any man*, her saga says.'

'There's an old Icelandic word, *skersa*, meaning "giantess",' Ari said. 'I bet Gudrun *did* die here, and that's why this place is called the Skairs. Nowadays *skersa* is an uncomplimentary word for a woman who looks a bit like a man, if you know what I mean.'

'So if you ever call me that, I'll know what you think of me.'

'That will never happen, *elskan min*. You're beautiful, a goddess, a ...'

To shut him up, she pressed her lips against his.

On Sunday Ari took the bus back to Aberdeen and Rona stayed behind for a couple of days to type up their translation. Borrowing Bert's wheelbarrow, she had hauled her father's 1950-vintage Imperial typewriter up from the gatehouse so that she could work in the Gordonhall library. Not having the full Icelandic alphabet with its accented vowels, its diphthongs and the consonants eth (ð) and thorn (þ), it would be impossible to properly render some of the personal names, but that was a minor issue.

She also completed the unfinished chapter, which dealt with an infamous Orcadian princess called Ragnhild Eriksdóttir, and included it in her typescript. For safe keeping, she put her work product in an envelope which she taped to the endpaper inside the back cover of the largest book she could find: a dusty copy of *Illustrated Natural History*, probably never taken down from its shelf in fifty years or more. She locked up, returned the typewriter, and caught the next bus into Aberdeen to rejoin Ari.

No thought occurred to her that this might be the last time she would ever see *Gudrun's Saga* – the old book itself or her typewritten translation.

Rona graduated M.A. with First Class Honours on 9th July 1966. Her parents attended the ceremony in the Mitchell Hall of

Marischal College but no one made the trip from Ardwhinzean. Coincidentally, Ari had his B.Sc. Forestry degree conferred on the same day in the same hall; *his* parents, Harald and Vigdis, and two younger sisters Margrét and Aslaug came all the way from Reykjavik.

That evening Rona went home to Gordonhall with her father and mother, while Ari and his family celebrated with a fine dinner at the Caledonian Hotel on Union Terrace. At eight o'clock he slipped away from the table to a payphone booth in the lobby.

'Rona, it's for you,' her mother said. 'Think it's your Icelandic fellow.'

'You know his name perfectly well,' Rona said, bristling. 'Ari Haraldsson.' Taking the handset, she waited until Aenea was out of range before putting it to her ear.

'Come with me to Iceland, *elskan*.'

'Ari, sweetheart, we've been over this a hundred times. You know I have to go through with this marriage, though the whole thing is a sham. Antony no more wants me than I him. But it's my duty to provide a legitimate heir to the Bracklinn and Fairfield titles; once that's done, I'm yours, if you'll still have me.'

'I don't see how you'll escape the clutches of that family. You'll never want to come away. And you certainly can't leave your child behind.'

'I will find a way. Just be patient, my love.' Rona knew she was asking a lot. And what she was proposing, to take a solemn vow 'till death us do part' with the full intention of breaking it, went against the grain. But she was inspired by some of the remarkable women she had read about in *Gudrun's Saga*. Women who took control of their destiny even in a world ruled by men. 'Wait for me. It won't be as long as you think.'

To her surprise, Ari responded by bursting into a familiar Ray Davies song:

Rona was transported back to the night a year and a half earlier, when she and Ari danced to that song at the Palace. It was the night they had fully confessed their love for each other.

14
ÅSA OF AGDER

WHEREAS THE FIFTH-CENTURY tale of Yrsa clearly belonged to the realm of myth, the next chapter of *Gudrun's Saga* related to a genuine historical figure, the ninth-century Åsa (or, as rendered in Rona Fay Swainson's typescript, Asa). She was queen of one of the petty kingdoms into which Norway was fragmented at that time.

Delia learned as much from a search on the Internet. As she continued reading the saga she found out a lot more about Åsa – but was it historically correct?

OF ASA, QUEEN OF AGDER

In the south of Norway, facing the stormy Skagerrak and, beyond it, the land of the Danes, lies the province of Agder. Once it was a kingdom, often at war with Rogaland to the west and Vestfold to the east.

The king of Agder, Harald 'Redbeard', was in want of a successor to continue the fight against enemies all around. Though not the wisest man ever to reign in Norway, he realised that to have a successor meant he must first find a wife.

'How should I do this?' he asked Ivar, his most trusted counsellor.

'Send me on a tour of the finest homes in Agder,' Ivar replied. 'I will find you the most worthy maiden in the land to be your queen.'

'Go then. But mind: she must be fair of face and lithe of limb.'

Ivar knew exactly where he would find this maiden: at his own farmstead on the land-between-the-fjords known as Lista. His daughter Gunnhild, seventeen years of age, had all the qualities the king demanded.

In addition, however, she was strong-willed and devious. 'I do not wish to marry a man I have never seen,' she told her father, 'even if he is the king. And in any case, as soon as you introduce me as Gunnhild Ivarsdottir, he will know you have presented your own offspring to him. It will be clear to him that you have disobeyed his order to search all over the kingdom.'

'I have thought of that, child. The king is too stupid to suspect such a thing. But just in case, we will change your name. Henceforth you shall be Gunnhild Ragnvaldsdottir.'

'And who is this Ragnvald, my father from now on?'

'I will tell the king that the noble Ragnvald Sigurdsson died in a hunting accident before you were born. Come, child, no future awaits you here on Lista. You will be safe at Harald's court, for I am there to watch over you.'

(NOTE: According to the 'Heimskringla' written in the thirteenth century, a certain Ragnvald Sigurdsson of Lista was the true father of Gunnhild.)

Reluctantly Gunnhild agreed to accompany her father back to the royal castle. She was pleasantly surprised to find King Harald a handsome man, not as old as she had feared. His famous slowness of wit was something she could live with; indeed, it promised her power, as he was constantly in need of advice. Within a month, they were wed.

Before long the king realised that, with his queen as counsellor in all matters, he could dispense with Ivar's services. Gunnhild's father was dispatched back to his farm on Lista and played no further part in royal affairs.

Within a year of their marriage Gunnhild bore the king a son and heir, Gyrd, and soon afterwards a beautiful fair-haired daughter, Asa. The queen loved both her children dearly and did all she could to protect them when the kingdom came under attack. By her constant vigilance she could anticipate where the next threat would come from, and advised her husband accordingly. As a result, Agder enjoyed peace and prosperity for twenty years.

A great sadness engulfed the king and all his subjects when Gunnhild took a fever and died. The news soon reached Agder's enemies. Also spread abroad was the great beauty of the princess who had just lost her mother the queen.

It was the king of neighbouring Vestfold, Gudrod 'the Hunter', who first saw the opportunity.

Gudrod was an aggressive and acquisitive ruler who, through earlier marriage to a Swedish princess, had extended his realm to the border of Sweden. His queen having recently died, he set his sights on the famously beautiful Asa of Agder.

First he sent a delegation to King Harald's court to propose marriage to Princess Asa. Harald, having lost his most reliable counsellor, his wife Gunnhild, rudely rebuffed the proposal. This enraged Gudrod, who promptly sent his warriors to invade Agder from the sea and storm Harald's castle. In the ensuing battle, both Harald and his son Gyrd were killed. Asa was captured and taken in chains to Vestfold. There she was forced into marriage with Gudrod who, as he deflowered her, commanded her to bear a son that would expand the kingdom of Vestfold to the whole of Norway.

While submitting to the king's basest desires, Asa began plotting her revenge. To her relief, Gudrod was frequently absent on military campaigns and, while he was away, she welcomed her servant Njall to her bed.

As a two-year-old Sicilian orphan, Njall had been seized during a Viking raid, brought as a trophy on a longship and given a Norwegian name. Now a handsome young man with sleek black hair and bronze skin, he seemed oblivious to the risk he was taking by cuckolding a warlike king.

In due course Asa bore Njall's son, whom Gudrod initially believed to be his own – the one he had demanded from his wife to be the eventual ruler of all Norway. He was given the ancient royal name of Halfdan; because of the boy's unusually dark hair and complexion he was soon known as Halfdan 'the Black'.

(NOTE: Some sagas treat Halfdan as the legitimate son of Gudrod.)

When Halfdan was just one year old, Gudrod began to suspect the child was not his. On being confronted with his suspicion, Asa denied ever having been unfaithful to the king.

He was not convinced. 'I am off to battle,' he told her, 'and when I return I will have you, the boy and every dark-haired man within a day's ride put to the sword, unless you can prove the child is mine.'

As the king set sail, Asa warned Njall of the threat. 'You must leave Vestfold now, and never return,' she said.

The battle was won by Gudrod and his men. Back in harbour, they were celebrating their victory, still on board their ship. Gudrod became very drunk. As he was staggering off the ship, Njall stepped out of the shadows and ran him through with a spear, killing him instantly. The king's men leapt upon the Sicilian and, before putting him to death, extracted the confession that the queen had warned him to escape before Gudrod came home.

The men immediately made for the castle to seize the perfidious Asa. But she had already fled with her black-haired son. She bribed a local boatman to take them to her Agder homeland, where she and Halfdan were welcomed with joy by her people. Asa was proclaimed queen, to rule in her own right, with Halfdan as her heir.

(NOTE: After Halfdan 'the Black' succeeded to the throne of Agder, he conquered many petty kingdoms throughout southern Norway. He might have realised Gudrod's ambition for him to unify Norway, had he not been killed by cattle dung. This came about when his sleigh, crossing a frozen lake, fell through a patch of ice weakened by the dung. It was Halfdan's son, Harald 'Fairhair', who by marriage treaty and further conquests became the first king of all of Norway.)

15
RESPECTABILITY

THE SUN HAD MOVED ROUND to the north-west but was still giving enough warmth for Ragna to stay outside. Around midsummer it never got dark in Akureyri, but soon the shadow of the hill behind her house would stretch over the garden, chilling the air and sending her indoors. No sign yet of Ari, though his boat should be in harbour by now. Any concern she might have had was allayed when he called her mobile to say he would be a little later than usual. He'd run into Bárður – his brother-in-law – and would have a couple of shots of *ákavíti* with him before coming home with his catch.

There was a curious blank in her otherwise encyclopaedic memory of the 1960s. Two full weeks passed between the night of her graduation, when Ari had serenaded her over the phone, and 23rd July 1966, when she walked up the aisle with her father, yet she could recollect nothing that happened during that time.

Even the wedding in St Kessog's church was a blur, as was the lavish feast in a marquee at Ardwhinzean. True, Rona (as she then was) had had a couple of drinks to steady her nerves beforehand, but not nearly enough to explain the amnesia. And, by choice, she had kept no photographs of the event, though an expensive album had been compiled by her in-laws.

What *was* seared into her memory was her first night of married life, in a luxurious suite in the Dunblane Hydro. The 'bedding after the wedding', as the occasion was indelicately referred to in advance by her new Argill family.

Antony was unable to perform.

'What's the matter?' Rona asked. 'Don't you fancy me? Am I a disappointment when you see me naked?'

'The problem isn't you, Rona. It's me. I ... how should I say this? ... I prefer a man.'

She sat bolt upright. Suddenly embarrassed by her nakedness she pulled the bedsheet up to her chin. It took a few moments for her shock to subside into anger. 'You're homosexual? *Now* you tell me. Don't you think this is something I deserved to know before marrying you?'

'If I'd told you, and you'd called off the wedding, my secret would be out. My father would disinherit me. And I thought maybe once we got started I'd find the ... the ...'

Rona turned away in disgust as Antony struggled to apologise. But another shock was to come.

'There's a solution,' he announced. 'I've discussed it with Dominic. He's the only person who knows my ... er ... problem, besides you – and, of course, Maurice.' He pronounced the name the French way: 'Mo-*reese*'.

'Who the fuck is Mo-*reese*?'

'My lover. All those "poker nights" I've been with him.'

'Jesus. You're such a shit, you know that?' Even as she spoke, she knew it was unreasonable to feel Antony had cheated on her, considering her years with Ari. 'So what exactly is your "solution"?'

'Dominic can bed you till you're pregnant. The child will be a legitimate heir to the Bracklinn *and* the Fairfield titles. Nobody but the three of us will ever know I'm not the father.'

'How nice of you and your brother to have cooked this up, to save worrying me with the details,' Rona said witheringly. 'I suppose he's okay with it?'

'You know Dominic. Never met a girl he didn't like. And I know he likes you.'

'How reassuring. Now, where are you going to sleep tonight? Because you're sure as hell not going to share *this* bed.'

'Father booked six rooms for wedding guests, but only five were needed,' Antony said. 'I'll head down the hall.' He pulled on his clothes and left her alone without a backward glance.

There was no prospect of sleep for Rona that night. What were her options?

She could tell her parents, and Antony's, what had happened. Secure an annulment – that shouldn't be too difficult under the circumstances – and get back together with Ari. But what if Antony denied everything? She was not a virgin, so could never *prove* the marriage was not consummated. And her parents would be ruined if their debt was called in. The Argills would get their greedy hands on the entire Gordonhall estate, lock, stock and barrel.

Or she could stay with Antony, refuse to play the charade he and Dominic had dreamt up. Accept a marriage devoid of any sexual relationship while Antony indulged his passion with Maurice or whomever. But that would mean never having the child that would be her passport to freedom. The child that would eventually inherit the Barony of Bracklinn as well as the Earldom of Fairfield. The child whose birth would cancel her father's debt. She would be locked in a charade of her own, at least until her childbearing years were over. Long before that, Ari would really have grown *tired of waiting*.

By the time daylight began to lighten the gloom, Rona had decided her only viable option was Antony's 'solution'. She would accept Dominic into her bed, conceive and give birth to a son or daughter who would be registered as Antony's, then as soon as possible bail out, hoping Ari would still have her. The sooner, the better.

A day or two after the 'honeymoon', the new arrangement was in operation. Antony and Rona had a comfortable, expensively furnished cottage in the Ardwhinzean grounds where, to all outward appearances, they lived as a devoted young couple. Antony continued to go out for his 'poker nights' while Rona stayed in to watch television – *Armchair Theatre* was her highlight of the week, together with lighter fare such as *The Saint*, *Z-Cars* and a new cop show, *Softly, Softly*. And while Antony was absent, Dominic took his place.

That September, a gossip piece appeared in the *Callander Advertiser* hinting at an improper relationship between the recently married Honourable Antony Argill and an unnamed young man. The pair had been seen emerging in a drunken state from the Crown Hotel bar, then staggering arm-in-arm along the pavement before indulging in 'an over-familiar embrace' in a Main Street shop doorway.

Ludovic Argill stormed into the *Advertiser* offices demanding a retraction. The editor tried to calm him, to no avail, but refused to withdraw the story.

'I'll sue your damned rag all the way to the High Court if necessary,' Argill ranted, his face red with fury. 'I'll shut you down, just watch me!'

'Please take a seat, your Lordship,' the editor said. Reaching into a filing cabinet, he produced a photograph and laid it in front of his enraged visitor. 'To spare the Argill family unnecessary embarrassment, we elected *not* to publish this picture. But, as you can see, the taller gentleman with his arms around his companion in what looks like a loving embrace is unquestionably your son.'

Argill spluttered for a moment, lost for words. Pulling himself together, he stammered that Antony had undergone hand-to-hand combat training as an army cadet and was just trying out some wrestling moves.

'I don't think so,' the editor said. 'I have some other photos securely locked in my safe that show this was *not* a wrestling match, but something else entirely.'

'Give me those photos, and the negatives, right now!'

'That I cannot do, Lord Bracklinn.'

'Then expect to hear from my lawyer before the day is out.' Ludovic Argill got to his feet and headed for the door.

He never made it out into the street. In front of the editor and his horrified staff, he made a gasping noise, grabbed his chest and fell in a heap on the threshold. He was dead before he hit the floor.

As soon as she heard the news, Rona saw her chance of escape. With Ludovic Argill's death, the deal he had struck with her father was surely off.

After the funeral service in St Kessog's, she announced to Antony that she would be seeking an annulment.

'Not so fast, Lady Bracklinn,' he cautioned her, taking obvious delight in reminding her she was now the wife of the 3rd Baron. 'Father's lawyer made sure the contract was enforceable by his heirs.' To emphasise the point, he spread the fingers of his right hand to show her his father's gold signet ring adorned with the Bracklinn arms of a wheat-sheaf and cow's head. 'And I for one will not let your dear Papa off the hook.'

'But why, Antony? This marriage has no meaning for you. It's better for both of us to put an end to it.'

'You don't get it, do you? Having a wife gives me the respectability I need, especially now that I'm to inherit Father's business interests.'

'Respectability, ha! How *respectable* is it to shag your boyfriend in the doorway of the Callander Co-op?'

It was the first and only time he raised a fist to her. She jerked her head backward and received only a glancing blow to the chin from the signet ring on his little finger.

Fighting to suppress tears – of anger rather than physical hurt – Rona stood her ground and said in a measured voice, 'You do that *ever* again and I'll see to it that your violent, abusive behaviour, and your affairs with men, will feature in every tabloid in Britain. The *News of the World* will love that story. It won't be just a couple of column-inches in the *Callander Advertiser*.'

He shrugged and walked out of the house, slamming the front door behind him. That evening, she wrote a long letter to Ari.

Rona had given no hint to her parents that marriage to Antony, now Lord Bracklinn, was a sham. Apart from anything else, she did not want any awkward questions if and when she became pregnant. Though they had manoeuvred her into this situation, she would not give them cause to think she couldn't hack it.

It was a surprise, then, when Aenea rang in the middle of the day.

'Is Antony at home, dear?'

'No, Mummy. Did you want to talk to *him*?'

'So you're alone?'

'Yes, why?'

'I am too. Your Daddy's off shooting somewhere. I wanted us to talk, woman to woman.'

This was most unlike her mother. Something was up.

'Talk? What about?'

There was silence on the far end of the line for a few seconds as Aenea tried to find the right words. 'Is everything all right, darling? I mean, between you and Antony?'

'It's okay. Naturally, he's upset at his father's sudden death, and now he has so much to think about with the inheritance and everything. But other than that we're fine, really.'

'So there was no truth in the story about Antony and that gentleman? What did the report say ... an "improper relationship"?'

'You *saw* that? Since when have you been getting the *Callander Advertiser*?'

'My friend Irene in Dunblane sent me a cutting from the *Stirling Observer*.'

'Irene – she's such a *clashbag*.' Rona had recently learned that wonderful Stirlingshire word for a gossipy woman from her cleaning lady and knew it would annoy her mother to hear her using it. 'No, it was a piece of malicious fabrication.'

'You're really okay, then?'

'What are you getting at, Mummy?'

'Your Icelandic friend … Ari … doesn't seem to think so. You wrote to him, didn't you?'

'Ari's been in touch with you?'

'He phoned – international, it was – but gave me no details, honestly. He just said he was concerned for you. Now you know your Daddy and I never approved of your relationship with Ari, but he did sound genuinely worried. He's to be at some kind of forestry conference in Edinburgh next week and wants you to contact him at his hotel. I have the number. He's reluctant to call you himself, in case … well, for obvious reasons.'

Rona managed to feign amusement. 'Ari – ha, ha! – he's such a silly, sometimes. Obviously he's read something into my newsy letter that wasn't there. Give me the number of his hotel and I'll give him a ring, put him right.'

Even before she'd hung up the phone, she had decided not just to call Ari when he got to Edinburgh, but to go and see him in person. She would tell Antony she was going shopping; Jenner's had their winter fashions in and she wanted to look the part of the new Lady Bracklinn.

When he met her on the Waverley concourse, it was as if they had never been apart. They sat in the station tearoom with eyes only for each other. Both laughed when she told him she'd been rehearsing this scene from *Brief Encounter* but she wasn't a patch on Celia Johnson.

Then it got serious.

She gave Ari a no-detail-spared account of her marriage, including her plan to have Dominic's child and pass it off as Antony's. And she told him Antony had punched her in the face.

'You have to get out,' Ari said. 'Murder the bastard if necessary.'

'Don't think I haven't considered it,' Rona said. 'But I want to spend the rest of my life with you, not in prison. A child's my only escape.'

'You could make it look like Dominic did it. He's got a motive, hasn't he? With Antony out of the way, he'd be Lord Bracklinn. All those grocery stores would be his.'

'And you think I would get away with it?' This was a pointless conversation, and Rona knew it. Yet in the days that followed the idea kept returning unbidden to her mind.

They left the tearoom and headed up the long flight of steps to Princes Street. 'I'd better go to Jenner's,' Rona said. 'Can't go home with nothing to show for my "shopping expedition".'

'My hotel's right there,' Ari said, pointing to the Old Waverley. 'I can think of a better way to spend the afternoon than trying on hats and coats. What do you think?'

Rona needed no further encouragement. As they lay together in bed with the sun streaming in through the window, it somehow felt like cheating on her husband whereas sex with Dominic did not. Yet it also felt natural, *right*.

'How long before we're a real couple, *elskan*?'

'We *are* a real couple.'

'You know what I mean. When can we be together like this, for all time?'

It was 3:30. She had to get going. Half an hour to grab a few things off Jenner's rails then down to the station for the 4:35 train. 'Give me two years, my darling,' she replied. 'Can you wait that long?'

'*So tired, tired of waiting, tired of waiting for you,*' he sang as he lay watching her get dressed.

16
REHABILITATION

FOLLOWING ÅSA OF AGDER IN Rona's translation of *Gudrun's Saga* was the life story of another remarkable woman of the tenth century, Gunnhild Gormsdóttir. Before beginning this new chapter, Delia consulted Wikipedia to learn what the known sagas said of her. The short answer: nothing positive. Few women in history have been as ill-served by their biographers; even Shakespeare's Lady Macbeth was benign by comparison. Though beautiful, Gunnhild emerges as a kind of pantomime villain.

Would *Gudrun's Saga* offer some rehabilitation? In spite of the late hour, Delia could not resist reading her tale.

OF GUNNHILD GORMSDOTTIR

(NOTE: The heroine of this story is not to be confused with Gunnhild, mother of Asa of Agder. According to the sagas, Asa's grandson Harald 'Fairhair', the first king of all Norway, had at least twenty children, one of whom took Gunnhild Gormsdottir as his wife, as we shall see.)

Gorm 'the Old', king of Denmark, and his queen, Thyra, had three sons. Succession was assured. They also had a daughter Gunnhild who, being as strong in body and spirit as any of the boys, when grown would not be marriageable as a princess should be. At the age of five, therefore, Gunnhild was sent away to the cold north land (NOTE: Lapland) to live a simple nomadic life with a Sami tribe and their reindeer. There, her parents thought, she would learn the feminine qualities of humility and obedience.

Things did not turn out that way. Two elders of the tribe took the child under their wing and instilled in her the wisdom of the Sami people. They taught her that life in their frozen land was possible only if women took their full share of responsibility for the wellbeing of the tribe.

(NOTE: According to the saga writer Snorri Sturluson, Gunnhild's sojourn in the north was with two 'Finnish wizards' from whom she learned the dark arts of witchcraft in return for sexual favours. Gudrun's Saga gives no such salacious detail, though its tale of the ordeal of Astrid Leifsdottir – see later – has certain similarities.)

When she was fifteen, Gunnhild returned to her father and mother. Aghast to find she was even more rebellious than before, they resolved to marry her off as quickly as possible, before she acquired a reputation for wickedness. Fortunately for them, she possessed a beauty that blinded men to her unwomanly manners.

Erik Haraldsson, one of the princes of Norway, had become famous for violence against his enemies, including any of his brothers who dared challenge his right to succeed his father as king. He was known far and wide as Erik 'Bloodaxe'. If any man could tame the wild Gunnhild, her father reasoned, this one would. He invited Erik to a grand feast at the Danish court, where a marriage contract was offered and accepted.

Erik's young and beautiful new wife set about repairing his relationships with his brothers. At her behest, he began making generous gifts to them of gold and silver he had plundered during his youthful days as a Viking raider. So friendly did she become with some of her brothers-in-law that people suspected her of infidelity to her husband. Malicious gossips even said that some of her eight children were not Erik's offspring. None of their stories were true: Gunnhild remained faithful to the man she had married.

(NOTE: Most or all of Erik's 'brothers' were in fact half-brothers. His father Harald 'Fairhair' had many wives and concubines bearing him children, all of them – the sons at least – having a legitimate claim to the succession.)

When Erik's brother Halfdan took ill, Gunnhild recommended a particular medicine she had learned about from her Sami tutors. For a few weeks his health improved, but despite her best efforts he took a turn for the worse and died. All of Norway mourned, for Halfdan was the best-loved of the sons of Harald. Gunnhild was accused of having poisoned him with her Sami medicine, but Erik threatened to take his axe to anyone spreading such lies.

Shortly afterwards, Harald 'Fairhair', King of Norway died and Erik 'Bloodaxe' came to the throne, with Gunnhild his queen. She had her servants become her eyes and ears at court. Soon she learned that three of Erik's brothers, each of whom had received valuable gifts from Erik, were plotting against him. When she told her husband, he resolved to kill each of the conspirators. The first, Bjorn 'the Seafarer', died in an ambush at Saeheim; shortly afterwards Olaf and Sigrud fell in battle at Tunsberg.

The nobles of the kingdom began to revolt against the persecution of the king's brothers. 'Bloodaxe' declared he would kill every man who spoke against him, but Gunnhild saw a better way out of the problem.

In King Harald's dying days he had fathered a son with his servant girl Thora. She named him Hakon and, to protect him from Erik's rampages, sent him to Jorvik (NOTE: York) where he was fostered by the king of England, Athelstane. Now Gunnhild believed that, of all Harald's sons, Hakon would be the fairest and most popular ruler of Norway, even though he was still a boy. She sent a secret letter to the English king, proposing that his foster-son Hakon return to Norway to be declared king, on condition that Athelstane grant safe passage to England for Erik and herself.

When Athelstane agreed, she next arranged a covert meeting with the most powerful of the Norwegian nobles. They gave their support to Hakon as Erik's successor and their word that Erik and Gunnhild would be allowed to sail to England.

Now all Gunnhild had to do was convince her husband that this was the best solution. That she did in bed one night.

(NOTE: No previously known saga gives credit to Gunnhild for the safe evacuation of Erik 'Bloodaxe' from Norway in favour of his half-brother Hakon.)

With a small band of supporters, the king and queen set sail across the North Sea. Storms delayed their progress towards England and they were obliged to take shelter on one of the islands held by the Earls of Orkney, who had been subject to the Norwegian crown since the rule of Harald 'Fairhair'.

Gunnhild saw that she could turn this diversion to their advantage. The Orkney Earldom was in those days split between two brothers, Arnkel and Erlend.

Playing one against the other, she argued that her husband was still the rightful king of Norway. Upon their eventual acceptance they became subject to Erik 'Bloodaxe', whose onward progress to Jorvik could now be as a reigning monarch, king of Orkney, rather than as a deposed former Norwegian ruler.

Erik and Gunnhild were accordingly welcomed with due respect; when they agreed to be baptised as Christians by the Bishop of Jorvik, they became even more popular. Soon Erik was named King of Jorvik, claiming to rule all of Northumbria from the Humber to the Forth.

But the Anglian nobles of Northumbria did not wish to be ruled by a Viking. They rose against him, engaging his forces in battle at Stainmore in the west. There the fierce 'Bloodaxe' was killed. Gunnhild tried to have their son Gamle Eriksson named as king, but the victorious Angles soon put her and all her family to flight, bringing Jorvik once again under the English throne.

Back in Orkney, she took tribute from Thorfinn 'Skullsplitter', by then Earl of Orkney in succession to his brothers Arnkel and Erlend. But soon she tired of the place, longing for a more prestigious home. Leaving her daughter Ragnhild in Thorfinn's care with a plan that she would marry one of his sons, Gunnhild left with her other children for Denmark, the land of her birth.

(NOTE: Ragnhild Eriksdottir's life in Orkney is the subject of the next chapter of Gudrun's Saga.)

At the Danish court in Roskilde, Gunnhild was welcomed by the king, her brother Harald 'Bluetooth'; she returned his generosity by lending her sons to him in military support. Until her youngest son Harald ('Greycoat') Eriksson was old enough to fight, the king became his foster father.

'Bluetooth' was constantly at war with Hakon of Norway; in one battle Gunnhild's eldest son Gamle was killed. Soon afterwards, 'Greycoat' and his remaining brothers slew Hakon at Fitjar, declaring Norway a Danish possession.

Now supreme ruler over both countries, 'Bluetooth' named his foster son King of Norway. With his mother Gunnhild, 'Greycoat' set up court there and ruled at her bidding. She was back in the land that had expelled her, now its reigning queen in all but name.

Having wealth and power, Gunnhild lacked only a man to love her. Although growing old, she gained the affection of a young Icelandic warrior named Hrut and scandalised her court by taking him to her bed. When he returned to his native land to marry a woman of his own age, her revenge was to replace him with an even younger man, his nephew Olaf.

(NOTE: Snorri has Gunnhild exact a different revenge. He writes that she cast a spell on Hrut, making him unable to consummate his marriage.)

After her son Harald 'Greycoat' was killed in battle, Gunnhild Gormsdottir returned once again to Orkney, rejoining her daughter Ragnhild. Under the protection of Thorfinn 'Skullsplitter', Gunnhild's last days were quiet and peaceful, unlike any other time in her long life.

17
TICKET TO FREEDOM

OPENING THE MAIL ON A Thursday morning, Antony announced to his wife that Jenner's bill had arrived. 'One hundred and sixty-two pounds seventeen shillings and sixpence,' he read to her from the bottom line.

'So?'

'So, I never saw what you bought.'

'I didn't realise that was necessary,' she said caustically. 'You'll find a coat and two dresses, still in bags in my room. Oh, and a hat, and some underwear.'

'It's over a week since your trip to Edinburgh. Shouldn't you hang those dresses up so they don't crease?'

She glanced up from her newspaper, gave him a withering look, then continued reading.

'Not that it will be of any interest to you,' Antony went on, 'but tonight's a "poker night". Dominic will be round later.'

'Do what the hell you like,' Rona replied without looking up.

That evening she settled in her favourite armchair with a glass of Blue Nun to watch *Top of the Pops*. As The Sandpipers' *Guantanamera* played over film of a Latin beauty strolling barefoot on a deserted palm-fringed beach, the doorbell rang.

Not Dominic. He always let himself in by the back door.

On the doorstep, in lashing rain, a young man with a slightly ragged goatee beard sheltered under an umbrella she recognised as Antony's.

'You're Maurice, aren't you?' she said, not bothering with the 'Mo-*reese*' affectation. 'You'd better come in, though Antony isn't here.'

He looked surprised. Whether he had not expected to be received with such courtesy, or to be so instantly recognised, Rona could not immediately determine.

In the warmth of her living room, she motioned him to sit down and offered him a drink.

He accepted a whisky. 'With lemonade, please, if you have any.'

She poured another glass of wine for herself. 'Maurice, I have to say I'm not in the habit of entertaining young men while my husband is out, but in your case I imagine I've little to worry about.'

His chin began to quiver. 'Mrs Argill ... I mean, Lady Bracklinn ... I'm sure you know about Antony and me.'

'I do, though it's a subject I don't care to dwell on.'

'We had a horrible row today and he told me it was all over between us.'

'And this affects me in what way?'

'I'm sorry, I don't mean to upset you, but I've seen him in one of these moods before. He gets alarmingly violent. I came to warn you.'

'Well, that was very thoughtful of you. But I'm going to be just fine. Antony's brother Dominic is coming over to visit in a little while.'

'In that case, I'll be off.' Maurice hastily collected the umbrella from a stand in the hall and stepped out into the rain.

What happened later that evening was etched in her memory, though now, fifty years on, it was more like a bad dream. Had she, Ragna Enjudóttir of Akureyri, Iceland, really been that Rona Fay Argill, Lady Bracklinn of Ardwhinzean near Callander, Scotland? And had it really played out just as she remembered?

Shortly after eleven o'clock, for the third time that week, Rona was trying her very best to buy her ticket to freedom – in other words, get pregnant. Dominic was a little more boisterous than usual in bed. Neither one of them heard the back door open and close as Antony let himself in through the kitchen.

A couple of minutes later he burst into the bedroom, his eyes blazing. 'Caught in the act, brother!' he yelled.

'For God's sake, Antony,' Rona said as Dominic heaved his body off her. 'This was your idea! You've no business barging in here like that.' She noticed his dishevelled hair, the wild look in his eyes. And oddly, that he was wearing leather gloves.

'No business, eh?' he slurred, obviously drunk. 'I'm Baron Bracklinn, lord of this manor. The arrangement with Dominic *vis-à-vis* my marital bed has ceased to apply, in light of the news we received today.' It was a pompous and complicated sentence to get his tongue around in his advanced state of inebriation but he had clearly rehearsed it and somehow managed.

'What news?' Rona asked, as much to Dominic as to Antony.

'The lawyer read our father's will to us this morning,' Dominic said. 'Your husband is miffed that the grocery chain, where most of the Bracklinn money comes from, doesn't go to him. He gets the title, I get the wealth. Seems fair.'

'Not to me, you bastard,' Antony shouted, his face becoming ever more twisted with rage.

By now Dominic, without a stitch of clothing, was on his feet facing his frenzied half-brother. 'I've been doing you a favour here,' he said, gesturing towards the bed. 'So just bugger off!'

With horror Rona saw a flash of steel as Antony drew a knife from his sleeve. He lunged at Dominic, who first recoiled then made a grab for Antony's wrist, hoping to force him to release the weapon. Rona pounced on Antony from behind and attempted a choke-hold, but he simply tossed her aside. The two brothers got into close quarters, chest to chest. The knife was in Antony's gloved hand between them, while Dominic maintained his tight grip on his brother's forearm. Suddenly it was over. The blade had found its mark. Antony slumped forward on to the floor, driving the knife further into his chest. He lay gasping for a few moments before coughing up a huge mouthful of blood, then was absolutely still. From the lifeless body, a rapidly expanding red stain spread across the bedroom carpet.

In a voice devoid of emotion, Rona said, 'You've killed him.'

'Don't say that, for God's sake! Shouldn't we check his pulse or something?'

'Look at him. It's all over for poor dear Antony.' She was in shock, yet preternaturally calm. 'Come on, Dominic. Get a grip of yourself. Go and clean up while I put some clothes on. We need to call the police.'

As she dressed, she thought, *He's dead, and they can't pin it on me! What a stroke of luck! Doubly so if Dominic's prints are on the knife and they put him away for murder. Except, what motive does he have? He already owns the supermarkets. All he gains by Antony's death is the Bracklinn title ... maybe that's enough.*

Coming through from the bathroom, a towel around his middle, Dominic put a sharp brake on Rona's train of thought. 'Good thing I never touched the handle of the knife,' he said. 'There won't be any question that I stabbed him.'

Then it struck her. That knife was from her block on the kitchen worktop. Though she would certainly have washed it after its last use, it might well still carry *her* fingerprints. Should she turn Antony over and wipe the handle clean? No, that would look even worse.

After she called the police, another thought came to her, just as awful. Dominic was now the 4th Lord Bracklinn. He could, almost certainly would, hold Rona's father to the deal. Antony was gone, but Dominic would insist on marrying her so that any child of theirs would be heir to both the Fairfield and Bracklinn titles. If she refused, her parents would be penniless.

It did not occur to Rona that she might already be carrying that child.

18
NOTHING, REALLY

THE AVENGER HAD TAKEN OUT e-subscriptions to a selection of local newspapers from towns and cities where the augmented packs of Fairfield's Premium Organic Muesli were sitting on supermarket shelves. Every day a dozen or so websites had to be scanned for news of deaths consistent with abrin poisoning. Once the first report appeared it would be time to move to the next stage of the plan.

A Twitter account had already been set up under the username @jequirityjo. It had proved surprisingly easy to establish the account untraceably. Certainly, it helped to have some geeky friends who knew about anonymization software and that kind of thing. What was not so easy nowadays was to find a variety of public computers on which to create and access the account. Using your own machine, whether laptop, tablet or smartphone, would be stupid. Internet cafés tended no longer to have computers for rent – those had become rarer than coin-operated telephones. Public libraries still offered them, but you had to show your library card: another no-no.

Fortunately there were still a few seedy pound-an-hour operations where you could sit on an uncomfortable stool before a scratched screen tapping a sticky, greasy keyboard without giving any kind of ID. Mostly they were within a block or two of major railway stations or port terminals.

To establish a following, @jequirityjo tweeted some mildly provocative comments about minor celebrities, footballers' WAGs and porn stars. Enough retweets showed up to confirm a small audience was out there. Small was good.

But still the papers gave no hint that a doctored box of Fairfield's had found a victim. That had to change soon.

On Friday at 2:15 pm the A&E department at Ninewells Hospital in Dundee was buzzing. Nothing like as busy as it would be twelve hours from now, but still having to prioritise new arrivals.

Dean Fegary was not a difficult decision for the triage nurse. Fourteen years old, he had collapsed on the school football field, vomiting blood. He was goalkeeper for the stronger team and, with most of the action going on at the opposite end of the pitch, it had taken a minute or two for anyone to notice him lying motionless in the goal mouth. As soon as the alarm was raised, the games master had run to his aid, ensured he was breathing and called for an ambulance. The game was abandoned and both teams sent to the showers.

The boy had regained consciousness on the way to hospital but the vomiting continued. Even before he was admitted to A&E he had been put on a drip for fluid replacement. Blood samples were taken in case transfusion would be needed, as indeed it soon was.

Dean's mother Alexis arrived at 3 o'clock, by which time the boy was in a coma. Dr Dilip Banerjee had a list of questions for her.

'How was Dean when he left for school this morning?'

'Fine ... no different from usual.'

'He didn't complain of feeling sick, having a headache, wanting to go back to bed, anything like that?'

'No. He's always a bit of a sleepyhead in the morning, but he gets himself going in time to catch the bus.'

'And today was no exception?'

'No.'

'Who else is in the household, apart from yourself and Dean?'

'It's just the two of us. I'm a single mum.'

'And no one else was there this morning?'

Alexis bristled slightly at what she thought the doctor was implying. 'No. Certainly not.'

'What about breakfast?'

'What *about* breakfast?'

'What did he have?'

'I didn't see. I was getting myself ready for work. I suppose it was the usual – a plate of cereal with milk and a banana.'

'What kind of cereal?'

'Cheerios. It's all he'll eat. Too much sugar, I know, but it's a way to get milk into him, for the calcium.'

'My kids are the same,' the doctor said.

'Oh my God, I forgot,' Alexis said. 'The Cheerios were finished and I hadn't managed to get to Tesco this week.'

'So what would he have had instead?'

'Dunno. Maybe just the banana.'

'When you go home, Ms Fegary, could you check the kitchen for any sign of what he might have eaten? It looks to me as if Dean has some nasty kind of food poisoning. His treatment could depend on us figuring out what the toxin is and where it came from.'

'But I want to stay here in case he wakes up.'

'We're keeping him sedated meantime. You'll do him much more good with a bit of detective work on what he had for breakfast. Check the bin. The dishwasher. Anything out of place in the fridge or the pantry.'

'Maybe it's what he had for lunch. He eats in the school canteen.'

'We're checking that too, Ms Fegary.'

An hour later, Alexis Fegary called Dr Banerjee's mobile number.

'Is he okay, doctor?'

'No change. That's good news, by the way.'

'The only thing I can see he might have eaten is some muesli. I buy it for myself and he never usually touches it. But since we were out of Cheerios, I suppose ...'

'How do you know he had some of your cereal?'

'You said I should check the pantry. The box was lying open, as if he'd just reached in and taken a handful. I never leave it like that.'

'Please keep the muesli and all its packaging, Ms Fegary, and don't eat any.'

'I've already had three or four breakfasts out of that same packet. And there's nothing wrong with me. It's organic,' Alexis added, as if that meant it had to be harmless.

The following morning, Dilip Banerjee received some troubling information. Dean's blood sample taken on admission had been tested against a battery of toxicological markers, and was positive for L-abrine, a sure indication that the patient had consumed abrin.

As virtually no possibility existed of accidental poisoning by abrin in the UK, the police had to be notified. Alexis Fegary was not yet dressed when two officers arrived with a warrant to search her house. Among the things they bagged and took away was a half-full packet of Fairfield's Premium Organic Muesli.

No trace of abrin was found in any of the materials retrieved in the search.

After three days and nights of intensive care, Dean turned the corner. Two more days in a regular hospital ward saw him ready for discharge, with no lingering effects.

A young female reporter from the Dundee *Courier* interviewed the boy and his mother. Dean confirmed he had eaten Fairfield's muesli on the morning he became sick.

'It was really expensive,' Alexis said. 'I thought it would be healthy, being organic and everything. You can't depend on anything these days, can you?'

'But the police said there was nothing wrong with it,' the reporter said. 'You're not so sure, are you?'

'*Something* in that cereal poisoned Dean. I thought for a while he wasn't going to make it, but thanks to the wonderful care he received at Ninewells, he's going to be fine.'

A rush of adrenalin made the reporter's scalp tingle. This could be the break she longed for: a news story on which she alone had the inside track! But everything rested on establishing a Fairfield's connection to the boy's close brush with mortality. If she had that, it could propel her into the national spotlight, maybe even a job in television! Without it, Dean's story was just an everyday human-interest piece.

She could not herself simply assert corporate malfeasance on Fairfield's part. What she needed was a quote from Alexis Fegary criticising the company. She thought for a moment before asking her next question. 'Fairfield's muesli is made right here in Dundee. Have you a message for the company?'

'Just double-check all your cereal ingredients. I wouldn't want anyone to go through what Dean had to suffer.'

Not quite strong enough, the journalist thought. Maybe the victim himself would be less forgiving. 'And how about you, Dean? How awful was this for you?'

'It was nothing, really,' the fourteen-year-old said stoically.

For one local beat reporter, the prospect receded of a glittering journalistic career in the national media.

The Avenger read the *Courier* story online next morning. It was headlined 'MUESLI MYSTERY BAFFLES DOCTORS AND POLICE'. The Fegary interview was the centrepiece of the report, which went on to say, 'At this point, there is nothing to suggest wrongdoing by Fairfield's' – a comment calculated to leave the reader wondering if indeed Fairfield's *was* somehow at fault. The cereal company's PR department issued a statement to the effect that its quality assurance procedures were second to none. Customers could continue to buy Fairfield's products with absolute confidence.

Later the same day a tweet was sent into cyberspace. It read:

> **Jequirityjo** @jequirityjo - Jul 6
> It's no longer a #mueslimystery. I spiked
> Fairfield's cereals. Dean was lucky. Others
> will die. Maybe already have.

19
DOUBLE-BARRELLED

OFFICERS AND FORENSICS staff of Stirling and Clackmannan Police had completed their examination of the scene of Antony's death by four in the morning. From the statements given independently by Rona and Dominic they seemed satisfied that the victim had accidentally stabbed himself during the struggle with his brother. Eyebrows were raised at the admission of the two witnesses: they had been engaged in sexual intercourse when Antony burst in on them. The absence of bloodstains on their clothing was explained by the fact that they were both naked at the time.

'Now, Lady Bracknell,' a police sergeant started to say, 'we're ...'

'This may look like an Oscar Wilde farce, officer, but I'm not Lady Bracknell.'

'Sorry, Lady Brack*linn*.' The sergeant raised his eyes briefly to the ceiling in an involuntary gesture of exaggerated patience. 'What I was about to tell you is that we're sealing off the room in case we need to come back for more fingerprints. Have you an alternative room you can use in the meantime?' He drew out the word 'use' accompanied by a leer that was not lost on Rona.

Even when the knife handle yielded Rona's prints but no others, the police found the need for only a perfunctory re-interview. There was a perfectly rational explanation for those prints. The sheriff, in due course, brought in a verdict of death by self-inflicted wound during a struggle while inebriated.

The Argills' family doctor confirmed Rona's pregnancy on 30th November. 'In normal circumstances,' he said in his self-important way, 'I would offer you my heartiest congratulations, as it appears you have an heir to the Bracklinn barony *in utero*. You must have conceived very shortly before your husband's untimely death, and I imagine this is a bittersweet moment for you.'

Well the doctor knew from newspaper reports that she was in an intimate relationship with her brother-in-law, the new Lord Bracklinn, indeed that Antony had caught them in the act before his demise. *What point is he trying to make,* she asked herself, *with this 'bittersweet' comment?*

To Rona there was nothing bitter about it. The child that would allow her to escape was on its way. She would give Dominic the news as soon as she got home.

His reaction was not quite what she was expecting.

'I was afraid this might happen,' he said. 'In fact I've been talking to old Whitfield.'

'Whitfield the solicitor? What were you talking to *him* about?'

'Hereditary peerages and the legitimacy of heirs.'

'What are you on about, Dominic?'

'Well, I suppose we're agreed I'm the father, right?'

'Who else could it be?' An uncomfortable thought occurred to Rona as she said these words. *That afternoon in the Old Waverley with Ari! What if ...?* She dismissed the idea. 'Of course you're the father. This is exactly what we intended to happen.'

'Yes, but circumstances are different now that Antony's dead. Whitfield says the law isn't exactly clear, but a child conceived while Antony was your husband would be presumed to be Antony's.'

'So what's the problem?'

'The problem is that *I* am now Lord Bracklinn, and any legitimate child *I* have would become first in line to that title. *Antony's* legal offspring, the creature in your belly, would be heir only to the Fairfield earldom. You see? The two titles won't merge the way my father intended.'

Rona shrugged.

'You don't get it, do you?' Dominic insisted. 'You have to get rid of this one and start again.'

She could not believe what he was proposing. 'You want me to abort the baby I'm carrying, just so that two peerages can be united? Is that it?'

'In a nutshell, yes.'

'But, Dominic, it's common knowledge you and I were having sex before Antony died. The newspaper reports more or less said so. No one can seriously suggest this baby isn't yours.'

'According to Whitfield, common knowledge and legal presumption are two different things. You were married to Antony when you conceived. That makes him the father, according to the law. So now, as only the first legitimate child of *mine* can be a Bracklinn and only the first of *yours* a Fairfield, we have to wipe the slate clean, as it were.'

'No! No! No!' she cried. 'I won't do it!'

'Then there's another solution,' Dominic said calmly. 'We marry immediately, and when the child is born we just pretend it's premature. Conceived on our wedding night, we'll say.'

'Who's going to be fooled?' Rona asked. 'The doctor knows I'm already pregnant. It'll be in my medical record – he estimated a due date in July.'

'Your records, and the baby's, are bound by doctor-patient confidentiality. Look, Rona, I *prefer* Plan A – abort and start again – because no one can ever question the child's legitimacy to inherit, but out of deference to you I'm prepared to go with Plan B.'

'That's big of you,' she said.

The wedding was a quiet affair in the registry office in Stirling. She wore a simple green dress, he an everyday business suit. On the little finger of his right hand was the Bracklinn family signet ring that not long before had caught Rona's jaw when worn by Antony. Besides the bride and groom, only two witnesses stood before the registrar: Dominic's mother Edith and his twenty-year-old nephew Fergus Argill-Hawke.

Back in the cottage at Ardwhinzean, Dominic was ready to assert his marital rights.

'Forget it,' Rona told him bluntly. 'I did you a huge favour by marrying you, but there's to be no honeymoon. I'll be in the spare room. You can have the master bedroom.'

'But ...'

'Don't "but" me, Dominic. I know you have girlfriends only too happy to oblige. I'm going to bear your brat, then I'm offski. Job done.'

'You're right,' he said, his temper rising. 'I *do* have other options. I'll ring Jenny and Freda, invite them over. A threesome on my wedding night – that'll be a lot more fun.'

'Suit yourself. Hope they'll like the bloodstained carpet.'

By mid-December, Lord and Lady Bracklinn had settled into their unconventional arrangement. Over lunch one day, Dominic said, 'You know, Rona, Fergus has been after me to take him shooting. Doesn't your father have land on that hill at the back of his place ...?'

'The Hill of Fare, yes.'

'Will there be good pickings up there this time of year?'

'I suppose so. We always had a hare for the pot in the run-up to Christmas.'

'Would he give us a day's sport, do you think?'

'Sure. He was willing to give up his daughter as a Bracklinn brood-mare, why not a few hares?'

Fergus Argill-Hawke had always been closest to Dominic among the Argill clan. The eldest son of Marjorie Argill and her stockbroker husband Angus Hawke, he had resigned himself to going through life with a double-barrelled surname. Marjorie was eleven years older than her brother Antony, now deceased, and her stepbrother Dominic.

Fergus had enjoyed dancing with Rona at her first wedding, and had been flattered by the attention she paid to him as a witness at her second. Their intimate conversation that day had been observed by Edith, the Dowager Lady Bracklinn. She was struck by the apparent warmth between Rona and Fergus: they *were* of a similar age, she supposed. Only when the bride glanced at her new husband did her smile turn to icy indifference. Edith worried that her son had fallen into the clutches of a man-eater. Might the beautiful Rona seduce Fergus next, and give Dominic the Antony treatment?

It was 21st December, the winter solstice and the shortest day of the year. Philip Swainson, Earl of Fairfield had given Dominic and Fergus some pointers as to the terrain above Gordonhall before sending them on their way up the hill. 'Stay above Corrichie,' he had advised them, 'and don't wander too far west, for safety's sake.'

Dominic had politely invited him to join them, but he declined. On such a frosty day, Philip had preferred to stay by the fire in the cosy gatehouse where he and Aenea were still living.

'Come by when you get off the hill,' he had told the two shooters. 'I'll pour a good malt whisky to warm you up. And I'll be interested to see what's in your bag. Good luck!'

At 3:30, just as it was getting dark, an urgent and insistent rapping came at the door. Fergus stood alone on the doorstep. 'There's been an accident,' he blurted out. 'Dominic's been shot. He's dead.'

'Shot? You mean *you* shot him?' Philip had turned pale.

'Not exactly. We were clambering over some rocks. I lost my footing and dropped my gun. It went off – both barrels.'

'Didn't you have the safety catch on?'

'I thought I did. He took it right in the face. I think he died instantly.'

'How ghastly! Rocks, you say?'

'Yes, on the hillside above where that ruined castle is.'

'Cluny Crichton. Oh my God, you were on the Skairs. I *told* you not to go too far west. That's off my land and it's ...' Philip almost let slip the word 'haunted'. Instead he finished his sentence with the words '... a dangerous place.'

'We have to go up there and bring him down.'

'It'll be pitch dark soon. No, we have to call the police. They'll prefer anyway that we don't disturb the body. It'll take them half an hour or so to get here.'

Aenea busied about making tea and stoking the fire. While the miserable young lad sat by the hearth waiting for the police to arrive, she beckoned her husband through to the kitchen. They talked in hushed tones.

'Who's going to break it to Rona?' she asked. 'She just lost her first husband, now her second.'

'Better you should call her,' he replied. 'God, what a tragedy!'

At that moment, a patrol car arrived at the door and three men from the Banchory police station emerged. Philip showed them in.

Fergus was not far into his account of what happened when the most senior officer said, 'We're going to have to continue this at the station. You say it was an accident, but we'll have to examine all the evidence. That could take a day or two. You may want to call your lawyer.'

Fergus was bundled into the patrol car. One officer stayed behind to interview Philip and Aenea. It soon came out that

Fergus was next in line to the Bracklinn fortune – indeed, since Dominic's death that afternoon, he already had a claim to be the 5th Baron. 'Quite a motive,' the policeman mused.

A Land Rover pulled up outside. Philip led the investigation team along rutted hill tracks to the Skairs, where the 4th Baron lay in the December darkness, most of his face blasted away.

When Aenea got her daughter on the phone, Rona absorbed the news with little emotion.

'I know this is a terrible shock to you, darling,' Aenea said. 'It'll take a little while to sink in.'

'No, Mummy, it *has* sunk in. And I'm all right with it, really I am.' *Actually,* Rona was thinking, *I'm over the moon. This couldn't have worked out better.* After putting the phone down, she did two things. First, she sent up a silent prayer of thanks to Gudrun, whose ethereal presence at the Skairs had (she was sure) used Fergus's gun to blast Dominic out of her life. And then, she switched on the Dansette and played the hit record she had bought that very day.

Good Vibrations by The Beach Boys.

20
RAGNHILD

'D ELIA? IT'S FRANK. I'M BACK in London. Had some funny results from blood tests and they want to see me in hospital. Nothing serious, I'm sure.'

'Hope you'll be all right, Frank. How is your wife?'

'More worried about this than I am. Listen, Delia, did I explain to you how I came by *Gudrun's Saga*?'

'No, but I'd really like to hear.'

Frank described finding Rona Fay Swainson's typescript in the back of a Victorian natural history tome somehow acquired from Gordonhall. 'From the bookplate I can see it was the property of the Earls of Fairfield, who had owned Gordonhall for centuries. Their family name was Swainson.'

'Rona's family?'

'Yes. I'm coming to that. Incidentally, I've just emailed you a copy of the bookplate.'

'Got it,' Delia said. 'I'm opening it as we speak. Mm, quite intricate, isn't it?'

'The "Faer Fjall" motto is apparently Old Norse meaning "sheep hill". Perhaps the original name for the Hill of Fare behind Gordonhall. See the pyramid in the centre of the bookplate? The one with a reflection beneath?'

'Yup. With its reflection, it looks like a regular octahedron. One of the five Platonic solids. Eight faces, twelve sides, six vertices.'

'If you say so,' Frank said, unable to conceal his amusement at Delia's slightly geeky knowledge of solid geometry. 'Could the octahedron have some significance for the Norse settlers in

Scotland? The Swainsons apparently believed they were of Scandinavian descent.'

'Don't know. It's interesting, though.' Oblivious to Frank's gentle ribbing, Delia mentioned her earlier investigation of a possible link between Taran's wheel and the carved stone balls found in Pictish sites all over the north of Scotland, but especially in Aberdeenshire. Most commonly they had six knobs, arranged exactly like the points of a Platonic octahedron.* 'But those are way older than Viking times,' she said. 'Probably iron age, some think even earlier.'

Frank drew her attention to the symbols on the octahedron.

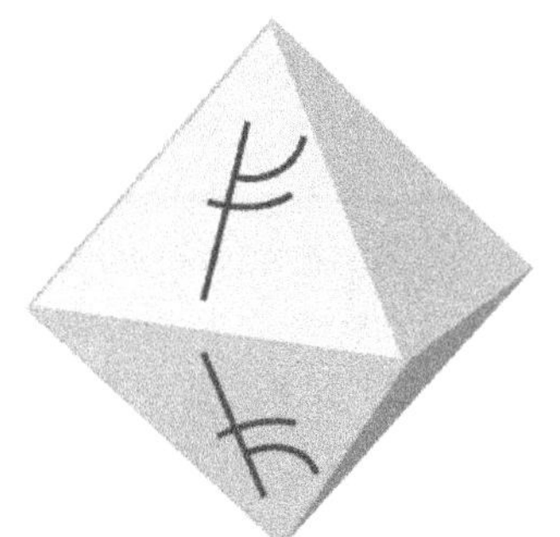

'Apparently, the upper one corresponds to F, the first of sixteen letters in the Scandinavian runic alphabet. The one below is a reflection, as you can see. "FF" – "Faer Fjall", I suppose.'

'Makes sense,' Delia agreed.

But she had another idea, one she was not yet ready to share until she did some more background reading.

'Anyway,' Frank said, 'the reason I called was to relay something I learned in Aberdeen before I came home. I was in the Central Library, going through *Press and Journal* reports from the late 1960s. I vaguely remembered there was some kind of scandal involving the Fairfield dynasty of Gordonhall. Now I know precisely what it was. Have you read the chapter of *Gudrun's Saga* that deals with Ragnhild, the daughter of Erik Bloodaxe and Gunnhild?'

'I'm just getting to it. Gunnhild was quite a lady. I hope Ragnhild's going to be as much fun. What's she to do with the Fairfield scandal, anyway?'

---

* See *Taran's Wheel* (*Incomers*: Book 1).

'As you read, think about what happened not in the tenth century, but in the twentieth. And for Ragnhild, substitute Rona.'

'Sounds interesting. Tell me more.'

What Frank told her of the 1960s scandal made *Gudrun's Saga* seem suddenly much more relevant. Eagerly Delia began the tale of Ragnhild, *alias* Rona.

OF RAGNHILD ERIKSDOTTIR

(NOTE: The Orkneyinga Saga portrays Ragnhild as a particularly evil woman. The version of her story told in Gudrun's Saga is in general agreement as far as the principal facts are concerned, but here the facts are as Ragnhild herself might have seen them.)

Thorfinn 'Skullsplitter', Earl of Orkney, was a gentler man than his nickname implies. Loving the young Ragnhild Eriksdottir like a father, he gave her a house by his palace at Reykjavik (NOTE: Rackwick, on the island of Hoy) and two maids, slave girls he had captured on a raid in the west of Scotland.

The land ruled over by the Earl in those days included not only the islands of Orkney but also Shetland and a northerly swathe of the British mainland including Caithness and Sutherland. Such an extended fiefdom was hard to hold together, but Thorfinn was a firm and effective ruler. Through marriage to a Caithness chieftain's daughter, he could rely on her kin to help keep control.

The Earl had five sons and two daughters, some by his wife Grelauga and others by various concubines. The sons were Arnfinn, Havard, Ljot, Hlodvir and Skuli, and the daughters were Thurid and Liv. While betrothed to Arnfinn, Ragnhild fell in love with Ljot, and implored the Earl to allow her to marry him instead of his elder brother. At first he agreed, but Grelauga did not like this new arrangement. Arnfinn, unlike Ljot, was her own son and, she told her husband, had first right to Ragnhild. Still Thorfinn preferred the marriage to be for love and refused his wife's entreaties on Arnfinn's behalf.

Arnfinn himself was unenthusiastic. 'Let her marry Ljot,' he told his mother. 'I do not care to marry any woman. My love is to hunt and to fight.'

This angered Grelauga. 'What kind of Viking would hand his woman to a lesser man? Do what your ancestors would have done: take her maidenhood, by force if necessary. Then you will own her.'

Afraid to disobey his mother, Arnfinn went to Ragnhild's bed as she slept. She awoke with a dagger pointed at her throat. After a few moments, sensing his lack of confidence, Ragnhild took charge.

'Come, Arnfinn,' she invited him, 'do what your mother told you to do. Lay down that stupid dagger and drop your breeches.'

When he had disrobed, Ragnhild saw he plainly had no desire for her. 'Is <u>that</u> what you intended to deflower me with?' she said derisively. 'I have seen your brother Ljot undressed for a bath, and he is ten times the man you are.'

'Well, you are welcome to him,' he replied, pulling on his clothes and heading for the door.

Now Arnfinn had to face his mother and admit his impotence. 'I might have known,' she said with disgust. 'Your uncle Erlend Torf-Einarsson was not attracted to women, but did his duty and fathered a child. It can be done. You <u>will</u> make Ragnhild Eriksdottir your wife, *in every sense of the word. How otherwise can you become Earl of Orkney when your father dies, as he must one day?'*

She then went to Thorfinn. 'Always remember, husband, that you are overlord of Caithness and Sutherland only through my family's support. If you do not make that girl marry our eldest son, they will give their allegiance to the king of Scotland instead.'

'Do not forget,' he responded angrily, 'that I am Thorfinn "Skullsplitter". If your kin desert me, I will go to war with them.'

'You and what army? Your warriors are off plundering in Ireland, France and Spain. You cannot split the skulls of a thousand men with your one axe.'

Thorfinn had to relent. A wedding was hastily arranged between Arnfinn and Ragnhild, and a great feast was laid on in their honour. But that very night, while Arnfinn was in a drunken sleep, Ragnhild stole away to Ljot.

'I will put a dagger through his heart while he snores,' Ljot told her. 'Then you and I can be one.'

'If you do,' Ragnhild said, 'Grelauga will call for your head. It is better that another man send Arnfinn to Valhalla.'

'Valhalla?' he queried. 'Odin's domain? Arnfinn shall instead go to Folkvang, where the goddess Freya rules. But who have you in mind to send him there?'

'Your brother Havard,' she replied. 'He makes no secret of his lust for me. If, by responding to his advances, I gain his trust, he will take care of our problem. And you, my dear Ljot, will have nothing to fear from Grelauga.'

Havard needed little convincing to dispatch his brother Arnfinn. He saw for himself that the beautiful

Ragnhild would be but a minor prize. A bigger reward awaited: he would become heir to his father's earldom.

It was planned that, while Arnfinn was hunting alone, Havard would lie in wait at one of their favourite coverts. He would take his brother by surprise and kill him on the spot, making it look as if Arnfinn had been set upon by a band of thieves. On the appointed day, Ragnhild advised Ljot to visit a group of friends so that he could not be suspected of the crime.

(NOTE: Arnfinn is believed to have been killed around 954. In the version of this story told in the Orkneyinga Saga, Arnfinn's death at the hands of his brother was entirely orchestrated by Ragnhild, and the following scene does not appear.)

That evening, Havard came to Ragnhild's chamber, still bloody from his dark deed. 'I am ready to claim my reward,' he said. 'For your sake I have murdered my own brother; now you must repay me with your body.'

'When we are married, Havard, my body will be yours and yours alone.'

'I will not wait, lady. Will you come to me tonight, willingly, or must I take what is now mine?'

Ragnhild could see he would not be refused. 'You will indeed have a night of pleasure beyond your wildest dreams,' she promised. 'But first, you must wash away my husband's blood. My Scottish maids will prepare a hot bath to soothe the troubles of your day. Whatever you ask, they will do for you. See how pretty they are.'

She rang a little bell to summon them, and spoke to them in their own language, knowing Havard would not understand.

'By Thor,' he whispered into her ear, 'these are pretty girls indeed! You say they will do _anything_? Both of them, at the same time?'

Ragnhild nodded conspiratorially. The gleeful Havard left her room anticipating a delightful cleansing experience. But once the maids had undressed him and set him in his bath, they stole all his clothes and ran away, giggling. Completely naked, he sat basking in the warm water, thinking it was all part of the game. But when the girls failed to return, he became angry, tore a tapestry from the wall to wrap around him, and stomped back to Ragnhild's chamber.

She was nowhere to be seen.

At that very moment, Ragnhild and her Scottish maids were outside in the courtyard being helped into a carriage. The driver cracked his whip over the backs of his team of horses and they took off into the darkness. After reaching the shore of the Sound, they boarded a small boat to take them to Stenness, the home of Thurid Thorfinnsdottir, Havard's older sister.

Thurid and her teenage son Einar 'Bread-and-Butter' welcomed the three women. For several weeks they fed and sheltered the fugitives. Though besotted with Ragnhild, Einar felt such a beautiful woman was beyond his reach. Instead he took one of the Scottish slave girls to his bed, where he learned of his uncle Havard's dastardly deeds. He plotted revenge: for killing Arnfinn and threatening to rape the widowed Ragnhild, Havard deserved to die. Then surely Ragnhild could not fail to love him.

(NOTE: The Orkneyinga Saga has Ragnhild promise to marry Einar and make him Earl if he kills Havard.)

The scheme was a dangerous one. Einar sent a message to Havard promising to reveal Ragnhild's whereabouts. They were to meet at the Ring of Stones on a narrow strip of land between two waters (NOTE: probably the Ring of Brodgar, which occupies the isthmus between the Lochs of Stenness and Harray).

At the Ring, Einar told Havard to stand alone in the very centre and call on the ancient guardian spirits. Just one of the stones would echo his call. In the direction of that stone he would find Ragnhild.

As Havard walked towards the centre, the younger man drew his bow and shot an arrow into his uncle's back, before finishing him off with a dagger. Leaving the body where it fell, he hastened home to tell Ragnhild what he had done.

Grateful though she was, Ragnhild declined a proposal of marriage from Einar 'Bread-and-Butter', offering him instead the hand of the Scottish slave girl he had already seduced. 'I will have Thorfinn, Earl of Orkney declare her free, and a lady worthy of his grandson.' With this outcome he was satisfied. (NOTE: Gudrun's Saga does not record whether the slave girl was content to exchange one kind of servitude for another.)

Now Liv Thorfinnsdottir had a son, also called Einar, who was jealous of his cousin's marriage to a slave girl reputed to be comely and compliant to her husband's every desire. Having lodged with 'Bread-and-Butter' in Stenness and witnessed for himself the beauty of his young wife, he sailed to Hoy, hoping to persuade Ragnhild to give him the second slave girl.

'No, Einar,' Ragnhild said, 'my life is difficult enough with only one maid. Would you leave me with none?'

At this, Einar 'Hard-jaw' flew into a rage, and threatened to burn Ragnhild's house.

'Do that,' she told him, 'and you will have your uncle Ljot Thorfinnsson to answer to. As heir to the Earldom of Orkney, he has sworn to protect me and deal harshly with anyone who becomes my enemy.'

With anger still boiling in his heart, he returned to Stenness. Ragnhild could keep her slave girl. Instead he would steal the bride of his cousin 'Bread-and-Butter'. A few days later, having drugged his unsuspecting host, he entered the bedchamber and hauled the young woman from her husband's side. 'Say goodbye to your bread and butter, wench!' he said to her as he set fire to the house, burning his still-slumbering cousin to death.

(NOTE: Again the Orkneyinga Saga says that Ragnhild put 'Hard-jaw' up to killing 'Bread-and-Butter', on promise of marriage and making him Earl.)

Not long after these events, Ragnhild and Ljot were married. When Thorfinn 'Skullsplitter' died of old age in his bed, it was Ljot who succeeded to the earldom. Like her mother Gunnhild before her, Ragnhild had such influence over her husband that she was effectively the ruler.

(NOTE: Nothing further is known of Ragnhild's life. According to the Orkneyinga Saga, Ljot was later killed in battle and the earldom passed to his younger brother Hlodvir, who established the dynasty leading to Thorfinn 'the Mighty', probably the most powerful of all the Earls of Orkney.)*

---

* Thorfinn 'the Mighty' features in *Scotch and Water* (*Incomers*: Book 2).

21
AN EMPTY TITLE

IN THE COOL EVENING AIR, Akureyri's ferocious midges had begun to bite. Ragna went indoors and opened the Chilean red wine bought that afternoon in the Vínbúðin monopoly shop on Hólabraut. As she enjoyed its complex flavour on her tongue and the back of her mouth, her thoughts turned again to the past.

Can it really be half a century since I got my life back? It's hard to pinpoint exactly when that happened.

Was it Christmas 1966 when Mummy called me to say Dominic was dead?

No, there was still the matter of my unborn baby. The baby who, if it grew up looking like Dominic, would be a perpetual reminder of the Argill nightmare.

It all fell into place on 3rd July 1967, when I saw my newborn son in Airthrey Castle maternity hospital near Stirling. In that instant I knew he was not an Argill. He was Ari's boy. Here in Iceland, his legal name would be Dónaldur Arisson. In Scotland, however, as the presumed son of Dominic Argill, 4th Lord Bracklinn (deceased) and his Lady, he was the Honourable Donald Swainson-Argill.

Ragna/Rona had never admitted to anyone except Ari and, eventually, to the boy himself that her son was not Dominic's. Such admission would deny Donny any claim to the Bracklinn title and the wealth that accompanied it. Her secret, that Donny was the product of a passionate afternoon with Ari in

Edinburgh's Old Waverley Hotel, gave her comfort. For all their power and money, she had triumphed over the Argill clan.

It worried her that the truth would out when the dark hair the boy was born with gave way to the blondest of blond locks, a feature unknown in the Argill family. But no one remarked upon it. Her own fair hair, though since pregnancy darkened to a deep golden colour, let people say, 'He takes after his mother in his colouring at least. But I see Dominic in him too.'

In the autumn of 1967, when the child was a few months old, Rona brought him to Gordonhall to meet his maternal grandparents for the first time. Aenea fussed over him as grandmas do, but Philip was strangely distant.

'What's the matter, Daddy?' Rona asked him. 'Don't you want to hold your grandson in your arms?'

'He's so small and fragile,' was his excuse. 'I'm afraid I might hurt him.'

Rona was the one who was hurt by his apparent lack of interest in the continuation of the Fairfield dynasty. Try though she might, she could not extract from him the real reason for his aloofness.

'I've some business to attend to in Banchory,' he announced. 'I'll be back before supper.'

It was time to feed and change the baby. Rona fetched his top-and-tail mat from the car but it was Aenea who insisted on washing and giving him a fresh cotton nappy. *She never said so*, Rona reflected, *but she would have loved a son of her own. All she got was me.*

Mouth wet and bum dry, Donny slept in his grandma's arms.

'Why haven't you moved back into the big house?' Rona asked. 'The roof's watertight now, isn't it? And you've so little space here in the gatehouse.'

'To tell you the truth, Rona Fay, it doesn't seem worth the effort. This may shock you, but I'm thinking about leaving your father – got my eye on a cottage in the Borders, not far from Connie and Keith's place.'

That her parents' marriage was disintegrating came as no surprise to Rona. They had few shared interests; with their only daughter married (twice, and widowed twice, in the space of a few months) there was little to keep them together. But, the *Borders*? 'Mum, you've had almost no interaction with Aunt Connie and Uncle Keith for twenty years! Suddenly, you want to be neighbours?'

'Connie *is* my sister. Sure, we didn't get along well as kids, and she wasn't keen on Philip, but recently we've talked a lot – both mellowed with age, perhaps. Anyway, enough about me. How are you managing on your own, dear?'

Better not seem too upbeat. 'It's okay. I have a woman from the village to help in the house three mornings a week, and a man who looks after the garden. But otherwise ... well, I'm just doing what you and Daddy set me up to do: raising the little chap who's going to be heir to both the Fairfield and Bracklinn titles.'

'It still rankles that we steered you in that direction?'

'Steered? What option did I have? You were going to lose everything you had if I married for love.'

'I suppose by "love" you mean your Icelander. What kind of life could he offer you? What was he, a forester?'

Rona's face flushed in anger. 'Yes, Mummy, that's what he was, and is. And let me tell you this: Ari and I will be together soon. I've done my duty by bringing another Argill into the world and now it's *me* time. If I want a forester, that's what I'll have.'

Aenea laid the baby in his carrycot, tucked a blanket around him and watched him settle. Silence had always been the best response to her daughter's flashes of temper, but there was a matter that had to be broached. When the moment seemed right, Aenea said, 'Fergus is now Lord Bracklinn, is he not?'

'I suppose so. What's your point?'

'If he has a son of his own, wouldn't *he* become heir to the title?'

'I've discussed this with the Argill family solicitor. Whitfield's his name. He's a bit doddery, but his opinion is that Donny is the *real* Lord Bracklinn. Fergus for sure will take a different view, but I'm not inclined to push the matter right now. At some point, I'll have to go to court over it.'

'Won't that expose you to a lot of difficult questions?'

'What, for example?'

'Well, some of the papers are hinting you might have put Fergus up to killing poor Dominic.'

'That doesn't make sense, Mum. If most of Dominic's wealth goes to Fergus, then – financially, at least – I'll have lost more than I can ever gain from his death.'

'Not to mention your personal loss of a husband of only a few weeks.'

'The Argills were your choice, not mine. Dominic can rot in hell for all I care. Antony too.'

Aenea's shock at such plain speaking resulted in another silence. The awkwardness was broken by the baby's stirring. Rona lifted him and rubbed his back gently to break his wind.

The fatal accident inquiry into Dominic's death at the Skairs returned an open verdict, leaving unsettled the question as to whether Fergus was criminally liable. That could only be resolved in a trial.

Through various legal manoeuvres, his lawyer engineered repeated postponements, but finally the case came before the High Court in Aberdeen in October 1968. Initially, the media paid little attention. That changed when an acquaintance of Fergus's, called by the defence as a character witness, came under cross-examination.

'You have testified that your friend the accused is neither impulsive nor calculating in a malicious way. Is that correct?'

'Yes,' the witness agreed.

'Could he be persuaded to act in a fashion that would normally be against his better judgment?'

'I don't follow …'

'What do you know of the relationship between the accused and Lady Bracklinn, the victim's wife?'

'I believe they are friendly, no more.'

'Did you not give an interview to a reporter from the *Press and Journal* in which you said the relationship was a little stronger than that? In effect, that the accused was, your word, "bewitched" by Lady Bracklinn? Sufficiently "bewitched", one might wonder, to kill at her bidding?'

On objection, the witness was directed not to answer and the jury of ten men and five women to ignore the questions. 'Lady Bracklinn is not on trial here,' the presiding judge intoned.

Suddenly, for the media, the case assumed a more interesting, salacious edge. Suspicions were aired not only that Rona had put Fergus up to shooting Dominic, but that she had previously incited Dominic to kill Antony, her *first* husband.

Rona became a tabloid villain. But in spite of the jury's 'not proven' verdict that might have encouraged further speculation, the spotlight quickly dimmed.

The attention of the media was mercifully diverted by a much spicier, sleazier case in the same Aberdeen courtroom the following month. One that knocked everything from the front pages for weeks: The Garvie Trial. A sensational *ménage à trois* where a wealthy farmer was killed by his wife and her lover. Lurid tales of three- and four-way sex in what was soon dubbed 'Kinky Cottage' made everyone forget about Rona. To her great relief, she slipped into obscurity.

Less than two weeks after Fergus was declared a free man, Rona received a letter.

Dear Lady Bracklinn:

I am required to inform you that the regrettable death of your husband the 4th Baron Bracklinn, at a time when he was without legitimate issue, leaves my client Fergus Argill-Hawke, Esq. as rightful holder of the barony, which will pass to his children or other legal heritors upon his eventual demise. This means that your son the Honourable Donald Swainson-Argill will have no immediate claim on the Bracklinn title or assets, although I am pleased to confirm that you, as the 4th Baron's widow, will retain the dowager appellation as Lady Bracklinn and are entitled by law to one-third of his estate.

You will understand, therefore, that your brief marriages to the 3rd and 4th Barons have not led to the merging of the Bracklinn and Fairfield titles as was envisaged in the agreement between your father and the 2nd Baron Bracklinn. The debt your father owes to the 2nd Baron's surviving heir, my client, under that agreement is accordingly now being called, with interest at 6 per cent per annum, compounded annually. I am simultaneously writing to your father, the Earl of Fairfield, to notify him of his obligation in this matter.

Yours sincerely, ...

The portion of Dominic's estate that Rona was to inherit included little in the way of cash or easily liquidated assets. She would have a one-third share in the chain of supermarkets and in the Ardwhinzean property, not enough to give her any degree of control but sufficient to provide a comfortable income.

She called Whitfield, who agreed to drop by the following day. No sooner was he settled in her drawing room than her barrage of questions began.

'Didn't I fulfil my side of the bargain? The deal was, if I married the Bracklinn heir and gave him a child, my father's debt would be cancelled. Well, I did both of these things. The marriage part, I did *twice*.'

'You did indeed, but the "deal", as you call it, required that your son be heir to both the Fairfield *and* Bracklinn titles. Your son will not automatically succeed to the Barony of Bracklinn. After yourself, he is second in line to the Earldom of Fairfield, but can only gain the Bracklinn title and its appurtenances if a court of law decides in his favour.'

'I thought as much. So, to cancel the debt, we must fight it out in court.'

'I'm afraid so. It will take time and a lot of money, and there is no guarantee you will win. Young Fergus is now a wealthy man and will no doubt hire a crack legal team, one with an unbeatable record of success in cases of this nature.'

'Still, we have to try. We have right on our side.' As she uttered those words, Rona thought, *What if a paternity test is demanded? It would come out that Donny has no Argill blood. Who am I to talk about having right on my side?*

'Case law, my dear, is littered with claimants who have "right" but don't win. I counsel you to hold your fire until your son is a little older and – how should I put it? – a more *credible* Lord Bracklinn.'

'If the only issue was my son's inheritance, I could wait, but my father will be ruined by this debt recall. Am I not entitled to one-third of the proceeds of that recall? I could at least reduce my father's liability by 33 per cent.'

'Not according to the way the agreement with your father was structured. All assets seized in event of a default become the property of Lord Bracklinn, whoever happens to be the holder of that title at the time. Fergus would get everything.'

'So, Mr Whitfield, there's *nothing* we can do?'

'For the moment, that is the situation.'

By July 1969, the Earl of Fairfield was declared bankrupt, his wife Aenea had left him and the house and estate of Gordonhall had been transferred into the name of Fergus Argill-Hawke, Lord Bracklinn. Included were the entire contents of the mansion, including the rare book collection. The Earl refused his daughter's offer of a roof over his head at Ardwhinzean and instead rented a room and kitchen in the Aberdeenshire village of Alford. There he lived as plain Mr Philip Swainson, a former naval captain down on his luck.

Fergus had wasted no time in evicting Bert and Ada from the gardener's cottage at Gordonhall and installing Ed Williams as caretaker. Williams was an ex-convict Fergus had met at the Ayr Races and was willing to accept the position for no salary but for whatever he could 'earn' from the property. He made an easy living by selling scrap metal from the big house, exacting payments from shooting parties, and felling ancient trees for firewood.

In that same month, Telford Argill-Elliott wed a society debutante from Appleby-in-Westmorland by the name of Penelope Dart. His cousin Fergus came to the wedding without a partner, though he could have called on any of half-a-dozen girlfriends to accompany him.

'So, where are you and Penny going to live?' Fergus asked the bridegroom at the bar after the meal.

'Strangely enough, that's a matter I want to discuss with you. How would you feel about leasing Gordonhall to Penny and me? Unless, that is, you have alternative plans for the property?'

'To be frank, Tel, I've been thinking of putting the whole estate on the market. It's a bit of a millstone round my neck, the income from it is negligible and, just between ourselves, the place gives me the creeps. You know, that's where ...'

'Quite,' Telford murmured tactfully. 'Perhaps, then, we might consider an outright purchase rather than a lease. How about we meet at Gordonhall in a week or two and see if we could come to some arrangement?'

On 19th August 1969, the newlyweds became the proud owners of the historic mansion and its lands on the Hill of Fare, and immediately began a programme of refurbishment. Two bathrooms were added, and central heating installed. Only the library was left untouched, the couple being unable to agree on what should be done with the books. Penelope was keen to sell the whole collection to an Aberdeen antiquarian dealer; Telford rather liked the air of baronial grandeur they lent to his new home.

While renovations were going on, the couple found a temporary home in a self-contained annex of Penelope's parental home in Appleby. The Gordonhall caretaker Ed Williams stayed on to keep an eye on the place until they were ready to move in.

Philip received a letter at his Alford digs, forwarded from his previous address.

My dear Philip:

I hope this finds you as it leaves me well. You have probably heard that a cruise of the northern and western isles of Scotland has been arranged for ex-naval servicemen, enabling them to revisit places they saw during the war that broke out exactly thirty years ago.

I do not think the organisers had in mind to attract 'enemy' officers like myself, but as soon as I found out about it I wanted to take part in this remembrance voyage. What would make it special would be if you were to be there. Can you make it? It's set for 8th to 15th September this year. And guess what? The itinerary includes a call at the island of

Philip would have loved to go, but could not afford the fare: over £200. When he mentioned it to Rona on the phone a week or so later, she told him, 'Go, Daddy. I'll pay for it.'

The north Atlantic that September of 1969 was unusually benign. The SS *Shearwater*, one of the 'Little Ships' that had evacuated troops from Dunkirk in 1940, was now refurbished as an inshore cruise vessel. She dropped anchor off the tiny island of Rona to send a party ashore in a lifeboat. Philip and Klaus, former adversaries but now comrade war veterans, made first for the remains of the chapel where the U-boat crew had sheltered in 1943.

'See if you can find any signs your men were here, Klaus,' Philip said. 'I bet some of them carved their initials or left some personal possessions. I'll be back in a minute. Have to answer the call of nature.'

Klaus spent half an hour among the chapel ruins, picking up a few discarded items, now bleached and weathered, his men had left behind quarter of a century earlier. Still Philip had not returned and was nowhere to be seen.

The alarm was raised. In ever-widening circles the party searched around the chapel. Then a shout went up: 'Found his coat!' It came from the east: a cliff-top spot near Mary's Geo, with a sheer drop of two hundred feet to the ocean below. Klaus was first to peer over the edge, narrowly avoiding a direct hit from a fulmar's foul-smelling projectile vomit. Though the swell on the sea was light, the contours of the shoreline somehow amplified the waves that crashed on the rocks far below.

Hoping against hope to see his friend safely on a ledge within reach, Klaus made his way along the cliff-top, looking gingerly over the edge every few yards, but of Philip there was no sign. The awful truth took little time to dawn: Philip had taken his own life by leaping from these cliffs to be claimed by the wild Atlantic.

A strange story came into Klaus's head at that moment, something Philip had recounted to him years before. A Danish warrior king – Helgi was his name, he recalled – tortured by his own earlier cruelty to his queen and Yrsa, his daughter, had a recurring dream of being lured to a cliff-top by an elf-woman who then pushed him over the edge. A dream that eventually became reality, in a way.

The body of the 22nd Earl was never found. In the instant of his death, Rona became the 23rd Countess of Fairfield. An empty title, without wealth, without influence, without joy.

22
BUSINESS AS USUAL

JEQUIRITYJO'S TWEET CLAIMING to have spiked Fairfield's muesli was quickly brought to the company's attention. Its offices in Dundee buzzed with speculation and debate; but most of the board were convinced jequirityjo had to be a prankster.

The police were under no such illusion. Only they knew that Dean Fegary had tested positive for poisoning by abrin, the toxic principle of *Abrus precatorius*, the jequirity bean. The tweet could only have come from the poisoner.

Twitter confirmed that, as expected, @jequirityjo was no longer an active username. The account had been set up fraudulently, making it impossible to establish the real author of the tweet.

Through collaboration with colleagues south of the border, Police Scotland identified something in common between Dean Fegary's non-fatal poisoning and at least one death by suspected abrin ingestion in Manchester: both victims had eaten from a box of Fairfield's Premium Organic Muesli. Further samples were analysed from the suspect boxes, and once again tested negative for the toxin. A forensic toxicologist voiced the theory that the poisoning agent was possibly whole jequirity seeds, which, she pointed out, would leave no trace of abrin in the package.

Yet, she noted, those seeds were typically bright scarlet, not easily missed in a breakfast cereal dish. As a remote possibility, the less conspicuous white jequirity could have been used, but this form of the plant was extremely rare. She had been able to find just one article from 2005 in an Indian medical journal that confirmed the toxicity of white jequirity, taken by a 42-year-old man believing it to be an aphrodisiac.

A breakthrough came when one of the Dundee forensic team noticed that the muesli box from the Fegary pantry bore a tiny mark, apparently made with a ball-point pen – a mark which was missing from the stock on the shelf of the local Waitrose. The suspect packet from Manchester had a similar identifier: a dot following 'g' (for grams) against one of the components in the nutritional information panel.   Further examination revealed that the bottom of each of the marked boxes had been carefully opened and re-glued – clear evidence of tampering.

Fairfield's were informed and immediately issued an order to recall all the company's muesli products and alert the public. In doing so they beat the Food Standards Agency to the punch by a matter of hours. The nature of the toxin was not revealed; only the company's managing director, Donald Swainson, was put in the picture. 'Keep it to yourself for the time being,' the police advised him. 'In cases like this lots of wingnuts will call in claiming involvement. It's best only the guilty party knows what poison was used.'

No national newspaper had picked up the *Courier*'s 'muesli mystery' story, but now it made all the front pages. Because of the seriousness of the crime, most headline writers resisted the obvious joke; only one tabloid, famous for its lack of sensitivity or good taste, splashed the two words over its cover: 'CEREAL KILLER'.

Of the thousands of recalled packets, the suspicious ball-point mark was found on only two more, one each from a Sainsbury's in Ripon and a Morrison's in Edinburgh. They were forwarded unopened to the police, who found a single white jequirity seed in each box.

The recall cost the company an estimated fifty thousand pounds, but lost sales of all Fairfield's products due to consumer worry was far more damaging than that – according to one analyst, over a million.

On learning of the forensic findings in Dundee, a detective in Durham constabulary convinced his superintendent that the death of bank teller Leona White by suspected abrin poisoning should be followed up. Having teased out a few inconsistencies in her boss's statements, he paid a call to Royston Perry's home one weekday morning. Happy to be distracted from her chores, Norma Perry invited the detective in and poured him a cup of tea in her kitchen. He did not miss the box of Fairfield's Premium Organic Muesli on the worktop.

'There's a recall on that product,' he said.

'I know,' Norma replied. 'That's why it's sitting out, to remind me to take it to Tesco for a refund.'

'I've seen it in Tesco, but the price put me off. Is it worth the money?'

'Oh yes. I love it. My husband claims he hates it, but he just grudges the expense. He's a banker, you see. I went to North Wales for a few days recently, and when I came home I found he'd opened a new box – that one, actually – and had eaten some. Now what was it you wanted to see me about?'

'Just routine,' the detective said. 'Do you know Leona White, by any chance? An employee in your husband's bank.'

'The woman who died? I've heard Royston mention her name, but never met her. Such a sad business.'

'Mm.' The detective drank some of his tea, giving Norma a few moments to add two and two. He stepped over to the worktop, picked up the Fairfield's box and began studying the nutritional label intently.

'Oh my God!' Norma cried. 'The muesli murders! You suspect my *husband*?'

'Of murder, no. Is it possible Miss White had breakfast here one day while you were in North Wales?'

'Why would ...'

The detective watched Norma's face as the truth dawned on her. 'I trust you've no objection, Mrs Perry, if I take this muesli box back to the station?'

FAIRFIELD'S CEREALS: PART I
MURDER IS 'BUSINESS AS USUAL'

By Toff Hammer

Nobody is buying Fairfield's cereal products any more. Not since the news broke that their muesli has killed at least two – and counting. The company is destined for the scrapheap. Bad news for the fifty or so employees at its Dundee plant and offices, but good news for the rest of us.

Why is it good news? You may not realise it, but killing is in Fairfields' DNA. For them, murder is 'business as usual'.

The company was formed by a very slippery lady, the 23rd Countess of Fairfield, otherwise known as Rona Fay Swainson. A toff from a titled family whose forebears were, wait for it, Viking plunderers and rapists. But crimes of a much later vintage foreshadow the recent poisonings.

In October 1966, Rona's husband of only three months, Antony Argill, was stabbed to death in his bedroom during a tussle with his brother Dominic. Rona was clearly complicit – she and Dominic were having an affair and Antony had just caught them in the act.

The Argill brothers were themselves toffs – though lesser toffs than Rona: third-generation descendants of a businessman who had bought his peerage (the Bracklinn barony) from Lloyd George. Antony had recently succeeded as 3rd Baron; on his untimely death the title passed to none other than Dominic.

It will come as no surprise to Toff Hammer's regular readers to learn that the adulterous couple got away with murder as members of the aristocracy usually do: Antony's death was ruled 'accidental' at the inquest.

Rona, already pregnant (by which of the two brothers is anyone's guess), married Dominic very soon after Antony's death. But within weeks she was plotting again. She arranged a day's shooting for Dominic and his nephew Fergus on her father's estate just before Christmas that same year, 1966.

This time Dominic was the victim of an 'accident', killed by Fergus's shotgun. And who stood to become Lord Bracklinn? Why, Fergus, of course. But if he was expecting to gain the hand of the fair Rona as part of the deal, in this he was disappointed. No matter, along with the title came the Argill family business, a chain of supermarkets that was doing very well, thank you.

Next, Rona turned her attention to her own father, the Earl of Fairfield. Had he been complicit in her plan to dispose of Dominic in that shooting 'accident' on his estate? For whatever reason, she bought a ticket for him on a cruise to the northern and western isles, where he would be joined by a German he had taken prisoner during the war. On a remote island – named Rona, if you must know – the earl fell to his death from a cliff, upon which Rona Fay Swainson (or Argill or Argill) became 23rd Countess of Fairfield in her own right.

By now, dear reader, you will be ready to agree with me that the imminent demise of the company started by the infamous Rona is not a cause for sadness. Yet there's more. Check this blog for the next instalment.

A twice-daily trawl of the Internet threw up Toff Hammer's latest blog within hours of its posting, sending Fairfields' public relations department into overdrive. Being head of PR, Faith Elliott was the first member of the board to be alerted.

Telford and Penelope Argill-Elliott had named their two daughters Faith and Hope. If a third had come along, she would no doubt have been Charity. As the elder of the two, Faith had succeeded to her father's position as a director of Fairfield's Cereals.

She had an excellent working relationship with her managing director, Donald Swainson. Though a cousin of her father's, he was only three years older than Faith.

At her beautiful home, recently built on the site of the old Gordonhall mansion, she received the call about Toff Hammer's blog. Before she had even read it all, she was ringing Donald in Orkney.

'Slow down, Faith, I'm not following you.'

'Don't you see, Donny? He's our man, this Toff Hammer as he calls himself.' Her voice had an excited, almost hysterical edge Donald had not heard before. 'He's out to destroy our company, he more or less says so. He *has* to be the one that's put poison in our muesli.'

'D'you think?' Donald was playing for time as he tried to grasp what she had just said. 'Seems odd that he would so deliberately attract suspicion. But I'll call the police, make sure they check him out.'

'Okay. Should I alert the media?'

'Not yet, Faith. If he becomes a suspect, reporters will soon pick up the scent. But we need to meet face-to-face on this. How soon can you get on a plane?'

'I can be there by tomorrow lunchtime.'

'Fine. Let's meet at Rolf's place, save you coming all the way out here.'

Rolf Swainson was Donald's 25-year-old son. With his live-in partner Amy Lister, he had opened a wine and deli shop in Kirkwall's Albert Street. The couple had met at an Argill family wedding. Amy was a niece of Faith's.

'So I'll see you at the shop?'

'No, I meant at Rolf's house – you know, out by the golf course.'

Faith knew well where Rolf and Amy lived: a restored and much-extended traditional Orkney farmhouse within a few minutes' drive of Kirkwall. She had visited on a couple of occasions and even stayed over once. 'Fine, Donny,' she said. 'I should be there by about one o'clock.'

'I'll pick up deli sandwiches and a bottle of something from the shop. It'll be a working lunch.'

23
BLUEPRINT FOR MURDER

OURING A SECOND GLASS of wine, Ragna Enjudóttir tried to remember if she had ever felt truly sad at the loss of her father back in 1969. Sad, yes, that he had been so distraught at the loss of Gordonhall and the break-up of his marriage that he was prepared to take his own life. But sorry he was no longer a factor in her life? No, she never felt that.

After the brief memorial service in Banchory East Church, Lidia had remarked over dinner, 'It's great to see you again, Rona, and you're as stoic as ever. If I'd just lost one of my parents in such a tragic way, I'd be crying my eyes out.'

'Why cry for someone who sold me into a marriage I detested? Who then refused to have anything to do with the child of that marriage?'

'Did you say *sold?*'

In a potted history of the previous four years of her life, Rona described the devilish pact between Ludovic Argill and her father leading to her brief unconsummated marriage with Antony, her even briefer marital union with Dominic, his death at the hands of his nephew Fergus, the birth of her son Donald, the recent dispossession of Gordonhall to Fergus, who had sold it on to Telford. Almost nothing was left out.

'Remember,' she said, 'when we read *Lady Chatterley* together? I wondered if my life would be like hers.'

'So was Dominic your Mellors?'

'No,' Rona replied, 'there was someone else I was in love with. Still am.' She felt herself blush and took a gulp of her wine. 'God, I must sound like a lovestruck teenager.'

'We can pretend we're sixteen again.'

The story of her relationship with Ari Haraldsson poured out, except for the important detail of Donald's paternity. Some things could not yet be shared, even with her oldest and dearest friend. 'So my life has turned out not to be Constance Chatterley's, but Ragnhild Eriksdóttir's.'

'Who is she?'

'A character from the Norse sagas who was said to have arranged the death of at least three husbands or suitors, all so that she could marry the love of her life.'

'But, Rona, you ...'

'Two down, one to go.'

Lidia looked horrified, then noticed a twinkle in Rona's eye.

'My first husband was stabbed, my second shot. Both deaths were accidental, though I *have* been accused of setting them up. Anyway, now I'm light of foot and fancy-free, as they say. No one else stands between me and Ari.' Rona noticed her friend wore no wedding or engagement ring. 'But Lidia, what about you? Is there a man in *your* life?'

'For the moment, no. I've had boyfriends, a couple of all-nighters if you know what I mean, but no one permanent. I have been busy in other ways, though.'

'Busy? How?'

'I was selected for the Olympic Games last year.'

'Wow! A track event, I bet?'

'The 800 metres. Went with the British team to Mexico City, ran 2 minutes 15 seconds in high-altitude training.'

'Brilliant! But how could I have missed hearing about this?'

'Didn't even make it to the heats. A dispute broke out at the last minute about my eligibility to compete for Great Britain. I'd gained citizenship two months before. Even some of my so-called team-mates said I'd switched from Polish to British just to qualify for the games. Called me a fucking incomer.' Lidia's tone was bitter.

'That's awful!'

'I threw a major tantrum in front of the TV cameras. That was the excuse they needed to disqualify me.'

'Bastards. What about the Commonwealth Games next year? They're to be in Edinburgh, aren't they?'

'That's right. Maybe I'll qualify as Scottish even if not British.'

'I would hope so. You still living in Banchory?'

'My parents are still here, but no, I teach PE in Inverness. Why don't you come up to visit?'

'I'd love that, Lidia, though Donny's a bit of a handful at the moment. Let's stay in touch.'

While in Banchory, Rona had another bee in her bonnet. She was anxious to retrieve her typescript of the *Gudrun's Saga* translation from Gordonhall. It would seem strange being a visitor there, at her childhood home and ancestral seat, but somehow she felt no great attachment.

Telford and Penelope had not yet moved in, but with some difficulty she persuaded a surly Ed Williams to let her into the library. Remembering exactly where she had hidden her precious translation, she made straight for the spot on the shelves where she had placed the heavy red tome bearing the title *Illustrated Natural History*.

The serried ranks of musty volumes had remained largely undisturbed since she was last here. Worryingly, however, the book inside whose back cover she had taped the envelope containing her typescript was not in its place. Instead there was a two-and-a-half-inch space. Rona could see from the absence of dust in the gap that the volume had been removed quite recently. *Maybe it's just been moved to another shelf.*

Looking around, she noticed other gaps, all similarly dust-free. 'Have Mr and Mrs Argill-Elliott disposed of some items from the library?' she asked the caretaker.

'Could have, I suppose,' Williams said evasively. He was not about to give away his secret to a stranger: that he had been using Gordonhall's rare books and other treasures as currency in dealing with local tradespeople. Suddenly regretting having given this visitor access to the house, he looked at his watch. 'Hate to rush you, but I'm meeting someone in town … need to lock up.'

'There's one other book I'd like to find,' she said, stalling for time. If her translation had gone, at least she could borrow the original copy of *Gudrun's Saga* in Icelandic. It could always be translated afresh.

But Williams hustled her out. *Never mind,* Rona thought, *I'll come back for it when Tel's at home.*

A little later, a darker thought crossed her mind. *The translation's out there somewhere, with my name on it. Anyone reading Ragnhild's story would think it's about me. God, it looks like a blueprint for murder!*

Then she began to feel better. *Ragnhild's tale had a third killing. At least mine has only two.*

It was the spring equinox, 21st March 1970, and on cue, a gale was forecast for much of Scotland. Right after *Listen With Mother*, Rona put little Donny down for his afternoon nap and sang a few nursery rhymes to him until he dropped off. Such moments with her fair-haired blue-eyed boy always made her happy, but at other times the world would look less rosy. She longed to be reunited with Ari, the father of her child.

Out on the back step at Ardwhinzean, Rona looked to the west. Banks of cloud were massing over Ben Ledi, heralding the coming storm. The cheerful kiddie-songs that had tripped off her tongue just a few minutes earlier gave way to the more introspective words and melody of a Joni Mitchell song. Judy Collins' recording of it had recently returned to the charts and was playing a lot on the radio.

Rows and flows of angel hair
And ice-cream castles in the air
And feather canyons everywhere
I've looked at clouds that way

But now they only block the sun
They rain and snow on everyone
So many things I would have done
But clouds got in the way

I've looked at clouds from both sides now
From up and down and still somehow
It's clouds' illusions I recall
I really don't know clouds at all

That night, high winds brought down trees and telephone wires across much of Scotland. The lower Dee valley around Banchory was particularly hard-hit. At the height of the storm, a paraffin heater at the foot of the main staircase of Gordonhall somehow started a fire, according to the official explanation. Flames spread quickly through the house. Firefighters were delayed by fallen trees; by the time they arrived the entire building was ablaze and could not be saved. Next morning, only a blackened shell remained.

Though the Argill-Elliotts had recently moved into Gordonhall, they were not in residence on the night of the fire. Penelope, at her parents' home in Appleby, received the news with equanimity. Telford was believed to be in Edinburgh at Fergus's flat; the cousins had tickets for the Calcutta Cup rugby match at Murrayfield. Scotland having beaten England by 14 points to 5, they were presumably celebrating somewhere, and could not be immediately contacted.

A call from Lidia a few days later alerted Rona to the disaster. 'The whole place was burned to the ground,' she said, her voice trembling. 'My Dad drove up to Gordonhall this morning. They've got a bulldozer in.'

Rona was in shock. 'What do you mean? Aren't they going to rebuild? What are they demolishing?'

'Everything. By the time Dad left, it was all reduced to a pile of rubble.'

'But ... why would they do that?'

'Apparently, after the fire, the building was dangerously unstable. So one of the demolition crew said.'

'The oldest part of the house was seventeenth-century. Where the library was, remember? Those walls were nearly three feet thick. I'm sure they would have been stable enough. Surely they didn't knock those down?'

'Not with the bulldozer, no. They used dynamite for that job.'

That night Rona cried, something she had not done on hearing of the death of her father six months before.

Late March of 1970 was an eventful time for the Argill-Elliotts. A few days after their home at Gordonhall went up in flames, news came that Telford's cousin Fergus was missing. His Citroën DS (the 'Goddess', he named it – from the French *déesse*) was found by the shore of Loch Katrine in the Trossachs. Inside were his coat, hat and gloves. His monogrammed gold watch lay on the front passenger's seat under a two-week-old newspaper.

A police search soon turned up one of his shoes among rocks at the edge of the loch some distance from the car. It was a foregone conclusion: Fergus had drowned in Katrine's chilly water. Yet no suicide note was ever found, nor any obvious reason – financial, psychological, physical – for him to kill himself or to fake such a thing. Divers were called to the scene but no body was found – unsurprisingly, given the depth of the loch, well over a hundred metres in places.

Newspaper and TV reports of Lord Bracklinn's disappearance prompted 'sightings' all over Great Britain and even abroad, one as far away as Auckland, New Zealand. None of these panned out.

As his bachelor cousin's sole heir, Telford himself was temporarily a suspect. His fingerprints were found in, and on, the 'Goddess'. That was to be expected, he told police. On 20th March Fergus had taken him for a spin to North Berwick, and he himself had taken the wheel on the way back to Edinburgh. He last saw his cousin 'chatting up' a girl in a Canonmills bar after the rugby game on the 21st. Telford had politely taken his leave of them and returned alone to Fergus's flat. Next morning there was no sign of his host, who had, he initially assumed, spent the night at the girl's place. A little later, he noticed that the 'Goddess' was no longer in its parking space outside.

Lack of compelling evidence meant no charges were brought; in the absence of a body it could not even be shown that Fergus was dead.

Rona had her suspicions. Telford had somehow lured Fergus back to Gordonhall, and torched the house around him. *That* was where Fergus met his end, where his remains now lay buried in a heap of rubble. In a stroke of genius, Telford had then driven the Citroën to Loch Katrine, and abandoned it there.

None of this was ever voiced. There was nothing to be gained by reminding the world that this was the *third* member of the Argill clan to die since she had joined them.

24
POWERS

SO FAR, DELIA KNEW OF ONLY the first two deaths, those of Antony and Dominic, Rona's first and second husbands. 'Don't keep me in suspense, Frank. *What* happened next?'

There was a moment's silence on the phone line as Frank considered how best to continue. 'Okay, fast-forward from 1968 to 1970,' he began. 'Fergus, the nephew who shot Dominic at Gordonhall, disappeared.'

'*Disappeared?*'

'Yes, just like Lord Lucan a few years later.'

Since Delia was unfamiliar with the allusion, Frank explained about the gambler and dilettante who famously vanished in 1974 after killing his children's nanny and attempting to murder his wife. 'Lucan was not formally declared dead until 2016,' he said.

'How about Fergus, though? Did *he* ever turn up?'

'No. Remember, he claimed the Bracklinn title on the death of Dominic. He had a cousin, Telford Argill-Elliott, who figured it should come to him once it was clear Fergus wasn't going to resurface.'

'His cousin, eh? You think Telford killed Fergus, the way "Hard-jaw" made toast of "Bread-and-Butter"?'

'It's possible, don't you think? He had a pretty strong motive, after all.'

'Yeah. A lot of wealth went with that title.'

'But if he stood to gain by Fergus's demise, so did Rona. Don't forget she wanted the barony for her son Donald.'

'Give me a break, Frank. You're not telling me Rona played a part in *a third* killing, are you?'

Frank hesitated before replying. 'Just saying we should keep an open mind.'

With that conversation replaying in her brain, Delia googled 'Telford Argill-Elliott' in her Aberdeen hotel room. She was surprised to find a newly posted item:

FAIRFIELD'S CEREALS: PART II
A KILLING TOO MANY

By Toff Hammer

If a house you recently acquired in a sweetheart deal from your cousin went up in smoke, and that same cousin disappeared without trace the very day of the fire, wouldn't you expect a call from the CID? Wouldn't the ashes be combed through for human remains?

Not, it seems, if you're a toff.

Not even if your cousin's vanishing act left you the apparent heir to his title and wealth.

Not even if you had already lost two uncles in quick succession, one stabbed to death, the other shot at point-blank range. And the former owner of the mansion had recently 'fallen' off a cliff.

For that is the truth behind the Lord Lucan-like disappearance of Fergus Argill-Hawke on 21st March 1970. His cousin Telford Argill-Elliott was the last to see him alive. It was at his behest that the burnt-out ruins of Gordonhall House were bulldozed with unseemly haste. But did the police come calling?

Nope.

You can bet that behind these suspicious events lurked the sinister Rona Fay Swainson, then Countess of Fairfield. There can be little doubt she was in on the act, as with all those other deaths in her family. I use the word 'sinister' advisedly: she seems to have possessed powers, like witches of old.

Now only Telford stood between her and her ultimate prize: the Barony of Bracklinn and the millions that went with it.

So did she bump him off too? I hear you ask.

Actually, no. Even for the scheming Rona, that would have been a killing too many. Instead she hired a smart lawyer (a crooked one, you may surmise – I couldn't possibly comment) to wrest the title and money out of Telford's reach and give it to her three-year-old son.

That little boy grew up to be Donald Swainson, Lord Bracklinn, Earl of Fairfield, chairman and managing director of Fairfield's Cereals. Destined, we can hope, to be the last chairman and managing director of that ill-begotten company.

Weep, if you will, for the innocent consumers sickened or killed by Fairfield's poisonous muesli. But shed no tear for the toffs who made and sold it. They are simply reaping what they have sown.

The same Toff Hammer blog and its earlier instalment were at that moment the subject of great interest to detectives in the West Bell Street, Dundee divisional headquarters of Police Scotland.

DS Greg Miller reported to his superior officer that the author of the blogs was at present the only suspect in the case. 'Toff Hammer and jequirityjo are one and the same person,' he confidently announced. 'These blogs contain thinly veiled threats against Fairfield's and their management. The timing of their release can't be coincidental.'

'Agreed.' DI John Howie said. 'And where is this person in custody?' He knew perfectly well the blogger was still at large.

Miller shifted uncomfortably in his swivel chair. 'Soon as we trace him through his web hosting company, he'll be brought into the nearest station for questioning.'

'Him? You're sure Toff Hammer is male?'

'Most likely.'

'But not sure?'

'Er ... no.'

'Then don't use language that rules out half the population,' Howie said, turning to walk away.

'No, sir.' Chastened, Miller returned to his computer screen. After another futile hour, he was forced to admit that his quarry had been very clever in hiding his (or her, he must remember to say) identity.

It was Webster's day off, but Miller called him just the same. Webster was the aptly-named forensic Internet expert on whom the Dundee force relied to break open cases like this.

'You've tried WHOIS, haven't you?' Webster asked after Miller explained his problem.

'Of course. But the name and address that come up are phoney.'

'And you've contacted the webhost?'

'Yes. With a warrant, I managed to get a bank account number from them. The one Toff Hammer's website is charged to. We're pursuing that, but so far it's not looking promising. The account's closed, and in the name of an untraceable company.'

'Leave it with me. I'll get back to you in a couple of hours.'

'Thanks, Webster.'

The 'outing' of Tim Heston as Toff Hammer did not take long, though the diligent efforts of Miller and Webster were not responsible. Monty Frome, an investigative journalist working for a popular national newspaper wrote a speculative piece about the blogger and was rewarded with a call from one of Heston's students at Glasgow Caledonian University.

This was a caller with a grudge – he was unhappy with the grades the lecturer had given him – but Frome was convinced that what he had to say was true. Heston, the student said, was a Marxist with anger-management issues. Though he avoided direct confrontation with those who disagreed with his political views, he would write scathing comments on work handed in. 'Passive-aggressive' was how the young man described him.

Toff Hammer's writing style was *exactly* like Tim Heston's, the student said. And the 'T.H.' initials could hardly be a coincidence.

The newspaper man sat in on one of Heston's lectures, then confronted him. To his surprise, Heston immediately admitted Toff Hammer was his *alter ego*. He vehemently denied, however, having anything to do with the spate of poisonings the police had linked to Fairfield's muesli. Unconvinced, Frome did two things: he put together a brutal personal profile of the Caledonian sociologist for his newspaper; and he informed the police he had positively identified the blogger who said Fairfield's deserved everything that was coming to them. Heston was in custody within the hour.

Frome's editor was nervous about publishing the piece. After all, his was one of the eight newspapers involved in the character-assassination of the innocent Christopher Jefferies, briefly a suspect in a famous Bristol murder inquiry in 2010. But the case against Heston seemed watertight, and it was too good a scoop to ignore.

While Delia brought herself up to speed on Rona's dramatic story as told by Toff Hammer, *Gudrun's Saga* had taken a back seat. Now she was eager to read the penultimate chapter.

<u>*OF ASTRID LEIFSDOTTIR*</u>

(NOTE: No counterpart of this story can be found in any other saga. It concerns a woman with no known connections to royalty or nobility, thus of little interest to the Skalds. But the eventful life of Astrid Leifsdottir was worthy of inclusion in Gudrun's Saga, as she was Gudrun's grandmother.)

When Eystein and Sigurd ruled Norway (NOTE: the joint reign of these kings lasted for twenty years from 1103), a period of prosperity arrived in Lofoten. The seas around the islands were alive with cod and the soil was fertile. Some islanders credited their good fortune to the Christian faith that Eystein entrenched by the building of churches and ordination of priests. Yet adherence to the old gods remained strong among most of the people. The tales they told their children of the cruelty of Olaf Tryggvason (NOTE: King Olaf I, who over a century earlier had forcibly converted the land to Christianity and tortured to death any who refused) bred a continuing distrust of the new religion.

In a village of south Lofoten with a sheltered harbour there dwelt a boat-builder named Leif, his wife and their young daughter Astrid. Leif's business prospered as his reputation grew: few could match the seaworthiness of his vessels. Astrid was not made to work in the fields or gut fish like most children of the village; instead she was given an education by the local priest. Though he taught her to read and write in the new alphabet introduced by the church, behind his back she learned the pagan runes she was forbidden to use.

Across the narrow fjord from her home a tall pyramidal mountain rose from the sea. In the gloom of a midwinter's day, with the sun never above the horizon, its snow blanket gave a ghostly shimmer; in July it was a mosaic of grey and green. More often than not its top was smothered by cloud, but in clear weather its sharp peak stood boldly against the sky. When the fjord was calm, an identical but inverted mountain appeared in its waters.

The last patch of snow to melt on the mountain each spring was in the shape of 'fe'. (NOTE: 'Fe' – pronounced 'fay' – is the first letter of the Scandinavian runic alphabet, corresponding to F; it is also an Old Norse word meaning 'riches'.) An upside-down 'fe' could also be seen on the upside-down mountain in the water below. Astrid believed the 'fe' was a sign from the gods assuring her village of continuing wealth year after year. If ever it failed to appear, bad fortune would follow.

Frank had emailed Delia a photo of just such a mountain: the 671-metre Skottinden on the island of Vestvågøya in southern Lofoten, where he had called on a summer cruise of the Norwegian fjords a few years previously. The sea was not smooth enough to show its reflection, and no snow patches remained on its slopes, yet Delia thought it possible this was Astrid's pyramidal mountain.

Visualising the reflection beneath, she immediately recognised the symbolic octahedron on the Gordonhall bookplate, complete with its runic character. She was excited at making the connection and amused to discover a pun in Old Norse, something the sagas were noted for. The double meaning of *fe* – rune or riches, take your pick – was further compounded by its pronunciation, a clue to the translator's middle name, Fay. Yet Delia was at the same time oddly disappointed.

She had conceived and become attached to a theory that the symbol on the Gordonhall octahedron was not a runic 'F' as

Frank had suggested, but, when turned on its side, a slightly deformed number 4. Together with its reflection, she had conjectured, it made 44, which she knew to be one of the octahedral numbers that form the series 1, 6, 19, 44, 85 ..., the fourth such number, indeed.* How fitting that this, of all numbers, should be inscribed on an octahedron!

Fitting, but coincidental, it was now clear. Gudrun had apparently adopted her grandmother Astrid's symbol of good fortune and passed it down through the generations.

> *One spring, the snow on the mountain melted so fast that the 'fe' never appeared. That summer, Astrid's father took a new boat out into the great fjord (NOTE: the West Fjord between the islands of Lofoten and the Norwegian mainland) for its first sea-test. Neither he nor the prospective buyers who accompanied him ever returned. Villagers speculated that the boat had gone down in the Moskenstraum (NOTE: the violent tidal current that develops at the south end of the Lofoten chain, called the 'Maelstrom' by writers including Jules Verne and Edgar Allan Poe), though Leif knew the danger of that stretch of water and would not willingly have gone there.*

> *Later the same year, while still grieving, Leif's widow died of a fever, leaving Astrid an orphan at the age of eleven. For a while the girl lived on her own, supporting herself by working as a fishwife, until the priest who had been her teacher arranged for her to go to Hinn (NOTE: the large island linking Lofoten to the Norwegian mainland) where she could have a home and domestic work in a monastery along with other orphan children.*

---

* Delia's interest in number puzzles was sparked at an early age, as recounted in *Taran's Wheel* (*Incomers*: Book 1).

For four years she lived in the monastery, enduring daylong gruelling labour and constant hunger. Sorely she missed her parents, her friends in the village, her view of the mountain and its reflection in the still waters of the fjord. Worse, she found that personal services were expected of her by the monks, whose concept of celibacy did not exclude taking their pleasure with young girls. Repeatedly she attempted to escape but each time she was found and brought back.

It was during this period that Astrid discovered her powers. Gradually she learned to use them to her advantage. When a monk had treated her cruelly, she would make a straw effigy of him and throw it on the cooking fire. Sometimes it would take weeks or even months, but eventually the man would succumb to disease or suffer a serious accidental injury. Several of her tormentors died.

When Astrid was fifteen, her bleeding began. Suddenly she was released from the attentions of the monks, who took seriously their vow never to be with a woman. But this relief would not last.

One spring day she was called to the chapel. There she was introduced to a stranger, a bearded man named Maddan. She reckoned him to be of similar age to her father when he died – about forty. Maddan announced he had just bought her from the monastery. She was to be his wife.

'But I cannot leave the monastery,' she told him. 'And I do not know how to be a wife. I am only fifteen.'

'You cannot stay here, Astrid. There is no place for you among men who have vowed to forsake all contact with women. You will come across the sea with me to my home in Caithness (NOTE: 'Katanes' in Old Norse).

Your life will be good, with Irish slaves to do your bidding, for I am a wealthy man.'

Though her education had come to an abrupt end four years before, Astrid knew that Caithness was a remote province, ruled by the Earl of Orkney but still part of the Norwegian kingdom. It was a land she had no desire to see, but she had no choice in the matter. If this Maddan treated her badly, she decided, she would use her powers on him.

Boldly she asked, 'Why have you chosen me? Did I carry the lowest price?'

'You were not cheap,' Maddan told her. 'You cost more silver than I expected to pay for an orphan girl. I got my last one from Hjaltland (NOTE: Shetland) for half the price but she bore me no children. You look strong and I think you will do better. First, though, I will have to fatten you up, get some flesh on those bones.'

'What became of her? The other girl?'

'I sold her last year to a merchant on Hrossey (NOTE: Mainland Orkney). I made a loss but it was worth it to get rid of her.'

'And will I meet the same fate if I do not satisfy you?'

'You ask too many questions, girl. Come now, my ship is laden, ready to leave.'

Astrid was pleasantly surprised to find that a tiny but private and comfortable space had been prepared for her aboard Maddan's knarr (NOTE: a traditional Norwegian cargo vessel). The crew of ten men treated her with courtesy and deference, as their master's intended bride.

They set sail from Hinn on a high tide, driven by a cold north wind down the great fjord towards the open sea. With her heavy cargo of timber, furs and reindeer hides the ship rode the waves calmly. Astrid was impressed; her father, she thought, would have been proud to have built a knarr such as this.

Soon, on the starboard side, a familiar mountain hove into view. For four years she had seen it only in her mind's eye. Her heart lifted as it drew closer and she could make out the 'fe' on its slope. The voyage was going to be smooth, it told her; perhaps even her future life in Caithness would be happy and prosperous.

Astrid decided to make the most of her upcoming marriage to Maddan. Her optimism persisted long after her beloved mountain disappeared from view forever.

The wedding was celebrated with great fanfare in Maddan's ha (NOTE: big house). Every landowner or noble in Caithness came to pay his respects; though Earl Paul and Earl Erlend, the sons of Thorfinn 'the Mighty', could not attend, they sent their blessing and a gift to Maddan's bride – the plans of a new longship for 44 oarsmen, to be named Astrid.

Forty-four. Delia pondered the significance of the number. Could the 'fe' symbols on the Gordonhall octahedron be 4s, after all?

By her nineteenth birthday, Astrid had borne two daughters. Maddan demanded a son next time, otherwise she would have to be sold off like her predecessor. Grievously upset, Astrid dreamed that night of meeting the ghost of Yrsa, who announced that it was her husband's seed that gave her daughters. She confronted Maddan with this revelation.

'Nonsense,' he cried. 'There is nothing wrong with my seed. The problem lies with you. With more weight

you would become fertile enough to produce a boy. So do not talk to me of Yrsa ever again. She was a wicked woman.'

He ordered his wife to stick rigidly to a diet he prescribed, and after a few months she became quite large, though not through pregnancy. No longer finding her attractive, Maddan took in a slender young woman as a concubine. Banished to rooms at the back of the ha out of her husband's sight, Astrid plotted her revenge.

'My bed is uncomfortable,' she told her Irish handmaiden one day. 'I need some Frigg's grass to pack my mattress.'

From a quick Internet check, Delia learned that in Norway the plant called Frigg's grass was sometimes used in infusions to enhance feminine attractiveness and to ease childbirth. Identified with lady's bedstraw (*Galium verum*), it has flea-repellent properties and was once a popular stuffing for mattresses.

But Astrid had other plans for the grass: an effigy of Yrsa was fashioned from it, and hidden in her husband's bed while he was not at home. On his return, his concubine came to him but he sent her away. This happened three times. Finally, he told her he no longer needed a woman.

Like Yrsa, Astrid had taken away her abuser's manhood. Only she had done it without a knife.

25
EMOTIONAL REUNION

SHORTLY BEFORE FERGUS'S disappearance in 1970, Rona had instigated legal proceedings to have Donald, then just three years old, declared the rightful heir to the Bracklinn barony and to the business interests that went along with it. By the time the matter came to court, Fergus was missing and his cousin Telford was acting as if *he* were the new Lord Bracklinn.

Rona's lawyer argued that it made no difference to the case whether Fergus was alive or dead. 'When my client's husband Dominic Argill was killed so tragically, she was already pregnant with his child. Had Dominic lived, Donald would have been his legitimate son and heir. Fergus would not have succeeded to the title, nor would Telford have any claim to it if Fergus was dead. The case is open and shut.'

Strangely, Telford did not put up much of a fight. His legal team's half-hearted argument focused on the lack of proof that Dominic was truly Donald's father. They challenged Rona to submit the child for a blood test.

She refused, using her lawyer's argument that no such proof was necessary. And the court agreed with her. It was long established, they confirmed, that a child born to a married woman was presumed to have been fathered by her husband. The fact that the putative father had died before the birth of the child was immaterial.

The court decided in favour of the three-year-old. Not only was he the true Baron Bracklinn, he was ruled to be the rightful owner of the entire Argill business empire. A trust was set up, into which the supermarket chain, the lands and buildings of

Ardwhinzean and sundry other investments were transferred. Rona was given stewardship until Donald turned eighteen.

Telford did not lose quite everything. The court stipulated that he was to become a non-executive trustee, and was still the rightful owner of the Gordonhall estate.

There were no sour grapes from Telford. Indeed, he made a statement saying, in effect, that he always believed Donald Swainson-Argill to be the proper Lord Bracklinn.

Ever the cynic, Rona thought to herself, *He would say that, wouldn't he?* By removing any possible motive, Telford deflected suspicion of involvement in Fergus's disappearance.

Donald's formal style of address, Lord Bracklinn, was not the real prize for Rona. It was what went with it that counted. Control of the supermarket empire, the land and buildings at Ardwhinzean. These assets were effectively hers to do with as she pleased while Donald was a minor – though as a trustee, Telford was entitled to a dividend from the income of the trust. But he could act only in an advisory capacity.

Losing Gordonhall was a price she was content to pay for exacting her revenge on the entire Argill clan. Now in charge of the Bracklinn fortune, she planned to turn as much of it into hard cash as she could.

But first, she and her little boy flew from Prestwick to Reykjavik on Loftleidir, the 'Hippie Express' as that Icelandic airline was known in those days because of its low-cost two-leg flights between the United States and Europe. There, on a bitterly cold snowy day, an emotional reunion occurred between Rona and Ari. For Donald it was a first meeting with his biological father, though he did not know that at the time.

Ari had arranged everything. All Rona had to do was fill out a few immigration papers and satisfy a short residence requirement. On Thursday 31st December 1970 she and Ari were wed in a brief civil ceremony at the *Þjóðskrá Íslands* (Registers Iceland) office.

In Ari's tiny apartment on Laugavegur in central Reykjavik, after little Donny was asleep, they toasted the New Year with *ákavíti*, then made love for the first time as a married couple.

Ari had secured a temporary job exchange with a silviculturalist from the Forestry Commission in Edinburgh – a fellow graduate of Aberdeen University. In the first week of 1971, he and Rona began planning their next move. Arrangements were made for her furniture and personal effects in the cottage at Ardwhinzean to be packed up for storage.

On seeing the removal vans, Edith, the Dowager Lady Bracklinn was taken aback; all she knew was that Rona and Donald were off somewhere on a winter holiday – no doubt enjoying balmy weather on the Côte d'Azur or somewhere equally expensive with their newfound wealth.

When she received an international call, Edith's mental image was of a luxuriously grand hotel room on the Corniche at the other end of the line. The reality was somewhat different: the source of the call was in fact a 50-square-metre apartment in a low-rent building in wintry Reykjavik.

'Just to let you know, Edith, I won't be coming back to live at Ardwhinzean. You said you wanted to move out of the big house now you're on your own. Why not have the cottage? It's yours, rent-free, for as long as you want to stay there.'

'But where are *you* going to live?' Edith asked. 'And where are you now?'

Rona ignored the second question, and in response to the first told her former mother-in-law she would send a letter with her new address as soon as she was settled. She had no such intention; she certainly was not going to tell Edith Argill that she and Donny would be setting up home in Edinburgh, nor that her household would include a new husband.

Mr and Mrs Haraldsson, an attractive young couple with a three-year-old boy, moved into their Edwardian terraced house in Kingsburgh Road, Edinburgh in March 1971. To their new neighbours they were simply Ari, Rona and young Donny; no one could have guessed that Rona was the Countess of Fairfield and her son was Donald Swainson-Argill, Lord Bracklinn. Ari appeared to be the breadwinner, with a job in the Forestry Commission at its headquarters a mile away on Corstorphine Road. He must be a good earner, Kingsburgh Road residents assumed, to afford a house on *this* street.

Donny and Ari bonded quickly, despite the father's misgivings about concealing their true biological relationship.

'We can't risk it getting out that he isn't Dominic's son,' Rona kept telling him. 'Once he's old enough to understand, and to keep a secret, we'll tell him the truth.'

The Argill stores had up to now been ably run by a salaried manager, an arrangement Rona saw little reason to change.

In June of 1971, she was contacted by an 'acquisitions executive' from Carrefour, then a rapidly expanding French retailer, interested in an outright purchase of the supermarket business. Seeing an opportunity to convert that asset to cash, she decided to travel to Paris to listen to what he had to say. Ari's younger sister Margrét was delighted to come from Iceland to look after Donald while his mother was away.

Marcel Fichet was suave and impeccably mannered, in his late forties with luxuriant dark hair just beginning to show streaks of grey. With no previous experience of serious business negotiation, Rona was initially apprehensive and very much on her guard. She need not have worried. Marcel turned out to be an honest broker – and a dedicated family man.

The conversation was conducted partly in English, partly in French. Within hours, they had reached agreement in principle for Carrefour to acquire the Bracklinn chain as a going concern. Half the purchase price would be paid in cash, the rest in stock, to the Donald Swainson-Argill trust. All jobs would be protected. It only remained for Carrefour's accountants to inspect Bracklinn's books, and for lawyers on both sides to validate the contract.

The takeover was completed by Christmas. Some of the board, faced with a *fait accompli*, resented what they saw as Rona's high-handedness, but were mollified with a payout from the trust's Carrefour stock holding. Only Telford Argill-Elliott, at his wife's insistence, held out for a more generous settlement.

'Here's the thing, Tel,' Rona said to him on the phone. 'You already got my personal inheritance – Gordonhall and its lands. I'm not bitter about that, but I don't think it's fair of you to expect more.'

Not one for confrontation, Telford replied, 'Honestly, Rona, I could go along with you on this, but ...'

'But what, Tel?'

Taking a deep breath, he launched into a speech composed by Penelope, his wife of little more than a year and now heavily pregnant. 'I have to think of our children, the first of whom will be born in less than a month. My lawyer tells me I have grounds for reopening the whole question of the Bracklinn succession.'

'I'm not sure, Tel, that you really want to press your case in court again.' There was no need for Rona to spell it out. The vexatious question of the 'disappearance' of Telford's cousin Fergus at exactly the time when Gordonhall burned to the ground was not one he would wish revisited while under oath. Furthermore, she reminded him, Fergus had not yet been declared officially dead; Telford therefore might have no legal standing to dispute her son's status as 6th Lord Bracklinn.

Still, he persisted with the words his wife had put in his mouth. 'You never provided a blood sample to prove Dominic was Donald's father. It wouldn't have been difficult.'

'I don't have to prove anything to anybody,' Rona said tartly. 'But if you want to make that lawyer of yours rich, bring it on. Let's go to court again.'

At this point Telford back-tracked. He had made his pitch – or Penelope's. 'I don't think that would be sensible, for either of us, Rona. We're family and should stick together.'

'I agree, Tel. Give Penny my best regards.' Rona was off the hook.

The stores acquired by Carrefour eventually became part of the Somerfield chain, which in turn merged with the Co-op.

In the summer of 1972, the Haraldsson family welcomed a new arrival, Kristin. Ari was determined to be involved in every aspect of the baby's care, having missed his son's first three years of life. His career began to play second fiddle; the work was unchallenging and his placement at the Forestry Commission temporary. Rona had made him joint custodian of the funds in Donald's trust, mostly derived from her deal with Carrefour, allowing them a comfortable income while the capital grew in various banks and other investments. By the spring of 1973 Ari had quit his job and become a full-time child-rearer. Life was uncomplicated, almost idyllic … but change was afoot.

That September, an unexpected letter arrived.

Dear Lady Fairfield:

Since we last met, I have parted company (amicably, I'm happy to say) with Carrefour, and am now seeking a business opportunity that allows me to become more of an entrepreneur on my own account.

I believe I have identified an investment that promises an attractive return. Could this venture be of interest to the Donald Swainson-Argill trust?

If we could meet in Dundee, I will expand on this proposition.

Warmest regards,

Marcel Fichet

Rona's first instinct was to crumple the letter in a ball and throw it in the bin. It reminded her forcibly of the 'investment opportunity' that had destroyed her father's life.

'Why don't you at least find out what Fichet has in mind?' Ari suggested. 'Take the train to Dundee and meet him. If the deal smells fishy, you can walk away.'

'I suppose ... but why *Dundee*, of all places?'

Having checked in for one night at the Angus Hotel, she met Marcel in the lobby. They exchanged formal greetings and repaired without further ado to the bar, where he ordered scotch and she opted for Grand Marnier.

Amongst other things, they talked about their respective plans for the future. Rona remained guarded, but Marcel spoke animatedly of a desire to start up a business in Great Britain.

'For goodness' sake, Marcel, if there was ever a *wrong* time to be setting up in this country, it's now. The government is powerless against the miners and dockers, the IRA is waging war in Belfast and will probably bring the troubles to the mainland, our prime minister is useless for anything except sailing and Christmas carols.'

'Mr *Eat*, yes.' Marcel's pronunciation of 'Heath' made Rona laugh. 'Not altogether useless. Don't forget he brought your country into the Common Market. *En tout cas,* my dear Rona, when all the analysts are saying "sell", *that* is the signal to buy. When everyone else is shutting down, *you* open up.'

'That takes guts.'

'Guts, and a long view. You know who has what it takes? Carrefour. My former employer has just opened the first *hypermarché* in Great Britain. In Wales, you may be surprised to learn. We have had them in France for twenty years ... but Rona, your glass is empty. *Encore un Grand Marnier?*'

'*Avec plaisir.* But this one's on me. Anyway, Marcel, what is it you want to open up?'

'*Demain, on va voir.* We will meet at breakfast. The place I want to show you is only ten minutes' walk from here.'

As they finished their drinks, Rona put her right index finger to her lips so they could listen to the music emanating from a speaker above their heads. 'You talk of the future, Marcel. *This* is the future of rock'n'roll.'

They were silent for the full seven minutes of a song that was charting that very week, with a plangent guitar accompaniment and an extraordinary piano coda: *Layla* by Derek and the Dominos.

26
SECOND SIGHT

ON A BLUSTERY JANUARY DAY, Donald and Faith got down to business over coffee and sandwiches as soon as she arrived at Rolf and Amy's home. Outside, squally rain showers blasted Kirkwall, but there was little time for looking out of the window.

'It's not good,' Faith said despondently. 'The worst PR a food company can ever have. We may have to close down completely for a month at least.'

The owner and managing director of the company was a little more sanguine. 'Don't think so, Faith. A week, tops. While you were on the plane this morning I already ordered Dundee to stop all production, pending our review. Staff have been sent home, except for essential maintenance workers. Pay will not be docked. I've informed everyone that I expect us to be back up and running in a matter of days.'

'But Donny, you obviously haven't seen the torrent of abuse on Facebook and Twitter. Even though people have been told it's a problem of post-production tampering, they still blame Fairfield's.'

'We don't need to let the Internet trolls intimidate us. Muesli is what fraction of our business?'

'Of net income, 36 percent.'

'Right. I see no reason to sacrifice our whole line. This is a muesli-only issue, isn't it?'

'As far as we know, yes. But can we bank on that?'

'Toff Hammer's in custody. He's not going to be spiking any more of our products.'

Faith Elliott thought for a moment. 'I suppose not, but what if they can't nail him? He could be back at his mischief very soon.'

Her negativity was beginning to annoy Donald. 'Look, Faith, there's something else you should be aware of. The police have confirmed that Toff Hammer's poison of choice is abrin.'

Her facial expression betrayed no reaction to this nugget of information. 'So?' was all she said.

'Can't remember where I read it, but abrin is destroyed by heat, is it not? All our products, apart from the muesli range, are designed to be cooked. For example, our biggest seller, porridge oats, would be harmless even if packed full of abrin.'

'Biggest seller, maybe, but with the smallest margin. You're not telling me, are you, that we could keep the company afloat just on porridge oats?'

'Of course not. Nor am I suggesting we should knowingly sell an abrin-contaminated product just because it's destined for cooking. My point is this: Toff Hammer presumably knows the limitation of his poison – that's why it's only our muesli he's targeted. We can resume sales of our microwavable, stove-top and bread-maker ranges almost immediately.'

'It's your company. Just don't say I haven't warned you about the PR disaster that will follow if we're seen to be taking chances with our customers' lives.'

'I hear you, Faith. We must have another string to our bow. And this is it. We introduce new tamper-evident or tamper-resistant packaging for *all* our products. It will be a differentiator, a way to stay ahead of our competitors. A meeting is already being set up with our packaging consultant, to review what's available.'

While that conversation was going on in an Orkney farmhouse, a drama was playing out in a remote part of the Cairngorm Mountains, 130 miles to the south. Terry and Anneka Fox, a couple in their thirties, had hiked seven miles from their car into the wilderness of Glen Eanaich, where Terry became unwell, complaining of severe gastric pain. Before long he succumbed to violent sickness and diarrhoea, and soon afterwards lost consciousness. His wife tried calling Mountain Rescue on her mobile but could get no signal. It was one o'clock in the day.

No one else was on the particular track they had followed. Anneka did the only thing she could under the circumstances: set off alone, back in the direction they had come, until she could find a spot with mobile reception. First, though, she scribbled a note to Terry in case he should wake, then removed one of her inner layers of clothing, a white tee-shirt, and tied it to a trekking pole which she stuck in the ground beside where he lay.

By about two, she was finally able to call for help. The response from Mountain Rescue was swift. Terry was picked up, still unconscious, at 3:45, taken by Land-Rover to Aviemore and whisked from there by helicopter to Raigmore Hospital in Inverness.

A blood sample confirmed Terry Fox as the fourth known victim of abrin poisoning. In the kitchen of the Aviemore timeshare owned by Anneka Fox's parents, where the couple had been staying for the last five days, was an open box of Fairfield's Premium Organic Muesli.

Anneka pleaded that she and Terry were unaware of the Fairfield's recall; the saturation coverage in the media had escaped them during their away-from-it-all holiday in the Highlands. She had bought the muesli in their home town of Sheffield.

Despite the best efforts of the Raigmore doctors, Terry never regained consciousness. He died three days after being picked up in the wilds of Glen Eanaich.

One more murder charge was laid on Tim Heston, *alias* Toff Hammer.

Despite Faith's pessimistic tone throughout the meeting with Donald, by the end of the day the two had agreed on a strategy for Fairfield's to weather the storm. The muesli range would remain off the market for several months, before reintroduction in new tamper-evident packaging. The company would take advantage of the present shut-down for a complete overhaul of all machinery and for routine maintenance and cleaning, including fumigation to prevent infestation by mites and weevils, always a hazard in the milling industry.

Production of straight oatmeal and oat-flake cereals would recommence in a week, followed shortly by a rebranding exercise with less emphasis on the Fairfield's name. A year or so earlier, Faith had quietly trialled a small number of new corporate identities with focus groups; she surprised Donald by telling him a new brand name, Caledonian Hills, had tested well, had been registered as a trademark, and could be rolled out within a month.

'You can't have known this was coming,' he said. 'It's great that you've prepared a new brand identity, but what made you do it?'

'Second sight,' she answered with a chuckle – her first light-hearted comment since arriving in Orkney. 'Seriously? I've always felt it was good to have plans for any contingency. Just didn't expect *this* one.'

'You did well, Faith, thank you. I think it would be appropriate to crack open the Pinot Grigio that's been chilling in the fridge.'

They had almost drained the bottle when the couple whose house they had commandeered arrived home. 'Hey, Aunt Faith!' Amy said, approaching with outstretched arms. 'You staying over, like last time? The bed's made up.'

'No, darling, I wouldn't do that to you on such short notice. I've a room booked at the Lynnfield. You guys want to join me for dinner there?'

'Can't tonight,' Rolf intervened. 'Having a bit of trouble with one of our suppliers in Bordeaux. Expect to be on the phone most of the evening. But I can give you a lift to your hotel, once you're ready to go.'

'Soon as I've made a quick visit to your loo.' Already Faith had grabbed her handbag and was making her way along the hall to the bathroom.

27
BREAKFAST WORTH GETTING UP FOR

IN 1973 MUCH OF THE INDUSTRIAL quarter near Dundee's docks was in a semi-derelict state. At its heart was the shuttered flour mill that Marcel now brought Rona to inspect. She was initially underwhelmed. Originally built in 1876 but updated and enlarged more than once since then, it still had bulk storage bins for grain and a partially preserved analytical laboratory, as well as office accommodation that would not satisfy 1950s, let alone 1970s, standards.

'Don't see the place as it is now,' he told her. 'Imagine a state-of-the-art processing plant *here*, a quality-control centre in the lab *there*, a packaging line at *that* end and an innovative marketing department in a new building at the back. We'll exploit a gap in the market. Premium quality ingredients put together in a new way to create a breakfast worth getting up for.'

'*We?*' Rona echoed.

'Your business, eventually your son's business, which I will run for you. Think of it this way: Countess of Fairfield, president; Marcel Fichet, general manager.'

'Sounds more like your business, my money.'

'Not at all. Here is my proposition: I set up the company in your name. You finance the start-up including purchase of these premises – which won't break the bank. I make all day-to-day decisions but defer to you in strategic matters. You pay me a salary and a performance-related bonus but the profits are yours.'

'Even if I liked your idea, Marcel,' Rona stalled, 'the money is not mine to invest. It's tied up in a trust for Donny and will be his when he reaches eighteen.'

'I'm coming to that. As soon as the trust matures, or as soon thereafter as young Lord Bracklinn is ready to take the reins, I will retire. Think of me as a caretaker until Donny finds his wings.'

'He may have no interest in running this operation you're talking about, whether with reins or wings.'

The Frenchman looked momentarily hurt by her gentle mocking of his mixed metaphors. 'Well, in that case, you can sell the company and let him have the proceeds. Look, Rona, I've a fully-costed business plan, which you can take to your financial advisor. Your return – I mean, the return to Lord Bracklinn's trust – will be far greater than you're able to get from cash in the bank ...'

'But riskier.'

'I can't argue with that. Though I *know* the food business better than most. If this is not for you, that's fine. I have several interested investors lined up. But I think you and I would work well together. Just give it some thought. Let's talk again in a week or so if you're ready to go into detail on the proposal.'

Rona had hitherto steered clear of 'financial advisors', believing them all to be charlatans concerned only with selling bonds or equities that would yield them a fat commission, regardless of their clients' best interests. However, her solicitor referred her to a consultant who, he said, would look at Marcel's business plan and give an unbiased opinion.

Mr Bremner, a condescending little man in a badly-cut suit with dandruff on the shoulders, did nothing to dispel her preconception. He did indeed render an opinion, but one so riddled with caveats and disclaimers as to be useless. 'This Marcel fellow, is he French?' he asked at one point.

'Yes, why?' Rona replied.

'As an incomer, he probably doesn't fully understand British ways of doing business.'

'Incomer or no, he has a very firm grasp of the British food industry at least. You know, Mr Bremner, Britain is going to need more people like Marcel Fichet now we're in the EEC.'

Bremner harrumphed. 'The EEC? That's not going to end well. You know what Continentals are like.'

Having delivered his equivocal 'opinion', he tried to sell Rona an investment package, claiming it would better preserve her wealth than this venture with Marcel Fichet.

'Thank you, Mr Bremner,' she interrupted half-way through his spiel, 'but I would prefer to live with my own financial mistakes than with any of yours. Good afternoon.'

That evening, she talked at length with Ari about the proposal. On 4th October 1973, she called Marcel. 'Let's do it,' she said.

Back then, the marketing of breakfast cereals was aimed almost exclusively at children – Rice Krispies, Frosties, Weetabix and so on. Grown-ups also enjoyed those, but the only products sold specifically with adults in mind were love-'em-or-hate-'em things like Grape Nuts, All-Bran or Shredded Wheat.

Marcel's concept was an oat-based range, from simple porridge flakes to multi-ingredient Swiss-type mueslis. Cartoon tigers or elves with chef's hats would have no part in his marketing message.

Rona initially proposed the brand name "Dr Johnson's" – an ironic take on Samuel Johnson's famous dictionary definition of oats: *a grain, which in England is generally given to horses, but in Scotland supports the people.* In the end, however, she could not resist calling the company Fairfield's Cereals, as a deliberate taunt to the Argill family, the original source of its funding.

In the spring of 1974, the Dundee plant produced its first batch of premium porridge oats, in packaging designed with understated elegance to differentiate it from its (literally) run-of-the-mill competitors. Plans were advanced for more upmarket products, including a variety of dry muesli mixes. This was where Fairfield's general manager Marcel Fichet believed the breakfast cereals market in Britain was headed.

(*And he was absolutely right,* Ragna Enjudóttir said to herself more than forty years later as she reflected on her remarkable life. *Putting my faith in Marcel was one of the best decisions I ever made.*)

When Fairfield's Premium Muesli was launched in October 1974, it quickly established itself as a top-shelf brand in supermarkets across Britain. Perhaps the best compliment was the appearance of a copycat from the breakfast behemoth Kellogg, which they named 'Country Store'. The Battle Creek, Michigan company was, however, unable to tempt its huge consumer base in the US to try this new-fangled European concept until about fifteen years later, with the launch there of a similar product under the brand name 'Mueslix'.

Marcel's marketing team sought various ways to differentiate Fairfield's lines from the mass-market offerings of Kellogg and the like. One of the most successful ploys, featured in much of their advertising, was to capitalise on their Dundee location by trumpeting that only oats grown in Scotland made their way into Fairfield's. Several studies by independent nutritionists were cited: slow ripening under the cooler conditions of a northern climate promoted higher levels of the proteins and oils that gave oats their health advantages over other cereals.

By 1976 Fairfield's were recording the kind of return on investment that Rona saw, to her satisfaction, was better than anything that Bremner could promise with his portfolio. She rewarded Marcel with a generous bonus to keep him motivated in growing the business to the benefit of the trust fund for her now nine-year-old son. Within a decade it would all be legally Donny's.

In their Edinburgh kitchen, Ari and Rona stepped around each other as he fixed himself a light lunch and she put away the groceries she had just bought.

'I had Leslie Macrae on the phone while you were out,' he announced.

'Mm?' Rona responded, her mouth full of loose grapes from a bunch she had rinsed.

'You remember Mac? My dissertation supervisor in the Forestry Department at Aberdeen? He's still lecturing, but has now got himself on to the Scottish Tourist Board. He's pushing a plan to open up Scotland's forests for leisure, sport and education. Hiking trails, campsites, wildlife observatories, rallying, you name it.'

'Orienteering?' Seeing Ari's blank expression, she expanded: 'It's a popular sport in Scandinavian forests and is starting to catch on here. I thought you'd have heard of it.'

Ari shrugged. 'Vaguely. Anyway, Mac says they're looking for someone to develop a "Nordic heritage" theme to attract tourists to the north and west. He thinks I would be ideal for the position.'

'And would you be interested?'

'Maybe, but I wanted to discuss it first with you.'

'Now you have.' She thrust three large grapes into his mouth. 'Aren't these delicious? Go on, give Mac a call. And knock his socks off with your knowledge of orienteering.'

To Ari's astonishment he was offered the job. 'How would you fancy living in Orkney?' he asked Rona.

'Orkney? There aren't any forests there, are there?'

'No, but this has nothing to do with trees. It's all about Norse history and culture.'

'Orkney's a land I feel I know, from the sagas. Yes, we could live there, for sure. It would be good for Donny and Kris to experience a more rural life … if the schools are good.'

'It would be quite a change from Edinburgh – you might feel isolated, after living in the city.'

Rona had to smile. 'Don't worry about that. I can handle it.' She was no stranger to loneliness. Only briefly had she known the joy of having a female friend – during her years at Banchory school. With Lidia she had shared secrets, laughed and cried, and voiced her hopes and fears for the future. But those halcyon days were brought to an abrupt end before she was nineteen. Forced to commit to a loveless marriage, her youth had been callously stolen from her. As a result, she had mastered the art of keeping people at arm's length, had steeled herself to forgo close friendships: that was the price of keeping the whole Bracklinn scandal buried deep in her past. Her sole confidant was Ari. He was her friend, her lover, her life. With him she would go to the ends of the earth.

Orkney? No problem.

28
GUDRUN'S KIN

ONE FINAL CHAPTER OF *Gudrun's Saga* remained. One that would bring the story up to date, at least to the twelfth century, the time of Gudrun herself. With a cup of hot chocolate, Delia settled down in her Aberdeen hotel room to read. The chapter was headed:

OF THE KIN OF GUDRUN LJOTSDOTTIR

In true saga tradition, it began with a detailed genealogy of the main players. As Delia read, her confusion grew. Paper and pencil were needed to scribble down the names and put them in some kind of family tree.*

She picked up the story at the accession of Hakon Paulsson to the Earldom of Orkney around 1103.

> *Earl Hakon had a cousin, Magnus Erlendsson, who believed he had a right to half the earldom, but whose Norwegian overlords mistrusted his devout Christian faith. Magnus therefore exiled himself in the South (NOTE: to this day Orcadians often refer to the Scottish mainland as 'the Sooth') until the king of Norway agreed to support his claim.*
>
> *The cousins ruled jointly for a number of years (NOTE: from 1105 until 1114) but eventually became enemies. Orkney's chieftains, meeting in secret, decided that only one earl could retain power and the other should die. In a battle fought on the island of*

---

* See facing page.

Gunnhild m. Erik 'Bloodaxe'
Thorfinn 'Skullsplitter'*
Ragnhild m. (1) Arnfinn (2) Ljot*
Havard
Hlodvir*
Thurid
Liv
Sigurd 'the Stout'*
Einar 'Bread-and-Butter'
Einar 'Hard-jaw'
Leif of Lofoten
Thorfinn 'the Mighty'*
Maddan m. Astrid
Paul*
Erlend*
Magnus*
Gunnhild m. Kol
Ljot 'the Ill-Behaved' m. Frakork
Helga (concubine of) Hakon* m. ?
Ingibjorg
Harald 'Smoothtongue'*
Paul 'the Speechless'*
Kali (Rognvald*)
Olaf of Duncansby m. Asleif
Thorljot m. Steinvor
Gudrun m. Thorstein 'Openmouth'
Olvir 'the Brawler'
Thorbjorn 'the Clerk' m. Ingirid
Sweyn Asleifsson
Sweyn
* Earls (sole or joint) of Orkney

Egilsay, Hakon's forces were victorious. Magnus was captured in a church and brought to Hakon, who had his cook summarily kill the prisoner with a cleaver blow to the head.

The pro-Magnus faction declared the murdered earl a Christian martyr. Soon he achieved sainthood with miracles attributed to his name.

Meanwhile, Earl Hakon consolidated his power and named two sons as his heirs: Paul (nicknamed 'the Speechless' on account of a stammer) and Harald (who talked with ease and was known as 'Smoothtongue'). Paul was born to Hakon's wife, while Harald's mother was the Earl's favourite concubine Helga. They were almost exactly the same age and became joint Earls of Orkney on Hakon's death (NOTE: in 1123).

Delia paused. How strange that the close timing of these births should be echoed by the twentieth-century arrival of the Argill boys Antony and Dominic, born to two different women on the same day!

Helga was one of the two daughters Astrid Leifsdottir bore to Maddan of Caithness. The other was Frakork, who married a man from Hjalmundsdal, Ljot 'the Ill-Behaved'. His father, also called Ljot, was a powerful chieftain whose lands in the next valley bore his name.

(NOTE: 'Hjalmundsdal' refers to the Strath of Kildonan in Sutherland; the name 'Helmsdale' now attaches to the river that drains the strath and to the village later established at its mouth. The neighbouring valley is Glen Loth.)

Frakork and Ljot had two daughters, Steinvor and Gudrun. It was Gudrun Ljotsdottir who collected the tales told in this saga.

Earl Harald permitted his mother Helga, his aunt Frakork and their offspring great influence at his palace, which stood near the Thingvollr (NOTE: Tingwall on Mainland Orkney, the place of assembly of the Earl's nobles and counsellors). Frakork in particular could dictate who among the nobles would be in or out of favour at any time. In this way she gathered friends – and enemies.

Harald 'Smoothtongue' had another estate over the hill at Orphir, where one Yule he invited his brother and co-ruler Paul 'the Speechless' for feasting and entertainment. As usual, Frakork was present to keep an eye on the proceedings.

One morning, she sat sewing with her sister Helga. Each was embroidering a linen shirt as a gift: Helga's would be presented to her son Earl Harald and Frakork's to the visiting Earl Paul. It was no ordinary embroidery. Helga used silk that had been seized during a Viking raid of Risa (NOTE: Reggio, on the 'toe' of Italy). Not to be outdone, Frakork's thread was spun from Hjalmundsdal gold.

While preparing for Paul's arrival, Harald happened upon the sisters as they sewed. He was immediately attracted to the shirt with gold thread that lay on his Aunt Frakork's lap.

'Who is to wear this beautiful shirt?' he asked.

The women looked at each other, not sure what to tell him, for they had intended to keep their gifts secret. Eventually Frakork replied, 'This one is for your brother Earl Paul. The garment your mother is embroidering with the most luxurious silk from Risa will be yours, Sire.'

'Am I not worthy of gold?' Harald demanded. 'Give me it, so I can try it on.'

Helga took the shirt from Frakork and put it behind her back. 'My son, do not be jealous of your brother, for he cannot speak properly like you.'

But Harald wrested the garment from his mother. He pulled it over his head and paraded around the room, till suddenly he was overcome by an intense pain.

'What is the matter with you?' Helga cried. 'Come, let us take you to your bed.' That same evening, Earl Harald died.

Frakork was distraught, believing the shirt she had made was the cause of his death. Her sister suspected sorcery. 'Our mother Astrid had such powers,' she said. 'Now you have used them to kill my beloved son. I will tell Earl Paul what you have done, when he gets here.'

'Do not, I pray, sister,' Frakork pleaded. 'For he will know the garment was intended for him.'

(NOTE: The Orkneyinga saga has Frakork and Helga collude in sewing the gold-embroidered shirt with the express purpose of killing Earl Paul.)

Harald's death (NOTE: around 1130) left Paul 'the Speechless' to rule Orkney on his own. Frakork and her daughters Gudrun and Steinvor made a hurried departure, spending the next few years in the territory of Ljot 'the Ill-behaved' in Hjalmundsdal. Gudrun by then had a son Thorbjorn. But it was Steinvor's son Olvir 'the Brawler' who was Frakork's favourite grandchild.

From far away in Agder, Norway, the partial power vacuum created by Harald's death was eyed greedily by a chieftain called Kali Kolsson, a nephew of the martyred Saint Magnus. Though he had never set foot in Orkney, he declared his intent to fight for the earldom. Frakork saw an opportunity to regain her position of influence.

With breathtaking audacity, she proposed that she would arrange the removal of Earl Paul if Kali granted her half the earldom. She knew she could gather ships and men for this purpose in the Southern Isles (NOTE: Hebrides), where her niece Ingibjorg was married to the king. Her warlike young grandson Olvir would, she reasoned, make a fine leader for the fleet that would do battle with Paul's ships.

But the forces of Frakork and Olvir proved no match for Paul's men, who were led by a warrior named Olaf Rolfsson, from Duncansby in Caithness. Frakork knew him: they had danced together at the wedding of her son Thorbjorn to his daughter Ingirid. The young Olvir vowed revenge. He besieged Olaf's house at Duncansby, then set fire to it, burning him to death.

(NOTE: The killing of enemies by 'burning' in their homes is a recurring event in the Orkneyinga as well as Gudrun's Saga: see, for example, the death of Einar 'Bread-and-Butter' in the Ragnhild story. It is believed that the victim was more often killed in hand-to-hand combat while trying to escape the burning building than in the actual fire.)

Meanwhile, Kali Kolsson had landed in Orkney. Through false promises and without Frakork's aid, he had become joint Earl with Paul. To ingratiate himself with the people he adopted the name of a former, very popular, earl – Rognvald – and began the building of a cathedral in Kirkwall dedicated to Saint Magnus, his uncle.

(NOTE: Rognvald was acclaimed Earl of Orkney in 1136 and foundations for the cathedral were laid the following year.)

Now Olaf of Duncansby and his wife Asleif had, in addition to their daughter Ingirid who married into Frakork's family, a son Sweyn. Upon his father's death the boy dropped the name 'Olafsson' and adopted his mother's as a matronymic. Sweyn Asleifsson became one of the most notorious Vikings of his era, and his exploits soon came to the attention of Rognvald.

'If you rid Orkney of Paul "the Speechless", he told Sweyn, I as sole remaining ruler will forgive all your crimes and make you rich. But you must do it in a way that will not arouse suspicion.'

The Viking went to Earl Paul and warned him that certain nobles were plotting against him. Feigning sincerity, he said, 'For your own safety, my lord, I will deliver you to the protection of your sister Margaret and her powerful Scottish husband the Earl of Atholl. There you can stay until your foes in Orkney have been dealt with.'

Sweyn took the gullible Paul by ship to Burghead on the Moray Firth coast, and thence to a famous standing stone (NOTE: almost certainly Sueno's or Sweyn's stone near Forres, a notable Pictish monument) a short distance inland. That was the agreed rendezvous for a handover; in the 'care' of the Earl of Atholl's men Paul 'the Speechless' was transported to the central Highlands of Scotland. He was never heard of again.

Now in total control of the earldom, the duplicitous Rognvald set about consolidating his hold on the mainland provinces of Caithness and Sutherland. By fostering Margaret's son Harald and naming him joint

Earl at the age of six, he gained control of Caithness. Sutherland was a thornier problem, as it was largely the fiefdom of Frakork and her kin.

It was time to engage the fearsome Sweyn Asleifsson again. 'Go to Sutherland,' Rognvald told him, 'and destroy that woman's home and her lands. I want her, and her entire family, to demand my protection so that all of Sutherland can be mine.'

Meanwhile Frakork had grown rich from gold in the streams of Hjalmundsdal. She had shared her wealth with the local farmers and villagers, as the price of their silence. If the Earl learned of the gold, he would want it all for himself.

(NOTE: The tale of the gold of Hjalmundsdal is not found in any other known saga.)

On his mission from the Earl, Sweyn seized hold of an old man and held a knife at his throat, demanding to know where to find Frakork's house. In terror for his life, the villager blurted out that he had none of the gold.

'Gold?' Sweyn asked. 'Is Frakork hiding treasure that should be Earl Rognvald's?'

'Of that I cannot speak,' the man stammered. 'But she lives yonder, by the river.'

Those were his last words, for Sweyn drew his knife across his victim's neck before making for Frakork's home.

'I know little of gold,' he said to himself, 'but this I do know. It can survive the hottest fire. I will burn the lady's house, then retrieve her hoard from the ashes. And Earl Rognvald need know nothing about it.'

With his small band of thugs, Sweyn Asleifsson imprisoned Frakork inside before setting fire to the house, where she burned to death. Afterwards, Sweyn returned alone to rake through the ashes. He found the gold close to her blackened body; evidently she had gathered it up in preparation for flight.

That pause to plunder Frakork's gold allowed Olvir, his mother Steinvor and his aunt Gudrun to escape to the mouth of the river. From there Olvir and Steinvor fled to the safety of the Southern Isles. Gudrun, meanwhile, sailed over the Broad Fjord (NOTE: Moray Firth) to Banff then travelled far inland where she believed Sweyn Asleifsson would never find her. On a lonely hill she built a house and named it Gudrun Ha. For years she led a peaceful life, pasturing sheep on the hill. Local people thought a giant had come to live among them and marvelled at the height of her ceilings and doors.

The only one of Gudrun's kin to remain in Rognvald's earldom was her son Thorbjorn. Because he was a close friend of the young Earl Harald, and took great interest in the boy's education – for which he became known as Thorbjorn 'the Clerk' – Rognvald initially tolerated his presence. But eventually Rognvald began to resent his influence over Harald and found an excuse to outlaw Thorbjorn – and, for good measure, his wife Ingirid. For safety's sake, Thorbjorn sent Ingirid, his son Sweyn and his three daughters Thora, Hilda and Ingibjorg to the South to live on the Sheep Hill near Gudrun Ha.

(NOTE: The Orkneyinga Saga makes no mention of the children of Thorbjorn and Ingirid.)

In the quiet surroundings of the Sheep Hill, Gudrun began telling Ingirid and her granddaughters tales she had learned at her mother's knee, weaving them into a saga that concluded with her own life-story. A travelling poet heard some of the stories and carried them to Earl Rognvald's court. The Earl was incensed to learn that the stories portrayed him as a cruel and deceitful man rather than the pious founder of Saint Magnus Cathedral. Torture forced the poet to reveal Gudrun's whereabouts, and two Scottish mercenaries were sent to silence her. They chased her from her house on to the Sheep Hill and slew her on a high place. By going into hiding, Ingirid and her children escaped the same fate.

(NOTE: According to Swainson family lore, the 'high place' where Gudrun was killed was the rocky slope now known as the Skairs – from 'skersa', meaning giantess.)

Hatred burned deep in the heart of Thorbjorn 'the Clerk'. The wicked Rognvald had first arranged the killing of his grandmother Frakork, now his mother Gudrun. Would Thorbjorn's wife and children be next?

It took him many years to exact his revenge, but the opportunity presented itself one summer day (NOTE: in 1158) in Caithness.

There he ambushed Earl Rognvald and his men. Thorbjorn was seriously wounded and captured in the battle that ensued, but not before he had extracted cold vengeance on Rognvald at the point of his sword and watched the earl die. Young Harald, now sole ruler of the earldom, ordered Thorbjorn to be brought before him. Though his advisors called for the killer's death, he decided to spare the life of the man who had been a true friend.

'Go in peace,' he told Thorbjorn. 'Join your wife Ingirid and your children in the South and no

Orkneyman will trouble you ever again.' But Thorbjorn's wounds were severe and, unfit for the journey, he died in Caithness.

(NOTE: Gudrun's Saga can be seen to restore to some extent the reputation of Frakork as well as women of longer ago such as Ragnhild and her mother Gunnhild, so callously destroyed by the more familiar sagas. The universal 'bad woman' of folk tales, from wicked stepmother to evil queen, deserves to have her side of the story heard.

Evening the score, Gudrun paints Earl Rognvald as cruel and duplicitous, in contrast with the Orkneyinga writers, who devote much of their saga to a reverential account of his life, travels and poetry. Where lies the truth? After so much time has passed, we can never know.)

THE END

A brief Internet search confirmed for Delia that Kali Kolsson, the Viking who became Earl Rognvald, was not quite the saint the *Orkneyinga Saga* makes him out to be.

Caithness remained firmly in the control of the Norwegian earldom of Orkney for most of the twelfth century, populated by farming people ('husbandmen' and their families) largely of Norse and mixed Norse-Celtic blood. The territory was, however, constantly coveted by the Kings of Scots and their nobles. Around 1196 the Earl began paying tribute for Caithness to King William I, effectively recognising Scottish sovereignty over the land.

William tightened his grip through the Church. A see or bishopric was created on the Thurso River at Halkirk (Old Norse *Ha Kirkja*) and a succession of Scottish bishops appointed with the right to raise a tax or tithe from the husbandmen in the form of butter. Resentment at this imposition by what was seen as a foreign power escalated into violence on numerous occasions. The most notorious such protest took place in 1222, following a doubling of the tax rate by the avaricious bishop of the time. A group of husbandmen seized and mortally wounded him, before finishing off the job by setting him alight in his kitchen – no doubt using the contentious butter to aid the fire.

When the king (William's successor Alexander II) heard this, he had eighty local husbandmen rounded up regardless of their involvement in the burning. Their fate was worse than execution: the king ordered that their hands and feet be hacked off. With Christian piety Pope Honorius III expressed great satisfaction at this mode of avenging his bishop's death.

Gilbert de Moravia (Murray), a cousin of the 1st Earl of Sutherland, was appointed to the now vacant position of Bishop of Caithness. He moved the seat of the bishopric to Dornoch, far to the south and a safe distance from Halkirk.

The status of Caithness was finally settled in 1266, when Norway formally ceded it to Scotland by the Treaty of Perth.

29
SNAEBISTER

WHEN DOMINIC ARGILL'S estate was wound up, Rona's one-third had taken the form of a substantial share in the family supermarket operation. After sale of that business to Carrefour, she had invested her own money cautiously: she did not, for example, take a personal stake in Fairfield's Cereals, the company owned by the trust fund for her son Donald.

In 1976 she used personal cash resources to buy an elegant former Church of Scotland manse at Snaebister, about eight miles north of Stromness on the western edge of Mainland Orkney. With sensitive extension and thorough internal remodelling, it would make a comfortable but prestigious home. It came with five acres of land, rentable to neighbouring farmers; a useful buffer against the possibility of any new building on her doorstep. Kristin was especially delighted, having visions of a paddock for a pony. Rona struggled to suppress her disapproval: girls with ponies were an unpleasant reminder of her earliest schooldays at Queen Alex's.

Just as the family was ready to move, the smallholding of Tannersquoy, adjacent to Snaebister, came on the market. It gave Rona an idea. 'Why don't we buy *more* property in Orkney? We could start with Tannersquoy, then other opportunities as they arise. Land's as good an investment as any these days, and we'll be right there to keep an eye on it. At Gordonhall, we had half a dozen tenanted farms. I know what's involved.'

Ari was sceptical. 'Gordonhall was in your family for centuries. It's different for incomers, as we're going to be when we get to Orkney. Buying up everything in sight will get us noticed, and not in a good way.'

'I didn't say *everything*.'

'Doesn't matter. We don't want to attract attention. You should appreciate that better than anyone.'

'I've gone along with *your* plans for the move to Orkney, but you think it's fine to pour cold water on *my* ideas for what we do when we get there.'

There was silence for a minute or two, till Ari said, 'Don't get me wrong, *elskan*. I'm not against buying Tannersquoy. In fact, it's perfect. We'll have a bit more land around us, means we won't have a nosey neighbour. But let's not make ourselves too conspicuous. Orkney's a small community. A bit like Iceland in that respect.'

Though she hated to give in, Rona could see he was right. One of the many reasons she loved him was that, when he got the better of her in an argument, he never treated it as point-scoring.

An offer for Tannersquoy went in next day and was accepted within a week. When the seller's solicitor began making stipulations that threatened to derail the deal, they simply added fifteen thousand pounds to the purchase price. All the difficulties miraculously disappeared.

The family moved first into Tannersquoy, as a temporary measure while the Snaebister manse was being rehabbed and extended. Soon they were able to decamp to the more spacious accommodation down the road.

Almost forty years later, Ragna Enjudóttir could reflect on her time at Snaebister as a happy one. With the kids at school in Stromness and Ari engaged in his Tourist Board work, she could immerse herself in the Norse heritage of that paradoxical land. Treeless yet fertile; wild yet civilised; peripheral to national and world events yet seminal to European culture for a thousand years. Orkney's vast skyscapes lodged in Ragna's memory, though not in a nostalgic way. Home now was Iceland's arctic coast, a place she loved and would never again leave.

When Donald turned twelve in 1979, Rona and Ari resolved to tell him the truth about his parentage. Up until then, he had been led to believe that his biological father was Lord Bracklinn, Dominic Argill, whom Rona married in 1966.

Now, the more complicated truth was presented to him. Ari, the man he called *Pabbi*, was his true father. Donald was still entitled to the Bracklinn barony and wealth, because under Scots law a child conceived by a married woman was deemed to be her husband's son or daughter, unless there was admission or proof to the contrary.

'Yet you've just *admitted*,' the boy said, 'that I'm *not* Lord Bracklinn's son.'

'Only to you, Donny,' his mother said. 'But now you know this, you must never mention it outside the family. Otherwise, someone else could lay claim to your title and the money in your trust fund.'

'Who would do that?'

'The man who called himself Lord Bracklinn at the time you were born. Telford. We don't want to give him a reason to open up the whole question again. You do understand, don't you, darling?'

'I ... I suppose so,' Donald said. 'But why tell me all this now?'

It was Ari's turn to speak. 'Two reasons. First, you're a big boy and can handle the truth. And second, I'm proud to be your *Pabbi* and I want you to know that. Plus, it's always good to know about your genetic inheritance.'

The boy's expression changed. 'What do you mean by that?'

'Nothing to worry about, just to be aware of. When I was about twenty – a student in Aberdeen – I was diagnosed with a form of gastric reflux disease that runs in families. If left untreated, it was going to be quite unpleasant and could lead to a more serious condition called Barrett's oesophagus.'

'Like *Afi* has?' Donald was referring to his Icelandic grandpa.

'Yes. The most effective drugs – PPIs, they're called – weren't available when he was young and he had a lot of trouble with some kinds of food.'

'Is it a PPI you take every day?'

'Yes. With it, I lead a perfectly normal life, as you can see.'

'So will I definitely get this reflux thing?'

'No, but there's about a fifty percent chance, according to what I've been told.'

'Kris too?'

'Possibly, yes.'

Ari and Rona looked at each other apprehensively as Donald processed the new information. They need not have worried.

'If that's all,' the boy said, 'it sounds like no big deal. I can take the pills, just like you do.' As for the biological father business, well, he had known for years. Miss Rendall, his teacher in Primary 6, had told him after parents' night how like his Daddy he was.

By the early 1980s, Ari had quit his job to set up in business on his own account, offering heritage tours for visitors to Orkney. He purchased a boat to include trips to the smaller islands; that led to fishing excursions, which were more lucrative. In his spare time he began cultivating some of the land at Snaebister and Tannersquoy, growing vegetables for local consumption and for the hotel kitchens of Kirkwall and Stromness. The ingredients for *clapshot* – a traditional Orkney accompaniment to haggis or minced beef, consisting of boiled swedes and potatoes mashed together, usually with chives – were in especially heavy demand during the winter months.

Donald finished secondary school in 1985 with six Highers to his credit, three of them A's. That same summer he celebrated his eighteenth birthday and the maturation of his trust fund. Now owner of the controlling share in a prospering breakfast cereals business in Dundee, a country house and lands at Ardwhinzean near Callander, and sundry investments, he was a very wealthy young man.

But he was not ready to take the reins at Fairfield's Cereals. There were oats of another kind he wanted to sow. The student experience beckoned and, at the end of September of that year he set off for the bright lights, big city of Aberdeen. Keen to be just 'one of the lads', he found a cheap flat to let in Ferryhill which he shared with two other students and began introducing himself as Donny Swainson, dropping forever the Argill part of his surname.

One of his flatmates was a pretty raven-haired girl called Isobel Craigie, an Orcadian like himself though he had scarcely known her before coming to Aberdeen. From a farm on Stronsay, she had attended Kirkwall Grammar School while he was a pupil at Stromness Academy. He was besotted with her, and the attraction was mutual. A year older than Donny and studious (the kind he dismissed in school as a 'swot'), she helped redirect his teenage energy more into coursework than partying. She liked to keep fit; each weekend saw them spend an hour together in the Kings College pool after Friday afternoon classes.

Isobel's pronouncedly left-of-centre political views held Donny back from telling her too much about his background. Only when she came to spend Christmas at Snaebister did she learn the awful truth: he was a rich kid, and a 'toff' to boot.

'Why didn't you tell me?' she asked him, both puzzled and hurt.

Donny launched into a prepared response. 'I'm not going to give you the "I wanted you to love me for *me*, not my money" crap. Well ... maybe I am. I figured if you'd love me poor, you wouldn't walk out on me when you found I owned Fairfield's Cereals and an estate in Stirlingshire.'

'Of course I'm not going to walk out on you. I just want no secrets, especially big secrets like this, between us.'

'Deal.'

'So show me your coat of arms.'

He reached out to embrace her. 'Will these arms do, for now?'

Rona and Ari took to Isobel right away. She was down-to-earth, smart and, most importantly, a good influence on their eighteen-year-old son.

Kristin, by then fourteen, was a little less enthusiastic. 'Why choose a brunette with brown eyes?' she complained to her mother. 'We're a fair-haired family. Pure Scandinavian. I hope he's not going to *marry* her and have little black-headed kids. Yuck!'

'Let me tell you a story, young lady,' Rona said, sitting down with Kristin in her bedroom. She launched into the tale of Åsa of Agder, the beautiful blonde queen who had a dark-haired son, Halfdan 'the Black'. It was almost exactly twenty years since she had translated that tale from *Gudrun's Saga*; thinking about it brought a lump to her throat.

She reached the end of the story. 'So Halfdan, whom his father had planned to put to death along with every dark-haired boy in his kingdom, became a powerful and much-loved king in his own right. Indeed, he would have gone on to be the first king of all Norway, if he hadn't fallen through the ice on a frozen lake.'

'Harald "Fairhair" was the first king of all Norway,' Kristin said triumphantly. 'He was *blond*, like us.'

'Yes,' Rona smiled, 'and Halfdan "the Black" was his father.'

'So Donny and Isobel might have fair-haired kids?'

'Fair or dark, what does it matter? And anyway, we're getting a wee bit ahead of ourselves here, don't you think?'

A couple of days after Christmas, Isobel went home to Stronsay to spend New Year with her family. And another visitor arrived at Snaebister.

Marcel Fichet kissed his hostess on each cheek in his Gallic way. It was a gloomy day, about two-thirty in the afternoon, when such daylight as had percolated through the clouds was already fading. 'This time of year, I should be off to Nice, not this dark wasteland,' he said with a twinkle in his eye.

'We make up for it in summer. I'm so pleased you've come.'

After a late lunch, Rona, Ari, Donny and Marcel got down to brass tacks. By five o'clock it was all hammered out.

Donny would henceforth devote part of each vacation to the Dundee operation, learning from Marcel how to run the business. He would spend some time on the shop floor to get a handle on every aspect of production and packaging, and he would accompany the sales manager on customer visits, making sure Fairfield's products were getting the right exposure on supermarket shelves. Not later than the end of 1989, six months after his graduation and four years from now, he would have to decide if he wanted to make that his career. If so, Marcel would stay on in an advisory capacity for twelve months before taking a retirement package. If not, the business would be sold as a going concern.

At 7:30 the family and their guest sat down to eat. A toast – 12-year-old Highland Park for the adults, apple juice for Kristin – was drunk to the continued success of Fairfield's Cereals. A bottle of Margaux from Marcel's cellar (he had laid it down seven years ago, he said) accompanied Ari's *boeuf en croute*.

With their coffee they had Grand Marnier. 'You drank this at our first meeting in 1972, Rona, when you told me about the future of rock'n'roll. Do you remember?'

In reply, Rona moved over to the entertainment centre graced by a brand-new state-of-the-art gizmo Ari had bought her for Christmas: a Sony CD player. But it was the old-fashioned turntable she switched on. Soon the unmistakable sound of *Layla* by Derek and the Dominos filled the room.

Kristin rolled her eyes.

30
TICKING

THE INTERROGATION OF TIM HESTON at Maryhill police station in Glasgow was ploughing on. His solicitor had tried to get him released on bail, but the gravity of the charges against him made that impossible. With no hard forensic evidence linking Heston to the poisoned muesli, the police had their own problem.

'Let's go over this once more,' DI 'Geordie' Neville said, a note of resignation creeping into his Newcastle-accented voice. 'You admit you are the author of the Toff Hammer blog?'

'Yes. So what?'

'I'll tell you what. Up to now you've kept the identity of Toff Hammer a secret, even from people who know you well. Your students, for example. Your colleagues in the Sociology department at Caledonian. How did you do that?'

'Not too difficult.'

'Not for a fellow as computer-savvy as you, right?'

'Your words, not mine.'

'But you agree you're familiar with the ins and outs of the Internet, how to post stuff under an untraceable pseudonym, that kind of thing?'

'Yes, me and many thousands of people in Great Britain.'

'So you'd be capable of setting up a Twitter account that can't be traced back to you?'

'Not something I've ever tried.'

'You *have* a Twitter account, don't you?'

'You know I do. Under my Toff Hammer pseudonym. But it's not untraceable. If your whizz-kids had done their work right, they could have figured it out in five minutes. You wouldn't have needed me to tell you.' A self-satisfied grin spread across Heston's face.

Neville's expression betrayed none of the exasperation he was feeling. 'So this jequirityjo name. That's another of yours, isn't it?'

Heston's solicitor whispered something in his ear.

'No, I hadn't heard of that name until you mentioned it earlier. But I'm aware jequirity is the plant you get abrin from. Is *that* the poison used in the "muesli murders"?'

'We are still investigating the precise cause of death.'

'I take it that's a "yes".'

'How do you know about abrin?'

'Doesn't everybody? It's not a state secret. All you have to do is look it up in Wikipedia. I suppose you could buy it on the dark web, like the Liverpool guy did.'

'That was ricin. Ali, the "Liverpool guy" you're thinking about, got eight years just for ordering it. Never got his hands on the real stuff. Imagine what's facing you, Mr Heston, for actually possessing abrin and using it as a murder weapon.'

'Whatever I am, Inspector, I'm not a murderer and I'm not a fool. You can't pin this on me because I have never in my life touched abrin – or the jequirity plant for that matter.'

'But you would know exactly how to cultivate this plant, wouldn't you?'

'Not very green-fingered, me.' He shrugged. 'I suppose I could have a go, if I got the seeds. Oh, wait a minute. Where am I supposed to have got jequirity seeds? At Dobbie's?'

'You tell *me*, Mr Heston.'

'Can't, because I had nothing to do with it.'

'I understand jequirity grows wild in parts of Indonesia. Ever been there?'

'On *my* salary? You must be joking.'

'You're a polytechnic lecturer. Not exactly on the breadline.'

'Glasgow Caledonian is a University, Inspector. It hasn't been a poly since 1993. You're showing your age.'

'Soil, pots, lights, plant food were all found in the cellar at your address. Everything you need for growing jequirity. Am I right?'

'Everything except jequirity seeds. Which you haven't said you found at Heston Towers. Let's stop playing games. You have *nothing* on me, and you know it.'

'So there's some innocent explanation for the little plant nursery in your cellar?'

'Innocent? Yes, though possibly not in your book.'

'What's that supposed to mean?'

'I occasionally grow a few cannabis plants, strictly for my own use. Charge me with that, if you like.'

The solicitor interrupted to say, 'My client is a humorist, Inspector. What he just said was not an admission of illegal activity.'

'No?' Neville countered. 'We'll have to see what it sounds like when we play back the tape. Mr Heston, let's talk about your vendetta against Fairfield's Cereals, shall we?'

Heston framed his mouth in an insolent sneer. '*Vendetta*? Inspector, if you want to sprinkle your conversation with Italian words, I suggest you first check their meaning.' Ignoring his solicitor's attempts to shut him up, he continued, 'Do you know what a *vendetta* is? It's a prolonged blood-feud conducted by two parties locked in a cycle of revenge. I am not *Cosa Nostra*. I don't do *vendetta*.'

There was silence, except for the ticking of the wall clock. Neville appeared to give his suspect's speech some thought before remarking, 'For an educated man, an intellectual even, you have some lowbrow tastes in reading material, Mr Heston.'

'I'm sure you know lowbrow when you see it, Mr Neville. Look, I see where you're going with this. It's the Kathy Reichs book, isn't it? Popular, I'd call it. Middlebrow, maybe, but not lowbrow. I like to relax sometimes, and, along with millions of my fellow-citizens, I enjoy a bit of crime fiction. Come to think of it, this is crime fiction you and I are engaged in right now. So why am I not enjoying it?'

'Have you read *Flash and Bones* by Kathy Reichs?'

'As you've discovered, it's on my Kindle and, yes, I think I've read that one. Not her best.'

'But you read it, at least as far as page 229. You bookmarked it.'

'So?'

'Let me read you a passage.' Neville lowered his glasses to the tip of his nose and picked up a photocopy of the page in question. 'She refers to jequirity as "rosary pea". Lowbrow that I am, I had to check. It's the same thing.'

> *"So, in all likelihood, it would take a deliberate act to obtain abrin, either from rosary pea seeds or from some other source, and use it to poison someone?"*
>
> *"In all likelihood."*
>
> *"If ingested, how much is required to kill a human being?"*
>
> *"Very little."*
>
> *Williams curled his fingers in a "give me more" gesture.*
>
> *"One seed would probably do it."*

'Your point, Inspector?'

'Why would you bookmark that particular passage?'

'Sometimes I finish reading in the middle of a chapter. Or I might accidentally add a bookmark. It's easily done, you know.'

'So Reichs is telling you all you need to kill somebody is a single jequirity seed. And you mark that very page.'

Heston rolled his eyes. 'It's *fiction*, Inspector. If I was planning to poison someone, I wouldn't rely on a work of fiction to get the dose right. Even if the author was a forensic anthropologist. Even if that forensic anthropologist was Kathy Reichs.'

'We're done for now. For the recording, Inspector Neville terminating the interview at 21:45.'

It had been another long day. But the Avenger was growing in confidence minute by minute, hour by hour. The police had no inkling of the time-bomb that was ticking, ready to destroy the whole Fairfield house of cards.

They could interview Toff Hammer all they liked, but it would never occur to them to question what was *next* on the agenda. Not that he would give them the answer, if they did.

The move was already in progress, from an indiscriminate assault on Fairfield's customer base to a precisely targeted attack at the heart of the operation. There was nothing more the Avenger needed to do. Only the timing was uncertain. The eventual outcome was not in doubt.

31
LIKE BEGINNING A NEW LIFE

To Rona's surprise, after Donald graduated in July 1989, he and Isobel decided to get married rather than continue just living together. A wedding date was fixed for mid-September of that year.

She had half-expected her son to walk away from the running of Fairfield's Cereals, because Isobel's heart was set on returning to Orkney. It was hard to see how this could be reconciled with a husband managing a business in Dundee.

Young Donald proposed a simple though expensive solution. Together with two other companies, Fairfield's would take a part-lease of a small plane, complete with pilot, enabling him to commute between Orkney and Dundee. Three days a week in the office should, he said, suffice; the rest of the time he would work from home, communicating by telephone and fax.

Marcel Fichet was none too keen on the idea. A managing director had to be hands-on five days a week, he said. Besides, the cost of the plane would blow a hole in Fairfield's balance sheet. Rona liked it even less, though her concern was for her son's safety rather than company finances.

But Donald got his way. By early 1990, married to Isobel and living in a modern house on Berstane Road in Kirkwall, he was in sole control of the business, soon spending no more than two days a week away from home. Marcel was forced to admit, at his retirement party in February, that the arrangement was working out much better than he had expected.

To the astonishment of many observers, most of all Rona, it was Telford Argill-Elliott who made the difference. The man who, twenty years earlier, had seen the Bracklinn title slip from his grasp, seemed to bear no grudge. He had, after all, received an income from Donald's trust for fifteen years, and had been a non-executive director of Fairfield's Cereals since 1985. Perhaps it helped that he had finally succeeded in having his 'missing' cousin declared legally dead; this meant Fergus's estate could at last be wound up, with Telford as sole beneficiary.

Contrary to Rona's inclination to exclude Telford completely from the trust, her lawyer had not minced his words. Lyndon B. Johnson's words, actually, referring to J. Edgar Hoover: 'Better have him inside the tent pissing out than outside pissing in.'

Telford proved an immense support in managing the company. During Donald's frequent absences, he supervised the business in Dundee, ensuring the young boss was informed on every issue that arose. Rona remained sceptical that Telford really had her son's best interests at heart. On the other hand, Donald himself placed great trust in the older man, and promised him that his daughter Faith, by then twenty years old, would be offered a position in the company once she had completed a business degree at Stirling University.

That year, 1990, brought another major crisis. Ari was with his mother Vigdis in Reykjavik, at the bedside of his father Harald who at the age of 76 was in the terminal stages of oesophageal cancer. At home with Kristin at Snaebister, Rona dived for the phone when it rang, expecting to hear her husband's voice.

But it was not Ari. The caller was a *Daily Record* journalist. Having written a piece on what he called 'the Bracklinn killings', he was offering her the chance to review it before publication. 'Fax it to this number,' she said.

Rona was horrified. The story rehashed yet again the whole twenty-year-old mess of the violent deaths of the 3rd and 4th holders of the Bracklinn peerage and disappearance of the man who claimed the succession, concluding that all three had been murdered. 'New evidence' was said to have been found (DNA analysis was hinted at but not explicitly stated) appearing to implicate Rona in all three 'crimes'.

She called her solicitor, who tried unsuccessfully to suppress publication of the story. Two days later, it was splashed across the front page and the centre spread. Suddenly she was bombarded with requests for interviews, all of which she dismissed. Strangely, none of those requests came from the police.

Harald died the same week. It was something of a relief for Rona to get on a plane from Kirkwall to Glasgow and from there to Reykjavik, even on such a sad mission. Kristin, Donald and Isobel made the journey a few days later, for the funeral.

'I hope you are still taking the medicine, Ari,' Vigdis said after the interment of her husband. 'If it had been available to your father when he was young, he would still be with us today.'

'Yes, *Mamma*, I take it every day,' Ari replied.

'And what about you, Dónaldur, and you, Kristin?'

Donald was first to answer his grandmother. 'So far, *Amma*, I haven't needed it.'

'Me neither,' his sister said.

The day after the funeral, Ari and Rona saw Donald and Isobel off at the airport then sat down for a coffee in the bar at the terminal. Kristin had stayed behind with her grandma.

'You know, sweetheart,' Ari said, savouring the aroma of the strong brown liquid in his cup, 'we don't have to rush back to Scotland. In fact, why don't we settle here in Iceland, far from all those bastards who are out to give you such a hard time?'

'Run away, you mean?'

'We don't have to. We're already out of the country. Look, Donny doesn't need us any more. He's got a great handle on the business. And Kris has talked about going to the University of Iceland. She loves it here.'

'I know. It's a blessing you insisted on bringing her up to be bilingual. But, Ari, we can't escape. The bastards, as you call them, will hunt us down, even in Iceland.'

'Maybe not.'

'What do you mean?'

'You're eligible for fast-track citizenship as the spouse of an Icelandic national. It would be like beginning a new life.'

Rona looked into his eyes. 'I would love nothing better, but we still wouldn't be safe. You know I could still be extradited back to the UK if the police there had a case against me. And what about my title as Countess of Fairfield? I want Donny to be Earl when I die.'

'To be honest, *elskan*, I don't think he cares too much about that, but I see your point. It would be a shame to give up on hundreds of years of history. What if you were to relinquish the earldom voluntarily, now, in favour of our son?'

'We could look into that, I suppose.'

'And as for the extradition thing, I think you worry too much. The police haven't shown any interest in the *Daily Record* story. It'll all die down again.'

'Until the next time somebody wants to rake over those old coals. There's no hiding place.'

'You're forgetting one thing. With Icelandic citizenship, you'll no longer be traceable under the Swainson name.'

'I know. I'll have to use the patronymic. Filipsdóttir, after my father, Philip. But it won't take a genius to crack that.'

'Remember *Gudrun's Saga*?'

'How can I forget?'

'What was the name of the Viking who kidnapped Paul, Earl of Orkney, at the behest of the evil Earl Rognvald?'

Rona wondered where this was going. 'Er ... Sweyn Asleifsson, wasn't it?'

'Yes, but Asleifsson wasn't his original name. He was Sweyn Olafsson until Olaf his father died. Then, remember, he took his mother Asleif's name. *You* can choose the matronymic, just like Sweyn did. Me too, now my father's gone to Valhalla. I'll become Ari Vigdisson.'

'But my mother ...' Rona paused, not quite sure what she wanted to say. Aenea, dowager Countess of Fairfield, had passed away at her Borders home two years previously; since the funeral in Melrose, Rona had not once visited her grave.

'I know,' Ari said. 'You don't want to recognise her in this way, do you? But it's not a question of honour or dishonour. In Iceland it's just an administrative process like registering the number of a car or the name of a boat.'

'So you're suggesting I take the name Aeneasdóttir? How would that be any less easy to hide behind than Filipsdóttir?'

'Well, Aenea isn't an approved Icelandic name. You'd be required to use the nearest equivalent: Enja. Your matronymic would be Enjudóttir.'

'So I'd be Rona Enjudóttir. One of a handful of Ronas in the whole country, I bet. I'd still stick out like a sore thumb.'

'You can't be Rona. Again, not an approved name. You'll have to become Ragna. Ragna Enjudóttir. See how different that is, yet still *you*?'

Rona/Ragna rolled the name around her tongue a few times. 'Yes, Ari, I quite like the sound of that.'

It was only later that she realised how close her new name was to *Ragnhild*, the tenth-century Norse princess whose life she often felt she was re-living.

32
A DELICIOUS THOUGHT

FAITH ELLIOTT'S SON OSCAR was an adventurous young man with a taste for danger. He had kayaked the Zambezi River rapids of the Batoka Gorge downstream from the Victoria Falls. He had parasailed off the top of the Eiger. While backpacking in the Swat Valley of Pakistan he had come within a hairsbreadth of capture by Taliban rebels. Nothing marked him as the kind of person who would happily run a food company; indeed, he had no idea that this was the future his mother was mapping out for him.

Oscar was the product of a brief fling in Faith's student days at Stirling with one of her tutors, a married man with three children. When she found she was pregnant, the affair was already over; she never bothered to inform him he had a son.

Back in 2009, Faith's father Telford Argill-Elliott – the one-time claimant of the Barony of Bracklinn – was killed in a car crash. Her grief was lessened by the realisation that she could now pursue a long-held ambition: to build her dream home on the footprint of the old Gordonhall mansion. Telford had been firmly against the idea – it would bring bad luck, he said. Now, with her father gone, the land was hers to do with as she wanted.

Though the then nineteen-year-old Oscar exhibited no interest in putting down roots, Faith fantasised that, when eventually he 'grew up' and became a company director, she would bequeath to him a property befitting his status.

While excavating the cellars of the old house that had been filled with rubble, a workman had come on what looked like human remains and called Faith to ask what he should do.

'Who else is with you?' she inquired.

'Nobody,' the man replied. 'Will I call the police?'

'Not yet. I'll be there in a couple of hours. Till then, carry on digging.' The possibility that this might be the skeleton of her father's cousin Fergus, who disappeared around the time of the fire, was not something Faith was ready to face.

A generous cash bonus bought the workman's silence. 'If the police get involved,' she told him, 'it could delay the project for weeks. An old tramp used to shelter in the cellars of the house when it was unoccupied, so I've heard. He could have died down there long before the house was destroyed.'

The gold signet ring, engraved with a wheat-sheaf and a cheese-wrapper cow, was quite a find for the contractor, as he carefully removed it from a finger-bone in the Gordonhall cellar. It was something he would treasure. Not too many homeless vagrants died wearing such a thing, he had thought at the time, but there was no point in letting on about it to his customer. It was, however, a proud trophy to flash in front of his mates at the Macbeth Arms in Lumphanan. Even after several pints with a whisky chaser, he would not be persuaded to reveal the precise location or circumstances in which he had come by it.

'Just one of the perks of my job,' was all he would say.

For Delia, a visit to Gordonhall was now a must. Frank had recently gone there, but she felt an irresistible urge to see the place for herself.

As she turned into the driveway she could not help but notice the two granite pillars, one on either side of the entrance. The elegantly carved finial surmounting each one was unmistakable: a Platonic octahedron, like the one on the Gordonhall bookplate.

The mansion that had been Rona Fay Swainson's home was long gone, of course, destroyed in a fire that coincided suspiciously with the disappearance of Fergus Argill-Hawke –

the twentieth-century *alter ego* of Einar 'Bread-and-Butter' from *Gudrun's Saga*. Faith lived there now, Frank had said, in a spectacular modern house on the same spot. And *she* was the link to Donald Swainson, Rona Fay's son, the managing director of Fairfield's Cereals.

Blissfully unaware of the 'muesli murders' making headlines at that very moment, Delia had no inkling that all was not well in the Fairfield's empire. Otherwise, she might have thought better of driving up to Faith Elliott's door and ringing the bell.

As it happened, no one was at home. Lifting the flap of the letterbox and peering in, Delia saw the floor littered with mail. *I'm here so I might as well have a look around,* she thought.

Among lawns, heath beds and rockeries she wandered, admiring the range of plants. Scattered tall trees were a reminder that this was an old-established country-house garden; these same Douglas firs, sequoias, oaks and beeches would have been familiar to Rona Fay Swainson as a child sixty or more years ago.

She came upon a lily-pond, by the side of which a large blue heron stood motionless, its eye trained on a frog or some other tempting morsel. Not wishing to disturb the bird, Delia turned back towards the curved driveway by which she had arrived. Out of sight now of the modern house, she found what had been the gardener's cottage, its windows boarded up and a wooden plank nailed crudely across its front door.

All but obscured by an overgrown hawthorn hedge, an iron gate gave access to the back of the cottage. With a push, Delia opened it just enough to squeeze through. Close behind was a high wall covered with rampant ivy, clematis and honeysuckle. A wooden door was partially hidden among the vegetation, and she could not resist trying its handle. With a creak the door swung back, and she found herself in the walled garden.

Box hedges delineated paths laid out in a regular rectangular pattern. What had once been well-tended vegetable plots were now mostly roughly-mown, weedy grass. Only an aluminium-framed greenhouse in the north-eastern corner showed signs of more careful attention.

Its door was firmly padlocked. Delia peered through the glass. *Those tomatoes are doing well*, she thought, *and can those be watermelons?* She had a momentary pang of homesickness for America, where summer wasn't summer without a watermelon.

In one spot stood a specimen that was vaguely familiar. *Where have I seen this before?*

Soon she had it: her Master's programme in environmental sciences had included a unit on poisonous plants. One species stuck in her mind, probably because of its extraordinarily high toxicity: *Abrus precatorius*, the precatory or rosary pea, also known as jequirity. And here it was, in a Scottish garden far from its native haunt in the mountains of Indonesia.

Only it was not quite as she remembered. The jequirity in the living herbarium in Boulder, Colorado had pink, perhaps mauve flowers; on this one the flowers were white. *Might its seeds also be white instead of scarlet?* A few pods had formed, but none had split open to reveal the answer.

Having collected her black BMW X6 from airport parking at Aberdeen, Faith Elliott at that moment was bombing along the road between Cullerlie and Raemoir. It would be good to get home to Gordonhall, though her Orkney visit had been productive, in more ways than one.

Poor old Toff Hammer, whoever he was, would be in the frame for the 'muesli murders'. As long as he was the prime suspect, the police would look no further for the author of the tweets posted under the name @jequirityjo. Shame, really, for the tirade against the Swainson clan in his blog was right on the money. Faith couldn't have written it better herself. That *she*, not Toff Hammer, was the Avenger who literally 'seeded' those

Fairfield's Premium Organic Muesli boxes with jequirity would never occur to Donald Swainson, to the police, even to her own flesh and blood – her son Oscar or her sister Hope.

And now the Avenger had set in motion the masterstroke, the *coup de grâce*. It might take days, weeks or months to play out, but no matter. Donald's son Rolf would die, leaving Oscar as eventual heir to the Bracklinn title and the Fairfield's Cereals company that went with it.

The long-term plan her father had vouchsafed to her, to be Donald Swainson's most trusted adviser over many years, then destroy his company at the moment of its greatest success, had taken time to come to fruition. 'The bigger they come, the harder they fall,' was Telford's not-exactly-original philosophy.

But the return of what should have been hers all along was a delicious thought. Finally, a great wrong would be righted.

As Faith braked on the approach to the turn-in for Gordonhall on the right, a small car pulled out of her driveway. She made out a young red-haired woman at the wheel, but it gave her not a moment's concern. Strangers often mistook the Gordonhall entrance for the Raemoir Hotel avenue a few hundred yards along the road.

Delia was disappointed not to find Faith Elliott at home: the white-flowered jequirity in the greenhouse had piqued her natural curiosity.

Well … probably best not to admit to sneaking into the walled garden without permission. But she was desperate to find out more about Rona Fay Swainson, the translator, maybe the original author, of *Gudrun's Saga*. Had she realised she had just met Ms Elliott she would have turned around and gone back up to Gordonhall. Luckily, Delia had no clue who was driving the black BMW.

33

IT SEEMS LIKE YESTERDAY

THE YEAR 1990, WHEN SHE turned 46, marked a clear dividing line in the story of her life.

Her new Icelandic identity as Ragna Enjudóttir would fit her like a glove. But before she could slip into it, she had one loose end to tie up as Rona Fay Swainson. In the briefest of trips back to Edinburgh she signed the papers prepared for her to demit her title to the ancient Earldom of Fairfield in favour of her son Donald, who on the last day of June became the 24th Earl. By another document she transferred to Donald ownership of the house and land at Snaebister, along with the next-door property of Tannersquoy, now generating a small income as a holiday let.

Then it was on to London, where she liquidated the proceeds of her one-third share of Dominic Argill's estate and transferred the cash to an account at Kaupthing Bank, one she had opened when she and Ari were newlyweds in Reykjavik almost twenty years before.

She took the night train to Aberdeen, where she closed her remaining UK bank accounts before boarding the *St Sunniva* for the voyage to Stromness in Orkney. Donald met her on the pier and drove her to Snaebister. There she gathered up a few items of clothing and prized personal possessions – enough to fill two large suitcases.

That night she slept for the last time in the place that had been her home for fourteen years, and would now become the official residence of Donald Swainson, 24th Earl of Fairfield and his Countess, Lady Isobel. Next morning it was back to

227

Stromness where an Icelandic trawler, the *Svanhildur*, was moored. The captain, Bárður Ingólfsson, stood ready to welcome her on board for an undocumented sailing to Akureyri. As the husband of Ari's sister Aslaug, he would take good care of Rona.

She would pose as a crew member for ease of re-entry to Iceland. Together with the only other female on the *Svanhildur* – Lísbet – she would share a tiny curtained-off section of the communal sleeping quarters. In preparation for the no-frills voyage, Rona's hair had been cut in a boyish post-punk style requiring less maintenance than the wavy tresses that had tumbled over her shoulders for most of her life. A touch of peroxide restored the flaxen blondness of her youth.

An additional element of the plan was revealed to her after embarkation: an intermediate stop in Torshavn, the capital and principal port of the Faroe Islands. 'Ari suggested this,' Bárður told her, 'to get you immigration papers that wouldn't immediately identify you as British. We'll pretend we have engine trouble and need to stay in port for a couple of days.'

In the event, a nasty North Atlantic storm was brewing when they left Stromness, giving the crew of the *Svanhildur* a genuine reason to take shelter in Torshavn. A Faroese immigration inspector boarded demanding ID. Rona was ready to show her British passport, but Bárður told her, 'Leave this to me.' An hour later, having bid good-day to the official who walked off carrying a case of Scotch whisky, Bárður presented Rona with a barely decipherable document in Faroese.

'What's this?' she asked.

'It says that Ragna Enjudóttir of Iceland has been legally admitted to *Føroyar* – the Faroes – and is now cleared for departure.' Bárður looked at her with a straight face then burst out laughing.

Rona assumed this was an elaborate joke on Bárður's part, but as she studied the document (Faroese being identifiably similar to the Old Norse with which she was familiar) she saw what he had said was true.

'Thank you, Bárður,' she said. 'I won't forget those twelve bottles of whisky in reckoning what I owe you for the trip.'

'They were really intended for the immigration examiner in Akureyri. Fortunately I have a few more cases down below, if they should be needed.' Bárður laughed again. 'Our secret, okay?' he said, tapping the side of his nose.

The *Svanhildur* put into Akureyri late in the evening and her crew were able to go ashore with only the most perfunctory of immigration procedure. Flashing the document she had received in Torshavn, Rona was waved through, to find Ari and Kristin waiting for her on the pier.

'What have you done to your beautiful hair?' Ari said after he had kissed her. 'No, don't answer. It kinda suits you, makes you look truly Icelandic. And young.'

'It's *so-o* 1980s' was Kristin's laconic verdict on her mother's new coif.

Exhausted and disoriented, Rona nonetheless had a strange sense of homecoming. After all she was Ragna Enjudóttir, an Icelander just returned from the Faroes.

It seems like yesterday, Ragna mused. Late in the evening, she sat by the window overlooking the blue water of Eyjafjorður and the sunlit mountains beyond, with their brilliant snow-patches. *Yet that was 1990, more than quarter of a century ago.*

They had talked about settling in Reykjavik, but her initial impression of Iceland's second city was so favourable that she had said, 'Let's see what's on the market here in Akureyri.' On their very first day of house-hunting, they had found a perfect spot on Ketilsgata on which to build their ideal home.

Over twenty-five years of happiness. Not bad for a woman in her seventies whose early years gave no promise of such a thing. Sure, I've had anxious moments.

The inevitable bureaucratic and judicial trauma of legalising my status as an incomer, so that I could finally take Icelandic citizenship.

A few health issues along the way – thankfully, none life-threatening.

Isobel's difficult pregnancy when I couldn't go back to Orkney – thankfully Rolf was safely delivered at Balfour Hospital in 1992 and Isobel recovered well. He's a fine young man, my grandson. But this Amy Lister he's living with – she's Telford's granddaughter, for goodness' sake – I'm not so sure about that. Another link forged with one of the Argill clan was something I didn't see coming.

The 2008 collapse of Iceland's economy that reduced our assets by more than half. (At least the rogue bankers here got jail sentences. Their counterparts in Edinburgh and London escaped with rapped knuckles and a modest reduction in their bonuses – and some senior executives of bailed-out banks are now heading up new ones.) I need no reminding of that catastrophe; it was all the more disgusting to learn in April 2016 that our prime minister Sigmundur Gunnlaugsson had squirrelled away an undeclared pot of money in an overseas tax haven. If I'd been younger, I'd have joined the crowd outside Parliament banging pot lids and demanding his resignation.

But the biggest regret in my life is that all those years ago my translation of Gudrun's Saga was lost. I used to worry about it turning up – that blueprint for murder, some might consider it. Now what upsets me is that it's gone forever, along with the precious original in Icelandic.

Those stories of Yrsa, Åsa, Gunnhild, Ragnhild – <u>especially</u> Ragnhild – are so familiar, they're almost part of me. Could I recreate them from memory? Maybe, but the mind plays tricks. A rewrite would be little more than a work of fiction. What would be the point?

It was after eleven now. The sun was somewhere behind Hvammsfjall, away to the north, yet still the sky over the fjord was bright.

The slam of a car door. The click of a key in the front door lock. *Ari's home.* Ragna greeted him in the hallway with a kiss.

'You met Bárður, didn't you? You could have brought him over for something to eat. What brings him to Akureyri, now he's retired?'

'Still has a financial interest in the trawler.'

'How is he? And Aslaug?'

'He's put on weight since I last saw him. Aslaug's feeding him too well. Otherwise, they're both fine.'

'Good. Didn't you catch anything in the fjord today?'

'A few nice haddock and some whiting. Our freezer's already full so I gave them to Adda at the café in return for supper. What have you been up to, sweetheart?'

'Reliving my life with the aid of Vínbúðin's best Chilean red. Bring a glass and I'll pour you some.'

34
A STRANGE COMPULSION

G*UDRUN'S SAGA* HAD DISTRACTED Delia from the purpose of her stay in Aberdeenshire: the search for a gravestone linking her ancestor Jane Wilson to Agnes Cromar. Since her accidental meeting with Frank Jamieson in Torphins, she had not crossed any more cemeteries off her list. Today she would resume the search, beginning with two old churchyards on the south side of the Dee: Glentanar and Birse.

It was at Birse that she found what she was looking for. Though badly weathered and lichen-encrusted, one stone let her establish a common female-line ancestry for Agnes and Jane. She took a few photographs to record the inscription. Job done.

Driving back to Aberdeen she once again passed by the Gordonhall road-end. On impulse, she took a detour up to Faith Elliott's house for the second time that week. Perhaps, she thought, she could persuade Ms Elliott to let her revisit the walled garden, giving her an opening to ask about the white jequirity plant in the greenhouse.

But once again, Faith was not at home. The day was warm with only a gentle breeze. On foot, Delia headed up the hill from Gordonhall, lost in thought about the original, twelfth-century mistress of what was then *Gudrun Ha*. She had met a violent end at the hands of a pair of mercenaries doing the dirty work of Rognvald, Earl of Orkney, right here on the Hill of Fare at a place known as the Skairs. A strange compulsion made Delia seek out the rocky outcrop where Gudrun the giantess was murdered.

On the rough track she encountered an elderly man and his dog. However much he tugged at the leash, the animal refused to approach the Skairs. 'She always does this. I have to take a detour through the heather to get past these rocks.'

'Is there something that scares her?' Delia asked.

'Ghosts,' he replied bluntly. 'This place is haunted. A man died here fifty years ago in a shooting accident. Dominic Argill, it was. Lord something-or-other.'

'How weird,' Delia remarked, 'because he wasn't the only one. The lady of Gordonhall met her end here nearly *nine hundred* years ago.'

'I wouldn't know about her,' he said, 'but one's enough to be going on with! Enjoy the rest of this fine day.' He and his dog set off across the heather, making a wide semicircle around the Skairs to return to the track some distance away.

Ghosts, Delia thought. *What nonsense.* Yet it was uncanny that Rona's second husband should have been killed at the precise scene of Gudrun's murder.

She remained where she was, taking in the dramatic view and watching a soaring hawk scan the landscape for its next meal. Something unearthly touched her at that moment: an overwhelming sense that Rona Fay Swainson was alive and well. Without knowing exactly *why,* she knew she had to follow Gudrun back to her roots.

Returning to her car, she noted a black vehicle now parked nearby. Faith was home. As she manoeuvred past the BMW X6, Delia heard an irate shout, 'You've no right to be here, young lady! This is private property.' A middle-aged woman with cropped grey hair was marching towards her, shaking her fist.

Ever so briefly, Delia considered making a grovelling apology. Instead, she put her foot on the gas and roared off down the drive, throwing up a strafe of gravel and a cloud of dust that rendered Gordonhall and its owner invisible in the rear-view mirror.

No longer had she any interest in Faith Elliott or that white jequirity plant of hers. An exploration of the twelfth-century origins of Gudrun, the *first* recorded owner of these lands, was now her obsession, for that would lead her to Rona.

That evening she called Frank Jamieson.

'What do you think about the latest on the "muesli mystery"?' he asked immediately.

Puzzled, she replied, 'I haven't been keeping up with the news.'

'Don't you watch television? Or pick up a newspaper sometimes? Fairfield's Cereals …'

Delia interrupted. 'Sure, the company owned by Rona's son. They've had an attack, something to do with product tampering, right? Reminded me of the Tylenol murders years ago in Chicago.'

'It's been announced that a man was charged yesterday. He's from Glasgow; Timothy Heston's his name. The police haven't given much detail – nothing about what poison he used or anything like that. But we know he writes a blog under the pseudonym Toff Hammer. Already the red-tops seem to think it's an open-and-shut case.'

'Red-tops?'

'Tabloid newspapers.'

'Oh. So do *you* think they've got their man?'

'Looks like it. He just posted an article in his blog saying Donald Swainson, the Earl of Fairfield, has no right to own the company and deserves all that's coming to him. It goes back to the Bracklinn affair of the 1960s. He says Rona Fay Swainson murdered or conspired to murder three successive heirs to the Bracklinn title and fortune.'

'Two brothers and their nephew, right? A replay of the Ragnhild story.'

'Exactly. It's still online. Google "Toff Hammer". I think you'll find he's got a point. And he doesn't even have the evidence *we've* got. *Gudrun's Saga.*'

'Frank, it's not evidence, and you know it. A woman who kills three men wouldn't write a story incriminating herself – that would be crazy! Rona Fay simply translated an old book with a different take on the story of Ragnhild.'

'Translated? Or made up?'

'Either way, she doesn't paint Ragnhild half as black as she was in the *Orkneyinga Saga*.'

'Maybe that was her whole idea. To make Ragnhild, therefore herself, seem less culpable. Or else it's a sick joke. Anyway, to come back to Fairfield's, if you're still trying to track down Rona, you might want to avoid Faith Elliott or Donald Swainson while they've got this muesli matter on their plate. So to speak.'

'Frank, I'm not going near Faith again, nor do I plan to speak to Donald. I'll find Rona through her writing. Gudrun's the key. Tomorrow I'm setting off for *Hjalmundsdal* – the Strath of Kildonan – where she and her mother lived before she came to Gordonhall.'

'You think Rona is there?'

'I don't know. But I've a feeling I'll learn more pretty soon.'

Delia could not explain the genesis of this 'feeling', only that the idea had come to her while she vacantly watched a circling, swooping hawk from that rocky slope of the Hill of Fare where Gudrun had met her end.

As Frank had suggested, she googled 'Toff Hammer', instantly finding the blog written by a man now charged with multiple counts of murder. Distasteful though she might find the ravings of a mad killer, Delia had to read his two pieces about the Bracklinn affair.

My God! Accusing Rona of masterminding the killing of three Bracklinn heirs is one thing ... but to blame her for engineering the death of her own father as a faked suicide? I'm not buying that.

Delia had to admit there was a certain logic – a slightly warped logic, perhaps – to Toff Hammer's theory that Rona had got away with murder in the deaths of Antony and Dominic Argill and the supposed death of Fergus Argill-Hawke. Yet what of his main thesis? That Rona had got off scot-free because she was a 'toff', a member of a privileged elite? It didn't ring true. *That* was what marked Toff Hammer, alias Tim Heston, as a nut job. The kind of nut job that might devise an elaborate plot to kill innocent people, just to make Rona's son Donald pay for her crimes.

Her mind in turmoil, Delia logged out of her computer, took a shower and packed ready for an early departure next morning. The Strath of Kildonan beckoned. Tired though she was, sleep eluded her. At midnight she was once again glued to her laptop screen, engrossed in an earlier Toff Hammer blog. Its title had jumped out at her, making her heart skip a beat.

A DUKE'S GREED FOR THE GOLD OF KILDONAN

by Toff Hammer

Regular readers: you will be familiar with the wretched history of the Highland Clearances and the central part played by the toffs of Dunrobin – Earls and Countesses, Dukes and Duchesses of Sutherland – in that episode of ethnic cleansing.

You might be excused for thinking that, after the murderous excesses of Elizabeth the 19th Countess and her husband the 1st Duke, the family would lie low for a generation or two. No point, you might think, in attracting <u>more</u> bad press.

But you'd be wrong. Number one, the toff-toadying newspapers of the day thought the Clearances were a jolly good thing. (Probably still do, though to say so would be a bit like denying the Holocaust.) Number two, what's bred in the bone *comes out in the flesh. The Sutherlands just couldn't resist taking <u>another</u> swipe at the few peasants who had survived their pogrom.*

Let me take you by the hand and lead you through the Strath of Kildonan, a wild and beautiful valley through which the River Ullie or Helmsdale tumbles to the sea. The strath was – still is – 'owned' by the toffs of Dunrobin in violation of the ancient udal system of land tenure in this once-Norse land. In 1819 the 19th Countess had her henchmen drive the people down from their crofts and pastures to what was effectively a refugee encampment in the village of Helmsdale at the mouth of the river. From a population of about 2000 only three families were spared. A few of the dispossessed were able to make a living in Helmsdale, mainly by fishing, but many left to face an uncertain future in the prairies of Manitoba.

Occasional finds of tiny flecks of gold in the Strath of Kildonan had been recorded since the sixteenth century, including a nugget retrieved from the river in 1818 that was large enough to make a ring. Somehow that ring found its way into the hands of the ever-acquisitive 1st Duke of Sutherland; it is still in the family's possession. The discovery in 1869 of the precious metal in two tributary burns led to a short-lived Gold Rush; the 300 or so prospectors who came in a vain search for riches left soon afterwards.

By 1886 the former crofters and their descendants in Helmsdale were starving and destitute because of a downturn in the fishing industry. With abject submissiveness they sought the 3rd Duke's permission to return to the strath to prospect for gold:

> *To His Grace the Duke of Sutherland:*
> *[This] petition ... humbly sheweth –*

That ... the present is here a time of great depression, and that many families are suffering severely from the want of the necessaries of life,

That ... it would be a ready means of giving a large measure of relief to a great many persons if they were allowed to try what gold they might get in the burns and adjacent places in the Strath of Kildonan,

That ... if [this petition] would be granted those having the liberty would be willing to bind themselves to any conditions thought necessary ...,

Trusting that Your Grace will take these premises into kind consideration, that the desired liberty may soon be granted, and that so a strong feeling of relief, of hope, and of grateful satisfaction may be spread throughout this large community, your petitioners now humbly submit their petition, and earnestly pray that their prayer may be granted.

Those words fell on deaf ears, just like a letter submitted earlier the same year to the petitioners' representative in Parliament, who was none other than the 3rd Duke's noble son and heir the Marquess of Stafford. In effect, the MP's reply was, 'My father is abroad just now and is unavailable to consider your request.'

(Stafford had been elected in 1874 in succession to his uncle, the foppish Lord Ronald Charles Sutherland-Leveson-Gower. Despite the Sutherlands' best efforts to delete Uncle Ron from history, his fame has persisted: having taken a young journalist, Frank

Hird, as his lover, he adopted him as his son. Oscar Wilde took him as the model for Lord Harry Wotton, an upper-class dandy in his only novel The Picture of Dorian Gray.*)*

On what important business abroad was the 3rd Duke engaged that precluded him from being distracted by a bunch of starving tenants back home? A visit to his family's awful 'museum' in the Dunrobin Castle grounds will swiftly answer that question. With their obscene wealth the Sutherlands made the world their playground. Rare animals were shot with gay abandon in Africa and India to provide carcasses for stuffing. Ethnic treasures from exotic lands were 'bought' or stolen to complement a collection of Pictish stones and artefacts from closer to home.

Stafford, meanwhile, finally began to feel the cold draught of unpopularity for his failure as an MP to do anything to relieve his constituents' hardship. In the general election of 1886 he stood down, freeing his parliamentary seat for a man who pledged to improve the crofters' lot.

What conceivable adverse effect could granting the 1886 petition have had on the Duke of Sutherland? Only the remote possibility that the crofters might have been successful in finding significant amounts of gold, thereby depleting the reserves that he believed were his family's birthright.

Recently (2015) in a much-publicised fit of generosity, the Sutherlands offered to sell 3,000 acres of land, even including mineral rights, to the Helmsdale community. Toff Hammer's verdict: too little, too late.

Delia had to admit to a sneaking admiration for the outspoken Toff Hammer. The world needed to know about the gross injustices and crimes perpetrated by the British upper class, the Dukes and Duchesses of Sutherland and the Earls and Countesses of Fairfield alike.

But there was no excuse for killing innocent people. Toff Hammer, she was sure, would deserve everything that was coming to him.

35
ABRIN, APPARENTLY

SEEN THROUGH HER PICTURE window, Ragna's colourful garden had turned monochrome in the eerie dim of the midsummer night. Beyond it, the Hvammsfjall ridge loomed dark against a still luminous sky streaked with pink clouds. Ari refilled her wine glass then poured what remained of the bottle into his tumbler.

'Donny rang when I was out on the fjord,' he said.

'Did he? I wanted to call him this evening, but thought he'd be too tied up with the muesli recall. How's it looking? Still pretty bad?'

'He sounded a bit more positive. Upbeat. Had a meeting yesterday with Faith.'

'In Dundee?'

'No, she flew up to Kirkwall. Seems they've worked out a plan to restart production with new packaging.'

'I wouldn't trust her as far as I could throw her. If it's *her* plan, Donny had better watch out.'

'You're a bit hard on the Elliotts.'

The wine had loosened Ragna's tongue, putting words into the air she might otherwise have kept to herself. 'Hard, Ari? I don't think so. It started with Faith's father ...'

'Telford, yes, who made a feeble attempt to take Donny's inheritance away. That was nearly fifty years ago, my darling. He admitted he was wrong and from then on did nothing but good for Fairfield's, right up until he died in that crash.'

'He set fire to Gordonhall, don't forget. Destroyed that priceless collection of Scandinavian literature, *Gudrun's Saga* included. Not to mention burning his cousin Fergus to death and disposing of his remains.'

'Ragna, sweetheart, you know that's pure conjecture.'

Ignoring his comment, she carried on. 'Faith built that monstrosity of a house on the precise scene of her father's crime.'

'Monstrosity? You've never been to Gordonhall since the fire. Never seen the new building.'

'There are pictures of it online.'

'So you don't trust her because she has an ugly house.'

Ragna ignored the twinkle in Ari's eye. 'I'm telling you, she'll stop at nothing to wrest control of Fairfield's Cereals out of Donny's hands.'

'Donny says she's come up with a thorough rebranding, proposes the Fairfield's label should go as it's tainted by the poisoning scandal. She's already tested a new name through focus groups. Caledonian Hills, I think Donny said it would be.'

'See what I mean? Next she'll try to bring that son of hers into the operation.'

'Oscar? He has zero interest in the business. Has too much fun on his intrepid adventures around the world. Incidentally, he's going to be visiting Rolf and Amy in Kirkwall soon, so Donny told me.'

'What's taking him to Orkney this time? Diving among the wrecks in Scapa Flow?'

'He wants to be the first person to climb the Old Man of Hoy with a set of bagpipes, and play them on the summit.'

She looked into his eyes, convinced he was pulling her leg. Simultaneously they burst into laughter.

'Seriously,' he said, unable to keep the grin off his face. 'Ask Donny when you speak to him.'

'Did he say anything about the bastard who wrote all those lies about me? Toff Hammer? They said on the BBC he's still being held by the police.'

'Just that he looks guilty as sin. Donny and Faith are pretty much agreed on that, too.'

'As are the British papers, from what I can gather. You should see what the *Mail Online* has to say about him. Funny thing is, I can't find anything on the Internet about the poison he used. Just a load of speculation. Have the police told Donny what it was?'

'Abrin, apparently. It comes from a bean of some kind.'

In their painstaking search of Tim Heston's chaotic tenement flat, forensic investigators were looking first and foremost for any evidence of abrin or of the jequirity plant from which the toxin is obtained. Even the contents of his vacuum cleaner bag were minutely examined for fragments of leaf, stem or flower – not that he did much housework, by all appearances. Microscopic pieces of marijuana were everywhere (that was no surprise) but of jequirity there was not a trace.

On the desk where Heston had pounded out his Toff Hammer blog was a well-thumbed red-jacketed Chambers dictionary sprouting Post-it markers. A pair of hands in blue surgical gloves was now fingering each of the marked pages. The Post-it nearest the front opened the book at the very location of the following entry:

> **ā'brin** *n* a poisonous protein contained in the seeds of the jequirity (*Abrus precatorius*).

Back at Maryhill police station Heston was asked, 'What was of interest to you on page 5 of the Chambers dictionary?' He was shown the book but not allowed to touch it.

'I don't remember,' Heston replied, 'any more than I remember the reason I stuck all those other Post-its on. How many are there? Twenty? Thirty?'

'Maybe we'll come to those,' his interrogator said patiently. 'For now, I'm interested in page 5.'

'Let me see,' Heston said, looking more closely. 'It's a fascinating page, for sure. You know what *abraxas* means? How about *abranchiate* or *abricock*? And by the way, do you realise this book was examined by your forensic officers *absente reo*? That means "in the absence of the accused", in case you didn't know. Read it for yourself.'

'Do you admit you marked that page?'

'Yes.'

'The one that carries a definition for abrin?'

'And at least fifty other words.'

'Yes or no?'

'Yes.'

'Why did you mark it?'

'I don't know. Maybe I wanted to use the word *abraxas* but had to check its meaning. Not that *you* would understand why intelligent people use dictionaries,' Heston added with a sneer.

'Traces of exotic plant species are in your Hoover bag.'

'Not true.'

'You deny having grown exotic plants in your flat?'

'No, I deny having a Hoover. My vacuum cleaner is a Henry. Check *Hoover* in that dictionary. I think you'll find it's a trademark.'

The solicitor sitting beside him whispered something in his ear.

'I'll antagonise him if I like,' Heston said. 'He's antagonising me.'

It was the solicitor's turn to speak. 'If all you have against my client is this dictionary and the contents of his Hoover bag ...'

'Henry,' the client said.

'... Henry bag, I think we're done here.'

'Not until I have an explanation for the exotic plants.'

'Provide me a list of the plant species you have identified in the Hoo ... in the Henry bag, and I'm sure my client will be happy to explain.'

'Marijuana, for one.'

'Ah yes.' Heston's tone was world-weary. '*Cannabis sativa.* I already confessed to growing small quantities of that "exotic plant" for my own use. But if you were to search a cross-section of upmarket homes in Bearsden, say, I think you'd find it's not as "exotic" as you're making out. And by the way, talking of exotic plants, *abricock* is just another word for apricot. Maybe Henry had some *abricock* divots in his bag. I'm a messy eater. Charge me with that, if you must.'

'Inspector,' the solicitor interjected, 'did you or did you not find *Abrus precatorius*, otherwise known as jequirity, in my client's vacuum cleaner or anywhere else in his flat?'

'This interview is terminated at 19:02.'

Faith Elliott had learned something important from her conversation in Orkney with Donald Swainson. The police had confirmed to him the nature of the poison used by the Avenger – the 'muesli murderer' of the tabloid headlines – though they still had not divulged it to the media. Pity they were all so slow on the uptake; the clue was obvious in her Twitter alias, @jequirityjo!

It was only a matter of time now before the information would leak and everybody would be on the look-out for jequirity. She strode purposefully to her greenhouse, where she gathered four or five potted plants and carried them outside. With a hot fire going in a perforated oil drum, she threw the plants in one by one, pots, soil and all. The smoke smelled curiously of refried beans until the more acrid stench of burning plastic took over. She stood by the fire watching and poking until nothing but ash remained.

Next she thoroughly swept, then hosed, the area of the greenhouse where the jequirity had been. Carefully she filled the gaps with some innocuous commonplace species. To admire her handiwork, she walked around the outside perimeter and looked in. The newly-arranged pot-plants had to look long-established there. The Avenger was nothing if not thorough in covering her tracks.

Just as she quietly congratulated herself, something struck her as not quite right. Puzzling. Worrying.

There were footprints in the soil. Smaller than her own. A woman's, she guessed – maybe even a child's. Whose?

Then she remembered. A couple of days before, as she arrived home from her trip to Orkney, a car had pulled out of the Gordonhall driveway. She had glimpsed the driver, a young woman with shoulder-length red hair. Yesterday, what might have been the same car was in front of the house when she returned from Banchory. It took off at such a speed when she approached that she had no chance to check the make and model or the registration plate. One of those identikit small hatchbacks, she thought. A Corsa, maybe, or a Polo or Fiesta, in a nondescript colour.

What had that redhead seen? Might she have taken photographs of the jequirity through the glass?

Damn! The Avenger's first slip. Well, as long as the police had the Toff Hammer guy as their prime suspect she had nothing to worry about.

Or had she?

36
STRATH OF KILDONAN

IT WAS A NEW VOYAGE OF discovery, except that Delia had selected a familiar stopping-off point for her first night as she drove north. Mrs MacNeil's B&B in Beauly, which she remembered fondly for its home comforts and delicious food.* It was a little off her route to the Strath of Kildonan, but would be worth the detour.

On the way, she made only one quick stop to see Sueno's Stone at Forres. According to *Gudrun's Saga*, this was where Sweyn Asleifsson handed over his hostage, Earl Paul of Orkney, to the men who would transport him to the central Highlands never to be heard of again. Just what the dastardly Earl Rognvald wanted. No wonder he hired Sweyn again, to dispose of Gudrun's mother Frákork, which he did with characteristic brutality, stealing her gold into the bargain.

Mrs MacNeil's welcome was warm and friendly. 'Where is it you're headed on this trip, Delia?' she asked. 'If I mind right, it was Strathconon last time.'

'Different strath,' Delia replied. 'The Strath of Kildonan. You know it?'

'Oh aye. Sad place.'

'Yes, I've just been reading about the Clearances. Tragic – so cruel.'

Mrs MacNeil opened her mouth as if to give an opinion, but thought better of it. Instead she said, 'On your way up there, you

---

* Delia stayed here while on a field trip for NEPA, her former employer (see *Scotch and Water, Incomers* Book 2).

should stop at Dunrobin Castle. It's the family seat of the Dukes of Sutherland.'

'And does Dunrobin tell the story of the Clearances?'

'Go and decide for yourself.' Her expression softened. 'Now, for dinner tonight, I have ...'

'Mrs MacNeil, whatever you have, I know it will be superb. Surprise me. Seven o'clock?'

Next morning, Delia was on the road by 9:30, heading north through Dingwall to join the A9 by the Dornoch Firth. Though a haze lay over the calm water, she could discern the angular shapes of oil rigs in the distance ... and was that a cruise ship making its way to the unlikely port destination of Invergordon?

When she reached Golspie, she *would* visit Dunrobin Castle as Mrs MacNeil had urged her. The stately home built by the family who essentially owned one of Scotland's largest counties and had so callously driven its people down to the sea to emigrate or starve. But why had the landlady been so reluctant to speak of that episode? Could it be that after almost two hundred years there lingered a kind of survivors' guilt? A feeling among descendants of those who somehow escaped the horrors of the Clearances that they were beneficiaries? Or was she just unwilling to admit the bitterness she and many others must still harbour towards the Sutherlands?

It began to make more sense once Delia actually set eyes on the castle.

Dunrobin's sheer scale and the ornateness of its architecture took her breath away. This was ostentatious wealth taken to an appalling extreme. Toff Hammer's words came to her mind:

> *No visitor to Dunrobin Castle who knows anything of the odious family whose seat it is, can fail to see it as an obscenity, a vulgar blot on the landscape of Sutherland.*

A busload of American tourists were clearly thrilled by the splendour of the place. 'Aren't you curious as to how this wealth was created?' Delia wanted to shout. But she kept her silence. And her distance; she would *hate* anyone to think she was one of *them*.

In room after room, walls groaned under the weight of portraits of Dukes, Duchesses, Earls, Countesses and minor Lords and Ladies of the Sutherland-Leveson-Gower nobility. Eventually she came face-to-face with the 19th Countess of Sutherland. There she was, the beautiful Elizabeth Leveson-Gower *née* Gordon, 1765–1839, smiling with abstract condescension from the oil on canvas, the chief architect of the Sutherland Clearances along with her shallow-browed husband the Marquess of Stafford.

No acknowledgement of the Leveson-Gowers' reign of terror was evident. It was as if nothing untoward had happened. Thrusting the omission into even sharper relief was a display of grovelling testimonials from 'grateful' tenantry addressed to later members of the dynasty.

Delia had yet to read another of Toff Hammer's tirades:

> *Even the 19th Countess herself found her displaced tenants, making such meagre living as they could from the unfamiliar seashore, to be 'unfailingly obsequious'. Good for them. On her arrival in Sutherland in 1820 she was delighted to find the 'hoped-for improvement' in place, with the straths 'entirely cleared'. Dunrobin was graced with 'large fat roses' in its flowerbeds, and gardens with strawberries, apples and greengages of richer flavour than any available in London. Wasn't that nice!*
>
> *Seven years later, Elizabeth was greeted at Dunrobin by her factors and parish ministers, who with some fanfare presented her with a gift of ornaments 'in the name of the tenantry' who had been*

'invited' to subscribe. In the absence of the subscribers themselves, she did not feel it incumbent upon her to pay them any compliments in return.

As a prominent pillar of the British establishment, it was not sufficient for her husband merely to be the richest man in the kingdom. In 1833 even more glory came his way when the king magnanimously created the Duchy of Sutherland for him, making Elizabeth a duchess as well as countess in her own right.

Who was the monarch who laid such honour on such undeserving shoulders? The reprehensible (even by the standards of his predecessors) William IV, last of the Hanoverian kings. Notorious for his anti-abolitionist views, he made known his appreciation of the Clearances by remarking that slaves in Britain's Caribbean colonies were 'fortunate' to enjoy a better life than the now-dispossessed Highlanders. Did he mean it would be a mistake to emancipate those slaves? Or that it would be a kindness to transport the population of Sutherland to provide forced labour in the sugarcane plantations of the West Indies? Either way, William doesn't exactly come up smelling of roses like those Dunrobin flowerbeds.

The newly-ennobled duke did not get long to enjoy his elevated status, for he died the same year. Yet, as Delia learned at Dunrobin, the honours kept coming for him. A colossal statue of the 1st Duke of Sutherland, facing the sea with his back to the land he had depopulated, was installed on a prominent hill overlooking the town of Golspie. Despite repeated demands for its demolition, it was still standing almost two centuries later.

'Melvich 40,' the sign indicated. The A897 led inland from Helmsdale into the Strath of Kildonan, scene of the short-lived gold rush, and before that the vicious expulsion of its crofters. Much, much earlier, the strath was the setting for the murder of Gudrun's mother Frákork at the bidding of Earl Rognvald of Orkney. Immediately outside Helmsdale village, the road abruptly narrowed to a single track, which continued with occasional passing places.

I have no idea what I'm looking for here, Delia thought. Yet the notion that had come to her at the Skairs above Gordonhall was as compelling as ever. If she traced Gudrun's life back from its end at the Skairs to its beginning in *Hjalmundsdal* – translated by Rona Fay Swainson as the Strath of Kildonan – she would *somehow* be led to Rona.

About six miles on she was forced to pull into a passing place while a flock of sheep was driven past her on the road. Turning off the engine, she consulted her Ordnance Survey map. Below her ran the Helmsdale River; on the other side was the railway to Wick and Thurso, and a forest plantation sloping part-way up to a rocky ridge. Beyond lay the head of Glen Loth.

Glen Loth? Was there not a mention of it in *Gudrun's Saga*? On her computer Delia opened the document file containing her scanned copy of Rona Fay Swainson's typescript and tabbed to the chapter titled *OF THE KIN OF GUDRUN LJOTSDOTTIR.* Sure enough, Rona had commented that Glen Loth was the valley next to Hjalmundsdal named after Ljot, Frákork's father-in-law. So the home of Frákork herself could have been very close to here.

Delia was startled by a tap on the glass. An elderly man with white hair and well-groomed beard was looking in. She lowered the driver's side window.

'You look as if you're lost. Can I help you?' From his accent, and even his trim appearance, Delia assumed he was a foreigner.

'Thank you, but I know exactly where I am. I recently read one of the old Norse sagas and I'm trying to pinpoint where the home of one of the characters might have been.'

'Really?' the rambler said, a sudden sparkle in his eye. 'Would you believe I'm actually Norwegian myself? Name's Lars. My wife is up ahead somewhere with the car. I originally came to Scotland to work in the oil business. Long since retired, of course.'

'I'm Delia. And I'm from Chicago.'

'Chicago, eh? Yet you're interested in Scottish history.'

'I know. Odd, isn't it?' *You've no idea*, Delia thought. *I feel like I've lived through Scotland's Bronze Age, Iron Age, the coming of the Angles and the Norse. All those incomers, and I'm an incomer myself.* She stepped out of the car to continue the conversation.

'The sagas have always fascinated me,' Lars said, 'the *Orkneyinga Saga*, in particular.'

'Then you may have heard of Frákork.'

'It's *her* home you're looking for? Frákork came from Kildonan?'

'Apparently, yes.'

'That I didn't know. What I do remember is a story about her making a poisoned garment for one of the Earls of Orkney.'

'Yes,' Delia said, that tale still fresh in her mind. 'But the wrong Earl, her nephew, put it on and died the same night.'

Lars warmed to the theme. 'A similar thing happened much later, very close to here, at Helmsdale. The earl in question that time was an Earl of Sutherland.'

'Is this about the Clearances?'

'No, long before the Clearances. It would have been the sixteenth century, I suppose, the time of Mary, Queen of Scots. The Earl and Countess were touring their vast domain and came to Helmsdale Castle to spend the night. It was the home of an aunt of the earl's, by the name of Isobel Sinclair. Now Isobel had an ambition for her son to inherit the earldom, so to pave the way she gave her noble guests a poisoned drink.'

'I think I know what's coming.'

'You can probably guess. Both Isobel's intended victims died, but the son she hoped would succeed to the title also drank the poison and succumbed.'

'Frákork cast a long shadow,' Delia remarked. Only much later would she learn *how* long. For a drama was playing out in Orkney at that very moment, in another strange echo of the tale of Frákork.

Lars set off at a brisk pace, and soon Delia was on the road again, continuing up the single-track A897 through the lonely strath. Still she had no idea how this trip was going to lead her to Rona Fay Swainson. The firm conviction that it would defied rational analysis. *Best not to question it.*

Once more she encountered Lars, on a narrow bridge gazing down over the parapet at the water below. He looked up at her approach, and waved her to stop.

'This is the Suisgill Burn,' he told her. 'One of the streams that attracted prospectors in the nineteenth century.'

'And the evicted crofters were refused permission to return here to pan for gold, when they were starving in Helmsdale?'

'I believe so, yes.'

'Given what the Sutherlands did just a few years earlier, I suppose it was very much in character.'

'You've obviously read about their part in the Clearances.'

'Yes. In fact, I visited Dunrobin Castle this morning. Not my favourite people.'

'Nor mine, Delia. Not at all. But, you know, the crofters who wanted to prospect for gold in Kildonan might have found nothing.'

'At least they could have hoped. After all, a thousand years ago Frákork had a hoard of Kildonan gold. Sweyn Asleifsson stole it when he burned her home and killed her.'

'Really?' Lars said. 'Is that in the *Orkneyinga Saga*?'

'Maybe not. I read it in *Gudrun's Saga*.'

'*Which* saga? I'm not familiar with that one.'

'*Gudrun's Saga*, based on tales told by Frákork's daughter Gudrun. According to her, Frákork was quite wealthy as a result of Kildonan gold.'

A cry from the bank of the burn made Delia and Lars look round. An attractive woman with straight grey hair in a neat bob waved to them. Despite her walking-stick she was having little difficulty in getting around on the rough ground by the burn. Lars's wife, obviously.

'Come up here, darling,' he called to her.

'I'm Delia Cobb,' the young American said, holding out her hand. 'Your husband and I were discussing something I've been reading about a woman who amassed a large quantity of gold from her land here in the Strath of Kildonan. It was written by one of her descendants, Rona Fay Swainson. She claims it's a translation of a Norse saga. *Gudrun's Saga*, it's called.'

The woman turned pale with shock and grabbed her husband's arm to steady herself. 'Rona Swainson was my best friend,' she said. 'My name is Lidia.'

37
HAGGIS PAKORA

COMING TO ORKNEY TO SEE his cousin Amy was always a pleasure, though Oscar had to admit that ninety percent of the fun was sharing a boys' night out with her partner Rolf. Tonight the two of them would knock back a few pints in one of Kirkwall's seedier pubs, heckle the resident musician and tell bad jokes. Amy was happy not to join them; she had paperwork from the shop to catch up with, plus *X-Files* was on the telly.

'You'll come to Hoy with me on Tuesday, Rolfie, right?' Oscar asked his host as they walked into town.

'Sure! Just don't expect me to climb that rock with you. Where the hell did you get the idea to take bagpipes with you? I didn't even know you played.'

'I'll give you my rendition of *Bonnie Gallowa'* when we get back to the house tonight. Wake Amy up.'

'Don't you dare, Osc! Seriously, have you been taking lessons?'

'Nah. I was in the school pipe band.'

'Won't you have enough to carry up the Old Man with your ropes and carabiners and what-have-you? Good thing it's not the piano you learned.'

In the pub, the two men soon gathered a small crowd around them, as Oscar regaled his audience with tales of earlier exploits and plans for new ones, including the imminent scaling of the Old Man of Hoy. By ten o'clock, Rolf was ready to call it a night, and with some difficulty managed to prise his companion away and head out into the street.

'I'm starving,' Oscar announced. What can we get to eat this time of night in Kirkwall?'

'Fish and chips. That's about it, probably.' Rolf steered a slightly unsteady Oscar in the right direction, and they ordered two haddock suppers. While these were frying Oscar noticed an item on the menu that took his fancy and ordered two.

'Haggis pakora?' Rolf questioned his friend's wisdom in ordering such a thing along with haddock and chips. 'Not for me, thanks.'

'No problem, Rolfie, I'll eat two.' Then, to the server, 'Give us some extra chili sauce on those, will you, darling?'

On the walk home, Oscar scoffed the lot, while the more cautious Rolf ate his fish and only some of his chips. Barely had they reached the house before Oscar was complaining of heartburn.

Declining Amy's offer of freshly-brewed coffee, he grimaced and placed his hand on his abdomen. 'This indigestion's killing me. Shoulda known haggis pakora and beer don't mix. You got bicarb or anything?'

'I'll get you some.' Amy turned to Rolf. 'Hey, why don't you give Oscar one of your pills?'

Rolf's prescription medication for the condition he had had since the age of sixteen was lansoprazole, a proton pump inhibitor in the form of large white capsules. He directed Oscar to a small bottle of them in his bathroom cabinet. 'One's all it takes. You'll feel better in half an hour.'

Sure enough, Oscar was much more comfortable by the time his host and hostess announced they were retiring for the night. They had early deliveries to the shop in the morning. 'I'll sit up for a while, if that's okay,' Oscar said. 'Think there's snooker on TV.'

When Amy came yawning out of the bedroom next morning, she found the television was still on, but Oscar was nowhere to be seen. Worried, she tapped on the guest room door. Her knocking was greeted only by silence. Gingerly she peeped in, to find the bed apparently unslept-in and no evidence of their guest. However, the bathroom door was closed and she could hear the extractor fan running.

'Do you think he's okay?' she asked Rolf as they began breakfast. 'I don't think he ever went to bed last night.'

'Give the guy some space, honey. He's spread up his bed, now he's having a crap, just let him be. So what, if he forgot to switch off the TV? It's no big deal.'

But after fifteen minutes, with still no sign of Oscar, Rolf made for the hall bathroom. The door was locked from the inside. 'Oscar!' he yelled. 'Are you all right?' *He's got up during the night and fallen asleep on the pot, I bet.* 'OSCAR! Answer me, dammit!'

No response. Becoming slightly alarmed, Rolf shouted, 'Okay, pal. You've had your fun, joke over. Just say something – anything. I'll give you five seconds.' He pressed his ear to the door, counted out loud, and waited. Still nothing.

Amy stood shivering beside him. 'God, what do we do now? Knock down the door?'

'The lock opens from the outside if we turn this little catch.' Rolf grabbed a screwdriver from the kitchen drawer. 'Oscar! I'm coming in!'

With a click the bathroom door unlocked, but Rolf could only open it a crack. Something was blocking it, something ominously heavy. Putting his shoulder to the door he pushed it far enough to be able to get his head in.

Unprepared for the rancid odour of vomit that met him full-on, he turned away for a deep breath before putting his shoulder against the door to give it another shove. Before he even caught a glimpse of Oscar, he realised what the dead weight had to be.

Recoiling, he stepped back into the hall. Amy made to go past him into the bathroom but he caught her arm. 'Don't go in.

It's bad. Really, you don't want to see … just call an ambulance.
Now!'

Around nine, Faith Elliott was in her BMW X6 on the Slug road
between Banchory and Stonehaven, heading for Fairfield's
Dundee plant and offices, when she got the call on her mobile.

'It's Amy, Aunt Faith. I'm afraid Oscar's in hospital.'

'What? Where? What's the matter with him?'

'He's in Balfour Hospital, here in Kirkwall. We don't know
what's wrong with him yet. He had a bad attack of indigestion
last night, but seemed to be getting over it when Rolf and I went
to bed. This morning we found him unconscious. He'd vomited
up some blood.'

Faith had heard enough to know immediately what had
happened. That idiot Rolf had given Oscar one of his capsules,
the very one she had refilled with ground jequirity and returned
to the bottle in the bathroom cabinet on her recent visit to
Orkney. The poison intended for Rolf had instead been
swallowed by Oscar.

'Are you still there, Aunt Faith?'

'Yes, Amy. Excuse me, it's a bit of a shock. What are the
doctors saying? Is he going to be okay?' Then, before Amy could
answer, 'What was Oscar doing up there anyway? He never told
me he was coming to see you.'

'He was planning to climb the Old Man of Hoy.'

'In God's name! He's got a death-wish, you know that?'

Amy was thinking more of Oscar's immediate health than of
the physical danger he would face on Britain's biggest sea-stack.
'It's food-poisoning, I'm sure. He'll get over it fast.'

'What had you given him to eat?'

'Me? Nothing. He'd had something in the airport before he
got on the plane yesterday. After he arrived he and Rolf went
into town. Apparently Oscar had a couple of haggis pakoras
from a chip shop. A fish supper too. And a few pints of beer.

Rolf gave him one of his lansoprazole pills, between ten and eleven last night.'

I knew it. 'Listen, Amy, best say nothing about the pill to the doctors. Rolf could be in a lot of trouble for giving his prescription medicine to someone else. In any case, it's obviously the rubbish Oscar ate, the haggis thing or whatever, that's knocked him for six. They need to close down that fucking chip shop.'

'But, Aunt Faith, surely it's better to tell the doctors everything. Maybe Oscar had a bad reaction to the medicine.'

'No, it wouldn't be that. Look, I'm coming straight up to Orkney. Until I get there, keep quiet about the lansoprazole. For your own sake, and Rolf's. Oscar's too – it'll just send the doctors off on the wrong track if they drop the focus on the chip shop. Indians, I suppose.'

Amy thought she'd misheard Faith's *non sequitur*. 'Say that again?'

'The chippy. Probably run by Indians. Or Pakis. Damned incomers, no idea about food hygiene.'

'Actually, I think they're from Peterhead. They're called Lawson.'

'Whatever. Not a word, mind! I'll call you back once I know what flight I'm on.'

'He has all the symptoms of abrin poisoning,' the young doctor said on the phone to the consultant, who was at that moment on his boat in the Loch of Harray, focusing on a trout he had just hooked.

'You think we've got a muesli murder in Orkney?'

'Could be, sir, though the patient just flew here yesterday. He might have had previous exposure to the poison.'

'Where did he come in from?'

The junior doctor looked at his notes. 'He boarded his plane in Glasgow. Ate something in the airport. Other than that, all he's consumed has been beer, fish and chips, and ... er ... haggis pakora.'

'Beer, eh? What often accompanies beer?'

'I dunno. Cheese and onion crisps?'

'Nuts. Easy to slip a jequirity seed into a bowl of peanuts. Have the police been informed?'

'I wanted to talk to you first, sir.'

'Call them. And get a blood sample off to Aberdeen to confirm your abrin theory. I'll be there in an hour.' *But first, I'm going to land this trout.*

The Avenger's mind was racing as she sat on the plane for the short flight from Aberdeen to Kirkwall.

How could such a perfect plan have unravelled in this way? What were the odds? She had put just one doctored capsule among Rolf's supply, even shaking up the bottle so that the lethal one wasn't sitting on top.

And Oscar. Her own son. What had possessed him to go to Orkney precisely at this time? And stay with Amy and Rolf. And get heartburn. And let himself be persuaded to take Rolf's medication. *The very capsule she had refilled with jequirity.* It was as if events were being steered by an Unseen Hand.

The Avenger was jittery. *She* was the one in control. Had to be. Otherwise unpredictable shit like this would happen.

Surely Oscar would survive this, big strapping lad that he is. Not a white-faced runt like Rolf Swainson. One capsule, with the abrin content of a single jequirity seed, would have been the end of *him*. But Oscar, no. He would pull through.

Wouldn't he?

On the Tuesday that Oscar should have been on the Old Man, he was unconscious in an intensive-care bed in Balfour Hospital. Results from the Aberdeen lab had confirmed abrin ingestion.

Though denied access to his bedside, his mother spent most of the day at the hospital awaiting developments. A police officer came to ask questions.

'You are a director of Fairfield's Cereals, Ms Elliott, is that correct?'

'Yes.'

'The company that's been hit by a series of tampering cases?'

'As you well know, officer, yes. The "muesli murderer" is in custody, in Glasgow if I'm not mistaken.'

'We do indeed have a suspect who has been charged in connection with those offences, as the media have reported. Is there any reason that you know of why he, or anyone else, might wish to harm you or your family?'

'He's laid it out for all to see in his blog, hasn't he? Toff Hammer, or whatever he calls himself? It wasn't enough just to kill our business – which he's done, pretty successfully. Now he's trying to kill *us*. My son first. Who's next? Me?'

'He's not trying to kill anyone just now, Ms Elliott. As you said, he's in police custody.'

'Sure, but he could have set this up ages ago.'

'Set what up, exactly?'

'No need to be cute with me, young man. I happen to know the muesli murders were committed with abrin, and it's abrin that my son has been poisoned with. Jequirity bean. I've read all about it. Somebody at that chip shop put it in his haggis pakora. Obviously in league with Toff Hammer. He has a lot of followers for that blog of his.'

'We've shut down Lawson's chip shop while our investigation is ongoing. But your haggis pakora theory seems unlikely. You see, abrin is destroyed by cooking.'

Faith Elliott knew more about abrin than this cop would ever understand. But it would be best for now to play dumb.

'Well, *somehow* his food was poisoned. It was the last thing he ate. Fell ill not long after.'

The interview in a corner of a waiting room in the hospital was interrupted by a young woman doctor. 'I need to talk to you, Ms Elliott,' she said, and pointed to a door marked CONSULTING ROOM. 'Let's step in here.'

Oscar was dead. The *Orcadian* published a respectful piece about him, mentioning also that police investigations were focusing on a Kirkwall chip shop, now shuttered for the time being. The *Scottish Sun* took a less restrained approach. 'BAGPIPE ADVENTURER FELLED BY BAD HAGGIS,' screamed its front page, a worthy contender for Britain's most unlikely headline of the year.

38
MEANT TO BE?

I
F THE AVENGER WAS TROUBLED by the Unseen Hand that had derailed her plans so tragically, a young American was feeling its more benign influence on her search for the author of a fifty-year-old typescript.

Here was Delia Cobb in the virtually deserted Strath of Kildonan, having just met – of all people – the childhood friend of the person she was seeking. One who would tell her all that she knew of the mysterious Rona Fay Swainson, one-time Countess of Fairfield, and, Delia hoped, would lead her to Rona herself.

Was it just coincidence that she should encounter Lidia here? No, *something* had driven Delia to this lonely valley, the notion that had implanted itself in her brain at the Skairs, the spot on the Hill of Fare in Aberdeenshire where, legend said, Gudrun had been killed. Had Gudrun's spirit, centuries later, *sent* her here?

Delia fought to dismiss that notion. She was a rational person. Ghosts had no place in her view of the world. Coincidence it was. A very happy one.

Lidia caught her looking at her walking-stick. 'Knee replacement,' she announced, answering the question that was obviously in Delia's mind. 'My second one. Did a lot of running when I was young, buggered my joints. Hope to get rid of this stick soon.'

'I'm sure you will,' Delia said.

'You mentioned this saga of Rona's you've been reading.'

'*Gudrun's Saga*, yes. Were you aware of it?'

'Not at the time. She told me about it at her father's funeral. Rona planned to revisit Gordonhall, where she'd hidden the manuscript inside a book. It was the only copy, she said.'

'An acquaintance of mine by the name of Frank Jamieson has her typescript, and the book she'd slipped it into. Don't ask how it comes to be in his possession. I don't know exactly. But we want Rona to have her saga back. If I can trace her.'

'We have so much to talk about,' Lars said, interrupting the dialogue. 'We're staying at Mackay's Hotel in Wick. Can you join us for dinner there?'

'I'd love to.'

It was agreed. Before they parted on the Suisgill Burn bridge, Lidia said, 'It's so strange running into you here, Delia. Lars and I had planned to make a day trip to Orkney from John o' Groats today. But last night I dreamt we were panning for gold, and I insisted on coming to the Strath of Kildonan instead. Otherwise we wouldn't have met. Do you think it was meant to be?'

Delia's rational self prepared to say something like, 'No, but it's a real stroke of luck, at least for me.' Instead, what came out of her mouth was the one word, 'Yes.'

Though Rona and Delia were of very different generations, backgrounds and nationalities, they shared a fascination with boundaries. In Rona's case, the fuzzy dividing line between fact and fiction, or between history and mythology as represented by the Norse sagas; in Delia's, physical, geographical and political borders. For a high school project, she had studied the mismatch between natural boundaries such as rivers or watersheds and the often arbitrary lines drawn on a map to delineate the states and counties of the US, particularly in the west and midwest.

Once she had made her father drive her the full 25-mile length of Lake Cook Road from its western end near Algonquin,

Illinois to its eastern terminus on the shore of Lake Michigan. In a virtually dead-straight line, it marked the border of two counties across a flat expanse of Chicago suburbia. What had interested her more than this administrative boundary was the precise location of the watershed between the Des Plaines River and Chicago River basins, for the ultimate destination of the water that flowed from these basins was very different. The Des Plaines emptied into the Illinois River, which downstream joined the Mississippi north of St Louis; its turbid flow was therefore destined for the warm embrace of the Gulf of Mexico. By contrast, the Chicago River fed Lake Michigan, whose waters would eventually tumble over Niagara Falls on their way to the chilly Gulf of St Lawrence. Delia reckoned the watershed boundary must lie near where Lake Cook Road intersected with the Tri-State Tollway, and fretted that the land was so featureless that it would be impossible to mark the dividing line with any degree of precision.

Now she was heading north through a landscape that could not be more different from the Illinois prairie. Watersheds here in the Scottish Highlands were easily mappable. (And there was no comparison between the broad highway that was Lake Cook Road and the barely one-lane track of the A897.) Near Forsinard, Delia crossed from the basin of the Helmsdale River that gave up its limpid water to the Moray Firth (the 'Broad Fjord' of *Gudrun's Saga*), into that of the Halladale River, which flowed into the Atlantic Ocean on Scotland's far north coast.

Forsinard, she had read, was a notable spot in the Flow Country, an ecologically significant expanse of peat bogs providing an almost unique habitat for bird life. Much as she would have liked to stop at the nature reserve managed by the Royal Society for the Protection of Birds, she had an appointment in Wick that was too important.

By five o'clock she was in the pleasant town of Wick (Old Norse *Vik*, meaning a bay or harbour, whence the *Vikings*) and soon located Mackay's on the south side of the Wick River. Shaped like the bow of a ship, the building faced east to the river on one side and west to the A99 and the railway terminus on the other. At its narrow end its two-metre-long frontage was called Ebenezer Place, certified by the *Guinness Book of Records* as the world's shortest street. The only address on the street was No. 1 – the bistro that served as Mackay's dining room.

Faded letters could just be made out on the river-facing wall reading TEMPERANCE HOTEL – the name of the inn prior to 1947, when Wick's 25-year 'dry spell' ended. That she would be spending the night in the very hostelry where Rona Fay Swainson had been conceived in December 1943 was a connection of which Delia had not the slightest inkling.

Her room, overlooking the river, was clean and comfortable; there was even a welcome tot of sherry waiting for her. Mackay's 'temperance' past had been well and truly buried.

At seven she joined Lars and Lidia in the hotel's quirkily-shaped bistro. The talk quickly turned to the subject of Rona. Lidia reminisced about her schooldays at Banchory, the sessions with Rona in the Gordonhall library, even her friend's teenage concern that she would be wedded, like Constance Chatterley, to a man who couldn't love her. 'And so it turned out. But ...' Lidia struggled to find words to express what she wanted to say.

Lars came to her aid. 'Rona's life developed according to a script not by D.H. Lawrence but by the Norse skalds who put together the *Orkneyinga Saga*. It's as if she became Ragnhild, a tenth-century princess who pretends to love her brother-in-law and persuades him to kill her husband Arnfinn – I think that was his name.'

'Yes, you're right,' Delia agreed. '*Gudrun's Saga* tells it similarly. Apparently Arnfinn wasn't much of a lover.'

'Neither was Rona's first husband,' Lidia broke in. 'Hence her affair with her brother-in-law Dominic. But she didn't arrange for him to kill Antony. It was an accident, while the two were fighting. She described the whole scene to me, and she certainly didn't engineer it.'

Lars raised a sceptical eyebrow. 'So you say, my dear, but in the *Orkneyinga* story, Ragnhild *does*, then has to get rid of her husband's murderer. So she tells his nephew she will make him Earl of Orkney if he kills Uncle Havard. You have to admit the two patterns of events are uncannily similar.'

Delia coughed. 'Hang on a minute. According to *Gudrun's Saga*, it was entirely the nephew's idea. He coveted Ragnhild, and hacked Havard to death in the Ring of Brodgar. But she wouldn't marry "Bread-and-Butter", as he was called. He had to make do with one of her slave girls.'

'Rona told me Dominic died at Gordonhall. Okay, he *was* killed by his nephew Fergus – in a shooting accident.' Lidia shook her head. 'And there the similarity ends.'

Lars laughed. 'Wrong, darling. For both women, there was yet another death. Ragnhild disposed of "Bread-and-Butter" by getting his cousin "Hard-jaw" to do the dirty deed.'

'It's true,' Delia put in, 'that "Hard-jaw" burned "Bread-and-Butter" in his house, but according to *Gudrun's Saga*, it wasn't at Ragnhild's bidding. It was because he wanted his cousin's slave girl for himself. And in the twentieth-century re-enactment, it's possible that Fergus perished in the fire that destroyed the Gordonhall mansion. His body was never found. The official version of events was that Fergus had drowned in a lake.'

'Loch Katrine, yes,' Lidia said. 'I remember reading about it … all sounded very fishy.'

'You said you saw Rona at her father's funeral. What year was that?'

'Let me think … 1969, I suppose. Nearly half a century ago. It must have been before the fire at Gordonhall, because she was headed there to try to retrieve her translation of the saga.'

'Have you spoken to her since then?'

'While she lived in Orkney, we exchanged Christmas cards, usually with a short letter, but that's all.'

'You don't know where she is now?'

'No. We lost touch completely after she gave up her title. It was still a shock to see what that Toff Hammer guy wrote about her. They need to lock him up! He's the muesli murderer, for God's sake!'

'*Allegedly* so, my dear,' Lars corrected his wife with a smile.

'Toff Hammer doesn't beat about the bush,' Delia said. 'He puts Rona in the frame for a whole string of deaths: two husbands, their nephew Fergus ... her own father, even.'

Lars raised his glass. 'Let's drink a toast to Rona, wherever she may be.'

'To Rona,' Delia echoed. 'Did you ever try to track her down, Lidia?'

'Not with any success. Obviously she didn't want to be found. Maybe she was paranoid, but who could blame her? I'm pretty sure she'll be in Iceland. That's where her husband Ari belongs. They have a daughter Kristin. Her son, the one she had to Dominic, is still in Orkney. He's the present Earl of Fairfield, but I gather he doesn't ever use the title his mother gave up for him. Just calls himself plain Donald Swainson.'

'I know about Donald,' Delia said, 'but I couldn't possibly approach him just now.'

'He wouldn't help you find Rona anyway,' Lidia said. 'I once wrote to him asking for her address but he refused, point-blank. Even when I sent him photos of Rona and me as teenagers.' She rummaged in her handbag and produced two creased and faded pictures. 'That's Rona on the left, me on the right.'

'Two pretty girls.'

'Rona, yes. Not me.'

'You mentioned her husband Ari. Would that be Ari Haraldsson, who helped her translate *Gudrun's Saga* from Icelandic into English?'

'Yes. It was a *long* time ago, before her *first* marriage in 1966. She and Ari had a thing going even then.'

'After dinner,' Delia offered, 'if you like, I'll bring my computer down to the lounge bar and show you their work over a drink. How does that sound?'

In concert, Lars and Lidia replied, 'Great!'

The bistro meal was excellent. Lars insisted on paying for all three. 'In that case drinks in the lounge are on me,' Delia said.

'It's a deal,' Lars said, 'but if you don't mind, we won't stay up too late. We're taking the ferry to Orkney tomorrow. No matter *what* Lidia dreams about tonight,' he added with a wink.

'Why don't you join us, Delia?' Lidia suggested. 'We're only going for the day.'

'Thanks, I'd love to.'

Wild horses could not have held Delia back. Already she was so excited, she wondered how she would ever get to sleep that night.

39
SMOKE HER OUT

THE AVENGER ABSORBED the news of her son's death in stages. Shock: even knowing how lethal the poison was – after all, her intent *was* to kill a young man – she had expected Oscar to recover. Resignation: Oscar, with his love of risk, was probably destined to die young anyway. Faith just didn't think it would be like this. Anger: however unreasonably, she blamed the doctors at Balfour Hospital, the chip shop owners, and most of all Rolf Swainson, her intended victim, for Oscar's death.

Anyone but herself.

Oscar, the intended beneficiary of the Avenger's campaign, had instead become its latest casualty. It had all been for nothing.

The shock faded, but her rage refused to subside. A few days after her son's funeral, that scattershot anger redirected itself on to a single target: the wretched Rona who had got away with murder. The Avenger would rectify that. She would find her, wherever she was lurking.

Smoke her out, as George W. Bush had resolved to do with Osama Bin Laden. Only, unlike Bush, she had no successor to accomplish the task if she failed.

The Avenger would not, could not fail.

She dialled Amy's number. Her sister Hope's girl, to whom she had never been especially close. But that would change, now that Oscar had been so cruelly taken from her.

'Amy, darling, I hope you don't mind me calling you. Just to talk.'

'Of course not, Aunt Faith. This is such an awful time for you, I know. For me, too. And for Rolfie. He and Oscar were great pals.'

They exchanged platitudes and reminiscences of Oscar's short but eventful life. Then Faith said, 'I never thanked you properly for allowing Donny and me to meet at your house that day. You really saved us time, let us get down to business faster. There was so much going on.'

'I know,' Amy said. 'Did you make progress with your plans to get production back up and running?'

'Yes. We've completely rebranded all our cereal products. No more Fairfield's. Now we're Caledonian Hills. Everything in tamper-evident packaging. Customers are coming back to us, faster than the analysts predicted.'

'That's great news. And with Toff Hammer in custody he can't do any more damage.'

'You know, even if they let him out – which I certainly hope won't happen – he can't hurt us again. We're pretty much Hammer-proof.'

It was time for Faith to change the subject. 'I've something else to tell you. An elderly man by the name of Frank Jamieson came to Gordonhall one day. Said he had a translation of a Norse saga that Rona Swainson had written long ago, and he wanted to return it to her.'

Amy was puzzled. 'But surely Rona already has a copy. You'd hold on to something like that, wouldn't you?'

'Apparently she didn't. If she had, Jamieson believes it would have been published before now. Yet it doesn't show up in any library catalogue. So I'm thinking I might present it to her. A kind of peace offering – our family and hers have never been the best of friends. There's bad feeling going back to ancient history. Time we put an end to it.'

'Hey, you're forgetting about Rolfie and me!' Amy countered. 'We get on pretty well together.'

'All the more reason for me to pay Rona a visit. This manuscript of hers would be a great olive branch.'

'But how are you going to find her? Rolfie has no idea where his grandma lives. Well, it's somewhere in Iceland, obviously. He's met her a few times, but always at a hotel in Reykjavik where I gather they have occasional family reunions.'

'We know her name. And the man she went off with: Ari Haraldsson. There are ways to find out where they live, at least what town or district they're in. Once I get to Iceland I'll make a few inquiries. Unless ...'

'Unless what, Aunt Faith?'

'A man will tell a woman anything for sex.'

Amy burst out laughing. 'Who exactly are you proposing to get into bed with?'

'Not me, darling. You.'

The laughter stopped as quickly as it had started. 'Me?' Amy said incredulously.

'I want you to use all your feminine wiles on Rolf, get him to tell you every little thing he remembers about his grandmother. I bet it'll turn out he knows more than he's let on up to now.'

'Aunt Faith, this conversation is getting a bit weird.'

'Okay, you don't have to tell me *how* you get the information. Just tell me whatever you can find out. It's for the good of our two families – the Elliotts and the Swainsons.'

'I'll see what I can do. No promises.' Quizzing her loving partner for information would feel almost like a betrayal, yet what harm could there be in helping unite their two families?

It was too much to hope that a phone number and address for Ari Haraldsson or Rona Swainson would be listed on the online Icelandic directory, but the Avenger gave it a shot. If Rona had adopted an Icelandic-style surname she would be Rona

Filipsdóttir. That yielded no fruit either. Ah well, she'd wait for Amy to get back to her.

After a week, no word from her niece. *What's the matter with that girl? No sex for seven nights?*

While she waited, the Avenger plotted how Rona would meet her end. Already she had decided it should echo the way Antony Argill, Dominic Argill or Fergus Argill-Hawke had died. What was it to be: knife, shotgun or water?

In her heart of hearts she knew Fergus had *not* drowned in Loch Katrine. Those bones that turned up in the foundations of the old Gordonhall mansion were almost certainly his. Telford, her own father, had set fire to the house, knowing Fergus was inside. Yet somehow the Avenger was irresistibly drawn to water as the best means for dispatching Lady Rona. Once she arrived in Iceland she would work out how it was to happen.

By the time the call came, Faith had already packed and booked a flight from Glasgow to Reykjavik.

'Rolfie really doesn't have an address for his grandma,' Amy reported, 'but he's told me a few things that might help narrow down your search.'

'What have you got for me, darling?'

'He's fond of his great aunt. Margrét's her name, no second "a". I take it she's a sister of Ari Haraldsson.'

'That's good,' Faith said, making a note of the name: Margrét Haraldsson. Then, realising her error, she scored out the surname and substituted 'Haraldsdóttir'.

'Rolfie thinks she never married, but lived in Reykjavik with her parents until they died.'

'Anything else?'

'He remembers when his grandma Rona was ill or having surgery, his father called the hospital every day to ask how she was doing.'

'Where was the hospital? In Reykjavik, I suppose?'

'No, Aunt Faith, that's the thing. It was in some other town, but I can't remember the name of it. I think it begins with "A".'

'Akureyri, maybe? It's the second largest city in Iceland, so probably has a pretty good hospital.'

'That could be it, yes. And ... Rolfie has a memory of hearing a conversation between his parents when he was just seven or eight. They were joking about Grandma Rona being from the Faroes.'

'The Faroes? That makes no sense. Maybe he misheard them talking about the Hill of Fare.'

'I suppose. Though they do make a big deal out of being descended from Vikings. But then, so does Rolfie's mum, though her hair is black as coal.'

'Well, thanks for those snippets, Amy,' Faith cut in abruptly. She had got what she wanted. No point in idle chatter. 'You didn't let on to Rolf why you were so curious all of a sudden, did you?'

'No, of course not.'

'Good. I want this to be a surprise for Rona.'

40
LUCKY LADY

THE FERRY CROSSING OF THE Pentland Firth from John o' Groats was unusually smooth. Lars had generously given his ticket to Delia, preferring (he said) to go sightseeing on his own along the north coast of Caithness and Sutherland. By the time they arrived in Burwick, on the tip of South Ronaldsay, it was as if Delia and Lidia had been friends for years.

As they boarded the coach waiting to take them on a whistle-stop tour, Delia confessed she knew virtually nothing about Orkney except for what she had read in *Gudrun's Saga*.

'You're ahead of me there,' Lidia said, 'but I do know they produce excellent cheese and whisky.'

The first stop, the Italian Chapel, was an eye-opener to both. A Nissen hut transformed by Second World War prisoners into a tiny but breathtaking place of worship using only the materials they had to hand, namely concrete, scrap metal and paint. A masterpiece of ingenuity and artistic vision by men removed from their warm Mediterranean homeland to this bleak northern outpost.

Next it was on to Skara Brae, the remarkably well preserved neolithic village on the Atlantic shore. 'When Rona and Ari moved to Orkney with their children,' Lidia said, 'they set up home near here. I believe Rona's son Donald still lives in the same house.'

'What was it called?' Delia asked.

'I don't remember.'

'Does Donald have a wife?'

'Yes, he married an Orkney girl he met at university. Their son Rolf lives in Kirkwall, must be in his twenties by now. I checked him out recently. He runs a delicatessen and wine shop with his girlfriend.'

Delia processed this information as she and Lidia viewed the excavated 5,000-year-old dwellings, a fascinating glimpse of everyday life from an era before the building of Stonehenge or the Pyramids of Egypt.

Heading back inland, the coach passed a handsome two-storey house set back a quarter mile or so from the road. On either side of the entrance to its driveway was a pillar surmounted by an octahedron, made from what looked like concrete. 'Snaebister,' the sign indicated.

'That has to be the Swainson home,' Delia stated confidently. 'The gate posts at Gordonhall have a similar design.'

'I didn't remember that,' Lidia said.

After a brief stop on the windblown clifftops at Yesnaby, with their distant view of the Old Man of Hoy, the tour proceeded to the neolithic sites of Brodgar, Stenness and Maeshowe.

Since her knee was giving her a little trouble, Lidia stayed on the bus at Brodgar while Delia went to explore the hundred-metre diameter ring of standing stones. This very circle featured in *Gudrun's Saga*: the teenage 'Bread-and-Butter', burning with unrequited love for Ragnhild, lured her wicked brother-in-law Havard – his own uncle – to his death here. A murder that anticipated by a thousand years Fergus's killing of *his* uncle, Rona's second husband Dominic.

A blast of cold air from the west brought a sudden rainy squall, making Delia run for the shelter of the waiting coach. The vast Orcadian sky, which moments earlier had been benignly blue with puffy white cumulus, now seethed with dark storm-clouds pierced by angled rays of sunlight.

At nearby Stenness the great stones, even older than those of Brodgar, stood unperturbed by the wind and rain as they had done for five millennia. The coach party remained in their seats while the driver spoke on the microphone.

'In 1814,' she said, 'there were more than you see now, including one known as Odin's stone. It had a hole through which the others could be viewed. Sir Walter Scott came to Stenness that year, and many visitors followed. The landowner, a man recently come to Orkney, objected to people tramping over his fields, so he began smashing the stones, including Odin's. Fortunately, he was stopped before they were all destroyed.'

'Were they originally erected for worship of Odin?' someone asked.

'No,' came the reply. 'Odin was a Norse god. These stones had already stood for four thousand years before the Norsemen arrived.'

'How about seeing some Viking sites now?' an elderly man near the front of the bus demanded. 'I'm neolithic'd out!'

It was pointless to continue to the chambered cairn that is Maeshowe. Experience had taught the driver that persistent rain led to disgruntlement among her passengers. With a pleasant smile, she announced that the tour would now proceed directly to Kirkwall, where they could have time on their own. 'And for Norse heritage, you couldn't do better than Saint Magnus Cathedral, the building of which was begun by another saint – Rognvald, Earl of Orkney – in 1137.'

Saint, my ass, Delia thought. Though the *Orkneyinga Saga* (which she had not yet read) may have portrayed Rognvald as a devout and virtuous man, she knew *Gudrun's Saga* was not unique in exposing his less saintly side. The underhand way in which he had Sweyn Asleifsson dispose of Earl Paul, thereby becoming sole ruler of Orkney and Shetland, was typical of Rognvald's machinations.

Lidia went shopping – Kirkwall's retail opportunities beckoned – while Delia visited the town's excellent, and free, Orkney Museum in Tankerness House opposite the cathedral. Barely forty minutes later, Lidia appeared by her side. 'Come with me,' she said, a note of urgency in her voice.

They went out together into the rain. Hurrying along the narrow lane that was Kirkwall's busy main street, suddenly Lidia came to a halt and leaned on her stick.

'Your knee bothering you?' Delia asked.

'No, I'm okay for a little while yet.' Lidia grasped her young companion's wrist with her free hand. 'See this shop behind me?' she whispered. 'It must be the deli and wine shop that Rona's grandson runs with his girlfriend. I bet that's him behind the counter. Don't stare.'

Delia made a point of gazing intently at an attractively-presented display of wines in the window before glancing beyond at the good-looking young man who was serving a customer. 'You think that's Rolf?'

'Could be,' Lidia said.

'And his partner is May or Amy, I suppose,' Delia ventured.

'How would you know that?'

'See the sign above the door,' Delia said. 'Fay Lordman. It's an anagram of "Rolf and Amy". Bet Rolf had fun with that, since he's the son of a lord. He's also incorporated his grandmother's middle name. Fay.'

Lidia smiled sceptically. 'Well, there's only one way to find out. Let's go in and have a word with Rolf – if that's who he is. I could tell him I want to see his grandmother before I die, show him the photos. It didn't work with his father, but I might have more luck here. It would be great if we could persuade him to give me her address in Iceland.'

'Worth a try,' Delia agreed. 'Best, though, if you talk to him alone. He'd be more likely to open up without me there. You'll find me back in the museum, okay?'

After sneaking another look at Rolf's handsome frame, Delia set off in the rain, back the way they had come. *May or Amy's a lucky lady*, she thought. A minute later, she began daydreaming about a trip to Iceland.

'It was Rolf all right,' Lidia said when they met up again. 'He said he'd think about it.'

'So you didn't get Rona's address?'

'No, but he says he'll talk to her and email me. Might have been better if you were there. He seems like the kind of guy who would fall for the charms of a beautiful redhead.'

'Yeah, right,' Delia said with a smile.

Lidia looked at her watch. 'The bus leaves in fifteen minutes. Come on, we'd better take a look in the cathedral before we go. Can't disappoint our driver!'

Two days later, Delia was back in her Edinburgh flat. Ploughing through a stack of laundry, she was quite pleased to be interrupted by the inane ringtone of her mobile.

'It's Lidia. Heard from Rolf this morning. Seems he spoke to Rona, told her about meeting me in Kirkwall. As we thought, she's in Iceland. Still nervous about giving out her address, but she would love to see me again, and will give me a call. Looks like I'll be going up there. Want to come?'

'Try and stop me!'

'Shall I tell her you'll be joining me, with a copy of *Gudrun's Saga*?'

Delia paused before answering. 'Can I get back to you on that?' she suggested. 'Frank Jamieson has the original typescript. He's really the one who should return it to Rona. I'll talk to him.'

The moment Lidia rang off, Delia called Frank at his home in London.

'This is wonderful news,' he said, 'but I'm afraid there's no way I can make a trip to Iceland. No travel, doctor's orders. I'm expecting to go into hospital any day.'

'Sorry to hear that.'

'But I'd really like you to take Rona Fay's typescript with you to Iceland. I'll send the original to you by courier.'

Much as she sympathised with Frank, Delia could barely suppress a surge of guilty excitement to think of carrying that precious cargo, and finally coming face to face with the mysterious, reclusive Rona Fay Swainson.

41
OUT OF THE BAG

T IM HESTON SIGHED LOUDLY as he sat down yet again in the interview room alongside his solicitor. 'What now?' he demanded. '*Another* murder you want to charge me with? Or have you rummaged through my recycling and found cardboard in the paper bin?'

DI 'Geordie' Neville let him finish his rant before turning on the recorder and reciting the obligatory date, time and names of those present. 'You travel quite a lot in Scotland, do you, Mr Heston?'

'Not lately. I've been in your tender custody for a fortnight.'

'Prior to that, what was the last trip you took of more than, say, eighty miles?'

'In Scotland? That would have been two or three years ago, to Aberdeen for a conference.'

'We have recent CCTV footage of your car in Dundee.'

'Dundee? Sure, I was there last month, but that's only 78 miles from Glasgow if you go by the Kincardine and Tay Bridges. You said more than eighty.'

'Okay, we've established you were in Dundee on ... let's see ... the 14th of June this year. What was the purpose of your visit?'

'Research for my blog. I needed to check out the Fairfield factory. It's an old building, in an industrial area near the docks, but it has pretty good security, I found. That was *before* the "muesli mystery" hit the headlines. I tried to bluff my way in to see their production and packing facilities, didn't get past the front desk. You can confirm with the receptionist if you like.

Nice wee Indian lassie.'

'We will, Mr Heston. So, you haven't been further than Dundee in recent months?'

'Not in Scotland, no.'

'The Orkney Islands are part of Scotland, are they not?'

'For a Geordie, your geography's not bad! I'm impressed.'

'When were you last there?'

'Oh, I get it. The bad haggis case. The son of one of Fairfield's directors died of food poisoning. You want to pin that on me now, do you?'

'Just answer the question, Mr Heston. When did you last travel to Orkney?'

'Nineteen ninety-five.'

'The chairman of Fairfield's lives up there. You didn't recently feel the need to go for some research?'

'No, but maybe I will, for my next article.'

'I wouldn't make any plans, if I were you.'

'Why would you think there's a connection between the muesli mystery and the bad haggis? Can't be abrin this time, can it? It wouldn't survive the cooking. Unless, of course it was ...'

The solicitor interrupted to remind her client that he should stick to answering the questions.

'Unless it was what, Mr Heston?' Neville asked.

'Added after cooking.'

'Or in something else that the victim ate?'

'Aha!' Heston exclaimed. 'So it *was* abrin again, was it? I've been nowhere near Orkney for over twenty years. You really have to look elsewhere for a suspect, Inspector, don't you? I'd like my life back now.'

Convinced that her prey was to be found in Akureyri, the Avenger had arrived in Reykjavik and planned to spend a day or two in the capital before travelling north. Not as a tourist – no

Golden Circle or Blue Lagoon fripperies – but on her mission to exact final revenge on Rona Swainson, the former Countess of Fairfield. And one route to the Lady Rona was through her life-partner and co-translator of *Gudrun's Saga*, the Icelander Ari Haraldsson, more particularly through his sister Margrét.

The online directory provided addresses and telephone numbers of twelve Margrét Haraldsdóttirs in the greater Reykjavik area. There was no guarantee that Ari's sister had a listed entry, but it was somewhere to start.

First the Avenger called each of the numbers; priority would be given to the five addresses where the phone was not picked up. At each in turn she rang the doorbell and knocked loudly to make doubly sure no one was at home. Breaking in was a simple matter – especially at one house, where the sliding patio door was unlatched and glided open with barely a touch of her gloved fingers. People here were pretty casual about security! Address books, phone lists, diaries and mobiles were what she was after. The temptation was to rummage through kitchen drawers, desks, briefcases or handbags left lying around; instead, she carefully leafed through any notebooks she came across, aware of the seconds and minutes ticking by, then quickly replaced each one precisely as she had found it. To give the appearance of a petty burglary, she pocketed whatever cash or small valuables turned up during her search.

Her luck held. At the third house on her list, she found an address-book entry for *Ari og Ragna*, Ketilsgata 44, 600 Akureyri.

Ragna? Had to be an Icelandic spelling of Rona.

Faith Elliott (or Stella Summer, the name on her Hertz car-rental contract) was already well clear of Reykjavik by the time the police received the first of three calls from unrelated women by the name of Margrét Haraldsdóttir, each reporting a break-in.

Now she had four hours' driving ahead of her. She would

check into a hotel in Akureyri – the Icelandair on Thingvalla Street had vacancies and should fit the bill. In the morning she would begin her surveillance of Rona's house. The Avenger's plan was on track.

The call from Ragna came the evening after Lidia received Rolf's email. It was an emotional reacquaintance for both women, who had last met in 1969 and had not so much as exchanged greetings cards for almost thirty years. In an hour-long conversation, the missing decades were filled in to some extent, but much remained to be said. Ragna was delighted that her friend would be in Akureyri that very weekend; Lidia's proposal to bring along a young American was less well received.

'You'll love Delia when you meet her,' Lidia said. 'Not only for who she is, but for what she's going to bring with her.'

'What's that?' Ragna asked nervously.

'Something of yours, from Gordonhall.'

'Gordonhall was totally destroyed. Nothing survived.'

'One little thing apparently escaped before the fire. Your translation of *Gudrun's Saga*.'

Silence on the Iceland end of the line.

'Rona? Are you still there?'

'But … how …?' Ragna's voice broke up.

'Delia will explain when we see you. What's your address?'

Ragna composed herself. 'Lidia, I haven't given out my address for over twenty-five years. I think you know why. Ari and I would love to have you round to our home here in Akureyri, but let's meet somewhere for coffee first.'

'Sure. Where do you suggest?'

'*Sundlaug Akureyrar*. The thermal swimming pool. It's one of the finest in Iceland, maybe the world. I'm a regular.'

'Rona! I was always the athletic one! Yes, we'll see you there this Saturday. At ten? Or is that too early?'

'Not at all. In my whole life, Lidia, you are the only person outside my immediate family ever to be my true friend. You can't possibly come too early. And *Gudrun's Saga* – I can't believe it. I'm *so* looking forward to seeing you again and to meeting Delia.'

Ragna need not have worried about giving Lidia her address. The cat was already out of the bag. Barely 200 metres from her house, the occupant of a Hertz car sitting innocuously at the park entrance had begun to keep an eye on her and Ari's every move.

'We're going to have a baby? Wow! I thought ...'

'So did I, Rolfie. But somehow you slipped one past the goalie. Hey, you look like you just got bad news.'

'No, sweetheart, not at all. It's wonderful news! I just can't believe it, that's all. I hope you're as happy as I am.'

'Honestly, I didn't mean for this to happen. Not right now, that is.'

'Somebody, somewhere, wanted it to happen. So let's celebrate!' Rolf took Amy in his arms and held her tightly for a full minute without saying another word.

'Orkney is supposed to be the best place in Britain to bring up a child,' she said, when eventually he relaxed his grip.

'And for a wedding, I hear.'

'A wedding? Is that a proposal, Rolf Swainson?'

'It is. Don't tell me I have to go down on one knee.'

'Only if you want me to say "yes".'

'Have you told your Mum? She'll be ecstatic.'

'Not yet, silly. You had to be the first to know. After me and Dr Martell. I'll ring my parents tonight, eh? And you should give yours a call, too.'

'Why don't we take a run over to Snaebister? They could do with some good news, for a change.'

'Before we do that, I have a confession to make. I don't want any secrets between us, especially now. I told Aunt Faith some stuff maybe I shouldn't have ...'

'What kind of stuff?'

'Rolfie, she's desperate to find your grandma's address. Spun me a story about having some old manuscript she wants to return. I believed her at the time.'

'You're worrying unnecessarily. Put it out of your mind.'

'Another thing. It was Aunt Faith who insisted we say nothing about Oscar taking one of your pills. I think that was a mistake.'

'Aim, we've been over this. Whatever killed Oscar, it wasn't that capsule. He was already feeling bad before he took it, remember? I've taken lansoprazole from that same bottle, every day since. And I feel perfectly fine.'

'You know the police said Oscar had abrin poisoning. What if the abrin was in the capsule he took? Abrin that was intended for you?'

Rolf grinned. 'You think Toff Hammer somehow sneaked a poisoned capsule into my prescription? That it should have been me, not Oscar, who swallowed it? Jeez, that's a bit far-fetched, isn't it? Lansoprazole is dispensed in tamper-proof foil packs. I break them out myself into that bottle, a month's supply at a time. I know you're not supposed to do that, but nobody's ever in that bathroom cabinet but you and me.'

'Faith used the bathroom when she was here last. And on her previous visit. What if she replaced the drug in one of your capsules with abrin?'

'Why would Faith do that?'

'Beats me. I know it sounds crazy. But we should tell the police about Oscar taking the medication.'

'Okay, I will, though I think you're off-beam with this. They can test what's left in the bottle.'

'And Rolfie, will you promise me you'll take your lansoprazole straight from the foil pack from now on? Our baby's going to need a daddy.'

42
WHAT'S THE WORST THAT CAN HAPPEN?

Monday. 9:15 R left house carrying canvas bag, walked alone towards town. 10:22 A drove away in Toyota 8-seater. 11:31 R returned, at home rest of day, sometimes visible in garden. 6:55 A returned.

Tuesday. Raining. Toyota in driveway. Both stayed in all day.

Wednesday. A in garden 10–12, cut grass & worked in vegetable patch. 1:45 Delivery from liquor store. 2:38 A & R left in Toyota. Followed them to Hagkaup s/market, home by 4:10.

Thursday. 9:15 R left as on Monday. Followed her on foot. 9:40 Arrived at swim pool on Thingvalla St. 11:05 R emerged, walked straight home. No sign of A or Toyota.

Friday. Both at home all morning. A washed windows. R visible at kitchen window from time to time. 2:10 R drove away in Toyota. Followed her to hair & nail salon, home by 4:45.

IT HAD BEEN FAITH'S INTENTION to monitor the comings and goings at Ketilsgata 44 for a full week. But on Friday evening she decided she had learned enough; there were other preparations to be made. If Rona was like most people in her age group, she was a creature of habit. Monday and Thursday were her swim days; the first good opportunity to strike would be next Monday. A short stretch of her walking

287

route to the pool was lined with thick bushes and free of overlooking windows; Faith had no doubt that she could easily overpower her elderly victim in a surprise attack, and quickly bundle her at knifepoint into the boot of her car. She would treat Rona to a dip of a different kind!

Saturday's task would be to identify a suitable quiet spot by the fjord to finish the job. The necessities were all in the car, including extra-long heavy-duty plastic cable ties and bags of rocks. And, of course, the shampoo bottle of chloroform she had brought in her checked baggage. It would be important not to overdo the anaesthesia. She wanted Rona to regain consciousness before she was put in the water.

Faith spent a peaceful night in the Icelandair Hotel, close by Akureyri's thermal pool. It crossed her mind that a drowning in that very pool would be appropriate, but impractical.

On Saturday morning at quarter to ten she was driving out of the hotel car-park when Ari's Toyota drew up. A smartly dressed Rona got out, waved to her husband and walked to the main entrance of the pool.

Change of plan. Faith turned around. In her hotel room she donned a shoulder-length chestnut-brown wig. Rona was unlikely to recognise her – they had last met more than thirty years ago – but there was no point in taking chances. In any case, Faith Elliott was the *last* person Rona would expect to see in Akureyri, Iceland.

By 10:15 Faith had entered and located her target in the café of the *Sundlaug Akureyrar* building, at a table with two women. One was of a similar age to Rona, with neatly bobbed grey hair and a walking-stick hooked over the back of her chair. The other was much younger, attractive, with ginger hair. She looked vaguely familiar.

In a moment it came to her. The same redhead who had been snooping around Gordonhall! From a table that gave a clear view of the party, Faith observed discreetly while sipping her cappuccino. Rona had been presented with a large envelope and was dabbing at her eyes with a tissue.

Carefully drawing out the fifty-year-old typescript, protected in a clear plastic folder, Ragna Enjudóttir felt her eyes well up. It didn't matter. No one could grudge her a few tears, as she leafed through these familiar old pages, unable to believe that she had been reunited with *Gudrun's Saga* after all this time.

'Someone at Gordonhall,' Delia explained, 'gave stuff from the library to a local mechanic. One of the books had your typescript hidden inside. Frank Jamieson, from London, inherited it years ago, but only recently discovered *Gudrun's Saga* tucked in the back. He wanted to present it to you in person but health issues prevent him from travelling, and he asked me to bring it to you.'

'You've no idea how much this means to me,' Ragna said. 'The original in Icelandic was almost certainly destroyed in the Gordonhall fire, so this translation is the only record that it ever existed.'

'Have you searched for other versions?' Delia asked.

'Many times, yes. I made the acquaintance of a professor at the University of Iceland, probably the leading authority on the so-called "lost sagas". He could find no listing for a *Gudrun's Saga* in any library or collection of medieval Scandinavian literature anywhere in the world. A Ph.D. student of his looked for references to the work elsewhere, but had to conclude no such saga was ever written.'

'But you know it was. And your translation is proof.'

'Not everyone will think so.'

Delia's eyes wandered around the room. Four or five tables in the café were occupied; at one a sharp-nosed, middle-aged woman sat alone, looking intently towards them. *I should know that face, those close-set eyes,* Delia thought, *yet I would have remembered that gorgeous chestnut hair.*

'Rona …' Lidia began, 'sorry, I should remember to say *Ragna*, how is your son? Donald, isn't it? Does he come to see you often?'

'We have a family reunion in Reykjavik every year, in May. That's where Kristin – she's our daughter – lives with her husband Jon Gunnarsson. Kris and Jon have a girl, Margrét, named after Margrét Haraldsdóttir, Ari's favourite sister.'

'Something I don't understand about Icelandic names,' Delia said. Why is your husband now Ari Vigdisson? Wasn't he Ari Haraldsson before?'

Ragna laughed. 'His father was Harald Tómasson, his mother Vigdis Erlendsdóttir. Ari changed his name from Haraldsson to Vigdisson after his father died. You can do that in Iceland.'

'Yet Margrét didn't?'

'No, that's true. However, like Ari, I took my mother's name. I could have been Ragna Filipsdóttir, but chose to become Ragna Enjudóttir when I applied for Icelandic citizenship. Makes it more difficult to track Rona Swainson down.'

'And are you quite close to Margrét?' Lidia asked.

'Yes, we get on really well. Ari and I are going down soon to spend some time with her in Reykjavik. Poor Margrét, her house was burgled just last weekend. Nothing much was stolen, but it's upset her a lot. It was a strange thing.'

'Strange? How?'

'Two other houses in the city were broken into on the same day. Both were homes of women also called Margrét Haraldsdóttir. No relation.'

'That *is* weird,' Delia remarked.

After a brief pause, Lidia said, 'I suppose when Donald comes he brings his wife and son?'

'Donny and Isobel never miss our get-togethers, though Rolf hasn't been for a few years. Not since he and his girlfriend started living together.'

'His girlfriend?' Lidia said. 'That would be Amy, am I right? Or is it May?'

Recovering from momentary surprise, Ragna responded, 'I was forgetting you'd met Rolf. I suppose he told you about Amy.'

'Actually, no. It was Delia who figured it out, from the name of their shop in Kirkwall.'

Ragna nodded knowingly.

'I've a bit of a history in decoding word puzzles,' Delia added. 'Number puzzles too.'

'Number puzzles, eh? Does 44 mean anything to you?'

Delia chuckled. 'I was going to ask you the same question! There's an octahedron in the middle of the Gordonhall bookplate.'

'I remember it well.'

'Then you'll remember it's marked with a rune on the upper half, reflected on the lower half. It could be *fe*, equivalent to F, or it could be a figure 4. The rune and its reflection can be read as FF – for Fairfield – or 44. The same octahedron, without runes, is on the gateposts at Gordonhall, and at what I assume is your son's place in Orkney, near Skara Brae.'

'Snaebister, yes. You're so sharp, Delia, you could be a spy or a news reporter! I'm just glad you came bearing *Gudrun's Saga*, or I'd be having serious misgivings about even talking to you!' Ragna laughed and came back to the subject in hand. 'So if FF refers to Fairfield, what about 44?'

'I've a feeling,' Delia said, 'the markings aren't really runes at all. The octahedron is a representation of a pyramidal mountain reflected in a calm sea. One that Gudrun's grandmother recalled from her childhood in the Lofoten Islands of Norway. The markings represent snow patches. But of course you know that, Ragna. You wrote it!'

'Someone else wrote it; I was just the translator. So, if I may persist, you think there's something special about 44?'

'In the series of octahedral numbers, 44 comes fourth.'

'Ari told me that, many years ago. It's been a lucky number for us.'

'The whole octahedral number series has four at its root.' Now Delia was warming to her subject, while Lidia looked on bemused. A complicated explanation followed on how the simple number 4 could be used to generate the whole series 1, 6, 19, 44, 85 and so on.

'Ari and I live at number 44 in our street.'

'You chose your house for the number?'

'No, of course not,' Ragna laughed. 'We're at the end of the street. The house next door is 36, but we bought some extra land in between so that our address would be 44, not 38. We cleared it with the Akureyri postmaster, who, it turned out, had been at school with Ari in Reykjavik. Iceland is like a small town.'

'I'm sure you're familiar with a famous book that has 44 chapters,' Delia said. 'Its action is largely set right here in Iceland, more correctly *under* Iceland. *Journey to the Centre of the Earth* by Jules Verne.'

'Probably hundreds of books have 44 chapters,' Lidia said, anxious to put an end to the number games. 'Nothing special about that.'

Delia was about to argue the point, but Lidia forcefully changed the subject. 'Hey, Rona, your grandson's a good-looking fellow. What's Amy like?'

'Er … never met her,' Ragna replied. 'I'll be honest with you, Lidia. I was none too happy when I learned Rolf had teamed up with Amy Lister. She's an Argill-Elliott, a granddaughter of Telford's. It was on his watch that Gordonhall burned down. Hearing about the destruction of the library was the worst news I ever had to bear in my life. Fergus's death was a shock too, though at the time I swallowed the official story that he'd drowned in Loch Katrine.'

'You've had more than your share of tragedy,' Lidia said softly. 'Donald too, losing his father like that.'

'I genuinely believe it was an accident on Fergus's part. To be brutally frank, I was glad to be rid of Dominic – I never loved him. He wasn't Donny's father in any case.'

Lidia was struck dumb for a few seconds. 'But I thought …'

'I'm tired of living that lie.' Ragna leaned forward and whispered confidentially, 'Donny was the product of an afternoon I spent with Ari in the Old Waverley Hotel in Edinburgh.' She allowed herself a little smile at the memory.

An awkward silence descended, till Lidia spoke again. 'What about the court case in Aberdeen when you challenged Telford's claim to the title? Didn't they ask about your relationship with Ari?'

'The subject didn't come up. The court decided Donny was the true heir to Dominic's title and estate.' Ragna smiled again, this time recalling her lawyer puffing out his chest as he intoned the principle rooted in ancient Roman law: *Pater est quem nuptiae demonstrant.* The father is he whom marriage so indicates.

'They didn't demand DNA testing?'

'There was no such thing back then, Lidia. Anyway, outside the immediate family, I've never admitted – until now – that Ari is Donny's biological father.'

'It's nobody's business anyway,' Lidia whispered.

'Honestly, it doesn't bother me any more,' Ragna said, a note of resignation in her voice. 'What's the worst that can happen? Donny loses the Bracklinn title and – maybe – control of the Fairfield's Cereals business in Dundee. But that's all turned to shit now, so who cares?'

'Yeah, the muesli murders,' Lidia said. 'Glad they got that Toff Hammer behind bars. Did they ever figure out how he did it?'

'He used poisonous beans, Donny told us. Jequirity, they're called.'

Delia's ears pricked up.

'They contain abrin, which is a potent toxin, I gather,' Ragna continued. 'Funnily enough, it was also abrin that killed Oscar Elliott when he was visiting Rolf in Kirkwall, though by that time Toff Hammer was in custody. What's the matter, Delia? Have you seen a ghost?'

'Faith Elliott,' Delia murmured, covering her mouth.

'Yes, Oscar's mother. What about her?'

'She has jequirity growing at Gordonhall. I've photographs on my smartphone.'

'Oh my God!' Lidia looked shocked. 'Surely it couldn't be her! No woman would kill her own son!'

'It was Rolf she was trying to kill,' Ragna said calmly. 'It's clear now: *Faith* is the muesli murderer, not Toff Hammer.'

Delia leaned forward. 'I don't want to alarm you, but she's right behind you. Three tables away, watching every move we make.'

43
BOUNDARIES

ARI WAS AT THE TOURIST information centre signing up a party of four for a day excursion to the lake area of Myvatn with its hot springs and lava formations. On receiving his wife's call, he returned to the swimming pool where she was waiting with Lidia and Delia by the main entrance.

In the car Ragna relayed to him what she had just learned about Faith Elliott. Meanwhile, flicking through dozens of pictures on her smartphone, Delia found one of the walled garden at Gordonhall with Faith's greenhouse in one corner. The next was a close-up of a potted plant visible through the glass. With finger and thumb she zoomed in. 'That's jequirity,' she asserted. 'A white-flowered variety, which is unusual but not unknown. It puzzled me at first, but there's no doubt in my mind. Faith is cultivating jequirity in her greenhouse.'

'Hope she doesn't realise you're on to her,' Ari said. 'Soon as we're home, I'll call the police.'

As she showed Lidia and Delia into the house at Ketilsgata 44, Ragna could not hide her agitation. She knew she was the next victim on Faith's list.

Ari immediately dialled 112 on his mobile and was quickly connected to *Lögreglan* – Icelandic police – at regional headquarters on Thórunnar Street, Akureyri. Simultaneously, Ragna placed an international call on the landline.

'Donny, you need to know something.'

'Are you all right, Mum? You sound breathless.'

'I'm fine, but listen. It's Faith. She's the one who's behind all these murders. And she's here, in Akureyri.'

'Oh my God! How ...?'

'Don't worry, your *Pabbi* is talking to the police right now.'

'Do you think she's in league with Toff Hammer?'

'No, Donny, I believe she's acting alone. She's warped, got some twisted plan for vengeance on the Swainson family, I suspect.'

'But abrin? Where could she have got hold of that?'

'Would you believe she's been growing jequirity at Gordonhall? We think she's been harvesting the seeds and planting them in packs of Fairfield's muesli.'

'So could she possibly have spiked one of Rolf's lansoprazole capsules with jequirity, the very one poor Oscar took for his indigestion?'

'It certainly looks that way.'

'Sounds like Rolf owes Amy a big apology. She suspected as much, but he told her she was imagining things.'

Ragna prepared to wind up the call, but a throwaway line from Donald completely transformed the tone of the conversation. One minute her brow had been furrowed; the next, a few casual words had her smiling. 'Really?' she said. 'That's wonderful news!'

Still holding the phone, she announced, 'Rolf and Amy are going to have a baby!'

'We're going to be great-grandparents!' Ari exclaimed.

Only after firing a dozen questions at her son did Ragna reluctantly hang up.

'So is there to be a wedding?' Ari asked.

'Yes,' Ragna confirmed. 'Right notes, not necessarily in the right order.'

'Congratulations,' Delia and Lidia said in unison.

'Thank you. It's a happy situation in more ways than one.'

'What, it's twins?' Ari was flummoxed.

'No, no. Don't you see? It's perfect!' Ragna could barely conceal her joy. 'Even if the truth about Donny's parentage gets out, the barony will pass to the descendants of Telford Argill-Elliott. But his eldest daughter, Faith, is now childless through her own actions. On her death the title will go to her sister Hope then to Amy, and on to *her* firstborn. The one she is now carrying. Rolf's baby.'

'Our great-grandchild will become Lord or Lady Bracklinn, regardless,' Ari added. 'The Fairfield earldom bequeathed to Donny will also eventually settle on that child's head. So it'll all be the same in the end.'

The police arrived. Their assurances that they would soon pick up Faith Elliott helped set Ragna's mind at ease. As she had done so many times in her life, she shelved her doubts and fears to focus on the present.

Ragna and Lidia needed some time alone to catch up. Ari went to the kitchen, and Delia joined him. Together they would rustle up a light lunch. From their forestry and environmental studies, albeit fifty years apart, they shared a lot of common ground. Ari explained his transition from forestry into tourism.

'And you still take visitors on excursions?' Delia asked, as she prepared a platter of herring and smoked salmon.

'Just a few these days,' Ari said. 'In fact I've two elderly couples from Germany (hear me, "elderly" – I'm over seventy myself) that I'm taking to Myvatn tomorrow.'

'Right – so that's why you have the minivan.'

'Yes. I also have a boat and sometimes do tours on the fjord. At midsummer I usually take a party to Grimsey, a small island forty kilometres out in the Greenland Sea, right on the Arctic Circle. If we're lucky we'll see the midnight sun. Ragna always goes with me on that trip. For some reason she's fascinated by boundaries, and loves being on the *heimskautsbaugur* – the "polar circle" – as we call it.'

'I'm a boundary freak too,' Delia said. 'But I've never been to the Arctic Circle. After graduation I was to go to the Canadian Arctic with my boyfriend at the time, but we split up.'

'That's a shame, but you're young. You'll have other opportunities. Listen, on the Myvatn tour tomorrow I'll be taking the Germans to a different kind of boundary. Maybe you'd like to come. To the east of it is the Eurasian Plate, to the west the North American Plate. The two sides are pulling apart at the rate of about three centimetres a year.'

'Wow, a tectonic plate boundary! That I would really love to see!'

'Well, we leave at 8:30. Actually, we should all go. I'd like to keep Ragna close by me while that woman's at large. The Toyota has eight seats, enough for everyone. There'll be plenty of room.'

That Saturday, detectives in both Iceland and Scotland were in possession of copies of Delia's pictures.

No record existed of Faith Elliott's entry to Iceland. Clearly she had travelled under a false identity. Thirty-nine British visitors were currently resident in Akureyri; of these only three were unaccompanied women. Police attention quickly turned to one Stella Summer, who had taken a room at the Icelandair Hotel but had unexpectedly checked out at noon that day. Hertz had a record of her renting a car in Reykjavik, and once again the contract had been terminated early with return of the car to Akureyri airport. No one of that name had booked a seat on any outgoing flight.

Until 'Stella Summer' could be tracked down, the house at Ketilsgata 44 would be kept under protective observation.

Meanwhile, DI Neville paid a visit to Tim Heston in his Glasgow cell. 'You're free to go,' he said. 'But I suggest you keep quiet online about your experience here. The case against you has now been dropped. We might still want to charge you with a drugs offence.'

'Is that it?' Heston said. 'You've put me through all this because of a trace of cannabis in my flat?'

'If you've any humanity, Mr Heston, you'll think about the victims of the muesli murderer and their families. For their sake, please don't compromise the case against the real perpetrator by sounding off in that blog of yours. Just give us all a break, will you?'

Having turned in her Hertz car at Akureyri airport, Faith needed a new set of wheels. She took a public bus into town and roamed the back streets looking for some hole-in-corner auto repair shop. In a light industrial area just north of the city centre, tucked behind a smart electrical supplies warehouse, she came across a dilapidated graffiti-defaced Nissen hut that seemed ideal. Framed in the open door was a lone mechanic, covered in oil from head to foot, bent over the engine of a battered red Fiat.

'Do you speak English?' she asked when he looked up.

'Of course,' came the sharp reply.

'I want to rent, or maybe buy, an old car, just for a few days. Cash payment, no questions.'

'This one's for sale by a customer of mine,' the mechanic said without batting an eyelid. 'He's at sea. Six hundred thousand. Bring it back within seven days and you'll get half your money back.'

He's stiffing me but I've no time to haggle. Six hundred thousand krona – about £3000, give or take. 'Call it five hundred thousand, cash, and you won't see me or the car again. You can report it stolen a week from today, collect the insurance. Deal?'

'Be my guest. Here are your keys.' It was his lucky day.

44
UNDERGROUND

THE DRIVE ALONG ROUTE 1 was beautiful. With the Toyota's heavy passenger load, it helped that Dieter, the bulkier of the two large German men, sat up front. Their mercifully slender wives occupied less than their fair share of the bench seats behind. Ari's running commentary in English was accompanied by an almost simultaneous German translation from Ragna.

'We are travelling to an area of volcanic and seismic activity,' Ari said. Our first stop will be at the large inland lake of Myvatn. I hope you all remembered to bring insect repellent, for the name Myvatn means "mosquito-lake".'

By ten o'clock, on the shore of the glassy-calm water, he was pointing out a series of volcanic craters. While the paying passengers clicked their camera shutters obediently, Ragna took Lidia and Delia aside to draw their attention to a strange white line on the distant southern horizon.

'The edge of Vatnajökull,' she told them. 'It's about eighty kilometres from here. One of the largest ice caps in the northern hemisphere outside Greenland.'

A dirty red Fiat clattered past them on the road, before executing a three-point turn and roaring by again in the opposite direction. 'Didn't expect to see Angela Merkel here!' Dieter chuckled. His compatriots agreed that the scowling woman hunched over the wheel of the Fiat bore a passing resemblance to the German chancellor. It was her mousey-blonde hair in an asymmetric short bob that did it, though outsized sunglasses hid most of her face.

At Dimmuborgir, an area of otherworldly lava formations, they all got out of the Toyota to follow one of the crooked paths that ran through the 'dark citadel'. On the approach to one much-eroded pair of rock pillars, these seemed to come together at the top, leaving a circular hole. The 'kissing trolls', they were called.

The next attraction was the one that really excited Delia. Unfortunately, at noon a touring bus was disgorging about forty people, and a dozen or so other vehicles sat in the parking area. 'Let's eat our packed lunches now,' Ari suggested. 'In half an hour they'll all have gone and we'll have the place to ourselves.'

'The red Fiat made it here before us!' Dieter exclaimed, pointing out the same car they had seen earlier, parked next to the bus. 'But no sign of Angela Merkel.'

From her collection of wigs, Faith had selected the Merkel bob; now, in the heat of the day, it made her head itch. Irritated, she snatched it off, throwing it on the passenger seat.

Her tourist map told her that Ari and his party would have to pass this way and would almost certainly stop for the obligatory photos at the tectonic plate boundary. All she needed to do was watch and wait. The large coach that parked right next to her provided great cover for melting into the throng of sightseers. Taller than most, she kept her head down and joined a group to duck into a cave-like opening alongside the gash in the ground that marked the plate boundary.

Down in the cavity formed by the great fault line was a deep pool which gave off an invisible sulphurous vapour. In the dim light filtering down from the entrance, she could just make out the cavern walls and uneven floor. She dipped her fingertips in the water and quickly recoiled. It was too hot for comfort.

This is the place, Faith thought, as the tourists scrambled up towards the sunshine again. She remained behind, lurking in a dark recess from which she could observe the entrance. *Twenty minutes I'll give them. It's about as much as I can bear down here.* She swallowed hard, suppressing the nausea brought on by the pungent atmosphere. From her backpack she withdrew a chef's knife stolen during one of her Reykjavik break-ins. Now she was ready.

Delia stood on the east rim of the fault line, Lidia on the west. Stretching out, they could touch each other's fingertips. 'I'm in Europe, you're in America,' Delia said. 'If we stand where we are for the next thousand years, we'll be three metres apart. After a million years, three kilometres. You'll have a long walk back to the van.'

'Yes,' Lidia said, entering into the spirit, 'and by then I'll need a lot more than a cane to help me.'

Ragna called to them from somewhere below. 'Come on down! We can go underground.'

'Be right with you!' Delia called back. *'Journey to the Centre of the Earth* begins here!'

'I'll go sit in the car,' Lidia announced. 'Knee's playing up a bit.' Leaving the Germans clicking their cameras at the tectonic boundary, she rejoined Ari at the Toyota.

First to enter the cavern was Delia, holding out a helpful arm to Ragna during the steep descent towards the water. Eagerly she stepped towards the edge of the simmering pool to take some flash shots on her smartphone.

Winded slightly, Ragna sat down on a smooth rock. 'Bit smelly down here, isn't it?' she remarked.

Delia was unable to answer. A hand was clasped tightly across her mouth and a knife-blade was at her throat.

Slowly the four Germans made their way back to the van, where Ari sat with Lidia. Pausing by the red Fiat, Dieter peered through its windows and passed a humorous comment.

Neither Ari nor Lidia understood Dieter's German but could see that there was general amusement. Dieter repeated what he had said: 'Angela Merkel lost her head!' He pointed to the wig lying on the Fiat's passenger seat. The laughter redoubled.

'Finally, Rona, we meet again. You know who I am, don't you?'

'Yes, Faith, I do.' In the gloom of the cavern, Ragna caught the flash of the blade. At that instant she was transported back to 1966 in the Ardwhinzean cottage, when Antony appeared at the bedroom door brandishing the knife that was soon to kill him.

'Listen carefully to me, Rona. Otherwise your young friend will die.'

'Let her go, Faith. Any dispute between us has nothing to do with her. We can settle this, just the two of us.' Ragna was amazed at her own calmness.

'No chance. She ensures that you will do as I say.'

Ragna's mind was in overdrive. *The woman's mad. She can't possibly expect to get away with this. Stall her off. As long as I'm still alive she won't harm Delia. But if I'm dead, she'll kill Delia too. Keep talking.* 'So what do you want of me?'

'You're a keen swimmer, Rona, so why don't you give this nice warm pool a try? Go on, put your hand in, see how pleasant it is.'

Ragna slowly crouched down and dipped her fingers momentarily in the steaming water.

'A little hot?' Faith said. 'I don't have a thermometer with me, but I reckon it's at least fifty Celsius. Sixty, more like. Must be quite a source of heat down below. And guess what? You're going to take a bath.' She pointed to a large flat rock a metre or so above the water's edge. 'Look, there's a nice spot to dive from.'

Ragna hesitated for an instant. There was a muffled yelp of pain as the blade pierced Delia's skin. A trickle of blood ran from the wound. In need of no further encouragement, Ragna climbed up on to the flat surface, followed by Faith and the captive Delia.

Now all three were perched on the rock, their backs to the light. 'Okay, Ginger,' Faith snarled at Delia, 'I want you to raise your left knee and place it on your friend's behind. She may need a little encouragement to go in the water. But wait until I tell you to push. We need to do this right, don't we?'

Delia remained resolutely motionless. She felt the cold steel of the knife pressed even harder against her throat.

'Not obeying orders, eh? Well, then, we'll have to try something else.'

A dome of lava rock protruded from the cavern wall immediately to Faith's left. *Getting one foot on the side of that thing should give me enough purchase to shove both of them into the water. Two birds with one stone. Save any mess with the knife, look more like an unfortunate accident.* She nudged Delia even closer to Ragna, who was now on the very lip of the platform. With her full weight on her right foot, Faith raised her left to rest on the dome.

So rigidly focused were Ragna and Delia on their predicament, and so intent was Faith on her purpose, that all three were unaware of Ari's entry to the cavern. Easing himself silently down from the entrance with the aid of Lidia's walking-stick, he approached them, his eyes adjusting to the semi-darkness. He tiptoed forward, hooked the handle of the stick around Faith's right ankle, and gave a sharp tug. With her weight-bearing foot snatched from under her, she fell sideways, her head smashing against the ground. The knife dropped from her hand and skittered away beyond her reach. Suddenly released from Faith's grip, it was all Delia could manage not to tumble against Ragna and send her headlong into the pool.

Ari rushed forward, holding out both arms. Ragna grabbed his left hand, Delia his right. Bracing himself, he pulled both towards him, safely clear of the hot pool. Ari held his wife in a tight embrace. All three shed tears of relief.

Gathering her wits, Delia stretched out a hand for the knife that lay on the cavern floor just a few feet from the motionless body. Suddenly she was sent reeling sideways from a violent push: her captor had reared up and made a lunge for the weapon. Half-blind with rage and concussion, Faith tripped on the uneven surface and tried to save herself. But instead, she stumbled forward until, with a bloodcurdling scream, she plunged into the scalding water.

In a half-hearted rescue attempt, Ari held out the walking-stick towards her.

'Leave her be, she's not worth it!' Ragna cried. 'Step back!'

At these words, Faith's head slowly slipped beneath the surface.

Trembling and gasping for air, they emerged from the cavern.

'How did you think to do that with the walking-stick?' Ragna asked.

'Old hockey move,' he said. 'In 1963 I once got sent off for pulling that stunt on a Glasgow midfielder, but I figured no ref would spot me this time.'

She managed a shaky smile, and kissed him. 'Always there for me, weren't you?'

EPILOGUE

HOMECOMER

RETRIEVING FAITH'S BODY from the underground hot pool was a difficult operation for the police; when eventually it lay on the pathologist's slab it was partially cooked. Lidia and Delia were requested to delay their departure for a few days while enquiries were completed on the circumstances of the death. Both were more than happy to prolong their stay in Iceland. Lars arrived from Scotland to join them.

Lidia's walking-stick was confiscated as a potential exhibit: a weapon used in what may have been an unlawful killing by Ari Vigdisson. He was assured this was simply 'procedure'; it was unlikely he would be arraigned, given the evidence.

On the patio at Ketilsgata 44, five wine glasses were raised in a toast. 'To our dear Ragna, or Rona,' Ari proposed, 'the reincarnation of Ragnhild Eriksdóttir.'

Lars coughed. 'Don't you mind, Rona, being compared with such an infamous woman? A ruthless schemer, who arranged a succession of murders, paving the way for her chosen husband to claim the Earldom of Orkney.'

'It doesn't worry me one bit. I choose to believe rather in the Ragnhild that Gudrun spoke of. A woman, abused by a series of men, who did what she had to do to make her life with the man she loved.' Ragna took Ari's hand in hers and squeezed it tight.

'Won't you consider coming back to live in Scotland?' Lidia asked. 'It's really where you belong.'

'Not any more,' Ragna said, no tinge of regret in her voice. 'I've been an Icelander for over twenty-five years, since I renounced my British nationality.'

'You could visit, surely?'

'Maybe I will, now that I'm to be a great-grandmother.'

'Then you might decide to come home for good. Even as Icelanders, don't you have that right?'

'We do, Lidia, but this is the place for Ari and me.'

'Wish *I* had that right,' Delia said. 'I'd love to make my permanent home in Edinburgh.'

A week later, Delia was back home. Not in Edinburgh but in Chicago. On checking in for a flight from Reykjavik, it was found that her British visa had expired a month earlier. Denied permission to board the plane, her pleas at the British embassy had fallen on deaf ears. As an 'illegal immigrant' – one who had overstayed her visa – she was denied permission even to return to Scotland for her belongings. Everything would have to be shipped to her.

'Yanks go home, is that it?' she had yelled angrily at consular officials. That did not go down well.

Once she had felt privileged to be a US citizen, if only through the accident of birth. Now, with such debasement of civic pride that a candidate for the presidency could garner millions of votes by proposing the building of a wall to keep Mexicans out, threatening denial of entry to others on the basis of religion, and condoning thuggish violence against protesters, she no longer felt she belonged there.

In the Chicago apartment which now seemed so foreign to her, she reflected wryly that generations of incomers – Beaker folk, Celts, Angles, Norse and many others – had made Scotland the nation it is. Yet, for a *home*comer from America, one who had contributed more than most to the land of her ancestors, the welcome mat had been summarily lifted.

It was a setback to be banished from the UK, but Rona was an inspiration. In keeping with her Viking blood, she had found happiness in a Nordic land. One way or another, Delia would return to *her* ancestral roots – in Scotland.

Of that she was sure.

AUTHOR'S NOTE

Characters and events featured in *Rona* from 1943 up to the present are fictional, except for some well-known public-domain figures and occurrences. Historical episodes are based on recorded fact, but if the reader detects a bias it is one that suits the fictional narrative. 'Gudrun's Saga' is my invention but its characters and tales, with a few exceptions, are drawn from Norse skaldic literature including *Heimskringla* and the *Orkneyinga Saga*. Familiar tales are given a novel slant in keeping with *Rona*'s themes but remain generally consistent with the semi-mythology of the source sagas. Only one story in 'Gudrun's Saga' is wholly invented: that of 'Astrid Leifsdóttir'.

Places mentioned in *Rona*, as in earlier novels of the *Incomers* trilogy, are almost all real. Exceptions are those named as homes of the principal characters: Gordonhall, Ardwhinzean, Snaebister, Tannersquoy and Ketilsgata 44. Banchory Academy is real, but not Queen Alexandra's School for Girls. The Tillybarnie estate where a youthful Rona cut broom is fictional.

Though no Gordonhall exists on the lower slope of the Hill of Fare near Raemoir, the house and its library were inspired in part by Craigmyle 4 miles to the west, at the edge of Torphins village. *Rona* tells of the destruction of Gordonhall by fire, bulldozer and dynamite in 1970; the real Craigmyle House suffered a similarly ignominious fate ten years earlier when it was deliberately blown to pieces by its owner. I clearly recollect visiting that elegant but unoccupied mansion a few weeks before it met its violent end, and looking through a ground-floor window to see books strewn on the floor. The bookplate illustrated in Chapter 2 is partly based on that of Lord Shaw of Dunfermline, one-time laird of Craigmyle.

While Gordonhall is fictional, the nearby rocky slope known as **the Skairs**, which features prominently in *Rona*, is factual. I leave it to the reader to decide whether that place is really haunted. I claim author's licence in proposing derivation of the Skairs from *skersa* (Old Norse: 'giantess'). Words beginning 'sk...' are often suggestive of Scandinavian origin, but a *skair* in Scots is a patch of steep hillside bare of soil and vegetation – a good description of the Skairs on the Hill of Fare. The word may, however, be ultimately of Norse etymology – compare it with *sker* (skerry), a rocky islet.

Does 'Fare' in '**Hill of Fare**' itself derive from Old Norse *faer* meaning sheep, as suggested in *Rona*? Several writers on place-names in north-east Scotland have held that no Scandinavian influence is detectable in that region. But is it not possible, even likely, that the Hill of Fare is etymologically related to Fair Isle and the Faroes? It is generally accepted, after all, that Fairfield in Cumbria, England's 13th highest mountain, is derived from *faer fjall* (Old Norse: 'sheep hill').

Torphins, a village at the foot of the Hill of Fare, is also redolent of Norse. Seductively similar to the name Thorfinn, it is nonetheless generally accepted to be a corruption of *torr fionn* (Gaelic: 'pale hill').

Sueno's stone, an intricately carved Pictish monument near Forres, predates Norse immigration by a century or more. The 'Sueno' its name refers to is unknown, almost certainly not Sweyn 'Forkbeard', invader and briefly king of England, as has sometimes been thought. The suggestion in *Rona* of a connection to Sweyn Asleifsson is a fictional device, though that Viking warrior probably did pass near Forres when delivering his hostage Earl Paul of Orkney to the dubious protection of the Earl of Atholl.

The **island of Rona** (from Old Norse meaning 'rough island') lies 45 miles from each of the Butt of Lewis and Cape Wrath and is the remotest island in the UK ever to have supported a permanent human population. (St Kilda, 40 miles from North Uist, is slightly less remote.) It is the closest land to the Faroes. The chapel or oratory, whose unmortared stone walls survive largely intact, may date from the eighth century. Lying in the centre of the island, it is surrounded by faint traces of habitation and lazy-bed cultivation.

In 1685 Rona was home to 30 people, but in that year a shipwreck brought an infestation of rats. The islanders' meagre food reserves were depleted and the entire population died through starvation, perhaps accompanied by plague. Having consumed everything edible, the rats died out in their turn. Since that time, farmers from Lewis have grazed sheep on Rona; it is recorded that during the First World War at least one German U-boat called repeatedly at the island to shoot the animals for meat.

Together with Sula Sgeir 11 miles to the west, Rona (on modern maps sometimes named 'North Rona') forms Britain's least-visited national nature reserve.

The turbulent life of **Ragnhild**, the tenth-century princess who forms the subject of Chapter 20, was the initial inspiration for *Rona*. Her ancestry can be traced in Snorri Sturluson's *Heimskringla* all the way back to the semi-mythical sixth-century **Yrsa** of Chapter 12:

Eadgils, King of Sweden + **Yrsa** (mid 6th C)
↓
Eystein, King of Sweden (late 6th C)
↓
Ingvar, King of Sweden (early 7th C)
↓
Anund, King of Sweden (mid 7th C)
↓
Ingjald 'the Ill-ruler', King of Sweden (late 7th C) + Gauthild
↓
Olaf 'the Woodcutter' (early 8th C) + Solveig
↓
Halfdan 'Whiteshanks' (mid 8th C) + Åsa
↓
Eystein 'Fart' (mid 8th C) + Hild
↓
Halfdan 'the Mild' (late 8th C) + Liv
↓
Gudrod 'the Hunter' (early 9th C) + **Åsa of Agder**
↓
Halfdan 'the Black' (c. 810–c. 860) + Ragnhild
↓
Harald 'Fairhair', King of Norway (c. 850–c. 942) + Ragnhild
↓
Erik 'Bloodaxe' (c. 885–954) + **Gunnhild** (c. 910–c. 980)
↓
Ragnhild (c. 940–?)

The fictitious 'Gudrun's Saga' of *Rona* disputes this direct line of descent, suggesting that **Åsa of Agder** bore Halfdan 'the Black' not to her husband Gudrod 'the Hunter' but to her servant Njall (Chapter 14).

The **Southern Isles** (Old Norse: *Suðreyjar*) were a Norwegian 'kingdom' of the twelfth century that covered the Western Isles from Lewis to Barra; the Inner Hebrides including Skye, Mull, Islay, Jura, Tiree, Coll and a host of smaller islands; the Mull of Kintyre and islands in the Firth of Clyde including Arran and Bute; and the Isle of Man. At times the 'king' was also overlord of parts of Argyll and Galloway on the mainland. His lands were ceded to Scotland in 1266, except that the Isle of Man was detached and came under English rule in 1334. Somehow left out of the United Kingdom created in 1707, it is still a self-governing dependency. The name *Suðreyjar* survives in the present-day Church of England diocese of Sodor and Man, which covers only the Isle of Man.

The **Fairfield and Bracklinn titles** are fictitious but their origins as given in Chapters 1 and 11 respectively are plausible. King Robert the Bruce might well have shown his gratitude for support in defeating the Earl of Buchan (John Comyn or Cumming) by creating the earldom of Fairfield. The Comyn family were related to and supporters of John Balliol, whom Edward I of England had installed as a puppet king of Scotland. They became implacable enemies of Bruce on the murder of the 'Red Comyn' (a grandson of Buchan's cousin) in a Dumfries church in 1306. In the 1308 battle of Inverurie (actually fought near Oldmeldrum), Bruce, though suffering from illness, defeated the militarily inept Buchan before launching his vicious 'harrying' campaign throughout north-east Scotland.

That Lloyd George (Prime Minister of the UK from 1916 to 1922) sold peerages for his personal enrichment is not much disputed; it does not defy credulity that a wealthy grocer might have bought the Bracklinn barony in 1918.

Mackay's Hotel, Wick is in reality every bit as hospitable as Delia finds it, and was indeed formerly the Temperance Hotel. The people of Wick had voted in 1922 to ban the sale of alcohol in their town, apparently convinced by preachers and others that 'temperance' – that is, prohibition – would lift the working classes out of poverty and debauchery. Pubs closed; inns could no longer serve beer or spirits to their guests. The Pulteney distillery on the south side of the Wick River struggled for a few years but was eventually shuttered in 1930. The town remained 'dry' for 25 years, the ban being finally lifted in 1947. The distillery reopened in 1951 and today produces one of the most highly regarded single-malt whiskies in Scotland: Old Pulteney.

Adam Gordon, husband of Elizabeth, 10th Countess of Sutherland, has occasionally been confused with his great-nephew of the same name. It was the younger Adam who was memorialised in the ballad *Edom o' Gordon* for a crime outrageous even for its time. Having besieged the Forbes stronghold of Corgarff Castle in the laird's absence, he demanded that the lady take him to her bed. Upon her refusal he set fire to the castle and burned her to death, together with all her children and servants.

Isobel Sinclair's intended poisoning victim John Gordon, 11th Earl of Sutherland was a cousin and supporter of the Earl of Huntly who was defeated by the forces of Mary, Queen of Scots at the Battle of Corrichie on the Hill of Fare in 1562; see *Taran's Wheel (Incomers: Book 1)*. Through his three marriages Gordon tried to ingratiate himself with the ruling Stewart dynasty: first with the Countess of Moray, widow of an illegitimate son of King James IV; then with Elinor Stewart, daughter of the Earl of Lennox; and finally with Mary Seton, one of the Queen's 'four Marys' – the wife poisoned with him by Isobel Sinclair.

The **Sutherland Clearances** of the early 1800s remain an emotive subject two centuries later. Literally hundreds of articles and books have examined this episode, with a perspective ranging from bitterly critical to cautiously supportive. My principal sources are listed in the Acknowledgments; of these the most authoritative is probably the recent (2015) book by James Hunter. Some writers have claimed to take a more 'balanced' view but have strayed into apologia or even denial of the indefensible. David Forbes (1977) opined that 'some credit is due the 2nd Marquess [of Stafford] and his wife [Elizabeth, 19th Countess of Sutherland] for their attempt to develop Sutherland when they could have easily ignored that county since their real wealth lay further south.' Of Patrick Sellar, who did their dirty work and became perhaps the most hated person in Scottish history, Eric Richards (1999) wrote: 'Perhaps the worst [*sic*] that can be said of him is that, in his zeal and impatience for improvement, he hurried a reluctant community to resettle thirty or so miles away from their usual homes.'

D.H. Lawrence's seminal novel ***Lady Chatterley's Lover*** was first published in Italy in 1928, but only expurgated versions were available in Britain until 1960, when Lawrence's full original text was released in paperback. The publisher, Penguin Books, was prosecuted under a 1959 act of Parliament intended to limit the banning of 'obscene' publications to those, lacking literary or other merit, that would 'tend to deprave and corrupt'.

At trial, the jury announced on 2nd November 1960 its unanimous finding that the book was not 'obscene' under the act. The opening remarks of prosecuting counsel Mervyn Griffith-Jones ('Is it a book that you would wish your wife or servants to read?') so encapsulated how out of touch the British Establishment was with post-war trends in everyday life and culture that the jury's verdict may have been inevitable from the start.

Put in historical context, the case is seen as a milestone in creation of a sexually liberated – detractors have called it 'permissive' – society. Millions of people have read the book, or seen film or TV dramatisations, that would never have known of it had the case not been brought to court.

The **Garvie trial**, a Scottish *cause célèbre*, took place in Aberdeen in November 1968. Maxwell Garvie, the farmer of West Cairnbeg near Stonehaven, was fun-loving with a taste for fast cars, aeroplanes and kinky sex. Having introduced his wife Sheila to group sex with a brother-and-sister pair, Brian Tevendale and Trudi Birse, he soon tired of the arrangement and wanted to replace them with more exciting partners. But Sheila had developed feelings for Tevendale, and together they plotted to kill her husband. When Garvie's body was found in a drain near Tevendale's home in May 1968, each tried to blame the other. After one of the most sensational trials in Scottish legal history, both were found guilty of murder and sentenced to life imprisonment. Following their eventual release, Brian Tevendale became a pub landlord in Perthshire and Sheila Garvie ran a B&B in Stonehaven. Both are now deceased.

In the **Tylenol murders**, seven deaths around the Chicago metropolitan area in September 1982 were linked to deliberate lacing with cyanide of Tylenol (acetaminophen or paracetamol) pain-relief capsules. A nationwide recall by Johnson & Johnson cost the company tens of millions of dollars. A man who demanded a million dollars to stop the killing was found guilty of extortion but the evidence was insufficient to convict him of murder.

The media character-assassination of **Christopher Jefferies**, innocent of the 2010 murder of Joanna Yeates, resulted in substantial damages for defamation being paid by the *Sun*, the *Daily Mirror*, the *Sunday Mirror*, the *Daily Mail*, the *Daily Record*, the *Daily Express*, the *Daily Star* and the *Scotsman*.

Believed to be the only Broadway song the Beatles ever recorded, **Till There Was You** was written by Meredith Willson for *The Music Man* in 1957. With Paul on vocals and Ringo on bongos, the band performed the song at the 4th November 1963 Royal Variety Performance, showcasing their remarkable versatility by following it with *Twist And Shout*.

Till There Was You had been included in the Beatles' audition the previous year at which Decca Records turned them down, famously telling them they had 'no future in show business' and 'guitar groups were on the way out'. In March 2016 a 78 rpm acetate disc of *Till There Was You* recorded in 1962 by 'Paul McCartney and the Beatles' was sold at auction for £77,500.

Eric Clapton's vocals and virtuoso electric guitar in Derek and the Dominos' **Layla**, a song Clapton wrote to express his love for the wife of his friend and fellow musician George Harrison, dominate the first half of the record. The second half consists of a remarkable piano coda contributed by Jim Gordon, the Dominos' drummer, a melody said to be derived from a composition by his (uncredited) ex-girlfriend Rita Coolidge.

Though not a stratospheric hit when released in the early 1970s, *Layla* is now a recognised rock classic. The acoustic version Clapton released in 1992 as part of his MTV *Unplugged* session was another popular music milestone.

Airthrey Castle, Stirling served as a maternity hospital from the Second World War until 1969. By 1968 (when Rona delivers her son there) Scotland's first new university since the sixteenth century was already being built in its grounds.

Octahedral numbers form the series beginning 1, 6, 19, 44, ...

Imagine a pyramidal bowl, square in section and coming to a point at the base. Now put a marble in the bottom of the bowl, then four more marbles to form a second layer, nine to form a third layer and so on. After reaching any desired number of layers, start decreasing the number of marbles again until the final single marble is in place. The marbles will form a regular octahedron, and the total number of marbles used is an octahedral number. Where the middle, largest layer is the fourth layer, the number of marbles in the octahedron is given by $1^2+2^2+3^2+4^2+3^2+2^2+1^2 = 44$.

To understand Delia's assertion that the whole series of octahedral numbers is underpinned by the number 4, begin with the exact multiples of 4, *i.e.*, 0, 4, 8, 12, 16, etc. Now, starting with 1, add these multiples of 4 consecutively to give a new sequence:

$$1 + 0 = 1$$
$$1 + 4 = 5$$
$$5 + 8 = 13$$
$$13 + 12 = 25$$
$$25 + 16 = 41$$

Then, beginning at zero, repeat the consecutive addition to provide the series of octahedral numbers:

$$0 + 1 = 1$$
$$1 + 5 = 6$$
$$6 + 13 = 19$$
$$19 + 25 = 44$$
$$44 + 41 = 85$$

Just as the numbers 6 and 66 (and 666) are a recurring theme in *Taran's Wheel*, likewise 5 and 55 in *Scotch and Water*, readers of the full *Incomers* trilogy will not have been surprised to find 4 and 44 featuring in *Rona*. Nor are the numbers of chapters in the three *Incomers* books (66, 55 and 44 respectively) entirely accidental.

Finally, **boundaries** are a source of fascination for both Rona and Delia. It has been said that everything that is truly interesting happens at a boundary. It's why we love the seashore, where land meets water; hogmanay, where an old year disappears and a new one begins; the cliff-hanger that carries the reader from one chapter to the next of a thriller or the viewer from one episode to another of a TV soap. Wars are fought over national borders, which are often arbitrary lines on a map. Boundaries feature significantly in many sports, including golf, tennis and cricket. The present is the evanescent boundary between a familiar past and an unknown future – and that's where we live.

Jim Forbes

ACKNOWLEDGEMENTS

Once again I owe a deep debt of gratitude to my ever-loving and ever-patient wife Elinor (the novelist Elinor Hunter) for reviewing and editing successive drafts of *Rona*. If errors or other shortcomings remain, they are mine alone.

I am grateful to Naida Forbes for her critique of an early draft and suggestions on certain plot points; and to Sandy Mowat for background information on Dundee, the setting for the 'Fairfield's Cereals' business.

Thanks also to friends who have read *Incomers* Books 1 and 2 for their patience and encouragement while this third and final book in the series was completed. I hope they consider it was worth the wait.

References to the *Orkneyinga Saga* are based on the translation by J.A. Hjaltalin and G. Goudie (edited by J. Anderson) published in 1873 by Edmonston & Douglas, Edinburgh.

For the *Heimskringla* (Sagas of the Norse Kings) by Snorri Sturluson (1178–1241) I have relied on the translation by S. Laing, published in 1961 by J.M. Dent, London.

Illustrated Natural History, as described in Chapter 2, was published around 1881 by Biggs & Co., London.

Sources for the Sutherland Clearances (principally Chapters 6 and 36) include:

David Forbes (1977) *The Sutherland Clearances 1806–1820: An Introduction.* The Northern Times, Golspie.

John Prebble (1982) *The Highland Clearances.* Penguin Books, London.

David Paton (2006) *The Clergy and the Clearances.* John Donald, Edinburgh.

Eric Richards (1999) *Patrick Sellar and the Highland Clearances.* Polygon, Edinburgh.

Eric Richards (2013) *The Highland Clearances* (3rd ed.). Birlinn, Edinburgh.

James Hunter (2015) *Set Adrift upon the World: The Sutherland Clearances.* Birlinn, Edinburgh.

The source for toxicity of white jequirity (Chapter 22) is 'Poisoning due to white seed variety of *Abrus precatorius*' by V.V. Pillai *et al.*: *Journal of the Association of Physicians of India* Vol. 53 (2005).

Chapter 30 contains a short extract from *Flash and Bones* by Kathy Reichs (2011: William Heinemann), which is gratefully acknowledged.

Previously in the *Incomers* trilogy
by Jim Forbes:

Taran's Wheel
(*Incomers*: Book 1)

What has become of the ancient talisman known as **Taran's Wheel**? A riddle from beyond the grave sets Delia on a hunt. Her search, which takes her from Chicago to the 'Pleasant Vale' of Cromar in Scotland, reveals the dramatic story of the Vale and its people.

But can this story lead Delia to Taran's Wheel, or will sinister forces deny her the prize, even threaten her life?

Scotch and Water
(*Incomers*: Book 2)

It's a time of drama for Edinburgh and the ancient land of Lothian, and Delia is in the thick of it.

A metal detector hobbyist is murdered just as he strikes gold. The discovery of cryptic writings sheds new light on a celebrated nineteenth-century Edinburgh family. A ruthless businesswoman exploits council corruption. Controversially, huge volumes of water are to be pumped to southern England. A violent ultra-nationalist cell plots mayhem in the wake of Scotland's 'no' to independence.

Like **scotch and water**, these apparently unconnected goings-on make a potent mix: a web of political, criminal and terrorist intrigue linked to a mysterious relic of some of Lothian's earliest incomers.

Also from Kinord Books:

A Bad Woman by Elinor Hunter

Though Queen Victoria's affair with John Brown raises barely an eyebrow, it's a different story for her working-class subjects. Two Scottish women discover the harsh realities of loss and single parenthood. Like Victoria, the supposed moral compass of the nation, Bella and Isa risk their reputations to survive tragedy and retain their sanity, only their efforts are met with public censure and humiliation.

The fates of all three share uncanny parallels, yet posterity will brand one of them *a bad woman*. But then nothing is ever as it seems ...

Sharpster by Elinor Hunter

It's the swinging sixties, and Kelton MacLeod is on a scholarship to Scotland. When Aberdeenshire farm girl Carol falls for his easy American charm, she abandons family, friends and fiancé to run off with him to Missouri.

Smooth as silk, slippery as soap, Kelton is driven by boundless ambition. Too late, Carol discovers she has sacrificed everything for a psychopathic womaniser. His lies and manipulation make him the husband – and at work the boss – from hell.

Yet what goes around comes around ... so will the long memories of those he has wronged prove to be his undoing?

www.kinordbooks.com